Thunder
In The
Capital

Thunder
In The
Capital

Rob Shumaker

To the Judge, Carla, and Stephanie
With thanks for your editorial assistance and friendship

CHAPTER 1

"We the People," William E. Cogdon said out loud in the law firm conference room as he thumbed through his pocket-sized copy of the United States Constitution. He might have been thinking out loud. "We the People. That is a pretty powerful phrase."

"Yes, it is." The tepid response came from Anthony Schumacher, Cogdon's law partner of ten years. His chin was buried in his left hand as he intently studied last night's box scores from around the National League. He really wasn't listening.

"We the People. Do you think that's the most powerful three-word phrase ever written?"

Slightly annoyed, Anthony stopped his search of baseball stats and thought for a second to appease his friend. "How 'bout 'In the beginning' or 'Do unto others' or 'Love thy neighbor' or maybe 'It is finished.'"

Cogdon sighed. "Yeah, those are good ones." He raised his eyes to the ceiling like he knew he had been bested. "We the People. We the People," he kept repeating.

"We the People," Anthony chimed in, lost again in his stats and hoping Cogdon would give it a rest.

"Schu, you ought to run for Congress."

The conference room suddenly grew quiet. The Friday afternoon sunshine peeked through the blinds and brightened the room, the dusty law books showing their age in the glow. Anthony Schumacher finished a swig of Diet Coke, set the can on the table, and let the idea rattle around his brain. Now this was something worth thinking about. It hadn't been the first time someone made the comment that Anthony should represent the good people of the Eighth Congressional District of the great State of Indiana in the nation's capital. Congressman Schumacher did have a nice ring to it. He could go from simply being a forty-two-year-old attorney to the Honorable Anthony J. Schumacher, Member of Congress. The twinkle in his eye indicated he might have already considered the matter, maybe even dreamt about it a time or two.

"Think about it. We could help fight the special interests, cut taxes, rein in spending, and fix the endless problems of big government," said Cogdon, friend, lawyer, and future hopeful for the Congressman's chief of staff. "We could finally put an end to all this mess in Washington." As if the world's problems would only be solved if Anthony Joseph Schumacher was a member of Congress and Cogdon his loyal sidekick was pulling the strings.

"I would like to tackle the tax code," Anthony said with great hope. "Cut the frivolous pork left and right."

Cogdon leaned closer to the table, his two cans of Red Bull emptied of their contents. His fifty-year-old face looked haggard, his loosened tie barely hanging on his neck. With his fleshy jowls and dark eyelids, he resembled a sad hound dog. He looked perpetually guilty of something, and no one ever knew whether it was because of his latest one-night stand or whether he was exhausted from staying one step ahead of the IRS. But, all in all, he really wanted Anthony Schumacher to be Indiana's newest congressman.

And he wanted to be the next Karl Rove.

"I don't know," Anthony said, playing the modesty angle. "What are my chances?"

"Hell, as good as anybody's." He counted along on his fingers. "You're young, a former FBI agent, good looking, with a hot wife . . ."

"Thank you," Anthony interrupted in agreement.

". . . three beautiful kids, and a conservative message that would resonate with like-minded Hoosiers in this reddest of red areas."

Anthony took another swig of his Diet Coke. The thought of running for Congress had consumed his mind lately ever since the local representative had decided twenty terms was enough in D.C. Maybe Anthony Schumacher was *the one* destined to replace the legendary Theodore Milhous Johnson.

Johnson was born in Terre Haute shortly before the Great Depression and earned the Congressional Medal of Honor for gallantry and intrepidity while leading the charge during the Normandy invasion on D-Day. After the war, he returned to Indiana a hero, its newest favorite son, and became a prominent and respected businessman. He won election to Congress in 1968 and promised to help Nixon end the war in Vietnam. Ted Johnson's plan, although not widely publicized, was to bring our boys home and nuke every last commie standing. Although his idea never gained much traction, he became a widely respected defense hawk and spent the rest of his years as the leading Republican voice on the Armed Services Committee. His booming voice and powerful delivery earned him the nickname of Congressman Thor, short for Theodore, as well as the Norse god of thunder. His ground-shaking rumblings on the House floor made him a legend among right-wing conservatives. However, at eighty-five, he couldn't press the flesh like he used to and sometimes even had to have an aide sign his name to documents.

Now was the time, Anthony told himself. Somebody had to step up to the plate.

Still, he had some lingering doubts. Did he really want to put up with the glad-handing, the baby kissing, and the fundraising just so the liberalized left-wing media could tarnish his reputation and drag his good name through the mud. It was a foregone conclusion that he would be no friend of the liberals. Or did he want to risk the chance of becoming embroiled in some tawdry sex scandal or bribery scheme whereupon he would most likely lose his wife, his kids, and perhaps even be required to take up residence as a guest of the government for five to ten years in some federal penitentiary.

"What about skeletons in the closet?" Anthony asked.

"Skeletons? You don't have any skeletons."

Anthony managed a sly smile. "I was talking about your closet."

Cogdon feigned shock, like his pride had been deeply hurt. "I've never been so insulted in my life."

"Come on, William. What do I have to worry about?"

Cogdon wasn't giving in. He wiped a river of sweat off his balding head. "If anything becomes an issue, I'll take care of it."

"That doesn't sound very reassuring."

"Trust me."

Anthony didn't like the sound of that either, but he really didn't want to know any more. The two looked at each other, one shaking his head no and the other nodding yes.

Anthony broke the silence. "I think I might just do it."

"Yes!" William said, pumping his fist in the air and exposing his sweat drenched pits. "I'll start laying the groundwork."

"Okay, but keep it quiet. I still have to run it by the Mrs."

Anthony hadn't mentioned the idea to his wife at all so he practiced what he was going to say once he got home. Maybe she'd talk him out of it. He had a feeling she'd go along with whatever he decided, but it was a big decision – for him, for her, and their family. Being away from home with three kids to feed and chaperone can be difficult for two parents let alone one full-time and one part-time. Still, he really wanted the job.

"Elle, I'm home," Anthony said, walking into the kitchen, resulting in a flurry of activity from all angles.

"Daddy, can I have twenty bucks?" asked Ashley Jewel, the Schumacher's fourteen-year old and oldest daughter. A.J., for short, she was blonde, beautiful, and an energetic whirlwind with places to be. She held out her hand and presented the sweetest, most irresistible smile she could muster.

"I'm just a walking ATM to you, aren't I?"

"Please, Daddy," she begged, her hands in full prayer mode. Begging wasn't necessary, however. She had him wrapped around her finger since the day she was born.

"Where are you going?"

"The movies."

"With who?"

"Kayla and ReAnn."

"How are you getting there?"

"Kayla's mom is taking us."

The interrogation completed, Daddy reached into his wallet and forked it over. "Here." She gave him a kiss on the cheek as a receipt. "No drugs, drinking, or odd boys," he was able to say before the door to the garage closed. It was a new experience for him. He was a teenage boy once and kept a close eye on her comings and goings.

"Dad, can we play some catch?" asked Michael, the middle child, age ten, with budding athletic talent. He idolized his dad, a former G-man and now a respected attorney. Michael pounded the ball in his glove with anticipation.

"Sure, Bud. Let me talk to your mom first."

Mom was sitting at the dining-room table practicing addition and subtraction with Anna, the youngest of the Schumacher brood, and a rising star in her first grade class. Danielle Schumacher, blonde hair down to her shoulders, sat contently in her red athletic pants and Wabash State sweatshirt. She was as gorgeous now as when Anthony first met her thirty seven years ago.

She was his Elle.

The love story that became Anthony and Danielle's started at a young age and tossed and turned until its present state of fifteen years of marriage, three kids, a dog named Frosty and a cat named Twinkie, and a comfortable life in Silver Creek. Danielle grew up right next door, the daughter of Roger and Martha Sexton. The blonde haired beauty caught the eye of Anthony when he was just five years old. He had moved in with his Aunt Meg after his parents died and instantly fell in love with his neighbor.

It was the start of a long and winding road to win her heart.

Anthony kissed Anna on the top of the head and did the same with his wife. He sat down at the dining-room table and looked Danielle over. She was forty one but looked twenty eight. How he had been so lucky to win her heart was still something that he marveled about. She was stunning in every way, and with her tender touch as a mother, even more so.

"What?" she asked looking at her staring husband.

He might as well get it over with. He leaned back in his chair and acted as nonchalant as possible.

"I've had some people tell me to run for Congressman Johnson's seat." Really it was just Cogdon and a couple of clients who were upset with Congressman Johnson's supposed lurch from far right wing to middle right wing. They wanted some new conservative blood. "He said he was retiring at the end of his term."

She sat back in her chair and dropped her red pencil. "So you want to leave us here while you go to Washington, D.C. and become a member of Congress." The tone in her voice was one of slight indignation, although it made her look even more sexy. What is my husband getting himself and his family into? she wondered.

"Does that mean Daddy is going to live in the White House?" Anna asked excitedly.

Anthony smiled. "No, sweetie, I wouldn't be President. I would be a congressman. Someone who represents the people around here in Indiana." Anna was disappointed. Being a congressman didn't sound as cool as being President. She went back to adding her numbers.

"Think of the time, the money, it would take to win a campaign," Danielle said. She taught third grade at Silver Creek Elementary School. Although Anthony had done well during his two years as the Wabash County State's Attorney and his subsequent days in the firm, the Schumachers still had bills to be paid and three college educations to eventually pony up for down the road. She was running the numbers in her head.

"I wasn't thinking about using our money or mortgaging the house or anything like that," Anthony rationalized. "I'd have to beg and plead for money just like every other candidate. Fundraisers, cookouts . . ."

"Parades, door-to-door campaigning," she interjected. "That's just to get to the opportunity to be away from home from Monday through Thursday for who knows how many months of the year." She was more up to speed than Anthony thought. Almost like someone had tipped her off.

"Cogdon said he'd run my campaign."

"Wiley?" She asked with an exaggerated roll of her eyes. "Great."

Anthony gave her that smile that said something was up and Cogdon was sure as hell in the middle of it. The Schumachers called William E. Cogdon, Esq., Wiley, as in Wile E. Coyote. Being twice divorced, Cogdon spent most of his down time at the bars, although he held his liquor well. The man was accident prone, restless, and always seemed to have a plan or hair-brained scheme up his sleeve. The schemes appeared to be legitimate, for now, and Cogdon thought he could change the world, or at least west-central Indiana, by putting Anthony in positions of power.

"He said I had a beautiful family." Anthony hoped the flattery would warm Danielle to the idea. He smiled. She smiled, closed her eyes, and shook her head. She knew her husband had made up his mind and his political aspirations were running in high gear.

"Just think about it." He got up from the table and gave her another kiss on the top of her head. "I gotta go play some catch."

The Schumacher family had jumped into the rough and tumble political whirlwind on two previous occasions. After law school, Anthony joined the FBI in San Diego only to be seriously wounded in a gun battle with bank robbers. He survived. The bank robbers weren't so lucky. His short tenure with the Bureau led to his marriage with Danielle and a return to their hometown of Silver Creek. His work at a local law firm led to a run for State's Attorney, the county's top prosecutor. Anthony and Danielle, supporters in tow, marched in the obligatory Fourth of July and Labor Day parades, knocked on hundreds of doors, and placed "Schumacher for State's Attorney" signs on every allowable corner and in practically every yard in the county. Their family picture even ended up on a billboard on the way into town. The hard work paid off as Anthony won with 69% of the vote in the heavily Republican section of Indiana. Four years later, he won reelection with 100% of the vote. The local Democrats, small band of brothers that they were in these parts, couldn't even bring themselves to place a sacrificial lamb on the ballot.

Anthony took the Office of State's Attorney seriously and worked hard to rid the county of a growing methamphetamine population. He aggressively prosecuted the meth cooks and mules who sought Silver Creek's forests lining the Wabash River to produce their nefarious cocktails and contraband. He even testified before a state panel to change the law regarding the purchase of over-the-counter cold medicines used in cooking the methamphetamine. Convictions skyrocketed and meth use plummeted. The voters liked his down-home style, his family values, and his tough-on-crime mantra.

Still, there were some naysayers that aggravated Danielle. One angry mother couldn't understand why her twenty-four-year-old son should be prosecuted for marijuana possession because "everyone does it." That her son was also selling to grade-school kids was a matter she was conveniently willing to overlook. Or when the mayor of Silver Creek came huffing and puffing to the Schumacher's door late one night after finding out his brother-in-law had been charged with driving under the influence. He was only three times over the limit, the mayor argued. Plus, he didn't hit anybody, just a parked car and a couple of mailboxes. "Give the guy a break" was a familiar plea.

Anthony took the criticisms in stride, almost oblivious to any ruckus, but Danielle didn't like it when the occasional idiot flipped the bird to the family while they walked in a parade or badmouthed her husband while she stood in line at the grocery store. She hoped Anthony would eventually decide to get out of the prosecution business and become a county trial judge. She hoped a black robe and a gavel would bring a little more civility from her fellow citizens. In the end, Anthony decided private practice would suit him for the time being – and still allow him a chance at the real action fighting the liberals in the state legislature or Congress.

"Well, did you ask Danielle?" Wiley asked when Anthony walked in the office on Monday morning.

"I'm not sure she's that into it."

Wiley was having none of it. He knew Danielle would have her reservations. He was ready. "But you're the best person for the job. The whole State of Indiana is depending on you. What would happen if those evil liberals were to take this seat? Indiana would turn blue right before our eyes."

"The Democrats aren't going to win here."

"Don't be so sure," Wiley said, as if he had the inside scoop on the liberal agenda. "The libs in Indianapolis and D.C. would love to spend big bucks here if they thought they could win. All they need is a moderate gun-owning Democrat to pull an upset and then make a hard left once he or she got to D.C."

"I'll talk to Elle again tonight."

The more Anthony thought about it the more he wanted the job. He would be just one of 535 members of Congress. But he would be getting off the bench and into the game. One where he could fight for lower taxes and less government and personal responsibility. All things he believed in and argued for to friends and colleagues. He could start at the bottom and work his way up, making the world a better place all along the way. He'd model himself after Lincoln and Reagan, a man of the people, for the common man.

It was already getting to his head.

"Why don't we take a walk," Anthony said to Danielle after the dinner table was clear. She knew the walk would be so he could talk her into okaying his run. Ashley had left early, Michael was staying over at a friend's house, and Anna was next door at the house of Danielle's mother, Martha Sexton.

The two held hands as they slowly made their way around their forty-acre spread on a bluff above the Wabash River. They had grown up in this area, canoed in the river, and hiked in the forest of trees. This was home to them. Other than a short time in California when Anthony was an FBI agent and Danielle taught third grade in San Diego, home had always been in Silver Creek.

"I think I want to run for Congress," Anthony said, breaking the silence. He wanted her blessing. His love for her was without bounds, and she was the only thing in life he wanted and could not live without. If she said no, he would drop the idea and never bring it up again.

"It's not that . . .," Danielle said before trailing off, her eyes scanning the river.

"What is it?"

"Can't you wait a few years?"

He kicked a few rocks out of their path. "There may never be an opportunity like this. The last guy served for forty years and who's to say the next person won't as well."

"I guess I wish you'd wait until the kids were older," she said, holding his hand tighter. "You would miss a lot of games and recitals. Ashley's going to be heading off to college in four or five years, and Michael and Anna love you so much I don't want them to have an absentee father."

The crickets were the only ones responding. Anthony just looked out over the river, flowing gently in the spring breeze. He was concerned about being away from home and then ten years down the road wondering how his kids grew up so fast without him knowing it. He still hadn't said anything.

"But I know how much you like politics," she said, looking into his eyes. "And if you think this is what you want to do, we'll make it work as a family."

Danielle had been a recipient of Anthony's love for over three decades now. Her ravishing beauty led many male suitors to her door in high school and college, but Anthony stood by patiently, hoping and praying she would one day see they were meant to be together. After high school, she up and left for San Diego with her boyfriend to attend college, while Anthony put on the freshman twenty and suffered ugly bouts of depression and loneliness at the loss of his best friend. The pain was excruciating for Anthony and only later did Danielle realize how much he really loved her, ached for her, and could not live without her. Danielle eventually dumped the boyfriend, found some others, and finally settled on a divorced podiatrist. They married, breaking Anthony's heart even further. The marriage wouldn't last, however, because of Dr. Foot's wandering eye, and the resulting divorce was a painful episode in her life that she wanted to forget. In swooped Anthony, now svelte and trim, with a badge, a gun, and a renewed mission to win her heart. Things eventually worked out and Anthony married the girl of his dreams. The American dream. He could already see the campaign commercials.

She put her arms around him. Her man. The guy who would do anything for her. Now it was her turn.

"We'll make it work," she said, planting a kiss on his lips. "And you'll make a great congressman." She smiled. Her eyes slightly moist.

He wrapped his arms around her and they kissed like they were newlyweds. They walked back home and, before Grandma Sexton brought Anna back over, husband and wife hustled upstairs and shook the bedroom just like old times.

The next day, Anthony walked into his office to find Wiley with a handful of Red Bull and a look that begged Anthony to run. Anthony gave him a sly smile.

"Make it happen, Wiley."

"Yeah, baby! We're going to Washington."

CHAPTER 2

The retirement of Old Man Johnson set off a flurry of activity inside the Beltway. Democrats were foaming at the mouth in hopes of winning the seat. The Eighth Congressional District of Indiana had never been represented by a Democrat, and the only moderate Republican to win the seat was easily defeated by the right-wing Johnson some forty years ago. The Dems had little chance of winning but sometimes judgment gets clouded in politics when personal animosity is bubbling over.

"Speaker's office," responded the receptionist.

"Yeah, it's Jim, is The Boss in?"

"Just one second."

The Boss. Speaker of the United States House of Representatives. Article I, section 2. Third in line to the presidency. Although the Speaker liked to say she was second in line because it was only her and the vice president standing around waiting for the president to keel over.

"Tell me something good, Jim," she said without saying hello. No pleasantries. All business.

"We think we can pick up a seat outside of St. Louis that has been historically Republican and the same goes for the eighth district in Ohio."

Jim Evans worked as the Speaker's election guru. He was employed by the Democratic National Committee but spent most of his time getting yelled at by the Speaker, the top Dem in Congress. He grew up in Boston, graduated with honors from Harvard, and went straight to the DNC to help plant the seeds of liberalism all across the fruited plain. He crafted the Democrats' attack strategy and managed the war room during any political crises. But all his hard work never seemed to satisfy The Boss. Now with her ten-seat Democratic majority in the House looking especially vulnerable, and thus her hold on power as well, every seat in every district, Republican, Democrat, or Independent, mattered.

"What about the eighth in Indiana?"

Jim hesitated ever so slightly. The eighth district in Indiana. Congressman Thor's district. Jim knew a volcanic eruption was sure to follow. "Very little chance."

"Damn it, Jim! Don't give me any of that red-state, Republican territory shit! I want that damn seat!"

Ever the whipping boy, Jim was unable to respond before the Speaker slammed down the phone.

Catherine "Kitty" O'Shea didn't become the most powerful woman in politics by not demanding results. She was the daughter of an Irish-Catholic family that had run Boston politics like the Daleys did in Chicago. Her great-grandfather was mayor, her grandfather was mayor then Massachusetts governor, and her father spent thirty years leading Boston politics as its longest serving mayor. The O'Shea name resonated in New England just as much as the Kennedy's and the Red Sox.

With such a distinguished pedigree, O'Shea was destined for political stardom. She graduated with a degree in political science from Boston College. Then, like many elite Boston Brahmins and budding politicians, added a Harvard law degree to round out her educational résumé. She could have been mayor of Beantown or governor of the Bay State but she was drawn to the power and prestige of Washington and the opportunity to solve the problems of every American by implementing her liberal agenda. She was elected to the House in November 1974, swept into power on the coattails of her father's fifth and final term and the Democrats' beat down of the Republicans following the Nixon debacle. She worked her way up the ladder in Congress, making backroom deals, scratching the backs of fellow Dems, and scratching the eyes out of anyone who crossed her. She headed the Appropriations Committee and directed hundreds of millions of taxpayer pork in Massachusetts' direction for roads, bridges, schools, lobster studies, duck boats for the Public Gardens, and extravagant bronze statutes for each of the family patriarchs, just to name a few of her pet projects. Once she was elected Speaker, she looked to expand Big Government and settle old scores.

Old Man Johnson was tops on her list.

Wiley was up early the next morning burning down the phone lines. He called the Wabash County Republican chairman and stated Anthony's desire to run and win Congressman Johnson's seat. Since Anthony was well-respected, had already won two county elections, and was the only legitimate candidate, Mr. Chairman should quash any other would-be hopefuls or Wiley hinted there would be hell to pay once Anthony was in Washington, an inevitable result. Chairmen from surrounding counties received similar calls and politely told to get on the Schumacher bandwagon. A declaration of candidacy was filed with the State Election Division. A campaign office was established, phone lines hooked up, campaign finance reports filled out, and volunteers contacted. A web site was in the works. Wiley the Whirlwind was a political machine.

Anthony paid a visit to Congressman Johnson's district office in Silver Creek. He had another one in his hometown of Terre Haute. It was a stroke of luck that the Old Man was actually in town. He spent most of his days in D.C., far away from the cornfields of Indiana, thinking he did not need to listen to his constituents because they would agree with everything he said anyway. They were "like-minded heartlanders" he was fond of saying.

Anthony had met Congressman Thor on several occasions, mostly on the campaign trail. They shared a stage together when county Republicans sought to honor those that had soundly thrashed their liberal opponents. The wall in Anthony's office once held a picture of him and the Old Man taken at the Wabash County Fair when both were glad handing for votes. The photo was still there, it was just sitting in the frame behind Anna's first-grade picture.

For as confident as Anthony was, walking into Johnson's office was enough to question his decision. The responsibility of the office was terrific. And whether the Old Man would approve was still a mystery. Johnson didn't handpick Anthony to succeed him, not because he didn't like him, but because he wanted to hang on to power until he croaked and really didn't think anybody could take his place. It was almost as if he thought his seat in Congress should remain vacant when he retired as an eternal monument to a man who had no equal.

"Schumacher, come in and sit down," the Old Man huffed as he waved Anthony through the walnut doors to his ornate office. The wood paneling reeked of smoke, a stale layer of Marlboro cigarettes covered by a fresh coat of Don Tomas Maduro Robusto. Meaningless awards hailed appreciation at the Congressman's hard work and dedication. A bronze bust of Lincoln gazed down from the bookcase, watching over all who entered. Pictures showed the longevity of the man and his influence. There were handshakes with Nixon, Ford, Reagan, the Bushes, the Iron Lady, and even His Holiness The Pope himself. The Old Man did not crave historical artifacts or priceless paintings. He craved what every politician dreamt of at night and crawled out of bed for each morning.

Power.

And the man who would succeed him stood in front of his desk.

Anthony gave a toothy smile to the decrepit miser and extended a hand. "Nice to see you again, Congressman."

The Old Man managed to pull himself halfway out of his high back leather chair to offer a cold hand. "Enough with the pleasantries. Sit down."

The Old Man was a tough and grizzled veteran of the political wars. He did not suffer fools lightly and the black pupils in his aged eyes zeroed in on the young whippersnapper looking to take over his seat. To him, it would always be "his seat."

"So, you want to start swimming with the big fish, now do you?" the Old

Man said, his voice reverberating around the room.

"Yes, sir. I've thought about it for some time now, talked it over with my wife, and decided I wanted to continue the good work that you have done representing this great district of ours."

It brought a smile to the Old Man's face. "No need to start blowing smoke up my skirt, Schumacher. I'm not going to stand in your way. I've been keeping my eye on you for some time now. Right now, you're the only one who could do it."

The Old Man liked Anthony, especially his conservative credentials. He was young and could solidify the conservative stronghold in Indiana for years to come. Plus, he thought he was sufficiently malleable enough that the Old Man could exert his influence and make sure Anthony was indeed continuing Johnson's work for another generation of Hoosiers. They chatted for ten minutes, and the Old Man rattled off a list of important issues that would arise in the next year or two. Anthony took it all in and offered his best wishes.

"What do you plan on doing in retirement?"

"Die, probably." He managed a smile, knowing even he wouldn't last forever. With his watery eyes and pale exterior, he was not the best picture of health.

Anthony shifted uncomfortably in his seat. "Well, I hope you'll stick around long enough so I can bend your ear every now and then."

"Sure," the Old Man garbled before unleashing his hacking cough. "Joanne, who you met at the front desk, can help you with the bitchers and the moaners."

"I'm sorry?"

"The bitchers, the moaners, the free-handout crowd. There's always some constituent out there wanting or complaining about something."

Anthony shook his head, knowing the Old Man liked the heat of political battle but not necessarily the everyday responsibilities of the office.

Joanne buzzed the phone at the Old Man's desk. His bloodshot eyes lit up when she told him it was the former president calling to wish him well and that they should get together. He told her to give him a second.

Anthony knew it was time to go and stood first. "Thanks for meeting with me. I'll keep in touch."

"You do that, Schumacher," the Old Man said as he slowly shuffled his way around the desk and extended his clammy hand for the final time. He pulled Anthony closer. Uncomfortably close.

"I want to tell you something to always remember."

Anthony could feel the Old Man's smokey breath on his face.

"You make sure you watch your back, young man. Those devils on the other side of the aisle are ruthless and will be out to destroy you."

The booming voice was gone but the whisper was just as powerful. The wise sage poked his bony finger into Anthony's chest. "They are not your friends. They are your enemies."

Anthony stood silent slightly stunned by the Old Man's frankness. The Old Man was serious and knew firsthand the viciousness of Democratic attacks on his character, his family, and his good name. Politics was not fun and games. It was war. And you either kill or be killed.

The Old Man then cleared his throat and spoke clearly. "There's just one thing I want you to do for me when you win."

Anthony felt the Old Man's cold grip tighten.

"Promise me you'll throw that liberal whore of a Speaker out of power."

Needless to say, the Old Man and the Speaker did not get along. They had been planning each other's downfall for years now. The Old Man always distrusted liberals, especially those from the New England area. How such hardy souls could advocate for government welfare and a lifetime of dependency always amazed him. The Old Man didn't get to know O'Shea during her first few terms in Congress, but he stayed away from most Democrats during that time period since he had been such a strong Nixon supporter. When O'Shea raised holy hell that Reagan should be impeached for the Grenada invasion, the Old Man took notice.

They eventually served together on the Appropriations Committee and that's when the lightning and thunder really started shaking the House chamber. He railed against her use of public funds for wasteful pork and under the table dealings with the unions. He once called her the terrorists' best friend after she cut off funding for his military projects. He even filed two ethics complaints against her alleging she lined her pockets and political coffers with bribes and kickbacks. The complaints went nowhere, which wasn't surprising given that the members of Congress weren't all that great at policing themselves. Besides using the classic Democrat talking points that the Old Man wanted to take free lunches away from starving kids, require elderly folks to live off dog food because they couldn't afford their prescriptions, and force poor pregnant teens into those ubiquitous back alleys for their abortions, she called him a war-monger who would risk Armageddon just to prove his point. Rather and Brokaw reported on their verbal volleys on a nightly basis.

Through certain back channels, Congresswoman O'Shea floated the rumor that the Old Man was a gay cross-dresser a la J. Edgar Hoover. She even showed a photo of the Old Man and Hoover, both shirtless, walking along the beach. That the two just happened to bump into each other on vacation one summer in Key West was conveniently left unsaid. Moreover, with Hoover wanting to keep all communists out of power and the Old Man wanting to run every last one out of the U.S., the two naturally developed a professional friendship that lasted until Hoover's death. Contrary to O'Shea's claims, the

Old Man's closet was empty on that matter.

When the Democrats took back power, Congresswoman O'Shea was in position to lead the liberal onslaught. The Old Man seethed with rage that some anti-war, big-spending, pro-tax, pro-choice Dem was the highest ranking official in the legislative branch. That she was a woman didn't help matters. As he aged, Johnson's verbal assaults grew nastier. Within the marble halls of the Capitol, he called her "that liberal bitch," although he cleaned it up for television appearances by referring to her simply as "that liberal idiot." Now he was retiring and she remained in power.

It gnawed on him every minute of the day.

CHAPTER 3

Anthony and Wiley talked over the upcoming campaign at lunch every day. The platform would be one of smaller government, lower taxes, and a strong national defense. A "common-sense" approach to governing that would focus on the needs of the citizenry not on the wants of the politicians. The flyers were about ready for mailing and a media guru would come tomorrow to film the first campaign commercial extolling the virtues of this young Indiana conservative. Things were running smoothly, and the campaign coffers had over a hundred grand waiting to be spent.

Anthony had already made an appearance in sixteen of the eighteen counties comprising the eighth district. Courthouses were always good stopping points, where candidate Schumacher could meet other elected officials – state's attorneys, county clerks, circuit clerks, and coroners. The local mayors bent over backwards to walk Anthony around the town square in hopes of someday being on the congressman's speed dial. Anthony also made a point to pop in at the local newspaper to flash a smile and offer a one-on-one interview. Now he just needed to meet his opponent.

Tomorrow, the challenger would make her much anticipated return to start the fall campaign.

Willow Widen-Wilbert drove her rented Saab through the dusty streets of Silver Creek, wondering why she had willingly returned to this middle American hellhole. The smell of hog manure infiltrated the car's interior offering her a hearty welcome back to Hoosier Land. More like a scatological slap in the face, the elite city dwellers would say. It made her want to win the election even more. If she was lucky, she would win a seat in Congress and spend all of her time with the liberal intelligentsia in D.C. If she wasn't so lucky, she'd be stuck in this middle of nowhere dump for another year.

California born and raised, she had accepted a teaching position at Wabash State University as a favor to a liberal friend, who was the full-time dean of admissions and part-time '60s radical holdout. A dying but still passionate breed indeed. Widen-Wilbert was essentially on loan from Cal-Berkeley for two years in hopes that she could bring a sense of "intellectual stimulation," as she liked to call it, to those who "have missed out on so much growing up in this neck of the woods." When she said "neck of the woods," she meant it too. She was *the* uber-liberal professor of Wabash State University and her radical leanings always provided great fodder for the student newspaper and coffee shops around town. Some of the locals looked at her like one of those giant fossils at the museum – interesting to gaze upon but hard to believe they actually roamed the earth.

Widen-Wilbert was fifty eight years old and once divorced. The hyphen connected her parent's names, a liberal hippie thing. She wore her graying hair in a tight bun. Some, especially her students, thought the bun was wrenched too tight and might have been the cause for her renowned bitchiness. She had no significant other, male or female, although the lack of a lesbian community in Silver Creek might have hindered any hopes of stoking a relationship during the school year. She had fought against every war she could, burned more bras than any woman alive, called for the legalization of marijuana, and advocated for the demise of the military. She was hard-core liberal.

And she was handpicked by Speaker O'Shea to take over the seat of Old Man Johnson. O'Shea could think of no greater insult, no better retirement gift, for that "arrogant son of a bitch."

Wiley had been digging deep into Widen-Wilbert's past the moment her name was bandied about as a possible candidate. He researched the university newspaper for articles, dug up her senior thesis, and even talked to a handful of her erstwhile students. The Internet revealed a treasure trove of material from leftist web sites extolling the virtues of this "legendary feminist." The NOW gang gave her its stamp of approval. Wiley's dossier topped out at one hundred and twenty pages and included a "For Eyes Only" stamp on the cover of the folder to make it look official.

"I'm a little worried about Widen-Wilbert, Schu," Wiley said as they sat at Anthony's desk at their daily meeting.

Anthony had his feet propped up on his desk and was fully engrossed in Wiley's top-secret file. It included a list of her marches and sit-ins and her arrest record (mostly disorderly conduct) from her "peaceful protests." Anthony focused on the Internet articles Widen-Wilbert had written over the last several years. Nationalized health care, abortion on demand, higher taxes on greedy corporations, redistribution of wealth, slave reparations, women reparations, a global community, a new world order, and on it went.

"Why am I not surprised?"

"Listen, the Speaker of the United States House of Representatives doesn't come to middle-of-nowhere Indiana for fun and relaxation. The Democrats mean business."

Speaker O'Shea had flown into the Wabash County Regional Airport in her spiffy government aircraft on Labor Day weekend to get Widen-Wilbert's campaign off to a roaring start. They met on the tarmac and rode with the Speaker's handlers and security entourage to the University amphitheater where a crowd of three hundred (most of them angry women bussed in from Terre Haute and Bloomington) yelled and screeched for the cameras. Thankfully, no bras were injured in the production. The Speaker went on and on about needing a "new tone" in Washington and a "new beginning" to raise the downtrodden from their forty years of oppression, a dig at the Old Man's four-decade tenure in the House. Widen-Wilbert promised to fight for the rights of women, minorities, gays and lesbians, the poor, animals, and "the millions of people around the world who have been kept silent for far too long." Not surprisingly, the unborn would be left to fend for themselves. Not once in her speech did she feel the need to utter the words "God," "Indiana," "family," or "jobs."

"I think as long as we focus on the issues we'll be okay," Anthony said.

"You're overly confident."

"No. I'm realistic. Give the people of this district *some* credit, Wiley. They're not idiots. It'll all work out in the end. Don't worry about it."

Wiley tapped his head nervously and downed another Red Bull. He said it was his job to worry. He jotted down a reminder to call the eighteen Republican county chairmen for the third time. Anthony just smiled.

The reverential view of the citizenry was not shared by the Democratic side. Widen-Wilbert's team, which had the benefit of the Speaker's D.C. public-relations firm, thought "these rural boobs" could be transfixed into voting for a liberal Democrat for the first time in their lives with fancy television ads and radio spots.

"Jim, I want a hundred volunteers going door to door nonstop for the next three weeks," Widen-Wilbert barked over the phone to Jim Evans, now on loan from the DNC per the Speaker's orders. "And get started registering those students."

The plan was to portray Widen-Wilbert as a moderate Democrat among the locals, one who would fight for any and every right they believed in. If she was talking to a business club, she'd be pro-business. If she mistakenly encountered a pro-life group, she'd sing the praises of adoption. Any minority gathering, affirmative action all the way. "Fake it 'til you make it" was the campaign's unofficial slogan. "Lie, cheat, and steal," might have been more appropriate.

Widen-Wilbert would focus most of her time on the students. The chances of converting the conservative base in the eighth district were slim to none. But the students, those open-minded wonders, hailed from metropolitan areas like Indianapolis, South Bend, Fort Wayne, and Evansville. Big cities where liberals and big government flourish. Those poor souls from Chicago, Detroit, and Louisville would be easy targets. To pull off an upset, she'd need every undergrad she could get. She handed out flyers around the quad, talked to women's sports teams, and even downed a few mojitos at a couple of sorority functions. Her campaign was a blizzard of e-mails, text messages, and tweets. "Hope." "Change." "Yes We Can."

Here we go again.

Anthony spent his time shaking hands and meeting the people at pancake breakfasts, church bazaars, and chicken dinners. He had fifteen fried Twinkies at as many county fairs in the district. For whatever reason, the local newspapers always liked a picture of political candidates enjoying the fried fare. Anthony tried his best to oblige, but he was growing tired of the elephant ears, funnel cakes, and pork chops on a stick. He had to pencil in extra time for exercise to combat the caloric explosion.

The Rotary Club, Chamber of Commerce, and the VFW all had him speak to their groups. He visited schools, the Boys & Girls Clubs, and the 4-H fair. At each stop, he would pass out pocket-sized Constitutions for all the kids. He loved seeing the eyes of the little ones light up as they thumbed through their new piece of history. He enjoyed listening to the voters' concerns, and they in turn liked his easygoing manner. His readily available and welcoming smile was one of his best assets.

The Republican County chairmen coordinated volunteers to hammer in yard signs all across the district. Anthony spent one Saturday cleaning up Silver Creek Park with a group of volunteers. It gave him a chance to meet the citizenry and receive a boatload of good press. An event at the Boat Club raked in ten grand for the campaign coffers. The family marched together in the Labor Day parade with their supporters in tow. Anthony even made his way over prior to the parade to shake the hand of his rival as well as the hand of every one of her rented union support crew. The campaign was rolling right along.

Then the tape showed up.

"Schu, it's Wiley." The phone call came in at two minutes before five on a Friday afternoon. Anthony was about ready to call it a day and head to the high school football game to be seen by the voters and shake some hands. Plus, A.J. was on the cheerleading squad.

"Hey, what's up?"

"We've got a problem."

Anthony had heard Wiley's claims that they had "a problem" a hundred times before. Everything was a problem to Wiley. Most of the time it dealt with such petty developments like Widen-Wilbert's yard signs being stolen or defaced or yet another union endorsement for her. But this time it sounded different. The tone in Wiley's voice was one of personal fear rather than simply just political worry. What now?

"I just got an e-mail with attachment from a private investigator who says he has in his possession a sex tape."

"A sex tape?" Anthony said almost laughing. "Who's the tape of?"

"It's not you."

"Well, I know it's not me. If it's not me, who the hell cares?" He tapped his pen impatiently on his desk. Anthony didn't want to worry about this type of stuff. And if it was a sex tape of Widen-Wilbert he sure didn't want to watch it or have to talk about it on the campaign trail. Just the thought of Widen-Wilbert and that tight hair bun in her moment of coital passion gave him the creeps.

"Wiley, is it you?" Given Wiley's past history of booze and babes, it was a valid question. Anthony wouldn't think twice about kicking Wiley off the campaign team if it was. He didn't want any part of Wiley's lifestyle causing a distraction.

"No, it's not me." He almost sounded disappointed that it wasn't him. He collected his thoughts for a second. He wanted to start crying.

"Well, who is it then?"

"Schu, it's your wife."

Silence.

The news cascaded onto his shoulders like a ton of bricks. The blood rushing up to his brain caused him to become slightly disoriented. Did he just hear correctly? His beloved wife? His Elle?

Nothing was said.

The pen dropped to the floor. Anthony's heart was now in his lap. A thousand thoughts were racing through his mind. He was madly in love with Danielle and had been forever. Didn't she love him too? Was she having an affair? Had the Democrat operatives followed her? Was it his fault for deciding to run? They had three kids. The perfect life.

"Anthony, the investigator said it was an old video, from many years back."

That helped a little, but the thought of people watching his wife having sex with another man made him want to puke.

"Have you seen it?"

"Yes. He e-mailed it to me. I've watched it once."

"Are you sure it's Danielle?" Anthony was begging, praying for mistaken identity. Maybe some hot buxom blonde that looks like her.

"Yes, it's Danielle." Wiley was sure of it. "The man said it involved some guy named Brock and it shows Danielle giving him a blow . . ., I mean, um. "

This was terribly uncomfortable for Wiley who cared deeply for both Anthony and Danielle. He squirmed in his seat at his desk.

"She's performing oral sex on him. After that Danielle starts stripping off her bra and panties. And then she's shown on top of the man having sex, um. . . , um, I mean, engaging in sexual relations. Um, full frontal nudity and um . . . loud sex talk, moaning and groaning."

Wiley was trying his best not to engage in some voyeuristic play by play.

"Then him on top. Different rooms. On the bed. In the shower. On the couch. In the kitchen."

Anthony couldn't believe what he was hearing and what he was seeing in his own mind. "Does it look like the camera was hidden? Maybe in a closet or something?" The old prosecutor in Anthony was thinking of what charges could be filed or what lawsuit could be slapped on the sleazy perpetrator.

"No, it's out in the open. It was consensual. He held the camera while he was on top of her. They were laughing about it. And they weren't leaving anything to the imagination. Close ups. Everything."

"How old is Danielle in the video? Is she underage?"

"I think it was made while they were in college. It looks staged. They were moving the camera around to film different positions. There also appears to be some marijuana being smoked. Looks like a bong."

Anthony rubbed his shaking hand across his forehead. He wanted to throw up but settled for slamming his fist on the desk. "That son of a bitch! I'd like to strangle that prick with my bare hands!"

That prick was Brock Harbaugh, Anthony's arch enemy in high school and beyond. Brock was the quarterback stud who every girl swooned over and stood in line for praying to do his bidding. With a hot body and her flowing blonde locks, Danielle was at the head of the line ready to be swept off her feet. They dated in high school, stayed out late partying on the weekends, and shared a bed when her parents were out of town. That bastard never missed a chance to take advantage of her and use her to satisfy his horny urges. As Danielle's neighbor, Anthony had to watch Brock's nocturnal comings and goings with an ever breaking heart. Anthony finally had enough one day with Brock's public fondlings of Danielle and his incessant sexual innuendos and punched him in the face outside a pizza parlor. Danielle stuck by the loser and followed him out to San Diego and the University of California. She eventually wised up and dumped him after walking in to find him boisterously banging some sophomore skank. Needless to say, Brock Harbaugh was persona non grata in Anthony's book.

"I'm really sorry, Schu."

Anthony was boiling with rage, pounding his fist on his desk again because there was nothing else to punch or kick or throw across the room. "What does that investigator want!? Money!?"

"No. He wants you out of the race."

"I'm not quitting!" Another pounding of the desk. Anthony was livid. Wiley had never heard him so angry. "I'm not going to let those bastard

Democrats run me out of this campaign!"

"I know. I know," Wiley said putting his political operative hat on again. "I don't think the Dems expect you to drop out. I think they want this tawdry revelation to come out in the last couple weeks of the campaign and try to knock you off your family values message. Maybe they plant some doubt in the minds of the voters, insinuate that there's more dirty laundry out there, that you're not ready, and they try to pick off some votes. Maybe enough votes to make a difference."

"Son of a bitch." Anthony barely managed a whisper. "I gotta go talk to Elle."

Those at the high school football game would have to do without Anthony that evening. With a pounding headache, he drove home and stopped at a secluded spot on his property overlooking the Wabash River. He turned the car off and cried his eyes out. He had run for Congress to make a difference, make the world a better place, all that good stuff. Danielle was reluctant for family reasons but she relented and gave her blessing. Now his opponents were prepared to drag his wife's good name through the mud. She had three kids under the age of fifteen and a classroom full of third graders. If the video spread across the Internet, her children, students, fellow teachers, neighbors, and maybe even a horde of perverts in Bangladesh could watch a congressman's hot wife getting high and nailed in all her stoned and naked glory. That's the image people would see when they saw her thumping melons at the grocery store, eating a footlong at the local Weiner King, or, heaven forbid, kneeling in church.

When Anthony walked into the house, he found Danielle and Anna sitting at the dining-room table working on her addition and subtraction problems. He almost starting crying at the sight of his beautiful wife, his best friend and the best mother in all the world. He kept it together and found Ashley in the kitchen making a pre-game sandwich.

"Can you keep an eye on Anna for a couple of minutes, I need to talk to your mom."

"Sure."

Anthony stuck his head back in the dining room and motioned to Danielle. "Elle, I need to talk to you about some campaign issues."

Danielle stepped into the kitchen and looked at Anthony's ashen face. "We need to go for a walk."

Once outside, he grabbed her hand and hustled her down into the trees away from the house and away from the kids. She wondered why they were moving so fast. Why did they have to go outside? Why couldn't they just talk in the kitchen? When they finally stopped, Anthony had tears in his eyes. He held her hand with both of his.

"What's wrong, Schumi?" The knot in Anthony's stomach reached over to hers. Now she was trembling. "What is it?"

Anthony didn't know of any other way to put it. Just come right out and say it. "Did you and Brock ever make a sex tape?"

The look on Danielle's face was one of utter disbelief. How did he know? It was years ago. That lying dirtbag promised her he erased it. She had all but forgotten about it.

That son of a bitch!

When she saw the tears dribbling down Anthony's cheeks, she started bawling.

"I'm so sorry, Schumi," she cried. She was borderline hysterical not knowing how the tape surfaced, who had watched it, and what was going to happen with it. She desperately tried to explain. She was young. They were in college. They were drunk and high. It was stupid. It only happened that one time. She begged Anthony to forgive her.

He threw his arms around her and squeezed her tight. He wasn't mad at her. He loved her and would always love her. He reminded her that he, not Brock, had been the winner of life's lottery, married the girl of his dreams, and had three beautiful kids with her.

"How did you find out about it?"

"A Democrat private investigator contacted Wiley and sent it to him in an e-mail."

"Oh my God! It's on the Internet! Schumi! My God!"

She tried to break away but Anthony held her with all his might. "Schumi, they're going to ruin us!"

"No, no they're not. We're not going to let them win."

In the last five minutes, Danielle went from loving wife and caring mother of three with a great job and a nice life to a woman panicked over the thought that her long forgotten momentary lapse into drunken debauchery was now going to be broadcast over the Internet for all the world to see.

"Schumi, what are we going to do?" she cried.

Anthony didn't have an answer yet. There were two weeks to go until Election Day. It was possible the Democrats would wait until the last minute and leak the video to the press. Anthony offered to drop out but Danielle would have none of it. They would need to be prepared if the bombshell landed. Anthony worried about Danielle. She worried about the kids. Both of them were growing a thicker skin.

CHAPTER 4

Wiley began sweating every detail. This was his big chance to show his mettle. If he could pull off a victory in a congressional election where his candidate survived a last-minute bombshell (and a sex tape at that), he'd be sure to join the political pantheon of great election gurus.

He called his contacts in hopes of gauging the mood of the electorate. It was going to be a tough year for Republicans all across the country, even in conservative Indiana. Wiley believed the numbers needed to be wide enough that they could take a hit if the tape surfaced. He convinced Anthony to spend some campaign cash on a voter poll two weeks before the election to get a sense of the way people were leaning. The results were not uplifting. A survey of five hundred registered voters showed Anthony leading 55% to 45%. Wiley wanted at least 60% to 40%. He worried about the undergrads and wondered whether they would skew the results. The Democrats smelled blood and poured more money into this race than ever before. Rumor had it the President might drop in to campaign for Widen-Wilbert.

Plus, the tape was always in the back of Wiley's mind. With a couple of phone calls, he saved his best bullet for last, two Saturdays before the election.

On a warm sunny Saturday afternoon, a boisterous crowd of two thousand swarmed the football field at Silver Creek High School, Anthony's old stomping grounds, for the largest political rally the locals could remember. Wiley pulled out all the stops. American flags blew gently in the breeze behind the podium. Red, white, and blue bunting decorated every fence, post, and railing. "Schumacher for Congress" signs for the adults. Balloons for the kids. Popcorn for all.

The Governor was in attendance along with the senior United States Senator. Wiley was even able to round up a Pacer, a Colt, and last year's winner of the Indianapolis 500. All Republicans! the partisan crowd was told much to their delight.

Anthony could barely believe the turnout as he stood behind the stage waiting for his big moment.

"Wiley, where did you get all these people?"

Wiley just winked. "They're all here for you." It was an exaggeration and

Anthony knew it. The free hot dogs and entertainment probably helped bring in a few extra people. Still, Anthony appreciated Wiley's work and the crowd's support. He thought he'd better deliver or there would be hell to pay.

The Old Man's ascendance to the podium hushed the festive crowd. He required no assistance save for an old wooden cane that once belonged to General MacArthur. The sunlight reflected off his pasty white face as he cleared his throat for what could be his last political rally. The previous speakers had all extolled the virtues of Anthony Schumacher and implored the crowd to send him to Washington, D.C. to fight for Indiana. Wiley didn't tell the Old Man what to say, nor could he have if he tried, but both Wiley and Anthony hoped he would keep it short and appropriate for the assembled throng.

"So this is it, my friends," the Old Man bellowed, his voice rumbling from the speakers. Nobody was sure whether that was a question or a statement. "It is great to be with you here today." The Old Man thanked his supporters for his forty years in Congress and ticked off all the good that America had enjoyed under his watchful eye and leadership. After fifteen minutes of rambling on in the hot sun, the Old Man lit into "those damn liberals" in Washington and the need to fight them at every turn.

Anthony glanced at Wiley standing offstage. Wiley was ready to tackle the Old Man if he turned any more profane. He took one step forward when the Old Man mentioned the Speaker, but Congressman Thor was still on his game and gathered the energy for one last booming peroration.

"Ladies and gentlemen, freedom is a fragile gift that has been bestowed on all Americans by our beneficent God. But the unalienable rights of life, liberty, and the pursuit of happiness are slowly being eroded by an ever encroaching government intent on telling you what to eat, what to drink, what to drive, and how to live your life. The rights fought for by our Founding Fathers and preserved by the courageous men and women of the greatest military in history from the battle fields at Bunker Hill and Gettysburg to the beaches of Normandy, the jungles of Vietnam, and the sands of Iraq will disappear if we don't continue the fight here on the banks of the Wabash to the banks of the Potomac and from sea to shining sea."

The American flags gained strength in the growing breeze. The crowd buzzed with intensity. And the Old Man finished with a resounding flourish.

"The fight for freedom must go on! The fight for freedom must be won! And if you want to continue freedom's fight in Washington you need to send Anthony Schumacher to represent the eighth district of the great State of Indiana in Congress! God bless America! And God bless you Anthony! Ladies and gentlemen, Anthony Schumacher!"

The crowd's applause shook the stage and could be heard four blocks away. Two Civil War cannons blasted away sending their echoes throughout the town and surrounding countryside. The U.S. Geological Survey would later report the moment actually registered on the Richter Scale. Anthony, a big softie when it came to patriotic crescendos, blinked his moist eyes dry as he shook the Old Man's hand and helped him to his seat. The Old Man triumphantly raised his cane to acknowledge his loyal subjects.

"Thank you very much!" Anthony said over the roar of the crowd. "Thank you!" He raised his hands to quiet the crowd. He once gave the valedictory address in the high school gymnasium just across the way, but the crowd in front of him was ten times as large. Young and old, man, woman, and child were cheering for the man they hoped would represent their interests in the nation's capital. He would have some big shoes to fill, but he felt he was just the Schu to do it.

"Thank you very much," he said settling in. "I just want to thank Congressman Johnson for being here today and his kind words. America owes a debt of gratitude to Congressman Johnson for his lifetime of public service, and we are proud that this American hero represented our great state of Indiana."

Anthony was energized by the festive crowd and launched into his campaign platform of education and family. The importance of loving parents and a first-class education were the two most important ingredients to a successful life. Parental discipline, along with love and encouragement, lead to children who respect their elders, their neighbors, and the law. Education inspires children to pursue their dreams and reach for the stars, and keeps them from falling into the trap of gangs, drugs, and a career of crime.

"It would be the highest honor to represent you in the halls of Congress," he said. "With your support, we can ensure the freedom of future generations and provide them with the opportunity to make the world a better place. Thank you very much!"

Both campaigns were now sprinting to the finish. Wiley unleashed a flurry of radio and TV spots. The latter showed Anthony at his desk, sleeves rolled up, and obviously hard at work along with pictures of Anthony talking with an elderly couple, listening intently to a group of police officers, and laughing with his beautiful family. Even Frosty the Snowdog looked happy. No negative ads. All positive. All American.

"I'm Anthony Schumacher and I approved this message."

Widen-Wilbert's ads were all about the Old Man and her claim that he was single-handedly responsible for every war, famine, and ghastly epidemic that the good earth had endured over the last forty years. One black and white photo of the Old Man slowly turned red as if a river of blood was running down his forehead. It's a wonder the Democrats didn't throw in a mushroom cloud for good measure. The last picture showed the Old Man and Anthony shaking hands, insinuating Anthony was nothing more than a dangerous clone of his would-be predecessor.

"Can we really afford two more years of Congressman Johnson?"

The one and only candidate debate took place on the Tuesday before the election. One week before the big day. One hundred and fifty people packed the American Legion hall. All of the prospective voters were given pamphlets from each campaign if they hadn't already been inundated with enough pamphlets in the mail and from door-to-door campaigning. Thankfully, the pamphlets could also be used to fan the voters in the stuffy heat. It was seventy five degrees outside on this Indian summer October evening and ten degrees hotter in the hall. It would only get warmer as the night wore on.

Anthony walked in early and shook some hands. He thanked the mayor for his support and greeted each councilman, the highway commissioner, and the district superintendent of schools like they were old friends. The chief of police used to be his little league baseball coach. Widen-Wilbert stood off to the side talking with a couple of fellow teachers who came to offer moral support. She didn't even know the mayor's name.

Danielle, the three kids, and her mother sat in the front row dutifully welcoming anyone who showed an ounce of support for their husband and father. Anna handed out "Vote for Schumacher" stickers to all who walked by, and no one refused the little blonde angel. Wiley worked the room with gusto, his right hand always in someone else's and his left hand holding his ever present BlackBerry, before taking his seat next to Danielle. He was nervous as hell.

When the moderator, the head of the Wabash State University political science department, called the debate to order both candidates took their places at their respective podiums. Anthony wiped a few trickles of sweat off his forehead with his handkerchief. He wore a dark suit, a red tie, and a smile. An American flag pin on his lapel glimmered in the light. Sans smile, Widen-Wilbert wore her standard gray pants suit. The bun seemed tighter in the humid air. No makeup. No American flag.

After a prayer and the recitation of the pledge of allegiance, the moderator alternated asking questions of each candidate on various topics of concern to the locals. The economy, jobs, health care, and national security. Anthony focused his responses on common-sense government, lower taxes, and allowing the people to make the decisions that impact their lives not some bureaucrat in Washington.

"The main job of the federal government is to keep all Americans safe, and I intend to make sure our military receives the funding it needs to protect us from those terrorists who seek to destroy us and our way of lives."

Widen-Wilbert questioned Anthony's experience, thought he was too young, and recalled several of her many marches on Washington. She used the word "change" thirty-seven times, almost in every sentence of every answer. She was short on specifics and came off as being slightly uppity and condescending. After an hour of back and forth, she had hidden her liberalism well. She kept telling herself to give the people what she thought they wanted to hear.

"I fondly remember my father taking me on hunting trips when I was a young girl growing up in California."

It was a lie, the part about her memory being a fond one, but she thought it sounded good and no one in the audience would know the truth. She hated those trips – her dad, her brother, and her camping in some dirty, smelly tent with a noticeable absence of running water but no shortage of blood-thirsty mosquitoes. At night, her gung-ho father would regale the children with gory stories of his hunting conquests and animal killings. He would then rise early and drag the two kids into the trees so they could watch him fire a slug into some defenseless animal's gut. Her little brother would cheer wildly when Pops bagged anything that moved. When Dad began the field dressing, she would throw up on herself at the sight of the bloody butchering. It was during these trips she learned to hate guns, hug trees, and gain an all-around aversion to capitalism, materialism, and conservatism.

After some more long-winded lies from Widen-Wilbert, the moderator asked Anthony whether he had any hunting stories he would like to share.

"I can't say I have ever climbed a tree stand or hidden in a duck blind," Anthony said with his words drenched in honesty. "Some people hunt, others play golf. I like to run and go to baseball games."

Widen-Wilbert thought this was her time to pounce. This was her big chance. She had yet to gain any points with this conservative audience. Now would probably be her only opportunity to zing a right-wing Republican on the issue of guns.

"How can Mr. Schumacher claim to be a champion of hunters when he's never enjoyed the thrill of the hunt?"

It was a feeble attempt to portray Anthony as soft on the Second Amendment. She thought Anthony was an idiot jock, maybe a charmer, but, all in all, only a tad more intelligent than the rural rubes that had elected him in the past. For goodness sakes, he only had a law degree from Wabash State University, she often snidely remarked to her supporters. With a full head of steam, she took another whack at the political beehive with her rhetorical stick.

"Maybe Mr. Schumacher isn't very proficient with his firearms and could enlighten us with his history."

If said opponent is not a hunter, the liberal play book reads, candidate must attack to make said opponent look weak in front of the voters and thereby cover for candidate's own shortcomings on guns. Unfortunately, the pages in

Widen-Wilbert's play book must have been stuck together. The first rule in politics is do your homework on your opponent's background or be prepared for a responsive ambush.

Wiley almost wet himself with glee.

"I'd be happy too." A slight smile escaped from Anthony's lips. The biggest softball imaginable was now lazily heading toward home plate ready to be belted out of the park. "I've been trained in various types of weapons – the 9-millimeter Glock, .44 Magnum, M-16, sawed-off shotgun, MP-5, M4-Carbine, Steyr-Aug assault rifle, Stoner SR-25 rifle, and the .300 Winchester Magnum rifle. I was a former assistant firearms instructor at the FBI field office in San Diego, and I've received expert certifications from Ruger, Colt, and Smith & Wesson. I also passed a preliminary sniper course."

He was on a roll.

"It's true I'm not much of a hunter. I'll leave the deer and the turkeys to the experts. My free time is usually spent playing basketball or baseball with my kids or running the trails in Silver Creek Park."

He paused and looked above the crowd as if trying to remember some little morsel, some little nugget from his past that might resonate with the voters. It didn't take long for him to remember that one moment because he thought about it every day. He still had the scars to prove it.

"Come to think of it. The last time I fired a gun was when I put a bullet in the chest of some wacko robbing a bank."

The assembled crowd grew hushed. Eyes widened throughout the gathered throng. None bigger than Miss Liberal's. Wiley leaned back in his chair barely able to contain himself.

"I would encourage Ms. Widen-Wilbert to ask that man his thoughts on my experience with guns but he was dead before he hit the ground. My gun, and the gun of my partner who shot the wacko's partner in crime, saved my life." His gaze was stern and his gestures emphatic. "And I will make sure that every American can enjoy the constitutional right to protect themselves and their family by upholding the Second Amendment!"

The crowd roared its approval. No seat was occupied. With his sweat drenched armpits raised for all to see, Wiley was jumping up and down like he'd won the lottery.

"Mr. Schumacher!" Widen-Wilbert interjected, thumping the microphone with her finger in a vain attempt to silence the raucous crowd. "Mr. Schumacher! I don't think your history of violence is appropriate in this campaign!"

Anthony stood silent and smiled. The crowd hooted and hollered. Some laughed. Half of them were probably packing heat at that very moment while the other half had sufficient amounts of small arms and long guns available out in the parking lot.

"Go back to San Francisco!" one yelled.

Thankfully, it wasn't Wiley.

The lone auxiliary police officer sent to keep an eye on the proceedings took a step closer to Widen-Wilbert. He had no heat, but his shaking hand was on his holstered radio ready to call for backup.

Anthony held up both hands to calm the frothing masses who were ready to charge if the bugle was sounded. He turned to Widen-Wilbert with a devilish grin. "I'll be happy to walk you out later on tonight if you want."

This electoral race was over.

CHAPTER 5

"Mr. Schumacher Goes To Washington."

That was the headline of the *Silver Creek Tribune* the day before Anthony was sworn in as a member of Congress. A variation of the headline probably ran in every freshman congressman or congresswoman's district newspaper. The article included a short biography, a picture of the family, and mentioned how Anthony was excited to start tackling the tough issues that were facing the country.

The Schumachers, along with Danielle's mother, flew to D.C. and arrived in the afternoon. Anthony had been to the capital for freshman orientation and to scout out living arrangements. He settled on a town house east of the Capitol building where several other lawmakers stayed. A few congressmen actually lived in their office, a roll-away bed hidden in the closet giving them a place to lay their heads in the evening. Anthony thought about it, mostly to save money, but worried about what would happen if the dirty laundry starting piling up. The town house had two bedrooms, a living room, kitchen, and bath. The furnishings were sparse, an old television and a computer, but Anthony thought it would be conducive to focusing on legislation.

Wiley packed up his U-Haul with what was left of his belongings (which wasn't much after two divorces) and left Silver Creek for the big city. In the southeast quadrant of the District of Columbia, he found a cheap dive in a low-rent district frequented by poor thirty-somethings also excited about changing the world and feeding from the federal trough. He had a refrigerator, a bed, and two folding chairs. He really thought he'd live out of the office or shack up with some other congressman's single and available chief of staff. He'd already made a list of available femmes, although he'd consider it a major coup to score a single congresswoman.

The third of January came with balmy fifty degree sunshine. Anthony snuck out shortly after dawn while the family slept. He made sure to pack his running shoes and they were getting a good workout. Around the Capitol, past the Supreme Court building, then down the sidewalks of an empty Pennsylvania Avenue. He slowed slightly as he ran by the J. Edgar Hoover FBI Building, his former employer. His pace quickened as he neared the White

House, a lap around Lafayette Square and then the Ellipse before turning west to the Lincoln Memorial and back east to the Washington Monument.

He stopped amongst the American flags surrounding the 536-foot obelisk memorializing the Father of the Country. There weren't any tourists around, just a few joggers getting in their exercise before the start of the work day and the Park Police patrolling the grounds.

For the political capital of the world, it was eerily quiet. Anthony had a little trouble comprehending the moment that was about to descend upon him. Because his parents died when he was young, he was raised by his Aunt Meg. She passed away when he was in college, leaving him without any relatives. He wondered what Aunt Meg would be thinking if she could see her nephew, really "her son," was five hours away from being sworn in as a member of Congress. He wished she could have been there with him but he said a prayer and thanked her for all her sacrifices to put him in this position.

The family was getting ready when Anthony returned. Ashley was complaining that her hair didn't look right and Anna was hungry and demanding pancakes. Elle commented sarcastically that she was the one who would get to hear the kids' complaints all by herself now that Anthony would be living in D.C. Her mother reassured Anthony and Elle that she'd always be available right next door back in Silver Creek and all would be well.

They all walked out together and headed the three blocks to the Capitol. Wiley called and said he'd skip the swearing-in ceremony to have the office ready to go. The House chamber was packed with members and their families all proud of the moment. Anthony and his crew settled on seats on the far right of the chamber. He spotted two of his new colleagues from Indiana and thanked them for their good wishes. They asked about Congressman Thor and gave him their cards. A freshman congressman from east central Illinois extended a hand and hoped they could work together on legislation.

At noon, Speaker O'Shea banged the gavel on the rostrum and called the House to order. Anthony and the other elected members stood, raised their right hands, and swore to uphold the Constitution of the United States. It was a humbling moment. Elle and her mother had tears in their eyes. Anthony gave them and his girls kisses and a hearty handshake to Michael. He also pulled out three pocket-sized Constitutions that he had inscribed with special messages for each of his three children on this special day.

After the speeches were finished and votes cast for Speaker and minority leader, the new members took turns for their ceremonial picture with the Speaker. It was an awkward moment for Anthony. He was taking over for O'Shea's great nemesis and the lack of love between them would surely carry over to now include Anthony.

Plus, the tape was still lurking out there somewhere.

Anthony and Danielle had talked little about it since the election. Anthony hoped Danielle's fear of its revelation would subside but it was always in the back of her mind. They knew the Speaker knew about the tape. They knew she knew they knew. It was not a comfortable situation.

Anthony approached the Speaker with a toothy grin and introduced the family. The Speaker had seen Danielle in action before, courtesy of the DNC investigators, and even replayed the video several times just to make sure it was her. O'Shea was amazed at how young and beautiful Danielle still looked, almost twenty years after the tape was made. She also commented on how Anthony had such a beautiful family – the good looking wife and the polite and respectful children. It was going to be a lot harder to tear down this conservative congressman as opposed to the old decrepit miser he was replacing. Elle held the Bible as Anthony raised his right hand before the Speaker as the photographers snapped away. The photo would later reveal the political smiles of Anthony and the Speaker along with Danielle contemptuously glaring at her. Anthony loved it and had it framed.

"Morning, Congressman Schumacher," Wiley said with the biggest smile.

"Wiley, call me Schu. I don't want to get a big head," Anthony said, extending a hand on their first full day as federal employees.

"Okay, Congressman Schu."

Wiley was having the time of his life, finally doing something meaningful he thought. Anthony decided on keeping the Old Man's administrative assistant and legislative aide to ensure a seamless transition. Joanne, the Old Man's former secretary, was setting up Anthony's new district office in Silver Creek.

"You need to be on the floor at eleven."

Anthony sat down at his desk on the fifth floor of the Cannon House Office Building, named after Uncle Joe Cannon, the former Speaker of the House and resident of Danville, Illinois, which sits just across the border from Anthony's district.

"Can you believe they put us in this labyrinth in the middle of nowhere?" Wiley asked, insulted that Anthony received the last office on the highest floor. "We're closer to the Potomac than we are to the Capitol. I think the Speaker screwed us over." Wiley was already making mental notes about how the Speaker was out to get them.

"You know, it's the oldest of the congressional office buildings." He sniffed around like he could smell the mold and mildew that had been lingering since the building was constructed in 1908.

"It was just the luck of the draw, Wiley, you know that." Anthony didn't care where they put his office, so long as they let him on the House floor he wasn't going to complain. His desk was surrounded by American and Indiana flags but the shelves remained empty for the time being. He'd get around to it later.

Betty Warner, the Old Man's former administrative assistant, was seated at her desk and ready to greet visitors who walked in and keep "the complainers" away. She didn't like the new digs either but she had five years to go until retirement and would suck it up until then. Stephanie Hamilton, the legislative aide, had a small office off to the side. She was a policy wonk and loved drafting legislation. Her eyes always seemed to be locked on a computer screen. Wiley's office had a door connecting to Anthony's just in case he needed to barge in with breaking news.

The first few weeks were a blur to Anthony. He was mostly a back bencher, intent on learning by listening rather than giving speeches nobody would care about. Michael sent a text one day and asked him to walk around the House floor so he could see his dad on C-Span. Dad obliged. His office helped a few constituents with questions regarding social security and veterans' benefits and processed forms to have American flags flown over the Capitol for special occasions. Most of the day was spent reading.

At night, the cocktail parties were never ending. Each day, a member of Congress or a lobbyist would have a get together to be seen or heard by somebody. Bad hors d'oeuvres and cheap wine would be served with promises to vote for certain legislation. Contrary to what most students learn in civics class, the legislative process doesn't take place on the House floor, it takes place in town homes and garden parties.

Anthony began to despise them.

"Congressman Schumacher, nice to see you," said the man unfamiliar to Anthony. He wore a well-trimmed beard and round spectacles. He was a first-class schmoozer.

"Hi, how are you?"

"I'm Ross Bridges, CEO of the Ethanol Production Alliance."

Anthony had no idea who he was. He also had no idea there was such a thing as the Ethanol Production Alliance. Wiley told him he had to go to the cocktail party at the agriculture secretary's house to meet the ag experts and talk some corn and soybeans. So Anthony went and was quickly cornered by Mr. Bridges.

"We've got some jim-dandy legislation about to be introduced and we want you to be a co-sponsor."

Anthony had read the proposed legislation. Increased ethanol production would reduce America's dependence on foreign oil and save the environment, the argument went. The bill would also vastly increase government subsidies for ethanol production.

"Congressman, wouldn't it be great to stick it to those rich fat cat sheiks in Saudi Arabia and grow our own energy?"

Anthony wasn't all that convinced. "I'd rather drill for our own oil here in America. We're going to need oil for the foreseeable future, why not use our own?"

"That's true, Congressman, no arguments with you there." Bridges came off like a used-car salesman, opening a new door when the old one closed. "But think of the economic benefits to your home state of Indiana. There's a lot of corn grown there."

"Yes, we have a few ethanol plants outside of my district. Many of the constituents there are complaining about the amount of water it takes to produce ethanol. They're worried their wells and aquifers are going to dry up."

Bridges looked like someone told him his dog had been hit by a car. He was talking to a rookie congressman from the Midwest. And a Republican! Republicans love farmers! And corn! Anthony should have been a reliable yes vote. But he was more up to speed than Bridges expected.

"Plus, if ethanol is such a panacea, a miracle cure for all our energy problems, why is it we need such large subsidies? Shouldn't the market dictate the growth of ethanol? And why is it that we get less mileage with ethanol? And what about the amount of energy it takes to produce it?"

Bridges didn't like to be lectured by some hotshot Republican who should have been in his back pocket. He reached into his suit coat and pulled out an envelope marked "Congressman Schumacher." He had ten envelopes inside with campaign donations for any member who needed to be "encouraged" to vote for the bill. Each envelope contained two thousand dollars, the amount allowed by the campaign-finance law. If Bridges did a good sales job, he would end the evening with the ten he started with and be able to use the money elsewhere. Unfortunately for most lobbyists, members of Congress had become more and more difficult to convince.

"Here, I've been meaning to send you a campaign contribution," Bridges said with envelope extended.

"Get that out my face, Mr. Bridges," Anthony whispered harshly. "Don't ever think you can stuff my pockets with cash in return for a vote."

"Don't be a Boy Scout, Congressman," the slickster retorted. "Everyone does it. It the way Washington works."

"Well, it's not the way I work."

Anthony flicked the envelope away from his face. He wanted no part of it. He made a beeline for the door and left the party. It would be the last cocktail soiree he would attend. Bridges would report the encounter to his fellow lobbyists and warn them about Mr. Clean from Indiana's eighth district. He smiled thinking the Republican leader in the House would someday twist young Schumacher's arm and force him to do the right thing on the ethanol bill. He made a mental note to thank Anthony once he came around.

With the spring recess approaching, Anthony planned a week long vacation for the family in Key West. Danielle and the kids would be on spring break and Anthony wanted to make sure they had extended family time together. He had only been home twice since January.

"Did you get my plane tickets for tomorrow?" Anthony asked Wiley, who was checking off the day's itinerary. Wiley planned on staying in Washington to "hold down the fort." Really, he just wanted to feel like he was in charge, boss the staff around, and then talk some political smack at the local hangouts during happy hour.

"Everything is ready to go. Washington to Miami. There will be an SUV for you at the rental counter. I've printed the map to your hotel off the Internet."

Anthony and Wiley made sure they had all the numbers necessary to stay in touch. Anthony would have his computer and BlackBerry and Wiley promised to report to work bright and early to e-mail anything important that couldn't wait until Anthony returned. Anthony was so looking forward to some time away from Washington and maybe fall into the arms of a bikini-clad Danielle on a nice secluded beach.

Anthony and Wiley were engrossed in the brochure from the Key West Palms Hotel when Betty barged into the office and interrupted their conversation. She had obviously started crying.

"It's Congressman Johnson!" she blubbered.

Anthony and Wiley looked up with great concern.

"He died an hour ago."

Anthony rose to comfort the woman, who spent the past twenty years helping to protect the image cultivated by the Old Man. She was a legend in the secretarial pool thanks to his stature and his good words. Now the man with whom she spent more time with save her husband was dead.

It was a slight surprise to Anthony. The Old Man had entered Walter Reed Army Hospital a week earlier after suffering a broken hip in a fall at his Georgetown home. Anthony visited him twice and listened to the Old Man curse his old age. Strange things were happening, he lamented. He even claimed he was being followed. Anthony worried the Old Man might be showing the initial stages of Alzheimer's or dementia. He kept him up to speed on what was happening inside the Beltway and threw in a few tawdry rumors about some Democrats in hopes of brightening the Old Man's spirit.

His condition took a turn for the worse, however, after he developed a staph infection and then pneumonia. Finally, and even with the best of medical care, his eighty-six-year-old body gave out. On April 15th, tax day (the Old Man's most hated day on the calendar) and the anniversary of the death of the Great Emancipator, the Old Man thundered for the final time.

Anthony told Betty to take the rest of the day off and he would get started on spreading the news. He and Wiley would come up with a statement and contact the Old Man's daughter to learn of any funeral arrangements.

"There goes your vacation."

Wiley was correct in that regard. Anthony was going to have to stay in D.C. to make sure the arrangements were taken care of and that the Old Man be given the dignified funeral he deserved. Danielle was none too happy when he called to tell her she and the kids would have to enjoy Key West without him, but news coverage showing the Old Man's replacement soaking up the sun during his funeral would not go over well with the constituents. Anthony hoped he could make it down by the end of the week.

Wiley e-mailed a statement to the press wherein Anthony offered his condolences to the Old Man's family and friends, stated how much respect he had for him, and thanked him for his patriotic service to this great nation. Wiley called a florist and a mortuary. He was already envisioning Anthony getting some valuable face time giving a speech at the funeral, maybe the cable news networks would even carry it live!

Anthony called the Old Man's daughter, Jacqueline, in California and told her how wonderful her father was when he needed advice. He told her nobody loved central Indiana more than the Old Man. She thanked him, told him to call her Jackie, like the O., and mentioned her father said nice things about Anthony.

Then she got down to business.

Jackie had looked in her file cabinet and found her father's will and burial wishes. He really wanted to lie in state in the Capitol Rotunda and have his casket rest on Lincoln's catafalque. After a nice patriotic ceremony, he hoped to then be buried at Arlington National Cemetery. He had always talked about it, she said. Apparently, the Old Man wanted all the "bells and whistles" to rightfully honor his contributions to America. Plus, he wanted to showcase the inspiring precision and spirit of the United States military by having its members ceremoniously haul his flag-draped casket all around Washington for the public to enjoy. Jackie hoped Anthony could get the ball rolling.

He told her he'd get right on it.

"Wiley!" Anthony yelled through the open office door. "Get me the Speaker's office!"

Anthony had no idea how to set up a funeral for such a celebrated lion of American history. Who was in charge of such an event? The House Sergeant-at-Arms? The Capitol Police? The Park Police? He was hoping the Speaker would have a three-ring binder or something detailing the necessary steps he should follow.

"Speaker's office. This is Marty Goldstein."

Goldstein was the Speaker's trusted chief of staff, more well known than most members of Congress because of his weekly appearances on the Sunday morning talk shows. His greasy black pompadour even had its own faux Twitter account. He was a hard-nosed, bare-knuckled political hack from south Boston and the Speaker's official arm twister and ball buster. The word on the street was he failed the federally mandated sensitivity training for government workers on three separate occasions.

"Yes, this is Anthony Schumacher, Congressman from Theodore Johnson's district."

"Yes, Congressman, I'm sad to hear about Mr. Johnson." Goldstein had been expecting Anthony's call. He wasn't really sad about the Old Man's death, and his reference to Johnson as Mister was a telling reminder that few in that office had any respect for the Old Man. The Speaker's hatred for Congressman Johnson rubbed off on anyone on her side. "What can I do for you?"

"I just got off the phone with Congressman Johnson's daughter and we discussed his burial wishes. She mentioned his desire to lie in state in the Capitol Rotunda and be laid to rest at Arlington."

Goldstein was shaking his head even before the word Rotunda rolled off Anthony's lips. He struggled to keep from laughing. The odds of the Speaker signing off on such an honor were slim to none. He didn't even need to run it by her.

"I think the Capitol Rotunda is reserved for presidents like Lincoln and Kennedy." He didn't hide his snarky tone well. Goldstein knew others had received the honor but hoped Anthony would get the hint that it should be reserved only for such giants as Honest Abe and JFK.

Wiley was on the ball, however, and threw a list on Anthony's desk showing the giants of American politics who have lain in state in the Rotunda. Anthony quickly looked down the list as he rattled off names.

"Well, representatives and senators have enjoyed the honor as well. Henry Clay, Thaddeus Stevens, Charles Sumner, John A. Logan, Taft, Dirksen, Pepper. Plus, military leaders like Pershing, MacArthur, and the Unknown Soldiers."

Goldstein was getting perturbed that the rookie congressman couldn't take a hint. Was he that naive? How did this idiot get elected?

"Yes, but those men were great leaders in American history," Goldstein snorted.

Now Anthony was getting irritated. "Congressman Johnson saved the lives of thirteen soldiers in World War II and was awarded the Congressional Medal of Honor. His expertise in defense matters helped bring down the Iron Curtain and prevent the spread of communism throughout the Western Hemisphere."

Blah, blah, blah, Goldstein thought. Wasn't a little communism good every now and then? After Anthony continued spouting off the highlights of the Old Man's legislative career, Goldstein finally had enough, his sensitivity training on full display. "Congressman, it'll be a cold day in hell before the Speaker allows for it. Maybe there's a chance he'll roll in over her dead body but, short of that, it's not going to happen."

"Well, let me talk with the Speaker then."

"She's not in the office right now. I'll tell her you called." Goldstein then hung up.

Anthony looked at the now silent receiver and then at Wiley standing in front of his desk. "That prick hung up on me. He said the Speaker wasn't in."

Wiley offered to call back and raise some hell. Maybe even head over to the Speaker's office and kick Goldstein's ass. No need. Over Wiley's shoulder, Anthony looked at the television on the wall in the back of the office. There in all her political glamour was the Speaker herself walking down the corridor to her office followed by a cadre of cameramen and reporters. She was rambling on about universal health care and whatnot and blaming Republicans for everything under the sun. No mention was made of Congressman Johnson's death.

"Maybe I'll just go pay her a visit right now."

Anthony hustled out of his office and down the maze of hallways in the Cannon Building. He skipped the elevator and bounded down the five floors of stairs. He sprinted across Independence Avenue and took the steps up the east front of the Capitol two at a time. He flashed his identification card to the guards at the entrance and slowed to catch his breath as he approached the klieg lights still illuminating the Speaker while she held court outside her office doors.

"Thank you all," she said. The Speaker had exhausted her minimal knowledge on health care and was ready for a stiff drink. The reporters finished their note taking and the camera crews switched off their lights. From his perspective in the back, Anthony could see the top of Goldstein's pompadour waiting for the Speaker behind the glass doors.

"Madam Speaker, what about Congressman Johnson lying in state in the Capitol?"

The Speaker had been followed by this same band of merry reporters for ten years now and knew every voice like it was that of her own children. This one didn't register. Who in their right mind would ask her about a state funeral for the most hated man in liberal America? Probably some smart-ass Fox News reporter.

The newsmen weren't sure who the voice belonged to either. Was there a rookie in their midst? Maybe a lackey with one of those late-night comedians sent to stir the pot?

"A what?" The Speaker pretended she hadn't heard the question. The Pompadour was now pacing back and forth inside the office.

"Yes, Madam Speaker, over here," Anthony said waving over the crowd. "Would you support a resolution allowing Congressman Johnson to lie in state in the Capitol Rotunda?"

The reporters whipped their heads back toward the Speaker. Nobody had even broached the subject. The lights were turned back on and the microphones were again thrust in front of her shocked face.

"Well, I . . . I . . . Congressman." She could think of no quick answer, one that would at least sound somewhat respectful of the Old Man on the day of his passing. Her big brown eyes bulged as if Bambi had been caught in the path of full-speed Mac truck. "Um, well, my staff and I were talking about it just this afternoon when the news came out. I'm not sure it will be feasible given the spring recess approaching."

The reporters looked perplexed. They had no idea who this "Congressman" was. A couple thumbed through their pocket congressional pictorial hoping to solve the mystery.

Anthony responded with a quick rebuttal. "Congress doesn't have to be in session for it to happen. It's for the people to show their respect to a great American patriot."

"I'm well aware of that, Congressman," she seethed. "I want to honor Mr. Johnson in a proper and fitting fashion." Again with the Mister. Some of the reporters almost chuckled. Only people living in a cave would fail to know of her animosity for the Old Man. Her way of honoring him would mostly likely consist of urinating on his grave. "My staff and I are working hard to make it happen, if feasible. Thank you everybody," she said as she reached for the door handle.

Off went the lights. No news here. The satisfied reporters closed up their notebooks. Time to trudge back to the office and type up their stories before the day's deadline.

One person, however, wasn't so satisfied. He was tired of the lies and the backstabbing of Washington. If she didn't want to honor the Old Man then have the guts to come out and say it. Anthony wasn't finished.

"Madam Speaker, your staff told me they'd have to carry Congressman Johnson's casket into the Rotunda over your dead body."

Uh oh.

The Pompadour behind the glass doors screeched to a halt. Two reporters almost tripped over each other at the statement. One on the phone told his boss at the office that he'd have to call back, something about some shit just hitting the fan.

Anthony regretted saying it once it left his mouth. He probably shouldn't have ambushed the Speaker without at least talking to her first in private. But he was pissed. Tired of the fake smiles and pleasantries. Even if the Old Man didn't deserve such a high honor, he still deserved respect for his service to the country.

The fiery daggers shooting forth from the Speaker's steely gaze were not lost on the assembled crowd of reporters. No one talked to Speaker O'Shea like that, especially some congressional newbie.

"Congressman, I can assure you no one from my office would speak of Mr. Johnson in such a manner." She was calm and dignified. The deer-in-the-headlights look was long gone. She made no mention of the high fives that took place inside her inner sanctum earlier that afternoon. "There is a step-by-step process that Congress has developed when dealing with requests to lie in state in the Rotunda. We will give Mr. Johnson our full consideration."

The Speaker wheeled around and headed inside her office and behind closed doors with the Pompadour where she could privately call Congressman Schumacher every name in the book. A few reporters asked Anthony about Congressman Johnson and his thoughts on a proper memorial. He hoped the Speaker would agree to the honor as a fitting tribute to a great American.

The Capitol Rotunda is under the joint control of the House and Senate. A person's remains may lie in state if Congress passes a resolution granting the honor or the congressional leadership gives its stamp of approval.

Anthony quietly worked behind the scenes hoping to generate support for the Old Man. He called the Republican leadership and they all said they were on board. He asked fellow Hoosiers to flood the House and Senate switchboards in support, and they gladly obliged. Some Democrats quietly stated they wanted to honor the Old Man but were afraid to anger the Speaker. The Senate majority leader, Jonathan Oldfield, a left-wing liberal from California, wasn't particularly fond of Congressman Johnson, who once referred to Senator Oldfield as a "limp wristed pansy" and a "spineless sad sack." Oldfield was a clear no vote.

Anthony even called the President's chief of staff to garner support. He would find none in the White House, given that President Jackson was almost as liberal as the Speaker. The official White House response was that it was a matter for the legislative branch to decide and, finding it convenient to hide behind the separation of powers, the president's press secretary stated he would not get involved. The reality of the situation was Washington was ruled by Democrats, and Congressman Johnson had pissed off almost all of them during his tenure. The honor wasn't going to happen.

Anthony picked up Jacqueline Johnson from the airport and gave her the bad news – it didn't look like a Rotunda viewing would be in the cards. She cried all the way to the hotel, heartbroken that her father's wishes were rejected. She was sixty years old and lived alone. Her father's memory was her only concern. Anthony told her he'd keep trying.

Wiley worked on a congressional resolution to honor the Old Man. The matter passed overwhelmingly as it does for most resolutions of the obituary sort. Anthony's speech on the House floor commemorating the Old Man's life and calling for a resolution allowing his body to lie in the Capitol Rotunda was heard by a smattering of colleagues. The final vote was 218 to 217, with the Speaker the deciding vote against the Rotunda honor. Her rationale was that the honor should be used sparingly and reserved for the greatest of great Americans. It was a disgusting display of pure partisan politics.

And Anthony didn't like it.

Although the Speaker twisted enough arms to keep the Old Man's remains out of the Capitol, she had no control over Arlington National Cemetery, which falls under the jurisdiction of the Department of the Army. On a cloudy and windy Thursday morning, a horse drawn caisson flanked by members of all five branches of the armed services marched the Old Man's flag-draped casket through the quiet grounds. His final resting place was at the end of a long column of white headstones. He wanted no grand monument or chiseled mausoleum. He just wanted a headstone like everyone else, "simple markers for monumental heroes," he liked to call them.

Jackie Johnson, the Old Man's only remaining family, sat in front of the casket and cried. Anthony sat on her right, the Secretary of Defense on her left. The Secretary was an old friend, and he offered to represent the Executive Branch at the burial. After a final prayer, the flag was folded, the bugle was sounded, the guns were fired, and four F-15s roared above the tree tops. Tears were shed as the mourners passed by the Old Man for the final time.

For a moment, Anthony paused to pay his respects to the man whose seat in Congress he now occupied. Johnson had been in office for most of Anthony's life and both shared a deep love of America and their home state of Indiana. Anthony remembered their conversations and the Old Man's admonishment that he was now fighting the Old Man's war. It was now up to Anthony to lead the battle for America.

A rumble of thunder could be heard in the distance.

CHAPTER 6

Following the dustup over Congressman Johnson's funeral, Anthony slowly became a thorn in the Speaker's side. After his reelection, he began to get his sea legs and felt more comfortable taking on the liberal establishment. The Left no longer considered him that annoying fly that they could simply swat away and be done with. Now, he was an angry hornet and his verbal taunts against big government were beginning to sting.

Fox News had him on every other night providing him with a countrywide megaphone to blast the Democrats for their government largesse and wasteful spending. He loved to inform the American people that their hard earned money was going to pay for such "necessities" like hippie museums in New York, the San Francisco habitat frequented by the endangered salt marsh harvest mouse, and an indoor rain forest display in Iowa. The public in turn would badger the Democrat representatives at town meetings, inundate their offices with angry e-mails, and berate them over the phone. The Speaker would then get calls from colleagues bitching about that rabble-rousing congressman from Indiana.

When the welfare debate made its yearly appearance, Anthony was thrust into the spotlight by the Republican leadership. His grasp of the facts and boyish good looks made him a natural in front of the camera.

He also became the Democrats' new favorite target.

The summer of Anthony's second congressional term also coincided with a major month's long heat wave. The hot air and humidity swamping Foggy Bottom made the House proceedings even more contentious. The Democrat plan for an expanded welfare program brought every liberal group to D.C. in support and every conservative one in opposition. Constituents flooded the congressional phone lines and overloaded the computer system. The debate had raged for two days. The members would wage their verbal wars on the floor during the day and then take the fight to the cable new shows in the evening.

"A.J., you ready to go?" Anthony asked.

"Yeah."

Anthony and his oldest daughter headed across the street to the Capitol.

She was using the summer months to work as a congressional intern – making copies, answering phones, running messages to members, and making sure the bills were ready to be circulated. With her blonde hair and cheerleader good looks, Ashley was a huge hit with the male interns. A senator's son even bought her a latte at the House cafeteria. It seemed every sixteen-year-old boy working on Capitol Hill suddenly had a burning desire to learn more about the great State of Indiana, especially the eighth district. The most used icebreaker was whether the Motor Speedway was in Ashley's district. Unfortunately no, she would say, although her initials and those of her dad stood for the legendary four-time winner of the famed 500, A.J. Foyt, Jr. The chatty, flirtatious Ashley was becoming a great ambassador for the Hoosier State.

Anthony was so happy to have her in town so they could spend time together. They went to museums and ran the National Mall almost every day. He hoped he could stay around Washington long enough to let Michael and Anna experience their federal government at work as well.

Anthony had stayed up all night reading the Democrats' welfare bill, all twelve-hundred pages of it. It boggled his mind that some bureaucrat deep in the bowels of federaldom actually wrote this gobbledygook. On the third and final day of debate, each side of the aisle braced for battle. The Democrats were finished with praising the bill and set their sights on destroying the Republican opposition. The GOP plan was to warn the Americans of the financial calamity the Democrats were proposing. The Blue Dog Democrats sat on the fence waiting to see how their constituents would lean.

Given the importance of the bill, the Speaker herself was in the chair. "The Gentleman from Indiana is recognized for ten minutes."

Anthony adjusted the microphone, "Thank you, Madam Speaker."

He then launched full bore into the bill, making the argument it rewarded irresponsibility and sought to increase the size of the federal welfare roles tenfold. Paying people not to work is a great way to keep people from looking for work. Then there were the earmarks, those handouts to congressional members to sweeten the deal in hopes of securing their vote. At the predetermined point in time, Ashley brought the twelve-hundred page behemoth to Anthony's side at the podium. He hurriedly went through the pork laden monstrosity, throwing a page at a time over his shoulder in emphatic disgust. Car museums, bike paths, and potato research – all items the country apparently could not do without even though it was trillions of dollars in debt. In summary, Anthony argued the bill would hurt the American worker and balloon the deficit even higher.

"We need more jobs not more welfare."

Representative Moeisha Robinson, head of the Congressional Black Caucus, was next in line to respond for the Democrats. A thirty-year veteran of Michigan's congressional delegation, she represented one of the poorest districts in the country, including a once bustling part of Detroit. During her tenure and those of the elected Democrats in the region, the Motor City plunged from the glittering jewel of the automotive industry to a bottomless pit of unemployment, homelessness, and despair. Nothing that couldn't be fixed with higher taxes and increased welfare payments, she told her supporters. Her promises of an extra hundred bucks a month in welfare led to her inevitable reelection every two years. Unfortunately, her support for higher taxes prompted companies to relocate out of state or overseas and take Michiganders' jobs right along with them. She learned quickly to blame everything on greedy corporations and white Republicans.

She had no response to Anthony's deficit numbers.

"Mr. Schumacher, why do you hate black people?" she asked smugly, as if she was doing a great service for her constituents. She was a front-row parishioner in the church of racial demagoguery, and bearing false witness against one's neighbor was a commandment conveniently tossed aside if doing so could somehow advance her cause.

Her reference to Anthony by his last name was also a breach of House rules on decorum and debate, but she was just getting warmed up.

"Why do you want black people to starve?" With an ever-increasing octave, she ranted on and on barely taking a breath. "Mr. Schumacher, why are you such a hate-filled racist!?"

Every Republican in the building had been branded a racist at one time or another in their careers by Congresswoman Robinson. It was part of her legislative *modus operandi*. When she couldn't think of anything intelligent to say, which was quite often, she shamefully flashed the race card because she thought it played well back home. Over time, Republicans learned to laugh it off. They would even share a congratulatory cake on a member's first time. The running joke among the GOP was that if Congresswoman Robinson hadn't called you a racist yet, you hadn't made it to the big leagues. As members of both parties had come to expect it, most paid no attention to her and some talked amongst themselves. Newsmen stopped taking her seriously years ago. The Speaker only tolerated her so as not to piss off the black community.

But one person was unaware of Congresswoman Robinson's standard operating procedure or that her racial barbs were just part of her political shtick. That person just happened to be sitting right next to her father, who was busily scribbling notes for his quick rebuttal. When the cameras turned to the right side of the aisle, they showed the young beautiful blonde with tears streaming down her face after someone called her dad, the sweetest, most caring man in the world in her mind, a wild-eyed racist intent on eradicating the black race.

Anthony didn't even notice until he heard Ashley sniffling uncontrollably in an attempt to keep her emotions in check. After Robinson finished spewing forth her worthless drivel, the cameras turned back to Anthony and showed him with his arm around his daughter, her eyes now red and her head shaking as she told her dad she didn't want to be there anymore. She wanted to go home. Anthony's Republican colleague sitting to Ashley's right passed over his handkerchief. Anthony told her they'd go as soon as he was finished.

"The Gentleman from Indiana is recognized for five minutes."

Anthony straightened his tie and took a deep breath. He stood tall, the pulsating veins in his neck constrained only by the collar of his white dress shirt. He closed his yellow legal pad full of notes and took another breath. His eyes were locked on Congresswoman Robinson. Ashley was still crying on camera behind him.

"Ladies and Gentlemen of the House," he said slowly. He said it again to grab everyone's attention. "I had prepared a few points in response but I now know I have won the argument. This bill is a fiasco and everyone knows it. The Democrats have no leg to stand on. But instead of offering reasons why their bill should be supported, the Democrats reach into their bag of dirty tricks and pull out their villain, someone they can demonize and destroy, in hopes of garnering just one last ounce of support. Maybe get a sound bite on the six o'clock news. We Republicans have come to understand that when the left side of the aisle starts throwing out that racial crap instead of answering the debate, we have won."

He then turned to the Congresswoman Robinson.

"To the Gentlewoman from Michigan. I can take your juvenile and petty antics. I don't take those things personally. None of us do. How many of us Republicans have been called a racist by the Congresswoman from Michigan?" He turned around and saw most if not all Republicans with their hands raised, one of whom was even an African-American, although according to Robinson, just another "Uncle Tom in a Brooks Brothers suit."

"But if you are going to drag my family's good name through the mud," he said, pounding his fist on the podium, "I would appreciate it if you would refrain from spouting your hurtful invective and calling me a racist when my daughter is on the floor of the United States House of Representatives!"

Uh oh.

The House chamber became eerily quiet. The idle chit-chat between members stopped. Tourists in the gallery leaned forward in their seats. The Speaker had been distracted by a couple of private questions from fellow members and didn't see the cute teenager bawling her eyes out behind Anthony. Microphones on the floor picked up her whimpering. This wasn't going to be good for the Democrats.

"I don't expect an apology from you, you're not that type of woman, but you do owe Ashley Schumacher an apology for mindlessly calling her father a racist just because you lost your argument and can't think of anything better to say!"

He waved his arm to the left side of the chamber. "How many of your colleagues think I'm a racist?" He paused for effect, pointing his finger to count any congressman who might respond. Some of the Democrats shifted uncomfortably in their seats. Others pretended not to be listening. A few slithered off the floor hoping not to be caught on camera. "I see no hands."

He went on.

"Some of your colleagues seem to be embarrassed by your display. Perhaps instead of giving your constituents a few hundred bucks extra a month you should try to create new jobs so they can support their families. That is compassion. You want to make people's lives easier in poverty, the members on this side of the aisle want to drive them out of poverty. And your track record has done nothing more than enslave poor minorities in Detroit to the demands of their big-government masters."

A wide-eyed Robinson high stepped it back up to the microphone, outraged that someone actually had the gall to call her out on the House floor. In a further breach of etiquette and House rules, she didn't wait for the Speaker to recognize her and grant her time to speak.

"You are a racist and a bigot, sir! Take your plantation ideas back to Whitetrashville, U.S.A., or wherever you're from!"

The discombobulated Speaker fumbled for her gavel before repeatedly banging on the rostrum trying to get Congresswoman Robinson to shut up, something to get her to stop making a fool of herself and her fellow Democrats.

"The Gentlewoman from Michigan is out of order! The Gentlewoman is out of order!"

A raging Robinson refused to heed the gavel and continued her racial attack, calling Anthony an "inbred honkey" and a "Jim Crow cracker."

"The Gentlewoman from Michigan must suspend her remarks!"

The slamming gavel echoed throughout the chamber. The Speaker was losing control. And with Congresswoman Robinson ignoring her commands, the Speaker now had no other choice.

"The Sergeant-at-Arms will present the mace to the Gentlewoman from Michigan!"

The what? Members on the floor looked at each other in amazement. Tourists and reporters in the gallery gasped. Did the Speaker just tell the man in charge of House security to mace the Congresswoman from Michigan?

Not exactly.

The mace, the ornate pole consisting of thirteen ebony rods and topped with a silver eagle stands guard near the Speaker when the House is in session. Upon order of the Speaker, the Sergeant-at-Arms is authorized to remove the mace from its pedestal and present it to "unruly and turbulent" members, as the

House rule states, to restore order. Only five members of the current class of representatives had served long enough to remember the last time the mace had been utilized.

The Sergeant-at-Arms, a short stocky man with a shiny bald head named John Rodgers, rose from his seat. With his broad shoulders and thick neck, he looked like a well-dressed bar bouncer. He had waited his entire twenty-year career to present the mace to restore decorum in the House, dreaming every night that maybe the next day would bring an unruly member to the House floor. With dignified confidence, he hoisted the mace from its position of prominence and marched it for the first time in a generation in front of a member of Congress. A shocked Congresswoman Robinson, her nostrils still flaring and her eyes ablaze at the mace staring her in the face, said no more and staggered back to her seat.

Anthony knew nothing more needed to be said.

"Madam Speaker, I yield back the balance of my time."

He left the podium, put his arm around Ashley, and walked her out of the chamber. The Republicans gave Anthony a raucous standing ovation. A few reached out to give Ashley an encouraging pat on the shoulder. For once, a Republican had fought back against the Democratic flamethrowers. Most of the deflated Democrats sat stunned.

The Speaker was furious. She banged the gavel for the mid-morning break and practically flew down off her perch. In the House cloakroom, she proceeded to berate Congresswoman Robinson for her stupidity. A fellow Dem stepped in, worried the Speaker might bitch slap her right then and there. Some of the cable news shows broke in live, replaying the shots of the racist congresswoman and the crying teenager in an endless loop. Bloggers feasted on the exchange like a bunch of starving piranhas. The YouTube viral was the most watched video of the day. O'Reilly raked the Democrats over the coals for their politics of destruction. El Rushbo even made time for Anthony on his radio show. Not only had the Democrats lost all support for their bill, but they were shamed as a political party – their race card exposed for all the world to see.

The Schumachers were becoming stars.

Wiley saw this as a great opportunity to get Anthony some national face time. He booked him and Ashley on the morning talk shows where the daughter could tell America how wonderful her father is and the father could call for a new tone in Washington, one that would encourage a civil debate to solve the country's problems. The *New York Times* wondered who was this Congressman from Indiana. Reporters found their way to Anthony's fifth-floor office and discussed his views on politics. Two of the major broadcast networks sent news crews to Silver Creek, where they filmed the corn fields, the Wabash, and the locals and all in all concluded it was not Whitetrashville, U.S.A. Wiley broached the idea of a book deal with a conservative publishing house. Now, the cocktail invitations didn't just come from members of Congress and lobbyists, they came from foreign embassies and the White House.

"I was able to get three invitations to the State Dinner on Friday," Wiley announced as he discussed the week's itinerary.

"Who's the State Dinner for?"

"The Queen of England."

"How in the world did I get invited to the White House by a Democrat president for a dinner with the Queen of England?"

"I made some calls. President Jackson's a lame duck with a soft heart. He felt sorry for Ashley. The British Embassy also heard about the story with you and Ashley and wanted to extend an invitation. Plus, I told them you were related to the Queen."

"You didn't tell them that, did you?"

"Hell, yes, I did. It's true," Wiley said with his mischievous smile. "At least I think it's true."

During one of the congressional breaks, Wiley spent time tracing Anthony's family tree in hopes of finding some famous blood lines. If he happened to be distantly related to Lincoln or Churchill, or maybe even Brad Pitt, it would make for good press and might even impress some voters. Wiley's research uncovered no A-list celebrity or giant of American history. He did find the name of Seymour in Anthony's family, and that line included Horatio Seymour, the governor of New York in the 1850s and 60s as well as the Democratic Party nominee who lost the presidential election of 1868 to U.S. Grant. Going back further, Wiley found the surname included a line shared by the Queen of England, including King Edward II. Unfortunately, King Eddie wasn't the great leader Wiley had hoped for. His reign was royally lampooned as grossly incompetent and known for multiple military defeats. Moreover, thought to be gay, legend has it his detractors took it upon themselves to shove a red-hot poker up Ed's rectum leading to his ignominious demise.

"You didn't tell them about my cousin Edward the Second, did you?" Anthony said with a big laugh.

"Hey," Wiley said, trying to be serious. "There's nothing to be embarrassed about. Everyone has an odd relative out there somewhere."

Anthony did attend the grand soiree with the Queen at the White House. It was his second visit to the Executive Mansion after the welcoming dinner the President gave to newly elected lawmakers. Accompanied by his two blonde beauties, Danielle and Ashley, Anthony was the standout stud of the evening. One slightly inebriated Brit attending the dinner remarked Anthony would make a "jolly good James Bond." Danielle felt like a fairy tale princess in her strapless red dress. She told Anthony all the lonely nights at home were worth it – she had her picture taken with the Queen of England! Ashley also wore red and said all the recent hubbub was worth it too – she got to dance with a prince! And they exchanged e-mail addresses!

The evening could not have worked out better for Wiley. There was his candidate, his electoral project, the toast of the town and hobnobbing with the elite and powerful – former presidents, ambassadors, and four-star generals. Plus, the morning newspapers didn't show the President and the Queen, they showed Anthony and the Queen!

The wave of Anthony's popularity coincided with a tsunami of bad public relations for the Democrats. They were taking a beating in the press and their poll numbers were sinking rapidly. Unemployment was rising, the deficit was skyrocketing, and the Dems couldn't stop spending the taxpayers' hard earned money. The President was of little help. He was on his way out after two terms and was getting tired of Washington and his fellow Democrats. That left one Democrat to take the brunt of the heat, to be the whipping boy or, in this case, the whipping girl.

Jim Evans called the Speaker every day at nine o'clock sharp to report on the previous day's poll numbers. The Speaker rarely cursed him out anymore, almost resigned to the fact that the upcoming elections would return the Democrats to the minority party in the House. Only a miracle could save her job as Speaker.

"It's Jim."

"Give me the bad news first," the Speaker said, taking a swig of bourbon. The drinking had started earlier and earlier in the day.

"We're going to definitely lose a seat in California and one in Florida. The six races we talked about yesterday are still neck and neck. Our candidates have been told they should lean right in hopes of catching some moderate votes. It's going to be really close."

The Speaker didn't need to be told her hold on power was hanging by a thread. She thought about it during her every waking moment.

"What's the good news?"

"I have no good news."

The Speaker wasn't surprised.

"There is that thing we talked about yesterday."

She took another drink. After firing round after round at the Republicans, the chambers in the Speaker's political revolver were all empty save for one last bullet.

The tape.

It was the one bargaining chip she had tucked away in her vault, a sort of "in case of emergency – break glass" type of thing. She didn't want to use it, mostly because she wasn't sure it would work. It was incredibly risky, one that could blow up in the Democrats' faces if the public discovered the Speaker of the House had ordered its release. Evans and the Speaker had discussed the pros and cons of releasing the tape on several occasions. Every night that Anthony went on television was another vote for a Republican candidate. He was becoming a conservative hero and moderates were drawn to him. The one-term congressman was campaigning in districts across the country where twenty-two months ago he was an absolute nobody. The line "U.S. Rep. Anthony Schumacher, R-Ind." seemed to run nonstop across the bottom of TV screens. *People Magazine* had Anthony and Danielle on the cover and voted them Washington's most beautiful couple in politics.

Democrat operatives told the Speaker her only hope of salvaging her career was to release the tape and throw Anthony off his family values message. The last thing Anthony would want to do would be to go on TV every night and talk about the tape of his wife having sex with another man. That it happened twenty years ago didn't matter. Even if Anthony took to the airwaves and gallantly tried to protect his wife and her privacy, the blurred out images of the nation's newest blonde bombshell humping some guy would probably be playing over his right shoulder. The words "Schumacher" and "sex tape" would now crawl agonizingly slow across the bottom of the screen. Instead of *Time* and *Newsweek* wanting interviews, tawdry skin magazines would offer big bucks for a pictorial spread of the Congressman's hot wife. Late-night comedians would have a new Lewinsky to fill up a week's worth of ribald monologues.

The Democrats just needed a distraction a couple of weeks before the election to stop the conservative juggernaut, or at least slow it down to give the party a chance.

The Speaker was out of options. She couldn't just hope for change. She had worked too hard in life to give up power now. If she lost the Speaker's chair, her fellow Dems would most likely seek new leaders to right the ship. She would go from third in line to the presidency with access to military aircraft, twenty-four-hour protection, and the most sought after office in the Capitol to a washed up has been. Unable to take the defeat and loss of power, she would probably resign, maybe write a memoir, join the lecture circuit, or host a talk show on MSNBC that nobody would watch.

She had thought about it enough. She wasn't ready to retire to Massachusetts.

"Release the tape."

CHAPTER 7

Thankfully, Anthony was in Silver Creek when it happened.

He was on a ten-mile run in Silver Creek Park the morning after Halloween. He liked a good long run in the clean air to clear his mind and prepare for the day's campaign schedule. Lunch at the Women's Club and then an afternoon assembly at the high school were both on the menu. He had no opponent in this year's election, but that didn't keep him from raising money and working up the Republican base for other candidates on the ballot.

As he admired the fall foliage, the phone on Anthony's hip buzzed. It was Wiley, and he was out of breath.

"Schu! The tape's out! Those bastards released the damned tape!"

Anthony ran his hand over his head.

"Son of a bitch," he whispered to himself. He didn't think the Dems would do it. He prayed they wouldn't. They didn't need to do it to defeat him in a campaign with no opponent. He should have known better. The Old Man would have seen it coming. These Democrats were his enemies.

The Democrats had planned it so the tape would hit the airwaves the day after Halloween when families would be at home after the ghosts and goblins had gone and plenty of candy remained to satisfy their hunger as they spent hours in front of the TV mesmerized at the sight of Congressman Schumacher's X-rated wife.

"Where is it?"

"I just got a call from a reporter who saw it on the web at the *D.C. Whisperer*. It's a social gossip site."

Wiley knew the site well. He often looked in to see what was going on after-hours in D.C. and learn where he might find some action. Now the site featured the breaking news of Danielle Schumacher and her sex tape. The accompanying article was purposefully vague – how the tape was obtained, when it was made, who the naked man happened to be. It also speculated Congressman Schumacher must enjoy his nightly romps in the sack with such a voluptuous wife and her apparent willingness to engage in "the kinky sex."

The lewd comments following the article were adding up quickly.

"Hot damn!"

"No wonder Congressman Schumacher always seems so happy."

"I'd tap that."

The heavy traffic caused the web site to crash after only twenty-nine minutes.

"I've looked at it. The quality isn't very good, but it's all out there for everyone to see." Wiley's head was spinning. He had to think of the cure. And quick.

"Schu, my BlackBerry's buzzing like crazy. The bloodhounds have found it and it's not going to take long for the whole world to find out about it."

Anthony's phone lost its signal out near the woods. He didn't need to hear anymore. He sprinted to his car. Silver Creek Elementary was less than ten minutes away. His heart was racing. His head was hurting. How was he going to break it to Elle that the Democrats sought to take down her husband by destroying her life?

He jammed the car in park and ran inside the school, still in his running attire. The secretary yelled at the stranger hurrying down the hall without checking in at the front desk. He didn't hear her. Outside the third-grade classroom, he saw his lovely wife overseeing her students working their math problems on the blackboard. She saw him and her heart dropped.

She knew what it was without a word being said. She told her students to continue working as she had to step outside for a quick second.

"It's out isn't it?"

"Yeah." He started crying and grabbed her in his arms. "I'm so sorry."

She showed little emotion other than a blank stare at what was about to transpire. Her former sex life was going to be the talk of the town. The locals might even conjure up the name of Brock Harbaugh and wonder what he's been up to lately.

"I'd really like to get you out of here."

"Schumi, I have classes to teach."

"Elle, the satellite trucks are probably heading here right now. We need to get the kids out of school and get home."

Anthony's words finally hit home. The thought of her kids finally unleashed her tears.

After being alerted by the school secretary, the principal sauntered down to investigate. Anthony explained their need to leave. Elle rounded up Michael and Anna while Anthony picked up Ashley from Silver Creek High. The dining-room table soon became the family base.

"Is anyone going to tell us what's going on?" Ashley wondered.

"Guys, your mom and I want to have a real important talk with you." All the kids listened intently, even seven-year-old Anna, who could sense something was wrong.

"I got a call from Wiley and he told me there's a video on the Internet. It's an old video of your mom. It shows her without any clothes on, but like I said it was taken a long time ago."

Ashley started crying and held her mom's hand. She knew this wasn't going to be good.

"It also shows your mom doing some other things." Anthony really didn't want to go any deeper lest he have to explain the birds and the bees to Anna.

Anthony blamed the Democrats and tried to tell the children that politics is a contact sport that oftentimes isn't fair and can be hurtful to innocent people.

Now they just had to wait for the fallout.

Wiley had called the sheriff and a deputy's car was parked at the end of the Schumacher's driveway. No one was to be allowed in. Anthony spent the afternoon on the phone with Republican leaders, apologizing for the mess and bitching about the Dems. He explained that the tape had surfaced during his first congressional campaign and he believed the Speaker had a hand in it.

The family reluctantly turned on the TV. The pontificators were having a field day. Democrat operatives tried desperately to paint all Republicans as horny perverts. Congresswoman Robinson not only called Anthony a bigot but a hypocrite. When asked how Anthony could be hypocritical given that he wasn't on the tape and it was made when Anthony and Elle weren't even married, it didn't matter to Robinson.

"God-fearing Republicans aren't supposed to be taping their sex acts," she crowed. "It ain't right."

For three nights, nothing was said of taxes, spending, deficits, or earmarks. Just sex.

Elle took Thursday and Friday off.

Anthony kept a low profile. Two elderly, blue-haired ladies stopped him at Wal-Mart one early morning and wondered how he and Elle could film their sex life and post it on the web. They apparently received their news from their hairdresser. Anthony's attempts to explain it was not him went unheard. "People go to hell for less things," the pious old biddies said, wagging their fingers as they lectured him.

On Friday morning, Anthony confronted the media in the parking lot outside his office. He asked that people respect the family's privacy. He also lit into the Democrats and their politics of destruction.

"I'd like to say one last thing. Nearly two years ago I decided to enter the political arena and run for a seat in Congress. I wanted to represent the great people of Indiana's eighth district in Washington and make sure they were getting the best bang for their buck. I naively believed Democrats, Republicans, and Independents could put aside their differences to make America a better place to live. Unfortunately, I learned the Democrats have no desire to put the American people first. Instead, their main goal is their own political survival. And what my family has been subjected to in the last forty-eight hours is the handiwork of a political party hell bent on personal destruction. My wife is a third-grade teacher and mother of three kids. The only reason her name has been dragged through the mud is because she's married to a member of Congress with an "R" after his name. The American people are tired of this type of political warfare and I will do everything in my power to make it stop."

The assembled media weren't sure how Anthony was going to make that happen. Anthony took no questions and walked back into his office. He was boiling hot and used every ounce of restraint to keep from promising to take down the Speaker for what she did to Elle. Publicly, the people's business was his first priority.

Privately, the war was on.

After a few days, the dust settled and the tape slowly made its way into political oblivion. The talking heads were now focusing on the results of Election Day. Anthony arrived at the polling station at the county fire department at 8 a.m. accompanied by Danielle. A few of the firefighters made their way out and shook the Schumachers' hands. Danielle had ventured out in public a few times since the tape was released. The locals went out of their way to make her feel comfortable. Some were furious at "those damn Democrats" and told her to keep her head up. The pair made their way inside and cast their votes.

Anthony decided not to have a big campaign shindig this year considering what transpired the last week. The Schumachers were exhausted and needed to catch a breather. Wiley came over at eight and spent the night in the den with a phone attached to each ear. The Wabash County Clerk called to say Anthony won his race with 100% of the vote and the Republicans were rolling to victory in the other local races. The other counties in the eighth district reported similar numbers.

The national news was also good for the Republicans. By eleven, it was clear the GOP would be back in charge at the White House. The Senate would stay in the hands of the Democrats, but only with a two-seat majority. The only uncertainty was in the House.

Jim Evans went through three cell phones and two shirts as he relayed the latest news to the Speaker. She spent the night at Legal Seafood in Boston eating snow crab and sweating bullets. Her political life was on the line and one or two races across the country could make the difference.

At two-thirty eastern time, after the lobster and shrimp were long gone and the bubbly was still on ice, Evans called for the final time. The last hotly contested race was over. California's tenth district went down to the wire but the Republican candidate looked at the numbers and made the call – to concede and congratulate her opponent.

The Speaker and the Democrats had survived. The Speaker's crew exhaled and exploded, sending a wave of liberal rejoice that resonated up and down the eastern seaboard. The balloons were falling and corks were popping. The raucous celebrations would last through the night, and the Speaker's hangover would linger through midmorning. But her job didn't get any easier. The Dems retained their majority – by one seat.

January brought with it ol' man winter and the presidential inauguration. January 20th started with snow showers and cloudy skies. As a great lover of American history, Anthony wouldn't miss the opportunity to view the inaugural from the congressional seats behind the presidential podium. He was able to score extra tickets from Democrat lawmakers who were taking the first flight out of town. They weren't in the mood to sit outside in the cold and watch a Republican being sworn in as commander-in-chief. The kids accompanied their grandma and sat amongst the VIPs. Anthony and Danielle sat huddled together, holding frozen hands and sharing hot chocolate.

Their early arrival time on the reviewing stand gave them time to reflect on their lives and the whirlwind of activity that had engulfed their world in the past two years.

"We're a long way from Silver Creek, aren't we?" Anthony asked.

"I never thought we'd be here."

The pulsating energy of Washington doubled on inauguration day. The pomp and pageantry made the enormity of the moment hard to comprehend. The city vibrated with power. You could smell it just walking down the street.

"I guess someday you'll want to be standing up there raising your right hand, huh?" Danielle asked, wondering what other types of messes her husband could get himself and the family into.

Anthony smiled. "Everybody sitting up here thinks they'll be President of the United States someday."

"Why would anyone want to put themselves through a ringer like that? Nonstop campaigning for a year or more. The media peering into every corner of your life." She was hoping he'd never want to subject himself and the family to a presidential campaign.

"It would be easier for us, we've already been through the ringer."

Danielle gripped Anthony's hand a little tighter and kissed him on his frozen cheek. As bad as the past couple of months were, she was still proud of her husband and his accomplishments. Things could only get better, she thought.

"Governor, would you please raise your right hand and repeat after me," the Chief Justice said as he read from the preprinted card held down at his chest.

"I, Ronald Jacob Fisher, do solemnly swear."

Those sitting nearby could see the breath of the Chief Justice and the President-Elect as they rattled off the thirty-five word oath set forth in Article II, Section 1 of the United States Constitution, the same one used by George Washington back in 1789 and every president since.

"That I will faithfully execute the Office of President of the United States."

Every member of Congress sitting on the podium had goose bumps running up and down their arms. The power they all craved was being bestowed on the man standing before them with the raised right hand and the other resting on the Fisher family Bible.

"And will to the best of my ability,"

Danielle took her hand away from Anthony's and snapped a picture of the panoramic vista, the Washington Monument standing sentry in the background amongst the hundreds of thousands of spectators. Her students would receive a historic slide show during next week's assembly.

"Preserve, protect, and defend, the Constitution of the United States."

The peaceful transfer of power was almost complete. President Jackson's belongings were boxed up and in a moving van heading out the White House gate. The presidential limousine bore new "USA 1" license plates. And the military aide with the nuclear football handcuffed to his wrist took one step closer to the new president. The clock read noon.

"So help me God."

Anthony soaked it all in. The crisp rendition of *Hail to the Chief.* The booming twenty-one howitzer salute. All spine tinglers for a political junkie. He hardly heard a word of President Fisher's inaugural address, too busy looking around enjoying the atmosphere. It was an exciting time with an amazing view of history.

The swearing-in ceremony was followed by lunch in Statuary Hall for the President, Vice President, selected Members of Congress, Supreme Court justices, and other dignitaries. It gave the powerful a chance to shed their winter coats and enjoy roasted Missouri quail with huckleberry glaze, rice pilaf, winter vegetables, and apple brown betty. Anthony and Danielle shared a table with Texas Senator Charlie Turner; Janice Harnacke, the incoming Secretary of Commerce; and Supreme Court Justice Pamela Anders. They were a delightful trio and the laughs they shared made the meal taste even better.

Anthony and Danielle skipped the inaugural parade. They weren't invited to the presidential reviewing stand anyway. The snow was picking up. Plus, they had to get the kids and Danielle's mom to the airport. They had school the next day and needed to get back to Silver Creek.

After a quick dinner, Anthony and Danielle gussied themselves up and headed for the State of Indiana inaugural ball. Governor Richard Armstrong put on quite a show with a black and white motif, tapping into Indy's checkered flag history. The guests sang *Back Home Again in Indiana* and *On the Banks of the Wabash* every hour on the hour, although by ten o'clock the free booze made the renditions less than noteworthy.

Anthony and Danielle shook every hand and thanked everyone for their good wishes. Requests for snapshots were never ending. They were in the company of friends and the evening was a terrific boost for their politically fractured psyche. The Governor told the crowd to party until the sun came up.

Anthony had other ideas.

"I don't think I've ever seen you as beautiful as you are tonight," he said, looking deep into her eyes. Her sleek and stunning ball gown and long blonde hair made her the envy of every attendee on that evening. She was so hot Anthony asked her to end the dancing early. They slipped out the back and hailed a cab, all the while surreptitiously fondling each other in the backseat as they headed to the town house. Once the doors were locked, their clothes didn't even make it to the bedroom. With the lights turned low, they made up for lost time and ran their hands over their naked bodies. They then made hot passionate love deep into the night.

And the Democrats heard every glorious bit of it.

CHAPTER 8

Gridlock gripped Washington.

With the Republicans in charge at 1600 Pennsylvania Avenue and the Hill still controlled by the Democrats, meaningful legislation ground to a halt. Democrats sent budget busting bills to the President, who promptly vetoed them and told Congress to start over.

Anthony was no longer the new Republican kid on the congressional block. He loved his job. He spent his evenings reading staff reports on upcoming bills and was selected for slots on the agriculture, small business, and judiciary committees. Fellow members of Congress would often see him leading a group of constituents through the Capitol and pointing out the paintings and rattling off trivia. A group of Indiana Girl Scouts even had a tour of the National Archives with their home-state representative. He always gave the kids autographed pocket Constitutions and told them to read and study it. Visitors from Indiana always remarked how personable and down to earth Anthony was. He tried to have his picture taken with at least a hundred people per week (Wiley's orders) and give the folks a reason to tell their relatives, friends, and neighbors about that wonderful Congressman Schumacher.

At the Friday office mail delivery, the keys arrived.

Jacqueline Johnson had called from California earlier in the week to inform Anthony that her father's D.C. apartment had been broken into. It had remained vacant for almost four years now. She had the power and water turned off after the funeral but could not bring herself to collect the Old Man's belongings so she left them there. She continued to pay the rent and thought one day she would gather the strength to fly out east and exact the final measure of closure.

Because of her advancing age, she wanted to know whether Congressman Schumacher would be so kind as to pack up the items and send them to her?

Wiley thought she had a lot of gall to ask a member of Congress to act as her moving company. Doesn't a U.S. representative have better things to do? Who the hell does she think she is? Anthony, however, understood that Jacqueline was old and alone and must have considered him her last dear friend who could help her.

"He had done such a fine job with the funeral," she was reported to have said.

"What about a moving company?" Anthony asked her.

"Oh no, no. Out of the question." Only Anthony would take great care with her father's possessions. She could not trust strangers.

"Just have Betty do it," Wiley said, tossing the thankless job to the hired help.

Anthony mulled the idea around for a second. Who knows how long it was going to take. "I probably should do it. I don't want someone thinking I'm using Betty for personal business on the taxpayers' dime. Why don't we do it on Saturday?"

"What do you mean we?"

"Yeah, both of us. We'll get it done Saturday." Anthony figured Wiley wouldn't have anything planned anyway, at least not during the day time.

Anthony and Wiley arrived the Old Man's Georgetown apartment at 10 a.m. wearing the oldest pairs of jeans they could find and a bucket full of cleaning supplies just in case the dust bunnies had overrun the place. A police officer tagged along after Anthony called the Chief of Police and made sure the coast was clear.

Anthony unlocked the front door and pushed it open. The stuffy air blew past their faces.

The officer checked each room of the residence. "Probably some kids saw the place had been uninhabited for a long period of time and thought they might find a hidden treasure or something," he said, as he opened the closets full of the Old Man's clothes. "It was hard for us to determine what if anything was stolen since his daughter didn't really know what Congressman Johnson still had in here. They made a mess of the den though."

"How did you guys find out about it?" Anthony asked, running a finger down the dusty counter top.

"Neighbor saw the blinds moving. Upon closer inspection, she saw the window had been broken."

"Any other burglaries in the neighborhood?"

"Not that I know of."

The officer found the place secure and let Anthony and Wiley get to work. They opened the windows to air out the place. Wiley carried in an armful of packing boxes and tape. They decided to start in the bedroom, box the Old Man's clothes, and then move to the den.

The Old Man had a closet full of dress shirts and dark pants. Wiley counted forty-four ties. They tried to write it all down just in case Jackie asked for an accounting.

"Why doesn't she just let us donate this stuff to Goodwill or the Salvation

Army?" Wiley wondered.

"I don't know. She probably wants to donate his clothes to the Smithsonian. Maybe start her own 'Theodore Johnson Museum.'"

"I'm sure she'll want you on the board of directors," Wiley said, laughing.

The bedroom took all of one hour. They were making good progress. Then they came to the Old Man's den. The shelves were lined with dusty books. Washington, Jefferson, Lincoln, Teddy Roosevelt, and Churchill each had their own separate shelves. The Old Man studied the greats and wove their teachings into his own Johnson Doctrine.

The Old Man's desk was a mess. It was a replica of the Resolute Desk, the original one made from wood of the HMS Resolute and gifted to President Hayes by Queen Victoria in 1880. A number of Presidents had selected the desk to occupy the Oval Office. The Old Man often told President Reagan how much he liked the desk, and the Gipper had the replica made in appreciation of Johnson's tireless effort to bring down the Berlin Wall. It was a beautiful piece of work. It probably cost five to six thousand dollars.

And the thieves had damn near destroyed it. Each drawer had a lock, and the robbers obviously didn't have the key. So they took a crow bar and a hammer (Wiley thought it might have been an axe) and pried them open. Obviously looking for the Old Man's secret stash of cash, Wiley surmised. Jacqueline had sent the three keys but they were useless now.

Anthony wasn't sure how this would go over with her. They took a picture of the desk and hoped she would agree to junk it since it was beyond repair.

A couple of more looks around the room made the former FBI agent think something else was going on here. On the windowsill were two glass vases full of the Old Man's loose change, probably a good five-hundred bucks worth. Petty thieves would have found a way to make off with that easy booty. The books on the shelves had not been disturbed, the dust covering the shelves a dead giveaway that they had remained in that position for some time. An autographed baseball from Yankee great Joe DiMaggio had rolled to a stop in the corner. Maybe the thieves weren't autograph collectors.

"Something just doesn't seem right here," Anthony said.

"I know. She really ought to have professionals come in and box this stuff up."

"No. That's not what I mean. The center of destruction is right here at the desk. Nothing else in the room has been disturbed."

"Like I said, they probably thought the Old Man had money hidden in his desk. Maybe a gold coin collection or something."

Anthony wasn't buying it. It didn't smell right. The FBI taught him to be curious, inquisitive, to look at a situation differently than the average citizen. Something was up.

"Or maybe they were looking for the Old Man's secrets."

Anthony chose not to press the matter. He didn't know what they were looking for anyway. He and Wiley had a job to do and Jackie was probably waiting impatiently for the Old Man's belongings. Twenty boxes full of clothes, books, and mementos were lined up ready to go. Anthony kept out the Old Man's Medal of Honor, the two pound chunk of the Berlin Wall, and an American flag that flew over the Capitol on 9/11. He wasn't going to trust those to strangers. He'd deliver them to Jackie himself.

The movers showed up at four. The boxes were loaded, even what was left of the desk, and shipped off to California. Anthony called Jackie and told her the stuff was on its way. She thanked him profusely and told him she would call when they arrived. She promised to send a check for his hard work but Anthony declined saying there was no need. He was glad to do it. Anthony and Wiley made one last inspection and concluded everything was cleaned out. They then locked the doors at the last home of an all-American hero.

The late Congressman Johnson wasn't the only recipient of strange happenings.

Anthony's congressional web site was breached. The hackers placed a picture of a marijuana leaf on his home page and wrote a professional piece pretending to show Anthony's desire to legalize cannabis. Both his D.C. and district offices were inundated with angry calls from law-and-order constituents. The House tech guys were looking into it.

On a quiet Wednesday evening in early July, Anthony was at his town home east of the Capitol. He was poring over health-care literature for an upcoming debate. The Factor was on TV but he had it muted while he read and took notes. He had already made his nightly call home via his web camera. Anna showed her dad the tooth she lost.

At 11:30 p.m., the car stopped at the corner. Jim Evans was driving the rented Toyota with the hooker in the front seat. She was battered, bruised, and disheveled. She had a fat lip and a torn blouse. She was all ready to go to work.

"Showtime, sweetheart," Evans said.

They had already driven by so Evans could point out where Congressman Schumacher lived. The hooker's name was Svetlana, and she was getting paid ten times what she normally took in during a week when Congress was in session. The bruises were real and of recent infliction. She got paid extra to endure that too.

She walked quickly but calmly up to Anthony's door, stopped to catch her breath, and started to cry. She mussed up her hair one more time. She then pounded on the door.

"Please help me!" she screamed. "Help me!"

Anthony put down his notepad. Was that at his front door? When he heard the woman yell again, he hustled out of his chair and looked out the window.

There he saw a woman in a short skirt and a ripped blouse.

"Help me, please!" she cried out.

"Just a second." Anthony turned the deadbolt and unlatched the chain.

The woman fell into his arms, screaming that she had been raped and begging him for help. Anthony pulled her in and closed the door.

"Who raped you?"

The woman was incoherent, blubbering on about some "son of a bitch" who beat and raped her in his car down the street. She tried to pull away to get away from the door. She even scratched at Anthony's arm.

Anthony told her to sit down on the sofa. It was going to be okay, he told her. He grabbed the phone and called the police. "Yes, this is Congressman Schumacher. A woman who says she's been raped just showed up outside my door. She looks like she's been beaten. Could you send a squad car over to this address?"

"Sir, they're already on the way."

Already on the way, Anthony thought. How could they already be on their way? Maybe the neighbors called it in.

Or maybe Jim Evans called it in when Svetlana made it inside.

The cops arrived in less than two minutes. And that's when things started to turn south. When the flashing red and blue lights could be seen through the front window, the hooker bolted out of the residence screaming for all the world to hear that Congressman Schumacher had raped and beaten her.

"He's inside with a gun!" she yelled to the two officers as she hid behind them.

Anthony had stopped in the middle of the front doorway. He didn't hear what she had said because he was getting her a glass of water. The cops drew their weapons and pointed them at Anthony, telling him to drop the glass and put his hands in the air.

"I called it in!" Anthony tried to explain.

The cops didn't know who raped who or who called who, but they had a hysterical woman begging for help.

"Turn around and put your hands behind your back! Now!"

Anthony could do little else but comply. The officers threw him up against the front door and handcuffed him. A search of his person revealed a container of ChapStick. A quick search of the residence showed no one else inside. Now the officers had the scene under control. The female one went back to the squad car to question the hooker, the male stayed with Anthony. Two more police cars showed up with lights flashing, drawing everyone's attention to Anthony's front door.

"Officer, I called the police. I was sitting down reading when I heard a banging at the front door. I heard a woman yell please help me. She didn't get past the front sitting room."

The officer walked the handcuffed Congressman through the residence. The officer noticed a throw rug that had been rumpled and displaced, but nothing else seemed out of place. The bed was still made. The Congressman's briefing materials were laying on an end table next to his recliner. A closed-captioned Hannity was excoriating Democrats on the TV.

"Where did you get those scratches on your arm?" he asked.

"That lady was trying to get away from the front door and I was holding her back. I didn't know if she was high or what. Ask my neighbors if they heard her yelling at the front door."

An officer who had arrived in the second wave of squad cars and had quickly canvassed the area stopped on the front porch to speak with Anthony and the other officer. He acknowledged that the neighbor across the street had come out to offer that he heard the woman yelling at Anthony's front door asking for help. He said the porch light came on and the Congressman had opened the door.

Both officers were beginning to believe Anthony. They wanted him to come down to the station so they could write up his side of the story. Anthony didn't like the idea. He hadn't done anything wrong. While they were standing on the porch, a Democrat operative hiding in the bushes two houses down caught the police questioning the handcuffed Congressman. Mission accomplished.

"I'll have to see if she wants to press charges," a female officer said. If she did, Anthony would need to go to the station for a more formal interview. When she got within fifteen feet of her squad car, she saw the empty backseat.

"Hey, she's gone!"

The other two officers and Anthony looked in each direction but the hooker was long gone. In fact, she was in the front seat of Jim Evans' Toyota heading back to her apartment so she could count her cash and ice her bruises.

The officers apologized for the misunderstanding.

"Get these handcuffs off me," Anthony snapped.

So ended a weird evening in D.C.

The Fourth of July brought a three-day weekend to the Capitol. Federal offices were closed on Friday. Tourists flocked to D.C. to visit the sites on Independence Day and enjoy the fireworks on the Mall. Anthony told his district offices in Indiana to knock off early on Thursday and enjoy the long weekend.

The Democrats planned to take full advantage of the layoff.

The two men dressed in white overalls and long-sleeved shirts parked two blocks from Anthony's Silver Creek office. Their painter's caps sat low on their foreheads. Their arms were weighed down with bags from Home Depot. One of them carried a paint roller. The crowd of festive Hoosiers walked east to the city park where the high school band would perform patriotic favorites before the fireworks lit up the sky at dusk. In the ninety-degree heat, the two men walked west. The locals carrying their lawn chairs and coolers to the park took little notice.

Congressman Schumacher's office had no elaborate security system. The two men knew that. The bald one had wandered into the office earlier in the week asking where the local Social Security branch was located.

Joanne was more than happy to offer directions. "Go two blocks south until you reach the stoplight."

The man nodded yes and pretended to point in that direction. He also saw no keypad next to the door. A wire running up the wall from Joanne's desk indicated she had a panic button for emergencies.

"Hang a left and it will be on your right."

No cameras. No motion detectors. No security guards.

"Thank you very much."

The man was out the door in less than five minutes but had scoped out half the office. Anthony's office would most likely have a panic button too. But the office had no money. It wasn't a cash business so a high-tech security system was not necessary.

This job would be a piece of cake.

They cut the power just in case. With the rockets' red glare and the bombs bursting in air, the pair broke the window in the front door and unlocked it. The booming fireworks didn't even require them to be quiet. They went straight to the Congressman's desk, ransacking its drawers and thumbing through the files. The light from their headlamps danced across the floor. Constituent services, health care, national security, federal taxation. They weren't finding what they came for. Out came the crow bar and the hand axe.

Where was that secret compartment?

The concussion from the fireworks shook the ground but the men were not phased. They were professionals. They had been in the D.C. offices of the Republican National Committee just last week.

The file cabinets were emptied and closets checked. They even felt along the carpet looking for a secret hiding place.

They found nothing.

But this time they weren't going to make the same mistake. Breaking up the Old Man's desk at his home in Georgetown raised some suspicions. This time they'd make it a little less tidy. Trash the whole place.

Out came the Home Depot paint, spray cans and gallon buckets. Blood red for a nice effect. By the time of the grand finale over at the park, the men were on their way back to the airport in Indianapolis.

Anthony got the call at nine on Monday morning.

"Schu, it's Wiley." Wiley had returned to Silver Creek to drop off a lady friend after a quick jaunt to Cancun for a weekend of tequila and romance.

"I received a call from Joanne about half an hour ago. Somebody trashed your office over the weekend."

"Is Joanne alright?"

"She's a little shook up. She noticed the front window of the door was broken and then the mess startled her a bit."

"How bad is it?"

"Most of the damage is in your office." Wiley looked around while a police detective took pictures. "They threw red paint all over the wall and carpets. They threw out all your files from your desk and file cabinets."

"Can you tell if they took anything?"

"Nothing jumps out at me. I think they were just vandals. They spray painted swastikas on the wall, "GOP Pig," and "GES.""

"That's odd."

"I'm not sure what GES means. GOP pig I can understand but not GES."

Anthony was now pacing the floor of his D.C. office.

"It stands for the Green Earth Society."

"Never heard of it."

Anthony had. During his stint with the FBI in San Diego, he was assigned to a task force to investigate the group – a fanatical organization comprised of violent green freaks who take great enjoyment in torching luxury car dealerships and million dollar homes in hopes of somehow saving God's green earth.

"It's a domestic terrorist group."

"I've never heard of them in Silver Creek."

"I doubt it's really the GES. They mainly operate out west. Somebody put it there to distract the investigators."

"What do you want me to do?"

Anthony looked out the window of his office.

"I'm coming home."

At six-thirty that evening, Anthony was met at the front door by the Chief of Police. The investigation was going nowhere and they had no suspects. Anthony was assured the police were making it a top priority. A pair of FBI agents said they'd return in the morning.

Anthony walked underneath the yellow police tape and encountered the outer office that looked like it had been hit by a tornado.

"They came in the front door. Probably Saturday or Sunday night," the chief reported.

Anthony's office looked like it had been destroyed by the tornado. He stood in the doorway with his hands on his hips surveying the crime scene. Red paint covered the Schumacher family portrait, the kids' school pictures, and Anthony's law degree. It was as if a starving artist had gone mad and decided to trash his canvas with the paint he had left.

"Most likely some punks got drunk on the Fourth of July," the chief surmised. "Probably liberals," he added to lighten the mood.

Anthony was beginning to believe he wasn't looking at the work of local punks. The books on the shelves were pulled straight down forming a circle around ground zero. His desk. He had seen the same thing minus the red mess in the Old Man's den. He rummaged through some of the scattered files and overturned drawers.

What were they looking for? He had nothing but files pertaining to congressional issues. He looked at the handles of the drawers with their "TMJ" nameplates. It was the Old Man's desk. Anthony had decided to keep it when the Old Man moved out. No need to buy new furniture if Johnson was just going to junk it. Except for the somewhat pungent cigar smell, it was a beautiful antique desk.

Someone obviously thought the Old Man kept his secrets in his desk. They had found two of them. One in Georgetown, the other in Silver Creek. The Old Man had one more.

And it was sitting in Anthony's office on Capitol Hill.

The Cannon House Office Building no longer offers free rein to all who enter. Visitors are screened by armed guards with metal detectors and hand wands. They must show identification and sign in. Surveillance cameras keep close watch of those entering, exiting, and those walking down the halls to a representative's office. Each representative has a panic button and a keypad to safeguard their office. The only people conducting business after hours are licensed and approved contractors.

Looking over his shoulder, Anthony walked briskly to the Donut Palace two blocks down from his office. He used to work there during his high school and college years. It was now a place of refuge after a long day in the office. The manager, Floyd C. Revson, was an old friend and fellow right-wing conservative. Over donuts and Diet Coke, the two would talk politics, and Anthony would get a good education on the business world and the impact of proposed small-business legislation. Always good for donations of donuts to the Schumacher campaign, Revson liked to say he was Anthony's conservative financier.

"Floyd, is the coast clear?" Anthony asked as he knocked on the door of the manager's office. The sweet smell of fresh baked goods wafted in and out.

The white-haired man with bifocals looked up from his daily log of donuts and dollars.

"Schu, how the hell are you!?" he asked with an outstretched hand. "You don't come in enough, my friend."

The two exchanged pleasantries. Anthony declined a free glazed chocolate cake donut, his favorite. No time, he said.

"I need to use your phone to make a long-distance call."

"Phone's all yours." Revson put his donut tally book under his arm and told Anthony he was going to personally box up an assorted dozen for the Schumacher family. "Take all the time you need."

Anthony didn't want to use his office phone or his home phone. He didn't really trust his cell phone either. The donut phone was probably safe.

"This is John."

"John, this is Anthony Schumacher."

"Schu, how the hell are ya!?"

Another old friend. Anthony had them scattered all across the country. But this old friend just happened to be John Rodgers, the House Sergeant-at-Arms. Rodgers also once served as the Special Agent-in-Charge of the FBI field office in San Diego. Along with being the bearer of the mace, he was responsible for the security of the United States House of Representatives, its members, and their offices.

"I just wanted to let you know about the break-in I had in my district office in Silver Creek."

"I'm aware of it," he said as he ran his hand over his shaved head. "It came across the AP wire a couple of hours ago."

Anthony gave Rodgers the details on the damages and also mentioned the incident at the Old Man's residence. Whoever was responsible was obviously searching for something in the desks.

"I have a feeling somebody wants to look at the desk I have in my office on the Hill."

Rodgers gave a slight chuckle, as if to say he wasn't surprised. "You may be on to something. A work order crossed my desk an hour ago to repair the overhead light fixtures in your office."

"I didn't authorize any type of work."

Rodgers ruffled through a stack of papers in his "Out" box and pulled out the pink sheet.

"It says Cannon House Office Number 536. Congressman Schumacher. Light fixtures. Requested and signed by Betty Warner this morning."

"That's funny. Betty's visiting her grandkids in Seattle this week."

Neither said anything. The third desk was now the target. And the ne'er-do-wells were planning on committing a felony right smack dab in the Capitol Hill offices of a member of Congress. All because of that desk.

"John, nobody in my office ordered that work. I want my office locked down. Nobody gets in until I get there tomorrow."

"Consider it done. I'll see to it myself."

Anthony hung up and then made one more call on the donut phone. "Wiley? Get us on the next flight to Washington."

The plane landed at Reagan National at six-fifteen. They took Anthony's car and sped into the city before the daily traffic nightmare. They rode the elevator up to the fifth floor of the Cannon Building and found it empty at that hour. Except for one solitary individual sitting at the end of the hall. His chair was pressed up against the door. His bald head reflected the white light of the hall.

It was the Sergeant-at-Arms himself.

"John, thanks for your help. I really appreciate it."

They shook hands, and Anthony introduced Wiley. With his starched white shirt and black tie, Rodgers had a pistol on his hip, an extendable baton on the other, and two sets of handcuffs begging for some guilty wrists to lock on to. He was hard core. He once spent three weeks shadowing a member of Congress who had received credible death threats. He even slept on the Congressman's front porch. Nobody was going to mess with his Congress.

"I was here all night. About twelve-thirty, I heard the elevator doors open and saw a man dressed as a janitor peek his head around the corner. He turned around and got back in the elevator. Must have spooked 'em."

"I'm not sure what's going on."

"Maybe you should contact our old friends at the Bureau."

Anthony was hoping it wouldn't come to that but the way things had been going it looked like some sort of federal prosecution was inevitable. Maybe a search of the desk would reveal nothing and Anthony could just donate it to the Old Man's future museum and be done with it for good.

"I had the locks changed. Here are four new keys."

Anthony thanked him again, and Rodgers told him to call if he needed anything.

CHAPTER 9

The lock to Anthony's office opened without any problem. Nobody had ransacked the place or entered through the windows. It was left just as they had last seen it the previous week. Still, Anthony and Wiley entered with apprehension. They locked the door behind them and tiptoed through the office. They said nothing and kept their eyes peeled for booby traps, hidden cameras, large angry thugs with metal pipes ready to spring out of the closet and bash them over the head.

They moved into Anthony's office and again locked the door. The desk was in one piece. Nothing had been disturbed. They checked the windows, the light layer of dust a good sign that it hadn't been opened. Fearing the place might be bugged, they moved Anthony's phone and desk lamp into the closet. They checked the carpet for any bulges. They checked the overhead light fixtures in the middle of the room. They found nothing suspicious. If they had checked the heating and air conditioning duct on the north wall they would have found a fiber-optic camera watching their every move. It, however, was being slowly recoiled by its operator at the other end.

"It looks like the coast is clear," Wiley announced in a whisper.

Anthony shook his head in cautious agreement.

"Bring those flags over here."

Being an admirer of American flags, Anthony had four of them in his office. Two behind his desk and two at each end of the bookcase.

"Put 'em around the desk."

Each flag pole stood eight feet high. Anthony and Wiley unfurled each flag and secured one to its neighboring pole. Old Glory now stood guard around the desk, sort of like a make-shift fort that kids would make in the basement on a rainy day. No one or no camera could see the two men and the desk behind the outstretched flags.

Now it was time to go to work.

Anthony pulled the key ring out of his pocket. He still had the key to the Old Man's desk that Jackie had given him. The bottom drawer in his desk was always locked, and Anthony had never felt the need to open it. Anthony inserted the key just below the "TMJ" nameplate. He looked around again, then up at the ceiling, and then at Wiley. He mouthed the words "Don't say anything" to Wiley, whose bald head was now a raging river of sweat. He thought he might pee his pants.

With a turn of the key, the locked clicked and the drawer opened. Both Anthony's and Wiley's eyes widened.

On top laid a copy of the Constitution, the kind on the fake parchment that you can buy at the National Archives gift shop for $6.95. A framed copy of Lincoln's Gettysburg Address was next, another gift-shop memento. Surely the burglars weren't looking for such modest tourist trinkets.

Then came the file.

Classified.

Top Secret.

For Eyes Only.

Federal Bureau of Investigation.

Central Intelligence Agency.

Anthony and Wiley looked at each other. Wiley wanted to throw up. His mopped his forehead with his handkerchief. Anthony picked up the inch thick folder and placed it on his desk. Again he looked around and up at the ceiling. He opened the folder and shook his head at what he saw.

The bright smiling face of the Speaker of the United States House of Representatives. The one and only.

Catherine "Kitty" O'Shea.

Oh shit.

Anthony was not surprised. The Old Man made no bones about his hatred for the Speaker. And with Republicans in the White House for a good part of the Old Man's tenure in the House, he had friendly relations with those conservatives heading every law enforcement, national security, military, and spy agency funded by the federal government. A secret file on a political opponent was not too hard to come by for the Old Man. Whether he found anything of use was still a question.

The banging on the outer office door startled both men. A white-knuckled Wiley yelped as he almost jumped out of his shoes. Anthony closed the file and Wiley peeked around one of the flags. Someone could be heard wrestling the lock, then pounding on the door. Anthony grabbed his phone, ready to summon the Sergeant-at-Arms, or the police, or the military.

"Open the door and see who it is," he whispered to Wiley.

Wiley tiptoed to the door and opened it two inches. Across the outer office he could see the bright red face of Stephanie Hamilton, Anthony's legislative aide, trying unsuccessfully to open the door.

"It's Stephanie," a relieved Wiley said. "Just a second," he announced to her. Wiley opened the outer door and explained that the locks had been changed. He didn't go into detail. He gave Stephanie a new key and told her they were in an important meeting. They were not to be disturbed. No phone calls.

Wiley returned to Anthony's office, locked the door, and exhaled as he took his place in the flag fort. Anthony opened the file again. The complete government history of Catherine O'Shea was right before their eyes. Birth date, social security number, children, acquaintances, what she did the night she became Speaker, and on and on. Wiretap transcripts of secretly recorded telephone conversations, political contributor lists, and even the layout of her Beacon Hill residence.

Then came the pictures.

There were no shots of the Speaker with current or former presidents, Hollywood stars, or foreign dignitaries. These pictures were black and white, taken undercover, behind trees, or in unmarked and unseen government surveillance vans. The subjects were known only to those in Boston's underworld. Paulie "The Pimp" Castellano. Johnny "The Jugular" Legani. Dominick "The Ice Pick" Andreotti. There they were, coming out of the Speaker's residence, her office, her back booth at Suldaner's in Boston. The Pompadour even showed up in a few shots. They showed her leading the picket's charge at the longshoremen strike, the city employees' sit-in, and the metal workers' march in Boston Common. Photos of union leaders were cross-checked with political contributors.

After the pictures came the bank statements. Boston, D.C., New York, Zurich. Entries of thousands of dollars in multiple accounts all freshly laundered. Unions, like corporations, are prohibited from giving campaign contributions to federal candidates. But that doesn't mean they don't try to sweeten a candidate's bank account under the table. Some unions forego the direct deposits and use cash, delivered in boxes of fresh seafood or vases full of flowers. O'Shea's accounts grew exponentially after she became Speaker.

"What are we going to do?"

"For right now. Nothing. I need to think some things through."

Anthony didn't like being in possession of classified documents, especially those pertaining to the Speaker of the House. If the FBI gave it to the Old Man, the FBI probably still had it. Anthony put the file back in the drawer and locked it.

Time to go back to business as usual.

Anthony and Michael had a father-son trip to Baltimore, and Anthony wasn't going to miss it. Because the engine light kept coming on in Anthony's car, he borrowed Wiley's beat-up Pontiac Sunfire. The thing belched blue smoke when it sputtered past sixty miles per hour and would have received top prize in the Cash-for-Clunkers sweepstakes.

Anthony and Michael visited Fort McHenry and the Naval Academy in Annapolis. They took in an Oriole game at Camden Yards and made up for lost time. Once Anthony put Michael on a plane back to Indy, he decided to return Wiley's piece of junk so he wouldn't be seen driving it on Capitol Hill.

Anthony had never been to Wiley's apartment. Wiley never invited him and Anthony never asked to come over. Wiley was blessed with a great political mind that Anthony found indispensable. It was as if Wiley had a sixth sense about liberals. He had the uncanny knack for knowing their next move and how best to counteract it. But his after-hours conduct always worried Anthony. The booze. The babes. The late nights. John Barleycorn was his best friend, and he showed his multi-cultural side by welcoming the likes of Jose Cuervo and Captain Morgan into his world every night. Anthony wondered whether Wiley's wild carousing would someday create problems for both of them. The Democrats would love to paint the conservative congressman from Indiana as being tolerant of his chief-of-staff's drunken debauchery even though he stayed well away from Wiley's sexual escapades.

At 10 p.m., the Anacostia section of D.C. was dimly lit, perhaps to save money for the street department or to cut down on light pollution. Or perhaps it was because the locals didn't want others in the neighborhood to see their comings and goings or with whom they were coming and going with. Right-minded people didn't dilly-dally in these parts, unless they were looking to get mugged.

Anthony held the scrap of paper that had Wiley's address scribbled on it.

"Howard Road. Howard Road. Where are you?"

After he found Howard Road (Wiley told him it was near the Anacostia Metro Station), he noticed the scarcity of available parking near Wiley's place. He pulled to the curb at the end of the block and decided to hoof it. Wiley's piece of junk was not out of place.

He was unbuckling his seatbelt when something caught his eye. Halfway down the block, even in the dark shadows, he could make out Wiley's portly bald silhouette stumbling up the sidewalk. He could hear him as well. He could also make out the shapely outline of a hooker on each of Wiley's arms.

This was going to be awkward.

Anthony wondered what he should do. He turned the car off and extinguished his headlights. He could tell Wiley was in no condition to chat on this evening. And he sure didn't want Wiley to invite him in. Being the nice guy that he was, he would undoubtedly offer up one of his whores for the Congressman's pleasure.

"I love women!" Wiley could be heard yelling. "I love beautiful women!"

Anthony worried about the neighbors, but they were either in the process of getting inebriated or out looking for hookers as well. He could see Wiley's congressional ID card hanging around his neck. Congressional employees were always warned that wearing their identification after-hours could cause questionable individuals to approach for questionable reasons. Somewhere that

ID showed Wiley worked for Congressman Anthony J. Schumacher. Wiley most likely wore his to impress the ladies or perhaps in hopes of getting a congressional employee discount from his hookers.

The hooker on Wiley's left wore black leather boots and a short skirt of the same material. The blouse was light, low cut, and loose fitting. She was on the skinny side with sagging, well-used breasts. She had trouble walking in heels while drunk. The plump hooker on the right wore white shorts that expended great effort to restrain her large posterior. Her tank top was pink, which conveniently matched her hair. Both her boobs and ass jiggled in rhythm as she stumbled up the sidewalk. She could not walk a straight line either.

"Babies! We're gonna have some fun tonight!" Wiley bellowed, breaking out in a half-wasted tune.

So this was how Wiley lived, Anthony thought.

Wiley and his hookers made it up the front steps of his apartment building. Each unit had its own entrance so Wiley and the girls wouldn't have to stumble through the hallways for all the tenants to see and hear. He removed one hand from the large hooker's bulging rear and fumbled around his pockets for his keys. Slowed by his drunkenness, his lady friends offered to assist him and promptly thrust their hands deep into his pockets, fondling him as they rummaged for his keys.

"I think we found what we're looking for!" one cooed, her hand on Wiley's crotch. The fat one laughed hysterically.

Anthony sat back in his darkened car and shook his head at the show. He wished he had a video camera so he could show Wiley how foolish he looked. He was going to have a heart to heart with Wiley on Monday. This could not continue.

"I'm gonna put it in the hole!" Wiley yelled. The hookers laughed again. Anthony thought he meant inserting the key into the lock. Wiley was having problems holding his hand steady enough to make the connection but eventually turned the knob and escorted his beauties into his Anacostia Shangri-La.

When the door closed behind, Anthony reached for the ignition key to head home. He'd bring the car back tomorrow. He suddenly longed for a quiet night with Danielle in Silver Creek. He saw the light come on in the living room. Thankfully the curtains were pulled. As he started to turn the key, he stopped when two shadows crept up the sidewalk. They were two males, both Caucasian and heavyset. They wore all black and mean faces. Neither one was drunk and they sure as hell weren't gay. They didn't walk like they were heading home or out for a night on the town.

Anthony slumped down in his seat. His eyes checked the side mirrors. He slipped on the Orioles cap that Michael had left in the car. A member of Congress was now conducting surveillance just like he used to twenty years ago when he worked for the FBI. Only this time he didn't have a badge.

Or a gun.

The two men stopped in front of Wiley's front door. They looked at the window and whispered something to each other. It was anyone's guess what the three occupants were now doing behind the curtain. If the two men barged in, they would probably find a naked Wiley with a smile from ear to ear. He most likely would be in no position to offer much resistance. The hookers would probably welcome the party.

One man with greasy black hair pulled out his cell phone and made a call. The other, a short stocky bald man built like a bowling ball, lumbered up the steps and pressed his ear against the front door. He gave a turn of the knob but it was locked. He shook his head to the other. He then took two steps to his right and peered in the window, the curtains preventing any type of peep show.

Anthony thought they could be pimps. They looked sleazy enough. Maybe making sure Wiley paid his fair share for his daily double.

Then Anthony saw the shiny silver pistol in the bowling ball's suit coat. Anthony didn't like what he was seeing. He flinched slightly when headlights filled his driver side mirror. He inched down as far as he could as slowly as he could. The car pulled to a stop outside Wiley's town house and the man with the greasy hair walked over. The car was black, possibly a 1980s Cadillac Deville, and Anthony surmised there were two people inside – the driver and the front seat passenger. It was too dark to get a plate number.

The bowling ball came over, pointed to the window, and held up three fingers. The passenger handed the man with the greasy hair a gun and a silencer.

"Aw, crap," Anthony said to himself.

He couldn't wait any longer. These guys weren't Boy Scouts selling raffle tickets or Evangelicals spreading the Good News. He reached for his cell phone and dialed 9-1-1. He was leaning toward the passenger side to stay hidden, the Oriole barely peering over the dashboard.

"D.C. Metro Police, what is your emergency?"

"Yes," Anthony whispered. "I live on Howard Road and I think there are a couple of prowlers outside my neighbor's residence. I think they might be burglars." He really wanted to avoid using his name and title at this point. Why a member of Congress was sitting in a car on a darkened street in a seedy part of town might raise some questions.

"Okay, sir, what makes you think they're burglars." The operator sounded bored, like she received these calls every ten minutes and knew they never amounted to anything, especially on that crime-ridden stretch of Howard Road.

Anthony didn't have the time to describe the situation. "Listen, lady, I see two males with guns. Two unidentified individuals in a black car. They also might be armed."

The woman snapped to it. "Okay, sir, I'll send a police unit to the location."

Anthony hung up the phone and noticed lights coming in his rear view mirror. Instead of popping his head up, he tried to turn his body around to look out the back window. Unfortunately, that caused his left elbow to graze the horn. The blaring noise pierced the silence and echoed off the facades of the apartment buildings. He froze. The Oriole froze. The two men in black froze. Anthony peeked up over the dashboard. Both men were looking in his direction when they saw movement in the car.

He had been spotted. Now Anthony was in trouble. Time for the Oriole to fly the coop.

On went the car and up popped his head. The two men were now sprinting toward him with their guns drawn. He leaned to the right and managed to open the passenger side door. He jammed the car in reverse and slammed the accelerator. Without looking up, he used the curb as his guide to keep it straight. The gunfire came fast and furious, the barrel flashes brightening the dark night.

The first shot blew out the passenger side window. The second hit the grill. The third one pierced the windshield and then the driver's side headrest. Anthony could hear the bullets whistling by him. Another in the windshield, shattering glass all over him. When he looked up from his position behind the dashboard, he saw the overhead stop light. He slammed on the brakes, whipped the car around one-hundred-eighty degrees, and floored it in the same direction he had been heading with the bad guys now behind him. A perfect J-turn, just like they taught him in the Bureau. The final shot hit the right tail light but Anthony was now speeding toward safety.

He hauled ass like the great Foyt speeding down the straightaway to win the 500. He saw the sign for Pennsylvania Avenue, made a hard right, and marched his way across the John Philip Sousa Bridge. His racing heart didn't slow until the two police cars passed him to check on those "burglars" on Howard Avenue. He fumbled for his phone and dialed Wiley's number.

It took five rings for Wiley to answer it. "Congressman Schumacher, how the hell are ya?" he stammered into the phone. He had no clothes on save for his white socks.

"Wiley, listen to me!"

"It's my boss," he slurred to the naked women passed out on his bed.

"Wiley, I think I'm having a heart attack!"

A heart attack! The Congressman was having a heart attack!

Anthony's words hit Wiley in the face like a cold glass of water. Wiley knew Anthony was in too good of shape to have a heart attack. He ran five miles a day, never smoked, never drank.

"I've had two spasms."

Then it hit him. Those were the code words. Trouble was brewing.

Ten years ago, Anthony and Wiley were in the process of getting Anthony elected as Wabash County State's Attorney. On a late night drive back from a fundraiser, Wiley started peppering Anthony for stories about his days at the FBI. Surveillance techniques, stakeout secrets, Bureau lingo. He then decided they should have some sort of code word that would alert either one to an emergency – political or marital – where secrecy was required. Upon hearing that the other was having a heart attack, they would either meet at the other's house or the police station. The code word for house was "help" and the police station was "paramedic." When Wiley asked Anthony what they should do if one of them was really having a heart attack, Anthony just laughed and said "Don't call me. Call an ambulance."

"What can I do?" Wiley asked. His stupor was wearing off quickly.

"I think I need a paramedic."

"Oh, God." Wiley knew he needed to leave. To make matters worse, all the booze he had consumed was weighing heavily on his bladder. He looked at his two hookers and then his keys on the night stand. "Schu, uh, I don't have a car."

Anthony was well aware of that. He was driving the bullet-riddled piece of junk. Wiley was in no condition to drive anyway.

"I'll send someone over to get you."

That someone was now banging on Wiley's front door, prompting him to screech in horror and drop his phone to the floor. Another loud knock caused him to empty half his bladder right there on to the bedroom rug. He threw on his boxers and rushed downstairs hugging the wall. Through the peep hole he saw the peaceful face of a patrol officer sent in response to the burglary call to check the premises. Wiley opened the door quickly, stuck his head outside looking for who knows what, and invited the officer inside.

Wiley was shaking, in part because a police officer was standing in his living room while two naked prostitutes were sprawled out across his bed in a drunken stupor upstairs. The officer noticed and asked him why he was so jittery.

Wiley managed a believable response.

"Well, I'm standing half-dressed in my living room with a police officer at eleven o'clock at night."

"Did you see anyone suspicious outside, like a prowler?"

Now Wiley was putting the pieces together. Anthony had come to return Wiley's car. He must have been parked outside and saw him with his two hookers, or in their secret code, two "spasms." Now the officer was asking about prowlers.

"Yes, I saw two of them." Wiley guessed at the number.

"Could you describe them for me?"

Wiley feigned fear of what lurked outside, even going to the curtains to see if the burglars were standing on the sidewalk ready to pounce.

"Officer, I'd feel much more comfortable if we could talk at the station. This isn't the best neighborhood and lately people have been acting strange. I'm a bit stressed out, and I really don't want my neighbors know I'm talking with the police. Perhaps I could talk to your sketch artist."

"Well, that might help." The officer didn't care one way or the other. He needed a cup of coffee anyway.

"Then maybe I'll just stay at a hotel tonight. I really need to find a new place. Somewhere safe."

Wiley hurried upstairs for a pair of pants, a shirt, shoes, and his wallet. He left the hookers on the bed. He had already paid up. He threw two twenties on the bed between them, a generous ten-percent gratuity he thought. If they happened to wake up before he returned, they would most likely leave. If they helped themselves to the contents of the refrigerator that was fine with him.

Wiley locked the front door and scurried to the police car. He scanned each direction, looking in parked cars and behind bushes. He didn't see Anthony or his car. He sat in the back and shivered in the cool evening air. He had ended the night in the back seat of a police car and still wasn't sure why.

The drive to the Metropolitan Police Department only took ten minutes. They went there because the sketch artist lived nearby. As they pulled into the parking lot, Wiley saw Anthony crouched low in Wiley's car in a dark spot of the public parking area. He had no front window and there were two bullet holes on the side. Wiley expressed the need to use the men's room.

The officer walked Wiley into the station and put him in an interview room. He told him the sketch artist would have to be called so it could be a few minutes.

"No problem," Wiley said. "How 'bout that restroom? With all this excitement, I gotta take a dump."

"Sure. Down the hall and to your left."

The officer went to grab a cup of coffee and start his paper work. Wiley opened the door to the men's room and saw Anthony pretending to dry his hands.

"Schu, thank God!" he said as he gave him a bear hug.

"Easy now, big fella."

They looked each other over. Wiley was still shaking. They stood at the sink and whispered.

"Schu, I'm so sorry. I shouldn't have asked you to return the car tonight."

"Don't worry about it. We've got bigger problems."

Anthony then motioned him closer. "Two men. All dark clothing. One greasy hair, the other looked like Mr. Clean, same build as you."

He handed Wiley a piece of paper with a description of each man and the car that pulled up outside the town house.

"Go back in and tell this to the officer."

Wiley nodded.

"Then I'll come in and pretend to be here to pick you up."

"Don't you think we'll be safer here?"

"Right now I don't know what's going on. Something a lot more serious than being caught with a couple of prostitutes."

Wiley couldn't look Anthony in the eye. "I'm sorry, Schu."

"Go."

Wiley went back in and gave the best description he could give based on Anthony's notes. The sketch artist's renderings would be of little use because Wiley "didn't get a real good look," he explained. He could, however, have given a nice detailed description of the sagging tits that had been flopping around in his face an hour earlier. The officer who brought him to the station took his statement and said they'd send more patrols to the area.

"Mr. Cogdon, Congressman Schumacher is here to pick you up," a police receptionist said with Anthony behind her.

"Oh, thank you," Wiley said as he stood and shook his hand. "Congressman, good to see you. Thanks for coming."

"No problem. How's my trusted chief of staff doing?"

They both looked at the sketch artist, who said it was the best he could do with the information given. He wasn't too happy to be called in at such a late hour for sketches of some low-level burglary suspects.

"Oh," Anthony said at the rendering. "Those guys look like bad news."

"That's all I need," he sighed.

"All right. Let's go," Anthony responded.

The two walked out the front door. It was twelve-thirty in the morning. The cool air brought on a developing fog.

"What happened to my car?" Wiley wondered, surveying the shattered glass and the bullet holes in the dim light of the parking lot.

"I'll tell you on the way."

"Where are we going?"

"We'll be safe at the office."

Anthony did his best to fill Wiley in. The two men, the car, the gunshots, and his escape.

"Schu, I'm sorry I won't get a hooker anymore."

"Two hookers," Anthony reminded him.

"I'm done, Schu. Not after what happened to you. I can't believe they'd come after two hookers. I had already paid."

"Wiley, they weren't there for the hookers." He looked over at a perplexed Wiley. "They were there for you. Or for what you might have in your house. They want the Old Man's file."

Wiley suddenly had the urge to urinate again. He still hadn't gone. He rolled down the window to get some fresh air. He thought he might puke.

"What are we going to do?"

"I'm going to pay a visit to an old friend tomorrow."

CHAPTER 10

Anthony made the walk up Pennsylvania Avenue from the Capitol. Both he and Wiley had slept in their offices last night. They were safe there, and Anthony could keep close watch on the Old Man's file. He showered at the House gymnasium and put on a spare suit that he kept in his closet.

He carried no briefcase or bag but kept a sharp eye out nonetheless. He hurried across the intersection at Tenth Street. A line of tourists was heading south from Ford's Theater. Anthony didn't notice anything suspicious. There weren't any Wilkes-Booths lurking in the shadows. He walked straight for the federal building at Tenth and Pennsylvania Avenue. He could see his reflection as he approached the glass doors. The sign inside brought a relieved smile.

"Welcome to the J. Edgar Hoover FBI Building."

He passed through security and stopped at the front desk. He handed over his congressional ID card.

"I'm Congressman Schumacher here to see Tyrone Stubblefield."

The receptionist smiled and made the call. Anthony took a look around the foyer. Fidelity. Bravery. Integrity. It brought back a flood of memories. He first pledged to support and defend the Constitution when he was sworn in as a special agent with the FBI. It was a pledge that he cherished even as a private citizen. An escort soon arrived and offered to take the Congressman upstairs to see Mr. Stubblefield.

As they made their way through the fifth-floor corridor, FBI employees walking the hall welcomed Anthony, formerly one of their own, with warm smiles and handshakes. They all knew Congressman Schumacher, his prior service with the Bureau, and his fervent support up on the Hill for the agents and support staff serving the people. Once you're in the FBI family, you never leave it.

The escort stopped Anthony outside the office occupied by Tyrone Stubblefield.

The Deputy Director of the FBI.

Anthony didn't have to wait long.

"Schu, my friend," he said with a broadening smile.

They hugged like long lost brothers. Their busy lives didn't allow them enough time together. Ty asked about Danielle and the Schumacher kids.

Anthony asked the same about Tina Stubblefield and their children, David and Tisha. The Schumachers and Stubblefields always exchanged Christmas cards and each were considered part of the other's family. Twenty years ago Ty and Anthony were inseparable.

And Anthony owed his life to the Bureau's second in command.

Ty and Anthony graduated from the same class at the FBI Academy. Their first placement was in sunny San Diego, and they were partners from the start. Fellow agents jokingly dubbed them the "Odd Couple." Anthony was a slim, white Midwesterner. Ty was a six-six African-American who had once played professional football. He was a massive individual with broad shoulders and bulging biceps. Even at the age of fifty two, he probably could have suited up for the Redskins if they were in need of a middle linebacker. The American people were lucky to have him on their side.

Ty and Anthony used to car pool to work, shared the front seat in numerous late-night stakeouts, and pushed each other to be better FBI agents. They listened to each other's family stories and sought out the other for advice on life. Their lives would change completely on one Friday afternoon.

Following a long day at the field office, Anthony asked Ty to stop at the bank. Anthony was in a full-court press to win over Danielle's heart at the time and had planned to propose to her that evening. The two masked men with semi-automatic assault weapons who burst into the bank had their own plans. As Anthony stood in line thumbing through his checkbook, the first shots rang out. They were just there for the money, they yelled. More shots. Screams of terror from customers and bank employees. Total chaos.

Anthony whipped out his gun, identified himself as an FBI agent, and dropped one with a single shot. The other robber fired off two and caught Anthony in the shoulder and the chest. Anthony crumpled to the floor. The gunman crept forward to finish Anthony off only to be thwarted by three bullets courtesy of Special Agent Stubblefield. Anthony almost died, and he and Danielle would be forever grateful to the man that saved Anthony's life and allowed them to live happily ever after.

After the shooting, Anthony retired from the Bureau and he and Danielle moved back home to Silver Creek. Ty continued his steady march up the FBI ladder. He became the first African-American Special-Agent-in-Charge at the San Diego field office. He then moved on to Washington, D.C. to become the first black Associate Deputy Director of the FBI. He was now one step away from being the head of the Bureau, and it would be another first when it inevitably happened.

Anthony told him everything. The break-ins, the Old Man's file on the Speaker, the shooting outside Wiley's town house. Ty said he was unaware of such a file, and he knew everything going on at the Bureau. At the time, three congressman were under surveillance for various reasons as well as the President's deputy chief of staff. If the Speaker was under surveillance, he would have known about it. He quizzed Anthony about the file, what was in it, and who knew about it.

Anthony pulled out a mass of folded papers from his suit coat. He had spent the early morning hours copying portions of the file, enough to get the FBI's attention but not so much that someone following him down the sidewalk would decide to pick him off before he made it to the authorities. Ty could barely believe what he was hearing. A secret file on the Speaker of the House of Representatives.

He didn't need to hear anymore. He reached for his phone and punched the red button on the left. "Carol, this is Ty. I need to talk to the Director. It's urgent."

Ty gave the Director a quick rundown of his conversation with Anthony. He stated more than once that he was dead serious. He had read portions of the file, he told him.

"He's sitting right here in front of me."

Thirty seconds later, the Director barged into Ty's office without knocking. Both Anthony and Ty stood.

Most people did when J.D. Bolton walked in the room.

Jack Daniels Bolton was the tenth Director of the FBI and the third longest serving one at that. He had survived four presidents, one terrorist attack, and two failed marriages. He had risen through the ranks, working to better the FBI at every level. His perfectly coifed white hair and tailored suits made him look like a distinguished senator, but he was a lawman through and through. Even though he had a stout team of four FBI agents protecting him twenty-four-seven, he still strapped on his shoulder holster and his trusted sidearm every day. Rumor had it he could score better on the firing range in the building's basement than eagle-eyed hotshots twenty years his junior. Under his starched-shirt, scorched-earth tenure as head of the Bureau, he had taken down sixteen suspected terrorists, three organized crime syndicates, two senators, nine congressman, and one crooked governor.

And he was always looking for more criminals to add to his tote board.

Anthony went through the story again, the Director's eyes widening by the minute with every turn of the Xeroxed page. Anthony mentioned the desks and the complete file tucked away in his office safe. When he finished, the Director was staring out the window. His eyes were full of energy. He sprang up from his chair and peered east down Pennsylvania Avenue toward the white dome of the Capitol.

"The Speaker of the House," he said softly. He didn't hide the smile in the corner of his mouth very well.

After exhausting all he knew, Anthony had his own questions.

"Why haven't you done anything with this information?"

The Director wheeled around with his hands in his pockets. He didn't like being interrogated. That was his job. "Congressman, this is the first I'm hearing of any such file," he snapped.

"How close were you with Congressman Johnson?"

The Director stared at the wall. "Congressman Johnson was an old drinking buddy. He shared my passion for the Constitution and keeping America safe."

Although Bolton was twenty years younger than Congressman Johnson, they both got along well. Johnson liked to call the Director "Bolt," as in lightning, and mentored him on the ways of Washington political circles. When Johnson would raise hell on Capitol Hill, Director Bolton could be counted on to respond in kind down at his end of Pennsylvania Avenue. Johnson liked to say it was the only time the thunder came before the lightning.

"But he got no such file from me."

"I don't know how he got it. He never told me about it."

"You have to realize Ted had no other life outside of politics. He lived it, breathed it. And he loved his country, shed blood for her. And if he thought anyone was out to harm her, he would do everything in his power to put a stop to it."

"But why would he sit on the file?"

"I don't know. Maybe someone got to him before he could put all the pieces together."

All three looked at each other. No one wanted to think the Speaker's goons actually had a role in the Old Man's death. "Natural causes," the death certificate read. But professionals trained in the lethal arts are often quite proficient in the natural causes of death.

"Congressman, I want the rest of that file," Director Bolton said.

It was not a request.

Not so fast, Anthony thought. "Listen, I think I'm being followed. I'm worried about my safety, my family's safety, and the safety of my staff."

"We'll take care of it," the Director promised. "I just want that file."

By the end of the day, two agents would meet with Danielle and take up residence at the end of the Schumacher driveway in Silver Creek. One agent would stay with Wiley, although he bitched that he wasn't assigned a team of hot female agents. Anthony spent the night at the Stubblefields.

Once the FBI had the file, a team of higher-ups, agents, and Bureau lawyers went to work night and day. The midnight oil burned bright at the thought of catching the third highest official in the federal government breaking the law. The search warrants came with amazing speed. The federal magistrate who signed off on the warrants could be heard to exclaim "holy crap" on a couple of occasions.

Word leaked out at about ten til five, just in time for the reporters to race to the Capitol and develop a storyline for the news at six. Cameras caught six FBI agents lugging boxes out of the Speaker's office and placing them in a black van. Six more were doing the same at the Speaker's office in Boston. Speculation ran wild. The reporters were elbowing each other for the best spot. The clamor in the Capitol hallways was electric.

The Speaker was nowhere to be found. The Pompadour either. No one was answering the phones. The office was empty save for a Capitol guard posted inside.

Anthony and Wiley were in his inner office watching the news unfold on TV. Wiley paced the floor wondering what kind of danger they were in. The three Red Bulls he had in the last hour didn't help his jitters. He had to use the restroom every fifteen minutes.

Anthony sat at his desk, the Old Man's former desk that had brought on this hysteria. He wasn't sure what was going to happen in the next twenty-four hours but he had to be ready. He had asked the Director to keep his name out of it as long as he could. But the press would eventually dig deep enough and find out. At some time, he was going to have to face the horde of microphones that would be thrust before him.

He called Danielle and told her everything. She started crying. She said she hadn't signed up for this. She had already been through Anthony being shot once in her life and the thought of him dodging bullets worried her. She wished he'd come home. He told her not to worry. The FBI was protecting him and the family, and he'd be home as soon as he could.

"It'll all be over before you know it," he said.

She didn't believe him.

After rampant press speculation and breathless commentary, the press conference took place two weeks after the initial meeting across the street from FBI headquarters at the Justice Department. Attorney General Claire M. Donovan led the charge. Behind the Attorney General stood a line of top-flight legal eagles and law enforcement heavy hitters – FBI Director Bolton, Deputy Director Stubblefield, two Deputy Attorneys General, the United States Attorney for the District of Columbia, three Assistant U.S. Attorneys, the Special Agent-in-Charge of the Internal Revenue Service, and the Inspector-in-Charge of the U.S. Postal Inspection Service. The members of the press sat on the edge of their seats, salivating at the red meat the Attorney General was about to toss into their cage.

"I will make a brief statement and then answer a few questions. At twelve-thirty this afternoon, special agents from the Federal Bureau of Investigation took Catherine O'Shea, Speaker of the United States House of Representatives, into custody at her district legislative office in Boston, Massachusetts." She paused slightly to let everyone digest what she just said.

"The United States Attorney's Office for the District of Columbia has filed a ten-count indictment against Ms. O'Shea, charging her with racketeering, wire fraud, mail fraud, attempted extortion, and conspiracy to commit extortion."

Another pause. The reporters were writing as fast as they could.

"It has been alleged Ms. O'Shea and several close associates conspired to enrich themselves at the expense of the American taxpayer. The charges were brought in conjunction with *Operation Racer*, a fast-moving investigation of public corruption, kickbacks, and the use of political power for financial gain. The Department of Justice takes allegations of public corruption seriously, and we intend to prosecute the conspirators to the fullest extent of the law."

She closed the folder containing the written statement and removed her glasses.

"Speaker O'Shea and her codefendants will be arraigned tomorrow before U.S. District Judge Rolando T. Casagrande at the federal courthouse here in Washington, D.C. I will take your questions."

The hungry lions pounced.

"One at a time, please," the Attorney General interjected.

How did the investigation start? How long had Speaker O'Shea been a suspect? What was the evidence against her? Will she spend time in jail if convicted? Are other members of Congress under investigation?

The Attorney General deferred most questions to the FBI Director and the U.S. Attorney. She did give the press one nugget to gnaw on.

"We were assisted in this investigation by a member of Congress and his information proved invaluable to us."

"Who is he?" one reporter begged.

"We will go into greater detail tomorrow. Thank you all."

The reporters had to shout over each other into their cell phones.

The nation's capital was in complete chaos. A political earthquake a magnitude of which hadn't been felt since Nixon and Watergate. The press sought out any member of Congress who could shed light on this bombshell. Former House Speakers shook their heads in disgust and disbelief. The three major television networks sent their best to D.C. to anchor the wall-to-wall coverage. The cable news shows had guests lined up for days in advance – legal experts, political historians, and constitutional scholars. History was being written by the hour. Would the Speaker resign? Who would replace her? Were the Democrats destined for destruction? What did the President think?

Outside the Speaker's Boston office, the crush of reporters caused police to close off the street and reroute traffic. Satellite trucks lining the curbs became permanent fixtures. Gawkers snapped more pictures of the Speaker's office than the Old North Church. Bostonians who had supported the Speaker walked around in a zombie-like daze. The long faces of liberals lining the bar at the Bull and Finch Pub on Beacon Street made the atmosphere less than cheerful.

Finally, the Speaker made an appearance. She put on her best pants suit, her best face, and came out swinging to save her political life. The whole world was watching. New Yorkers stopped in Time Square to watch. Californians scurried off the freeways to get to a TV. Everyone else across the fruited plain was holding their breath in anticipation. Anthony and Wiley were glued to the TV in their Capitol Hill office.

"I have a short statement to make." She showed no hint of frayed nerves. She was feisty and focused. Her team of five-hundred-dollar-an-hour attorneys stood in a protective semi-circle around her ready to fight and bill twenty-four hours a day. Her family was sequestering themselves at the Cape. The Pompadour was laying low.

"I want to start by saying I am innocent of the charges that have been filed against me. This is nothing more than a smear campaign by political enemies. I have served my home state of Massachusetts and my country with distinction for over thirty years, and I will not let the opposition party destroy my reputation for political gain. I take this matter seriously and I will fight it to my death."

The first shouted question was thrown out before she was done speaking. "Will you resign, Madam Speaker?"

"Why would I when I know I'll be vindicated. I am confident I will be completely exonerated."

"Any comment on the rumor that former Congressman Johnson had a secret FBI file on you."

The Speaker's eyes narrowed. That old son of a bitch wasn't going to take her down from the grave. "I know Mr. Johnson and his replacement have been out to get me for some time now. It is a calculated conspiracy to remove me from power and deprive the good people of Massachusetts of their elected representative. They will not succeed."

"That bitch!" Wiley yelled at the screen as he watched the Speaker march back into her office.

An incensed Anthony slammed his fist down on the Old Man's old desk. He wanted nothing and had nothing to do with the file's existence. And now the Speaker insinuated he and the Old Man conspired to take her down. She was dragging his name in it simply to save her own skin.

"I can't believe this," Wiley fumed. "She's lying through her teeth."

Director Bolton was pissed too. He didn't like somebody trying to discredit the FBI or a former FBI agent in good standing. If somebody committed a crime, that person ought to stand up and take his guilt like a man, the Director believed.

But he and others had planned for the Speaker's defiance. He contacted the U.S. Attorney and suggested the other shoe should drop. That legal shoe was a sealed indictment wrapped with a big red bow that federal prosecutors looked forward to opening with great anticipation like eager children on Christmas morn – one where they could rip off the wrapping paper and tear into the box and then show off their new must-have possession to all their jealous friends.

An hour after the Speaker made her statement, the U.S. Attorney dropped the hammer.

"Today, in an unsealed indictment, a federal grand jury has indicted Antonio Rinaldi and Eduardo Liuzzi on five counts of the attempted murder of Congressman Anthony J. Schumacher. On September 7th of this year, Congressman Schumacher was returning a car to his chief of staff in southeastern D.C. when Rinaldi and Liuzzi allegedly fired five shots into the car driven by the Congressman. We believe this was a coordinated effort to silence those who had knowledge of criminals acts including those involving the Speaker of the United States House of Representatives."

Attempted murder! The headlines screamed.

That shut the Speaker up.

Even though she was not charged or even mentioned in the indictment, everyone knew Rinaldi and Liuzzi weren't lone wolves who get their kicks trying to pick off members of Congress. "Unindicted co-conspirator" would soon become the most repeated phrase of the week. Anthony's official congressional photo was plastered above the fold across the country. Even Londoners and Parisians were introduced to Congressman Anthony Schumacher and his brush with the criminal underworld of American politics.

Reading the articles in the paper, Anthony now knew the names of the two men who had tried to kill him. Rinaldi was the grease ball, Liuzzi the bowling ball. Both were shown shuffling into the federal courthouse with their ankles and wrists in chains. Detention orange was not a good color for them.

The Schumachers were beginning to have more protection than the President. The FBI had four agents chauffeuring and shadowing Anthony every minute of the day. Four more along with two Wabash County sheriff's deputies kept close watch on Danielle, her mother, and the kids.

Anthony and Danielle worried life would never be the same.

CHAPTER 11

Anxious news reporters rushed the black Chevy Suburban as it pulled to a stop on Constitution Avenue outside the E. Barrett Prettyman Federal Courthouse one block west of the Capitol. Anthony didn't wait for his FBI security detail to open the door for him. He waded through the mass of tape recorders, microphones, and television cameras.

"Congressman, what are your thoughts about today's proceedings?"

Anthony smiled as he inched his way forward. He said he was hopeful that this would all be over soon. It had been six long months since the shooting. "Then I can go back to the time when you folks never sought me out for questions."

Anthony was the star witness in the criminal case of *United States of America v. Rinaldi* and *Liuzzi*, the first trial of the attempted murder of a member of Congress that anyone could remember. The Speaker's goons were the first on the prosecution's chopping block. The Feds hoped they could take down Rinaldi and Liuzzi and then build the case against the Speaker and her cohorts in crime. They were charged with five counts under Title 18 of the United States Code section 351, which makes it a federal offense to kill or attempt to kill a member of Congress as well as other notables such as major presidential candidates and Supreme Court justices. Anyone convicted of making such an attempt faced a sentence of up to life in prison.

At precisely 10 a.m., District Judge Casagrande paraded into the courtroom with his two law clerks following closely behind – so close they could have held the great jurist's robe as he ascended the bench to rule over his legal subjects. This was his kingdom. His law clerks had other work to do, but they begged him to be allowed to watch the highest profile case they might see in their lifetime.

After neatly situating his materials on the bench, the Judge called the trial to order. The Republican appointee ran a tight ship with a no-nonsense style. His half glasses sat low on his nose, and when he glared over them with his piercing black eyes attorneys were known to shiver in their loafers. The ex-Marine was tough as they come, as demonstrated when he was once asked whether he feared making a decision that might be unpopular with the general public. He simply responded that "federal judges have no fear."

"Mr. Officer, bring the jury to the courtroom."

The prosecution team was led by W. Jackson Bennett, the United States Attorney for the District of Columbia. He had been nominated by a Democrat, approved unanimously by the Senate, and asked to stay on by the current Republican administration. He was a polished, straight-laced Stanford grad with a hard nosed legal mentality. He took no prisoners, and if he brought charges against someone, they were guilty and going away for a long time. His three assistant U.S. attorneys accompanying him, all equally dapper, were Ivy Leaguers relishing the power that came with the office. They sought out convictions like rock stars seek out women. Any time, any where.

The gallery was a packed throng of media types, lawyers, and a handful of lucky citizens who had waited in line for three hours just to sit on hard wooden benches and take in the judicial spectacle. The buzzing crowd warmed the room ten degrees. Rinaldi and Liuzzi sat with stiff backs and thick necks at the defense table surrounded by four high-priced legal sharks who were being paid by a secret arm of the Democratic underground.

Their lead counsel, the esteemed John Jay Marshall, Esq., wore a striped silver suit over his 300-pound frame. His wavy blonde hair jostled just below his shirt collar with every demand he barked to his underlings. He was the son and grandson of self-important lawyers. His parent's decision to name him after the first Chief Justice of the United States Supreme Court, John Jay, as well as the longest-serving one, "the great Chief Justice" John Marshall, only instilled in their son the belief that he would someday join the legal pantheon of judicial greats. His likely ascent to the high court, however, was put on the back burner when he realized he could rake in ten times what the Chief Justice makes just by defending the richest of the scoundrels. And there were a lot of rich scoundrels out there. John Jay Marshall did however fashion himself as important and as gifted as all Chief Justices combined and graciously allowed his associates to call him "Chief."

Marshall and his girth were well-known around the Beltway and he had gained a national reputation for defending serial killers, spies, and disgraced congressman. With his win-at-all-costs legal ability, the guilty had gone free on more than one occasion. His plan was to take control of the trial and portray the government's case as full of holes, lies, and innuendo.

The all-white jurors, six men and six women, paraded in and took their seats in the jury box. After careful scrutiny by both sides in their attempt to find a favorable panel, three union members, two low-level government secretaries, a school teacher, and six retirees had been selected. The elderly gentlemen with the slight hearing problem sat closest to the witness stand. The jury had endured two hours of opening statements yesterday afternoon and were anxious to hear from real-life witnesses. The men looked around at the packed gallery. The women did not make eye contact with the defendants sitting across the courtroom. The Judge told them they would not be sequestered during the trial but it wasn't a guarantee. The news accounts of the trial would be worldwide, and they were directed to stay away from newspapers, radio, TV, and the Internet. Don't talk to your friends and family about the case until it's over, the Judge admonished. They each had a yellow note pad and a freshly sharpened number-two pencil. They were ready to go.

"Counsel, call your first witness," the Judge directed Joel Clarkson, the first assistant U.S. attorney.

"Thank you, Your Honor, we call Congressman Anthony J. Schumacher."

All eyes in the hushed courtroom turned to the door being opened by the plain-clothes U.S. marshal sent to keep an eye on the proceedings. Two more were sitting in the gallery behind the defense table. The eyes widened as Anthony walked confidently through the wooden gate separating the parties from the spectators.

"Congressman, would you please step forward and be sworn in," the Judge instructed.

Anthony was no stranger to the courtroom. He had tried cases, defended the accused, and testified as a witness during his time with the FBI. Now he had his right hand raised swearing to tell the truth as the "victim" of a criminal act. Once sworn, he took his seat in the witness chair and gave a welcome nod to the jurors. They did the same. The rising star of the Republican Party sat before them in his dark suit with red tie and American flag lapel pin.

"Counsel, you may proceed."

"Would you please state your full name for the record."

"Anthony Joseph Schumacher."

"And how are you so employed?"

"I am currently the elected United States Representative from the Eighth Congressional District of Indiana."

The women on the jury smiled. This was the type of guy they wanted their daughter to marry. The men gave another nod of approval. Anthony was the guy they wanted their sons to grow up to be. The prosecutor made quick work of Anthony's background and got to the heart of the matter.

"Congressman, do you remember the events of late evening on September 7th of last year?"

"I do."

"Could you tell us what you were doing at approximately eleven that evening?"

Anthony related the story of how he and his son had returned from a trip to Baltimore. After dropping Michael off at the airport, Anthony proceeded to his chief-of-staff's apartment in southeast D.C. to return his car.

"Were you familiar with the Anacostia area?"

"I was not."

"Ever been in that area before?"

"Just to see a Nationals game."

Anthony went on to state it was dark and that Mr. Cogdon's street was dimly lit. He pulled the car to a stop at the end of the block and saw Mr. Cogdon walking down the street toward his residence.

"Did you approach Mr. Cogdon?"

"I did not."

Anthony and the prosecutor had been through this questioning before in the latter's office. Anthony hoped to keep Wiley's hookers out of the story as much as possible – for Wiley's sake as well as his own. Although he figured the defense team knew about them because the defendants had followed Wiley home. It was inevitable the story would come out at some point in the trial.

"Why not?"

"From what I could tell, Mr. Cogdon was inebriated and occupied by a couple of his friends."

"He was drunk," the prosecutor surmised.

"Yes, from my perspective."

Anthony told the jury he decided to return the car in the morning as he did not want to disturb Wiley that evening. Once Wiley and his friends went inside, he saw two men coming up the sidewalk.

"What were the men doing?"

"Objection, Your Honor," Marshall bellowed with great authority in the hushed courtroom. "The witness cannot testify to state of mind."

"Overruled," the Judge said, dismissing the objection out of hand. "He didn't ask about what they were thinking. He asked about what they were doing. You may answer, Congressman."

"They walked up the sidewalk and stopped outside Mr. Cogdon's front stoop."

"Could you describe the men?"

Anthony looked over at the defense table and rattled off the characteristics of the only two nonlawyers who sat in front of him. "The first male was about five-ten with black greasy hair. The second male was about five-eight, stocky, with a clean shaven head."

"Congressman, do you see the two gentlemen you described in the courtroom today?"

"I do."

"Would you please point them out and describe an article of clothing they are wearing."

Anthony pointed the index finger on his left hand over to the defense table and noted the grease ball's silver tie and the bowling ball's pinstriped suit. Given the absence of television cameras in federal courtrooms, the evening news that night would show the sketch artist's dramatic rendering of the patriotic Congressman fingering the two cartoon-like thugs who tried to kill him.

"What happened next?"

Anthony described how the two men stood outside Wiley's apartment complex until a car pulled up. They talked to the occupants and the one with the greasy hair was handed a gun. The bowling ball already had his own weapon. Anthony then called the police. After he was discovered in the darkened car, Anthony told of how the two men ran toward him and fired several shots in his direction. Several bullets hit the car and shattered some windows. He then sped away in the car to safety.

"And you saw these two men chasing after you with guns," the prosecutor said pointing his finger at the two defendants.

"Yes."

"I have no further questions, Your Honor."

"Mr. Marshall, you may cross-examine," Judge Casagrande said.

Marshall unfurled his large body slowly from his seat.

"Mr. Schumacher," he snorted. He gave no deference to any occupational titles. "What were you doing again on Howard Road in southeast D.C. in the dark of night?" His tone dripped with disbelief. Only people looking for trouble or illicit activities would be hanging around that area at that time of day.

"I was returning Mr. Cogdon's car."

Marshall took his glasses off and threw them down on his legal pad. He pinched the bridge of his nose like it gave him discomfort. He waddled around the defense table and rested the left side of his five-hundred-dollar pants on the edge. "Mr. Cogdon was in the company of two prostitutes, wasn't he, Mr. Schumacher?"

"He was indeed."

Some of the jurors leaned forward and raised their eyebrows. Others scribbled the word "prostitutes" on their note pads.

Marshall tapped his index finger on one of his double chins. "Was one of those prostitutes meant for you?"

"Objection! Your Honor!" came from U.S. Attorney Bennett. "This is uncalled for!"

Marshall had no qualms about throwing mud at a witness, true or not, congressman or jail-house snitch. His job was to win. If he could make it a trial about hookers and whores, the jury might forget about the evidence that the defendants had shot at a member of Congress.

"Sustained."

"How much did Mr. Cogdon pay for his prostitutes?"

"Objection, Your Honor. Again, it is irrelevant."

"Sustained."

Marshall put his glasses back on. He cleared his throat and looked at the floor for inspiration. He then raised his head slightly as he threw a mischievous glance at Anthony.

"Mr. Schumacher, you've had a prostitute over at your residence before, haven't you?"

"Objection!" shouted the prosecution team in unison. Bennett stood and wagged his finger at Marshall. "Your Honor, this is irrelevant. Counsel's questioning is demeaning to this witness and solely an attempt to badger the Congressman."

Anthony held his tongue to let the prosecutors handle it. Marshall smiled knowing he had the pictures to prove it. And a nice black-and-white shot of the Congressman in handcuffs to boot.

Judge Casagrande's mood was turning sour. His view of defense attorneys had deteriorated over the years and he thought mudslingers like Marshall brought the judicial process into disrepute. "Counselors, approach the bench," he growled.

Out of the earshot of the jurors, Judge Casagrande told Marshall that he had better clean up his act or he would come up with an appropriate sanction – he was leaning toward reporting him to the disciplinary committee.

What me? Marshall wondered. He pretended to apologize and said he meant no ill will. He was only trying to defend his clients. The Judge looked over his glasses with his icy glare.

"Listen here, chief." The reference to "chief" was not one of respect. "It better not happen again."

The attorneys returned to their battle stations with Marshall trying to hide the smile of a school-aged troublemaker who just weaseled his way out of detention.

"The Government's objection is sustained. Let's move on."

Marshall relented for the time being. He could always come back to it later and try again.

"Mr. Schumacher, it was dark at that time of the evening?"

"Yes."

"The streets aren't well lit in that area either, are they?"

"No, they're not."

"Mr. Schumacher, you didn't see these two men shoot at you, did you?"

This was going to be another one of Marshall's defenses. No eyewitnesses saw the actual shooting, and with his head hiding behind the dashboard, Anthony was more worried about getting out of there than looking at the color of the gunmen's eyes."

"No, I was preoccupied at the time."

Huh, Marshall remarked to himself, mumbling ever so softly as he strutted near the jury box that the witness didn't see the men who supposedly shot at him.

"Mr. Schumacher, you didn't call the police after you allegedly had been shot at, did you?"

"I did not."

Marshall paced the floor deep in thought. The whole courtroom was his stage and he took his time in delivering his next line for the audience. "Let me get this straight. Two guys with guns on a darkened street in a bad neighborhood take a few shots at the car you're driving and you apparently barely escape with your life. But you don't call the police? How can you not call the police?"

Anthony gave it a quick thought. He told the jury he had become privy to highly classified information and he did not know who to trust. He believed the defendants were looking for the material and would stop at nothing to get it.

"But you decided to not call the police?"

"I thought about it over night and the next morning I contacted the FBI."

Marshall had no where else to go. Anthony was a believable witness, and Marshall wanted to save the mud for the less than savory characters that would follow him.

On redirect, Bennett asked Anthony whether he had any doubt that the two men sitting at the defense table were the same ones who shot at him on that evening. Anthony responded he had no doubt in his mind. Bennett had no further questions for the Congressman.

Anthony left the stand and walked between the defense and prosecution tables. To Rinaldi and Liuzzi, he gave a quick wink and a sly smile, unseen by the jury but noticed by the two U.S. marshals sitting behind the defendants. The marshals had to bite their tongues to suppress their smiles.

The prosecution called several police officers and an evidence technician concerning the car they scoured over for clues during their investigation. After the prosecution showed pictures of Wiley's battered and bullet-ridden Pontiac to the jury and played Anthony's call to 9-1-1, the U.S. Attorney rested his case.

Marshall had three subpoenas issued for the only witnesses he planned to call. On the second day of the trial, Wiley was first up. He took the stand with a conservative blue suit and matching tie. Anthony had told him earlier that morning to just tell the truth and everything would be okay. The trickles of sweat on his forehead reflected nicely in the warm courtroom lights. His hands were shaking and he suddenly felt the need to urinate.

"Mr. Cogdon," Marshall started off with a smirk, "my, my, my, two prostitutes on that September evening?"

The prosecutors sat still. It was Marshall's witness, and they were going to have to try and clean up the mess after he was done roasting Wiley over the coals.

Wiley could do nothing more than simply say, "Yes."

"Did you see Mr. Schumacher, the Congressman you work for, on the evening in question?"

"No, I did not."

"Because you were drunk and looking to have to sex with your whores."

"Objection, Your Honor," Bennett said. "Counsel needs to ask a question."

"Sustained. Put a question to the witness, Mr. Marshall."

Marshall led Wiley from the bar where he picked up his two hookers all the way to his apartment. Wiley had some difficulty remembering their names and stated he never saw them after that evening. Marshall grilled Wiley on every detail. Did he see the defendants? Was he concerned for his safety as he walked down the dark street with his hookers? For half an hour, Wiley endured his public flogging. After it was over, he limped out of the courtroom drenched in sweat with his tail between his legs.

Next on Marshall's witness list were Wiley's two hookers. Shelana Rondo, the one with the large rear end, mystified the jury with her nearly incoherent testimony. She had a few drinks for breakfast to calm her nerves and didn't remember much from that night. Judge Casagrande suggested Marshall quickly wrap up her slurring testimony.

"Call your next witness, counsel."

"Your Honor, we would call Miss Candi Kane."

The audience swiveled their heads as Candi sauntered in through the courtroom doors swaying her saucy hips back and forth. Her grand entrance reminded those old enough to remember of the great Carson strutting through the late-night curtain to a wave of adoring applause. "Heeere's Candi!"

She was the younger of the two prostitutes and was ready to put on a show. She swore to tell the truth and paraded her high heels up to the witness stand. Judge Casagrande told her to lose the gum before she started testifying. Candi simply swallowed it like a pro. Marshall had paid her an extra five-hundred bucks to dress the part and she didn't disappoint. Along with her low-cut top and push-up bra, her decision to go commando with a thigh-high leather skirt gave the six men in the jury box a free peep show. The old goat on the end had to reach into his pocket for his nitroglycerine. The men took no notes during her testimony but listened intently on the edge of their seats. The six women didn't take any notes either, too busy shaking their heads in disgust at Candi and the knuckle-dragging Neanderthals in their midst.

"Miss, would you please state your name for the record?"

"Candi," she responded proudly. "With an 'i.'"

"How are you so employed, Candi with an i?"

She smiled so innocent and sweet. "I'm a personal services representative," she said seriously.

A few chuckles could be heard throughout the usually quiet and dignified courtroom. The ever reserved Judge Casagrande bit down hard on the inside of his lip and pretended to write down something of extreme importance on his legal pad. Even Rinaldi and Liuzzi smiled.

"I see." Marshall kept going. "Miss Kane, you get paid to have sex with men, correct?"

"Yes, sir," she responded. She then interrupted the awkward silence. "Unless some women want to join in too."

The women on the jury were rolling their eyes. The drooling men were licking their lips. Judge Casagrande didn't wait for an objection. "Let's keep this moving, Mr. Marshall."

Candi testified to her evening with Wiley, although she didn't really remember his name or him for that matter. She had a lot of work to do since that night with Wiley. Marshall was, however, able to keep the jurors' minds off the defendants for fifteen minutes as he descended into the seedy world of D.C. prostitution. She never saw Congressman Schumacher that evening but, she confessed, she had no idea who he was or what he looked like. She also did not see Rinaldi and Liuzzi while she was with Wiley.

Every seat in the courtroom was occupied for closing arguments. U.S. Attorney Bennett thanked the jurors for their service and told them the evidence in this case was clear. Congressman Schumacher was returning Mr. Cogdon's car when he saw two men, identified as defendants, coming up the sidewalk. He saw one with a gun, and an occupant of a car that pulled up gave the other man a gun. When they saw the Congressman, they chased after him and fired multiple shots.

"Congressman Schumacher testified these two men were the ones with guns running after him when he backed away in Mr. Cogdon's car. The multiple bullet holes in the car do not lie. The evidence shows the defendants attempted to kill the Congressman. Find them guilty."

Marshall rose and unbuttoned his jacket, exposing his Brooks Brothers draped belly. He paced the floor for ten seconds without saying a word, his head pointed toward the floor in deep thought.

"May it please the Court and counsel," the Chief began slowly.

He started with a recitation of the history of the jury system in the United States and its importance to the presumption of innocence and the right to a fair trial enjoyed by every American citizen. He pointed out Jefferson specifically mentioned King George III's deprivation of the colonists' right to a trial by jury in the Declaration of Independence. The Bill of Rights to the United States Constitution was meant to protect the people from the all-powerful government and the Sixth Amendment right to a jury trial was an accused's best hope for a fair hearing. He punctuated sentences with a slamming fist on the podium. He noted the Founding Documents, those historic documents revered by all Americans, sat less than four blocks from that very courtroom, and the rights afforded the People to protect themselves from the Crown did not lose their power simply because the parchment had faded over the last two centuries.

"Only you, the jury, stand in the way of government tyranny!" the Chief roared.

He paced some more, deep in thought and in no particular hurry, sweat forming on his brow. He then went through the time line of events. Wiley at the bar with his hookers. Wiley walking to his apartment with his hookers. Congressman Schumacher's observance of Wiley and his hookers. Wiley inside his apartment with his hookers. Prostitution. Illicit sex. Hookers, hookers, hookers.

"Nobody saw these two men shoot at Congressman Schumacher. Not Mr. Cogdon, not Ms. Rondo, not Ms. Kane, and not even the Congressman himself. Nobody proved my clients even knew Mr. Schumacher was a member of Congress. The Government has not proven its case. These two men are innocent, and you are their only hope for justice."

Bennett's rebuttal was short and quick. Congressman Schumacher saw Mr. Rinaldi and Mr. Liuzzi chasing after his car. The bullets that came flying through the air didn't just happen to magically appear from out of nowhere. Also, the federal statute doesn't require the Government to prove the defendants actually knew Anthony was a member of Congress. The men were guilty. Find them so.

The jury took two hours to deliberate, just long enough for them to enjoy their brown bag lunch courtesy of the American taxpayer and, for some, a second cup of coffee.

"Has the jury reached a verdict?"

"We have, Your Honor," the foreman said, standing at the end of row two in the jury box.

"Hand the verdict forms to the bailiff."

Judge Casagrande took the forms and sifted through them. He saw the twelve names of the jurors signed neatly down the page. He showed no emotion at knowing the jury's decision on the fate of the two men sitting at the defense table.

"I am going to read the verdicts. I want to remind those in the gallery that there shall be no outburst once the verdicts are read. No one will be allowed to leave the courtroom until the jury has been discharged." The outbursts usually came from a guilty defendant's family, shocked that their relative would soon be sent up river. But Rinaldi and Liuzzi had no family, or at least none that would claim them. Judge Casagrande straightened the mess of papers and then looked over his glasses.

"Would the defendants please rise?"

Rinaldi and Liuzzi rose and stuck their big muscular chests out in defiance.

They knew what was coming. Marshall also stood. He was counting the billable hours he was racking up and wondering if the Dems would pay for his clients' appeal. He'd take it all the way up to the Supreme Court if they'd make it worth his while.

"We the jury find the defendants guilty of attempted murder."

The jury sat still. Some looked angry. Others looked exhausted. They had just made the decision that would likely result in the defendants spending the rest of their days in a cramped eight-by-ten cell in federal prison. But they had done their patriotic duty and were now ready to go home.

Judge Casagrande thanked the jurors for their service and excused them.

"Judgment entered on the verdicts, bond is revoked, sentencing in sixty days," he rattled off. He then looked at the two guilty thugs sneering at him. With a wave of his hand, the Judge gave his final order. "Custody, Mr. Officer. Take them away."

Anthony was sitting in his office when the verdicts were read. Wiley came in to tell the news. He nodded. The result was expected.

The news media came the next day for a statement from the Congressman and he obliged. He was ready to move on. Two months later, Judge Casagrande handed down the sentence. Rinaldi and Liuzzi were sentenced to life in prison. In one last insult to the defendants, a final poke in their guilty eyes, the Federal Bureau of Prisons assigned the two goons to spend the rest of their lives behind the high walls and razor wire of the United States Penitentiary in Terre Haute, Indiana – located in the home congressional district of one Anthony J. Schumacher.

CHAPTER 12

The world was slowly beginning to close in on the Speaker. Her circle of friends was getting smaller and smaller. Editorial pages were calling for her resignation. With this black cloud hovering over her, she could no longer serve her party, her state, her nation as Speaker of the House, the editors wrote. Democrats were scared of what the mid-term elections would bring. It was sure to be disastrous. Many wanted to throw the Speaker overboard and show they had rid the ship of the rats.

But the Speaker had no desire to leave quietly. She would fight to the end.

The Speaker tried to go to work as usual, but it was difficult with the throng of reporters huddled around her and hounding her with questions. She really wanted to pass health-care legislation for all Americans, she said in hopes of changing the subject. She came off as nicer, more congenial, like she thought a softer image would help her in the court of public opinion and whatever criminal court she might someday face.

She spent her time sequestered in her office phoning representatives and counting votes.

"Congressman, I want to move House Bill 121 quickly," she told a Democrat legislator from Maryland. The bill would expand government health care at the expense of the American taxpayer. Every Democrat should have been on board. "Now is the time. Our majority may not last much longer."

"Madam Speaker, I don't think we can get the votes. All the Republicans have to do is attach your name to a bill and it's poison."

She offered no response of damning condemnation at her colleague's forthrightness. Still, she pushed. She gathered her Democrats together in conference and told them to focus on the fight for the average American. Partisan politics must not get in the way of necessary reforms. It all sounded good, but the Democrats were afraid to even be seen with her let alone go along with anything she was promoting. No one wanted to get too close to this lightning rod.

At the opposite end of Pennsylvania Avenue, the mood was much more optimistic. President Fisher's popularity seemed to rise any time the Speaker's name was mentioned. It wasn't that Fisher was doing anything spectacular, he just wasn't hounded by scandal twenty-four hours a day. The moderate New York Republican had spent the first year and a half trying to bring the economy out of the doldrums and keep the terrorists from committing acts of war on the country. With the Speaker now on the verge of ouster, he wanted to step up the attacks and win back Congress.

At fifty nine, the President looked young for his age. The pressures of the presidency had yet to gray his movie star dark hair. He came from a New York family of great wealth and privilege – mostly American-made steel. At the height of their wealth, the Fisher forefathers left the steel industry before it tanked and turned to philanthropy. They relished the power of their money, which never seemed to dwindle. The Fisher family weren't just members of multiple country clubs, they owned them. They then moved on to gobbling up skyscrapers in Manhattan.

The President had been chauffeured around since he was a little boy and got everything he asked for. His father was once a powerful New York senator and twisted enough arms to get his spoiled brat of a son appointed Ambassador to Brazil. The son spent most of his tenure at the U.S. Embassy in Rio chasing hot Latin women. Following his skirt chasing south of the equator, Fisher returned to New York City and threw the family's money around. A library here, a new hospital wing there. He lived the high life in New York City and then bought the chief executive's seat in the Governor's Mansion in Albany – where he enjoyed taking the taxpayers' money and spending it as he saw fit. He called himself a Republican, but that's what every rich blue blood fancied themselves as. Calling oneself a liberal had fallen out of vogue after LBJ. Not content with counting his family's money, Fisher bankrolled his own presidential campaign. Following his victory, he brought his lavish lifestyle with him down to D.C.

Sharing the White House residence but not the same bed was First Lady Susan Randolph-Fisher. She was an attractive woman, ten years his junior, and liked to flaunt herself as the social doyenne of D.C. high society. She too came from money, so she was not in awe of her husband's fortune. Susan Fisher rarely talked with her husband, who had quit hiding the fact he enjoyed the occasional call girl, but she kept busy attending parties and obliging the paparazzi.

"Congressman, good to see you," President Fisher said to Anthony as he was ushered into the Oval Office.

Anthony had become a more frequent visitor since the trial. His poll numbers had also been on the rise. A *Gallup* survey of registered voters found 85% of voters nationally had a favorable opinion of him. Indiana voters gave him a 94% favorable rating. Numbers hadn't been seen this high since the first President Bush's numbers after the first Gulf War. With such high approval, politicians clamored for time with him – a picture here, a fundraiser there – hoping the good press would rub off on them. The White House was no exception. The President's handlers invited Anthony for coffee and political discourse several times a week. Anthony had somehow surpassed the Republican Minority Leader in the House and the Minority Whip as the Republican point man on Capitol Hill. The Minority Leader and Whip could do little more than grumble together in private.

"Nice to see you, Mr. President." Anthony would often tell people that walking into the Oval Office never got old to him. It was the most historical office in the world. And it was difficult not to be intimidated by the power that vibrated throughout the room.

"I thought we could have lunch with the Vice President today and discuss strategy," the President said.

"Sounds like a plan to me."

What else was Anthony going to say to the President of the United States? Anthony was not the President's biggest fan however. President Fisher was more moderate than conservative and, to Anthony's dismay, thought government was the answer for many of the problems confronting individual citizens. He was wobbly on abortion, squeamish on the rights of gun owners, and soft on illegal immigration. Plus, he had a green streak and thought global warming was a looming disaster that we could forestall with more government regulation. As if the American people could somehow change the entire climate of the earth and turn down the thermostat on the sun with a few wind farms and solar cells. Like most politicians, the President could tell one group he was for their cause and then turn around and tell another group he was for the exact opposite platform. But his good looks and smooth delivery charmed enough from each group to get him elected.

The President and Anthony took the elevator to the second floor of the residence where the Vice President was waiting in the President's private dining room.

"Mr. Vice President," Anthony said. "Always good to see you."

"Congressman, always a pleasure."

Contrary to his tepid feelings for the President, Anthony might have been Vice President Sutton's biggest fan.

Vice President Robert Sutton was seventy-two years old with a head of hair as white as the paint on the outside of the Mansion. He was a staunch conservative from Missouri, or as he called it, "Mizzorah." He had spent what seemed like a lifetime in politics, first as a young congressman from Missouri and then moving on to Governor, United States Senator, Secretary of the Treasury, and now Vice President of the United States.

He left the Treasury Department once the Democrats took back the White House and headed west to the Show-Me State. There, he returned to his hometown of St. Louis to help further the world dominance of Anheuser-Busch. With his collection of beer distributorships, he made himself into a wealthy man and thought he would retire and spend the rest of his days watching the Cardinals. When then Governor Fisher needed a strong conservative to balance his moderate credentials, the Republican base strongly suggested he place Sutton on the ticket. He did, and the Fisher-Sutton campaign carried forty states to victory.

For a quick getaway, Anthony would often take the family to St. Louis for a weekend of good food and baseball games. His House colleagues from Missouri introduced him to Sutton and they hit it off from the start. They were small-government conservatives who advocated for lower taxes, balanced budgets, and a strong national defense. And the Cardinals had no bigger fans.

"It's a glorious day, Congressman," the Vice President said to Anthony.

"How so?"

"The Cubs have officially been eliminated."

They both shared a hearty laugh at the expense of their National League rivals and expressed the desire for postseason tickets. They sat down for lunch. The President had a bowl of tomato soup and a salad. The Vice President enjoyed a plate of ravioli and a Bud Light. Anthony settled on a hamburger and a Diet Coke. Then the strategizing began.

"Congressman, we want you to campaign for us this election season," the President said, wiping his lips. "The Republicans have a shot at huge gains and we need you out there as much as possible."

Vice President Sutton was quick with the poll numbers. "We think we can pick up Senate seats in Illinois, California, and New York. There are thirty House seats that could go our way. You are someone whose argument for cleaning up Washington will resonate throughout the country. You are the face of the Republican Party in Congress."

Anthony placed his Diet Coke on the table. He wasn't sure if he wanted to campaign cross country. He was growing tired of Washington. At the start of congressional recesses, he was the first congressman to Reagan National for the flight home. A part of him just wanted to go back to Silver Creek and live out his days with Danielle.

Republicans however kept pulling him back into the limelight. Hoosiers were telling him to run for Senator or Governor. A conservative grass-roots organization conducted a straw pool and concluded he was the future hope for the Republican presidential nomination. He couldn't retire if he wanted to.

"I don't know. I've been thinking about cutting back and focusing on legislation."

"I understand," the President said. "We just need you in a few states to rev up the base and keep the conservative tide rolling."

"You and I can campaign together in the Midwest," the Vice President promised. "And we'll make sure we're in St. Louis for the World Series."

Anthony smiled. "I'll think about it."

Anthony declined the offer of a ride back to the Capitol. He decided to walk the mile and a half to get some fresh air. As much as he had been on TV, a good pair of sunglasses still allowed him to walk incognito as he blended in with the rest of the bureaucrats and professionals. He gave some thought to what the President and Vice President said. Maybe he'd see what Danielle had to say.

He walked into his office and grabbed his messages from Betty. He then went to Wiley's office and slumped in a chair. Wiley put down a copy of the budget numbers. He was a changed man. After the embarrassment of the trial, he quit drinking. He spent thirty days in a alcohol rehab center where he lost twenty pounds and his thirst for hard liquor. Since then, he was living a clean life and had a new friend named Bill, who was always willing to offer an ear if Wiley had the urge to return to the bottle. Wiley was also in a committed relationship with a recovering alcoholic who worked as a Senate staffer. There had even been talk of wedding bells. Although he might not be attending church every Sunday, it was a giant step forward for a man who lived the past thirty years under the influence of the bottle and in a quest for casual sex.

They talked about Anthony's conversation at the White House and the thought of campaigning for the next two or three months. Wiley thought it was an excellent idea, giving Anthony plenty of face time across the country. The people are going to love you, he kept repeating. He started making mental notes of places he wanted Anthony to go. Big states with large blocks of electoral votes. This was the next step to 1600 Pennsylvania Avenue.

"We'll win the presidency in a landslide," he beamed.

"Easy now, big fella. Let's not get ahead of ourselves."

Their moment of lighthearted banter was interrupted when Betty walked in the door.

"Congressman, I think you need to turn on the TV."

Wiley grabbed his remote control and flipped through the channels – CNN, MSNBC, and settled on Fox News. Each network shared a single camera shot of a car in a wooded area with yellow police tape around the perimeter. "Breaking News " flashed across the bottom of the screen. Wiley turned up the volume.

"At approximately ten-thirty this morning, a jogger passing through the park became suspicious after noticing a car that was idling between two trees," the reporter said, looking at his notes. "Upon her approach, she observed a white male in the driver's seat with an apparent gunshot wound to the head. She then called the police. Authorities have cordoned off the area and are looking for clues." Crime scene investigators with their latex gloves and brown evidence bags were combing the area around the car. "The Associated Press is reporting the deceased individual is Jim Evans, the Deputy Director of the Democratic National Committee."

Anthony looked up to the ceiling, closed his eyes, and sighed.

"Here we go again."

The FBI had begun to ratchet up its investigation of the Speaker since the Rinaldi and Liuzzi trial. The two gunmen weren't so tough after spending a couple of weeks in prison. Moreover, they had no loyalty to the Democrats or the Speaker, both of which threw them under the bus without a second thought. Rinaldi and Liuzzi's hopes for better accommodations and more yard time in prison had them singing like canaries.

For thirty minutes extra phone time per month, Liuzzi gave FBI investigators the name of Svetlana Gorginski, a poor Russian immigrant and now full-fledged American prostitute who was made available to him by Democrat operatives. Whenever he was finished receiving his thirty minutes of sexual services from Svetlana, she would call this guy named Jim Evans to come pick her up. This happened on four or five occasions.

FBI agents confronted Evans outside the grocery store last Saturday morning and asked if he would be willing to answer some questions about Miss Gorginski. He started sobbing uncontrollably right there in the parking lot. He had a Harvard degree, a loving wife, and two young kids. But the Democrat war machine had caused him to do things that he was ashamed of, that would forever tarnish the reputation he had worked so hard to achieve. He was intimately involved in the release of Danielle Schumacher's sex tape, he coordinated the break-in at Congressman Schumacher's Silver Creek office, and helped orchestrate the scheme to catch the Congressman with a prostitute. This wasn't the way his life was supposed to go, he bawled. He was going to be a successful political consultant, advising senators and presidents on ways to win high office and implement the liberal agenda.

Now he was a broken man, ashamed of himself and who he had become. The wife yelled at him for an hour after FBI agents came to the house with their search warrants. How could you lead this double life! she screamed. What about me? What about the kids? She demanded a divorce.

Fearing an arrest and further public scrutiny, he bought a bottle of gin and drove to the park. He placed pictures of his kids on the dashboard. He could barely see them through the tears flooding his eyes and running down his cheeks. Once the bottle was empty, he put a bullet in his brain to end the pain.

The reporters were starting to put the pieces of the puzzle together. Veterans of Capitol Hill knew Evans was the Speaker's election confidant at the DNC. She declined to make an appearance on TV because she was so distraught. Her office issued a written statement which said she was deeply hurt by the news of Evans' death and her thoughts and prayers went out to his family.

The vice around the Speaker was slowly tightening.

The FBI took the information they received from Evans and moved in on the Pompadour. He would not break easily. The Speaker had entrusted him with some of her innermost secrets, and Goldstein promised her he would take them to the grave.

The FBI had him under surveillance for the past three weeks. Goldstein would often meet his girlfriend Dorene Thompson, who was married, at his apartment for a late night of drinking and lovemaking. He liked to take her down to Boston Harbor and show her around the Speaker's yacht. If the Speaker wasn't in town, he and his babe would hop on board, set sail on the Atlantic, and fool around for a couple of hours.

When the Speaker went on a scheduled trip to California, Goldstein called Thompson and told her they'd meet at the apartment and then head to the docks. The night before last, she brought a backpack that the FBI figured contained a change of clothes. When she and the Pompadour walked off the yacht the next morning, they were wearing the same clothes. The backpack, however, was clearly empty. Their plan was the same for the next evening.

As usual, Goldstein parked his car on the first floor of the wharf parking garage and he and his beauty headed down to the docks. She was carrying the backpack, again stuffed to the gills.

The FBI didn't let them get out of the parking garage. Two agents appeared from unmarked cars and approached from behind, two other agents approached from opposite directions, and the lead agent came right at them.

"Mr. Goldstein, I'm Special Agent Barnes, FBI," he said with his badge raised for all to see. "We're going to need you to come with us."

Goldstein stuck out his chest and held his head high. He was ready for battle.

"Fuck you, feds! I ain't going nowhere with you little pieces of shit." He held Thompson's hand who appeared to want little to do with the backpack. She wanted to run but Goldstein held on tight. "I'm a federal employee. I know my rights."

The four other agents closed in and surrounded them. Agent Barnes spoke clearly without raising his voice. "Mr. Goldstein, I'm going to need you to come with us." He held up the arrest warrant. There would be no negotiation here.

"Fuck you, feds," he whispered as the agents slapped the cold steel of the handcuffs around his wrists.

FBI agents drove the Pompadour to the field office and he proceeded to curse them during the entire ride. After they read him his *Miranda* rights, he refused to speak with them and lawyered up.

The girlfriend was a different story.

The FBI transported Thompson in a separate car to the federal lockup. There, they fingerprinted her, took her mug shot, inventoried the contents of her purse, and had a female correctional officer strip search her. After telling her to bend over, the latex-gloved officer even manipulated her bare butt cheeks and checked her crack looking for who knows what. For thirty minutes, Thompson sat shaking and shivering next to three large females who looked like they had been repeat customers. It was a humiliating experience for her, and it would only get worse when her husband found out she was screwing around.

In the interview room, Agent Barnes read her rights to her and she pleaded with him to let her tell her story. She was having an affair and it would kill her if her family found out. Agent Barnes couldn't care less about her secret affair.

"Ms. Thompson, I want to know why you had files pertaining to violations of federal law in your backpack."

"What?" Federal crimes? She didn't know what he was talking about.

Agent Barnes didn't like to be jerked around. "Ms. Thompson," he said as he pulled the backpack out from under the table, "the backpack you were carrying contains five files full of evidence of illegal transactions between various labor unions here in Boston with the Speaker of the United States House of Representatives. This is evidence of bribery and kickbacks involving federal officials. Do you know how much trouble you're in?"

Thompson's eyes almost came out of her head. She knew the Pompadour was the Speaker's chief of staff and the Speaker was in legal trouble, but she had nothing to do with it. She was in love with Marty. She was just there for the sex and the candlelight dinners on the yacht. Now Agent Barnes was calling her a co-conspirator and telling her she was facing charges of obstruction of justice, lying to federal agents, and conspiracy.

"No, no, no," she pleaded. "I was just fooling around with Marty."

"Where'd you get the backpack?"

She looked at the table and the blue backpack. Her head was spinning. Should she ask for a lawyer? Should she rat out her boyfriend? They had already put her in a orange prison jumpsuit that smelled like it hadn't been washed in three years. Prison would only be worse. Her hands started shaking and she began to sob, her mascara dribbling down her cheeks.

"Please God," she cried to the ceiling.

"Ms. Thompson, where did you get the backpack?"

She took a deep breath. She only had one real option. She was going to be strong. For herself. For her family. "It's my backpack. Marty told me to bring it so he could take some reading materials on the boat with us. He asked me to do the same this evening."

"Did you see Mr. Goldstein read those materials while you were out on open waters last night?"

"No," she said, trying to remember. Her tone was dour. The tears had sapped the emotion out of her. "We had dinner, drank some wine, and then had sex. I don't know what he did after I fell asleep."

At the same time as Agent Barnes' interview with Thompson, a team of FBI agents armed with a search warrant was boarding the Speaker's boat. They didn't find any documents. The Pompadour had dropped them into the bottom of the Atlantic the previous evening. Bank accounts, wire transactions, and illegal contracts were now soaking up the salt water and fading into oblivion.

But the backpack provided a treasure trove of goodies that would give the FBI just the ammunition it needed against the Pompadour. The grand jury quickly indicted Goldstein on charges of conspiracy, obstruction of justice, and bribery. Other charges were possible if he didn't start talking. Save yourself or share a cell for life with the Speaker, the feds told him. He, however, was too much of a prick to know what was good for him.

With the mid-term elections just two months away, the Democrat leaders in the House could not wait any longer. The Speaker's lawyers were stalling for time, hoping a deal could be reached on the charges against her. But every day the Speaker remained in power the Republicans ran commercials reminding the voters of the leader of the Democratic Party. Ads portraying the Speaker as the ring leader of the band of corrupt politicians galvanized voters to support anyone who didn't have a "D" after their name.

In a secret meeting attended only by the House Majority Leader Kenneth Williams, the House Majority Whip Walter Nixon, and various Democrat committee leaders, the group considered their options. Asking the Speaker to resign for the good of the party was out of the question because she wouldn't do it. She wouldn't even think about stepping down as Speaker and keeping her seat in the House. They could reprimand or censure her, but the public would most likely conclude that was nothing more than a slap on the wrist imposed by her corrupt colleagues.

There was one other way. However much the group hated the idea, they could implement the "nuclear option" set out in the Constitution. Unlike Presidents and federal judges, members of Congress are not removed from office by impeachment tribunals. Instead, Article I, Section 5, clause 2 provides as follows:

"Each House may determine the Rules of its Proceedings, punish its Members for disorderly Behaviour, and, with the Concurrence of two thirds, expel a Member."

Only five members of the House of Representatives have been expelled throughout the history of the country, and none of them had reached the pinnacle of being Speaker. Representatives Clark, Reid, and Burnett got the boot for disloyalty during Civil War times, Congressman Myers from Pennsylvania was kicked out for a bribery conviction in the 1980s, and the colorful Congressman Traficant from Ohio made the trek to federal prison after being expelled in 2002 for his convictions on conspiracy, racketeering, and taking kickbacks.

Curiously, all of them were Democrats.

Expulsion could take place before a criminal trial or conviction and it would not prevent future criminal prosecution. The path to expelling members would start in the Ethics Committee, a.k.a. the House Committee on Standards of Official Conduct. Upon the formation of an investigatory committee, a hearing would be held to admit evidence, question witnesses, and consider whether the House member then in the docks committed the charges against him or her. Since it was not a criminal trial, the charges would not have to be proved beyond a reasonable doubt. If the subcommittee found the member committed the acts in question, the Ethics Committee would determine the appropriate discipline. A decision by the Committee to expel a member would then be referred to the full House for a vote on the proposed expulsion.

Majority Leader Williams felt sick even talking about it. Everyone in the room owed some aspect of their careers to Speaker O'Shea. None of them assumed their current position in the House of Representatives without her blessing. And now they met in secret to stab her in the back and save themselves.

"Would we get two-thirds of the members to vote for expulsion?" Walt Nixon asked to those at the table.

"All the Republicans will vote for expulsion," Williams said. "That's 217 votes right there." He then sighed. "It would take 290 votes to expel her so we're looking at a lot of Democrats who are going to have to make a tough decision."

Congresswoman Robinson, she of the Congressional Black Caucus, refused to even think about expulsion. "They ain't proved she did anything wrong yet."

Williams shook his head. "But they will. And when they do we'll lose even more seats than we are going to lose during this election."

Robinson dismissed the truth, unwilling to recognize the writing on the wall. She didn't have any concerns with her reelection, and short of the Speaker killing someone on the House floor, nothing called for her expulsion. The Republicans are just going after the Speaker because she's a woman, she huffed.

Walt Nixon had known the Speaker for twenty-five years. He oftentimes looked the other way with the shady characters she dealt with. But his career and the life of the Democratic Party were hanging in the balance. He knew they could not sit around and do nothing.

"I think we know what must be done," he said. "Let's start the expulsion process and see where it ends up. If the House votes to expel her, then it's over. If not, then we try the best we can to stop this sinking ship."

A majority of the group agreed. After a resolution to expel was drawn up, the Ethics Committee would start first thing tomorrow morning.

CHAPTER 13

Anthony took the Vice President up on his offer to tour the country searching for Republican votes with the condition that Danielle got to tag along. It gave them some time together and crisscrossing America on Air Force Two was not an inconvenience. Chicago to St. Paul to Kansas City with an evening stopover in Denver. Then they'd be off to Boise, Seattle, Portland, and Sacramento. The Vice President took to calling Anthony "Super Schu" for his boundless energy and his apparent ability to survive speeding bullets. Danielle got along well with Candace Sutton, the Vice President's wife. They were like two long lost sisters who loved shopping and children. Ms. Sutton was a former school teacher and took Danielle under her wing to offer ideas on how to cope with the long lonely nights of a politician's wife. She even invited the Schumachers to the Vice-President's Mansion for Christmas. They enjoyed each other's company and the couples' evenings together were a load of laughs.

"Good afternoon, Las Vegas!" Anthony said to the throng of Republican supporters and fat cats enjoying the annual Nevada State Republican Convention on the north end of the Strip. Anthony and the Vice President had been on the ground for two hours and just finished an hour long meet and greet with those willing to plunk down five-hundred bucks for a picture and a handshake with the two of them. Those not wanting to fork over the cash had waited for three hours to listen to their fellow Republicans lambast the Democrats and tell them how it would all be better come November 4th.
Anthony began each speech by laying out the agenda after the anticipated Republican take back of Congress.

"We're going to make sure that every dollar you send to Washington is being spent on projects that we need, not on those some bureaucrat in D.C. wants. We will balance the budget and keep taxes low so you can decide how best to spend that money and take care of your family."

Anthony interspersed his speech with lighthearted barbs and good humor. "It's true. We Republicans have taken some hits over the years," he deadpanned. "Heck, I've even been the recipient of a few shots myself."

The crowd busted up laughing. Here was a member of Congress making light of the fact that someone had tried to kill him on more than one occasion. He was as down to earth as any politician in the country. He rarely spoke of Speaker O'Shea, mainly focusing on all Democrats in general. The press would try to get him to bite on the proceedings in the House but he just smiled and said he'd let the situation play itself out.

"The power of the people should not be concentrated in a select few in a faraway land in D.C.," he said to these independent-minded Westerners. "That's why I will sponsor a constitutional amendment to limit the terms of members of Congress to twelve years in the House and twelve years in the Senate."

The Republicans roared their approval. The idea of a forty-year incumbent was anathema to most in these parts. For every lifelong incumbent like the Old Man, who tried his best to return power back to the states and the people, there were two like the Speaker, who tried to gain more power for their political party and enrich themselves as well.

Anthony hadn't run the idea by the Republican leadership, many of whom had been in the House for twenty plus years. But he liked the idea because it would send him home at the end of his next term.

His last duty in his speech was to introduce the Vice President. "Ladies and gentlemen, it's time to bring to the microphone someone I have a great deal of respect and admiration for. He's a great American patriot and the Republican Party is lucky to have him on their team. Las Vegas, please welcome the Vice President of the United States!"

The dynamic duo, as they were called by their wives, revved up the base and headed for Phoenix, Albuquerque, and Santa Fe to do the same thing. Anthony had to take the stage by himself in Austin and Little Rock because the Vice President was fighting fatigue. He teasingly cursed Anthony for being so fit.

The investigatory subcommittee got down and dirty into looking at the actions of its fellow member – something none of them relished because they feared that someday they might be on the receiving end of an ethics investigation. FBI Agent Lee Paige testified to the affidavit filed in federal court in the Government's case against the Speaker.

"It is alleged Speaker O'Shea personally took $10,000 in cash from each of three union leaders in Boston in exchange for passage of the pro-union card-check bill before Congress. She is alleged to have bribed certain business officials by trading official acts and influence for things of value – including a yacht, construction of an addition to her vacation home, and a brand new Jaguar for her husband."

The members of the committee sat in stunned silence, some shaking their heads. Photographers snapped pictures of Agent Paige as he read from allegations for fifteen minutes.

"It is alleged she influenced a congressional employee, Mr. Martin Goldstein, to destroy evidence and to provide false testimony to a federal grand jury. It is also alleged Speaker O'Shea filed false income tax returns for nine of the past ten years, and all nine of those years correspond to her tenure as Speaker of the United States House of Representatives."

It was not looking good for the Speaker.

After each day of subcommittee hearings, the Speaker's office would send out a press release rebutting the claims against her. She believed her best chance was to try the case in the court of public opinion. She called the proceedings a sham and a witch hunt and promised to fight these baseless charges and clear her name.

Across town, the feds were still working hard on the Pompadour. He would refuse to talk in any interviews, but afterwards, his attorney would always ask the U.S. Attorney what could be done to resolve his client's matter in the best way possible. The U.S. Attorney always said he wanted information on the Speaker. Whether that would put the Pompadour in a favorable light was something that would have to be decided later.

Two days before the start of the Pompadour's trial, he had a change of heart. One of the Speaker's press releases hinted several of the criminal charges against her were the handiwork of her staff. Since the only member of her staff that had been charged was Goldstein, the writing was on the wall. She would throw him under the bus before she would take the fall.

Goldstein's attorney, Jonathan Petro, took the lead with U.S. Attorney Bennett after extensive negotiations.

"My client is willing to plead guilty to lying to a federal grand jury."

"I want to know of Speaker O'Shea's involvement," Bennett responded. "Names, dates, numbers."

Petro conferred with the Pompadour. He had bargained hard and the possibility of a good deal finally won Goldstein over. He wanted to smell the sweet air of freedom before he died. If he went to trial and was found guilty, it's likely he'd be collecting social security while in prison. He acted tough, like he was in control, and he was still a prick.

But he wasn't stupid.

The air in the committee hearing was thick with anticipation. Every seat was taken. Photographers squeezed together on the floor in front of the witness table readying their long lenses and bright flashes. Sound technicians tested the microphones. The committee took their seats with trusted staff in tow. They were all dressed in their best business attire. This was the day their faces would be on every TV in America. The committee chairman rapped his gavel and called the hearing to order.

"Mr. Goldstein, would you please rise and raise your right hand to be sworn," the Chairman said.

The Pompadour stood erect, his wavy do shining in the lights. He wore a silver-striped suit, the type worn by old-school gangsters. So much for conservative attire when you're on the hot seat. He raised his right hand and the flashes nearly blinded him.

"Do you swear that the testimony you are about to give is the truth and the whole truth, so help you God."

"I do."

"You may be seated."

The Pompadour returned to his place on the hot seat next to his attorney. He began with a prepared statement.

"It is with great shame that I come before this austere body today. It is a day that I never thought would occur, and I would not wish it on anyone. Yesterday, I pleaded guilty in federal court to one count of lying to a federal grand jury. Sometime in the future I will be sentenced to prison for my criminal act. I would like to use this time to apologize to the American people and ask for their forgiveness. It was never my intention to break the law and I am sorry for my lapse in judgment. I will be happy to answer your questions."

Each member on the subcommittee had ten minutes to ask the Pompadour what he knew about the allegations against the Speaker. Goldstein told them the Speaker asked him to lie to the federal grand jury to keep her from being indicted. He was also in on her falsifying tax returns. As to the bribes and kickbacks, he had been the intermediary between her and the money men. Boxes of money disguised as birthday gifts would show up at the Speaker's office. Suitcases stuffed with cash would be swapped at airport baggage carousels. Goldstein was then directed to steer the legislation as directed by the Speaker's associates.

The questioning had gone on for two hours. The testimony was damning but some members of Congress wondered whether this evidence justified an expulsion. While bribery and kickbacks had led to expulsion before, they worried about the finality of the matter, especially since Speaker O'Shea had not even been tried or convicted of a crime at that point. Perhaps a strong censure and removal as Speaker would be more appropriate.

The last subcommittee member was Representative Jeb Lovejoy, a Republican from the Fifteenth District in east-central Illinois, and a former federal prosecutor. He had spoken with Congressman Schumacher, who asked not to testify before the subcommittee because of the pending trial, and he was curious about something other than the Speaker's kickback and bribery scheme.

"Mr. Goldstein," Congressman Lovejoy stated, "did you have any knowledge of files kept by the late Congressman Theodore Johnson?"

The Pompadour's back stiffened. He turned to his right and whispered in his attorney's ear. Attorney Petro responded with his hand over the microphone.

"Congressman, on advice of counsel, I respectfully refuse to answer that question based on my constitutional rights."

The reporters leaned in closer. A few of the photogs caught a drop of sweat, or perhaps hair gel, sliding down from the Pompadour's right temple. He took a drink from the glass of water in front of him.

"Mr. Goldstein, did the Speaker know of the file?"

Goldstein gave another glance to his attorney. Petro whispered something and nodded his head.

"Yes, she did."

"That file has been the subject of great speculation and is at the heart of the Government's case against the Speaker, isn't that correct?"

"Yes, that's correct."

In the silence that followed, the spectators could hear the electricity buzzing out of the hearing room's lights. Blood pressures were surely on the rise. Lovejoy only had one more question.

"It has been alleged that one of our colleagues was the target of an assassination plot because of his custody of the file. Did Speaker O'Shea order the hit on Congressman Schumacher?"

Some of the spectators gasped. Reporters had never heard of such an explosive question concerning an elected official. The tension in the room made it feel the walls were collapsing in on its center. The floor itself seemed to be vibrating. It was as if the pounding of the hearts in that room was causing the ground to shake underneath them. People were holding their breaths for Goldstein's response.

He looked again at his attorney and then stared down at the microphone. He took a deep breath.

"She did not order the hit," he explained, causing the crowd to exhale. What a relief, they mumbled.

Goldstein, however, wasn't finished. After the Chairman gave a slight tap of his gavel to quiet the growing murmur, Goldstein gave one last answer.

"But she knew about it beforehand."

All hell broke loose on press row. Fingers were tapping furiously on BlackBerrys. Camera flashes tried to catch the expression on the Pompadour's face after his damning bombshell. Some reporters bolted from the room and were seen running through the hallways like madmen to be the first to reach their fixed camera location and make a breathless on-air statement to the world. The murmur in the crowd turned to a rumble of white-hot noise. The Chairman banged his gavel, not to quiet the crowd, but to end the hearing. That way the members could scurry out of the room and keep their stunned faces off the TV screens.

"Speaker O'Shea Knew of Hit Attempt on Rep. Schumacher"

So blared the headlines of the next morning's newspapers. The late-night political roundtables from the previous day morphed into the morning news programs. Anchors, reporters, and commentators refused to take a break fearing they'd miss out on something earth shattering. Caffeine wasn't even necessary. This was history in the making.

The committee met one last time later in the day. By clear and convincing evidence, they concluded the Speaker had engaged in repeated and serious breaches of the public trust and her continuing abuse of her congressional office had brought the House of Representatives into disrepute. The committee recommended the Speaker be expelled and referred the matter to the full House for consideration.

The House took up consideration of the resolution the next day. Every member was on the floor. Some quietly chatted amongst themselves. Others sat in their seats with their hands folded. Today they would consider House Resolution 613 and decide whether to expel from office the third highest ranking official in the United States Government.

The House Majority Leader, Kenneth Williams, occupied the chair as Speaker *pro tempore*. He banged the gavel three times.

"We will now take up House Resolution 613," he said. "The clerk will read the resolution."

"House Resolution 613. Be it resolved, pursuant to Article I, Section 5, Clause 2 of the United States Constitution, Representative Catherine O'Shea, Speaker of the House, be, and she hereby is, expelled from the House of Representatives."

Representative Williams noted the solemnity of the occasion and stated the Democrats and Republicans would each have one hour for statements. By agreement, the Speaker herself would be allowed to close.

Majority Whip Walt Nixon was first up for the Democrats. It would not be an argument in support of the Speaker.

"The evidence disclosed in the subcommittee over the past several days has shocked us all. These charges are some of the most serious that this body has considered since those who took up arms against the Union during the Civil War. The Gentlewoman from Massachusetts has brought great shame upon herself and this great House. We must make the hard but only choice to expel her from office and then work to restore the dignity of the House of Representatives and rebuild the confidence of the American people."

The Republican leadership had asked Anthony to give the closing argument for their side, but he declined. He didn't think it was appropriate. Representative Lovejoy would handle the duties.

"It is with great sadness that I rise today in support of House Resolution 613. As spokesman for the men and women on this side of the aisle, we share the disappointment and outrage mentioned by our Democrat friends as to the allegations against the Gentlewoman from Massachusetts. The use of one's public office for personal enrichment is greatly offensive to all Americans. Even more disturbing are the allegations that the Speaker of the House knew of a plan to kill our colleague from the great State of Indiana. The decision before us is one of the most serious that we will confront during our time in Congress. The evidence justifies expulsion, and I ask for an aye vote."

The moment of the vote was drawing near, but one last person would have the floor. It would most likely be her last speech there.

"The Gentlewoman from Massachusetts the right to close."

The Speaker rose from her seat in the front row. She wore a blue pants suit with a large American flag broach on her left lapel. She didn't bring any notes or prepared statements to the podium at the clerk's desk.

She started off with her first campaign for Congress when some voters back home didn't think she could represent their views in Washington because she was a woman. She then rose to the highest peak in the House of Representatives because of hard work and determination. And women were better off for it. She then ticked off her accomplishments as Speaker – expanded health care, increased welfare, and consumer-protection regulations. And the poor were better off for it.

But then she took a turn to the nasty side. The Republicans had hated her since she showed up. Her angry railings against the Right had a certain Blagojevich bluster and bravado to them.

"That bastard Johnson from Indiana has spread lies about me for the last ten years," she howled. "And now he's doing it from the damn grave."

The Speaker *pro tempore* rapped the gavel. "The Gentlewoman will suspend and avoid profanity or indecent language."

The Speaker threw a visual dart up to the Speaker's chair. Her chair. She argued she has been convicted of nothing, not one charge has been proved against her in a court of law. The right to the presumption of innocence would be nullified if she were expelled. They were taking the word of a convicted felon, she said slamming her fist on the podium.

"I have done nothing that justifies expulsion. I have been duly elected by the voters in my home district, and they should be the ones to decide whether I serve in the United States House of Representatives."

Her impassioned plea at a close, she didn't wait around for the vote and headed straight out of the chamber.

Representative Williams then made the call for the vote. "The voting is now open."

Anthony punched in his vote. He never thought he would be voting on whether to expel the Speaker of the House. No one in the chamber took any joy from it.

"The Clerk will call the roll."

"On House Resolution 613, there are 388 voting yes, 30 voting no, 10 voting present, and 7 not voting. As two thirds of the House have voted in favor of the resolution, it is hereby passed."

That was the end of it. All 217 Republicans voted for expulsion. Thirty Democrats voted no, some wanting to wait until the Speaker was convicted in a court of law and others worried about getting expelled themselves. The Speaker refused to vote, stating she would not acknowledge this sham trial.

The reporters were hot on the trail of any member they could find. Headlines across the country the next morning would blare:

"Speaker Expelled from Congress"

"O'Shea, O'Shame!"

"Catherine the Great Booted from House"

The reporters couldn't find the Speaker, she was on a private jet to somewhere. Representative Williams said he cried after the vote. The Democrats were visibly shaken and most refused comment.

The scene outside the Capitol was part funeral and part circus. Car horns could be heard blaring up and down Independence and Constitution Avenues. Democrat staffers wept. Republicans hid their smiles with a muted spring in their step. They were looking forward to a night of celebration at the local watering holes.

A saddened Anthony sat in his office with Wiley. They only allowed in one reporter, an old friend from the *Silver Creek Tribune*, who was sent all the way from Indiana to cover the historic vote. He stated his hope for a political renewal of American togetherness, one where Democrats, Republicans, and Independents could put the interests of the American people first and foremost on the legislative agenda. He hoped the country could just move on.

"If I could be permitted to quote our 38th President," he said, "'Our long national nightmare is over.'"

Anthony and Wiley ended the evening at Arlington National Cemetery. There they placed a small American flag at the Old Man's head stone. They talked about all they had been through in the last year. They brought up the Old Man and wondered what he would be thinking right now. "That liberal whore" was out of power, just like he wanted. Anthony didn't know it would take a political earthquake to do it but she was now history.

Their moment of silence was shortened by the start of a falling rain. A faint clap of thunder rolled over the tree tops.

CHAPTER 14

Anthony felt he was finally able to settle into work as a legislator. The Republicans enjoyed a landslide victory across the country, vaulting them back into power on Capitol Hill. They won a five-seat majority in the Senate and had a twenty-nine seat advantage in the House. Carlton J. Spencer, a Republican from Kansas, was elected Speaker of the House. Some conservatives wanted Anthony to take the helm, but he declined stating Representative Spencer had the experience and leadership qualities to do the job. Plus, without the extra duties of being Speaker, Anthony was able to return to Silver Creek on a consistent basis.

When Anthony did return home, the world seemed much more peaceful. The cacophony of political discourse was drowned out by crickets and the gentle breezes rattling the sycamore leaves. The days didn't fly by as fast anymore. Anthony made sure to take more time with the family.

"When we were on the road campaigning, you kept saying you were going to introduce term-limit legislation," Danielle said as they sat on the back porch swing looking at the Wabash River lazily flowing passed them. "Were you serious about that?"

"Absolutely. Twelve years in the House should be enough for any representative. If they're that good, they can represent their entire state for another twelve years in the Senate. That's almost a quarter century on Capitol Hill. That's plenty."

Danielle had been wondering if she was going to get her husband back. Maybe then she could make some concrete family plans. Maybe they could even take an extended vacation with no cell phones or BlackBerrys. She held his hand like he so often enjoyed.

"So does this mean, you're coming home at the end of this term?"

He turned to her and smiled. "Yes, six terms are enough for me. I'm tired of all the traveling anyway."

She turned to look at the river and smiled too.

"Unless you don't want me to come back," he offered.

She backhanded him in his ribs. They cuddled in the cool breeze and watched the stars take light in the evening sky.

The push to limit the terms of members of Congress is always the strongest in the months preceding an election. A candidate need only point to some tax-evading, pork-receiving, revenue-wasting incumbent as the poster child for why members of Congress should only serve a set number of years in Washington. Poll numbers routinely showed the strong support of citizens in limiting the ability of incumbents to become career politicians. Returning the legislature to the people proved to be a strong rallying cry, with "Throw the Bums Out!" a less subtle but still effective war whoop.

States had tried to limit the terms of their congressional members only to be beaten back by the Supreme Court in *U.S. Term Limits v. Thornton* in 1995. The Republicans' hope for a constitutional amendment limiting congressional terms in the mid '90s *Contract with America* failed to receive the necessary votes for passage.

Anthony thought now was the time to finally get the job done.

Back in Washington, Anthony and Wiley started working on the proposed constitutional amendment, an opportunity both political junkies relished. Article V provides one of two avenues for amending the Constitution.

> *"The Congress, whenever two thirds of both Houses shall deem it necessary, shall propose Amendments to this Constitution . . . which . . . shall be valid to all Intents and Purposes, as Part of this Constitution, when ratified by the Legislatures of three fourths of the several States."*

The task they set out to complete would be a long hard journey. The chances of success within Anthony's last term were slim given that three fourths of the States would have to go through the process of ratifying the proposed amendment. Still, they were psyched, thinking they could actually be the engineers in attempting to change, in only a small way, the very document they both revered. They would be responsible for the ratification of amendment number twenty eight.

Anthony ran the idea by the Republican leadership and they gave their blessing. There would be some Republicans in the House and Senate that would most likely vote against it. They had been there for twenty-plus years and liked their power. The title of Senator or Congressman gets one into many a fine restaurant and on the dais of important civic functions. Incumbents didn't want to have to look for new jobs, and their government paycheck courtesy of the American taxpayer was something they cherished.

In what was billed as a major policy announcement, Anthony stood in the House press room and made the pitch for term limits surrounded by a group of like-minded Republicans and Democrats. His dark suit and his ubiquitous red tie, along with his boyish good looks, made him stand out against the more seasoned members. He grabbed the podium with both hands and went to work like a veteran of the political stage.

"Once again the American people have clamored for a change in the way their elected leaders do business. Far too often, the people of this country have felt the men and women they have sent to Congress have failed to be responsive to their needs and instead focused solely on their next election campaign. It is time to return Congress to the citizen legislature that was intended by our Founding Fathers, one that is accountable to the people and ensures their representatives and senators listen to their concerns."

Anthony then read off the proposed amendment to Article I of the Constitution. "No person who has been elected to the House of Representatives six times shall be eligible for election to the House of Representatives." The corresponding Senate language made a senator ineligible if he or she had been elected twice.

The press questioned Anthony on the chances of success for the measure. He said current members would not be forced to retire if they had served longer than twelve years but would be eligible to serve the full amount after the amendment's passage. He noted his predecessor had won twenty consecutive terms and had done much good during his forty years. He did not impugn the integrity of those who may have overstayed their welcome, but argued a citizen legislature would be more in tune with the everyday problems confronted by Americans on Main Street and not just those financial wizards on Wall Street and bureaucrats on Pennsylvania Avenue. One reporter asked Anthony what he thought if he was forced by the amendment to "retire" at the end of what would be his sixth term.

"It is something I have thought about. I guess I am going to use myself as the guinea pig in this project. This will be my final term in the House of Representatives," he declared.

A few of his colleagues raised their eyebrows and glanced at each other. This was the first they were hearing of Anthony's decision. The reporters suddenly took a greater interest in the story. They had come to know this young Republican from Indiana, and he had quite often proved to be front page material.

"If the people of Indiana want me to continue in Congress, there's always the Senate. Moreover, there are other jobs available in politics if I find I still have the fire in the belly."

Anthony denied he was running for governor of Indiana. He also dismissed one reporter's question that he would be a candidate for president in four or eight years.

"That's not something I'm thinking about right now."

That was enough to keep the door open.

Anthony went on the national news shows to promote the term-limits amendment. He was usually paired with a member of Congress who thought the idea took away the choice of voters and would place the decision making in the hands of lobbyists who would prey on congressional neophytes. Plus, the opposition argued voters already have the power to implement term limits on House members at the ballot box every two years.

Anthony would respond that limiting the President to two terms in the White House was not in the original Constitution that was ratified in 1787. Instead, following the near four-term reign of Franklin Roosevelt, it was changed by the Twenty-Second Amendment in 1951, thereby depriving future voters of the ability to vote for certain incumbents. Thus, limiting the terms of a member of Congress was not a radical idea. As to the power of special interests, he said he had more faith in the American people and the representatives they choose to send to D.C. and reiterated his long-held belief in a return of smaller government, one where the decisions were based on common sense and could be made by those who hadn't spent forty years learning the bureaucratic jungle of federal red tape.

While Anthony focused on the amendment, Wiley was hard at work watching the poll numbers – for term limits and for Anthony. He was always on the phone to political donors and grass roots leaders in various battle ground states. He would send out feelers to various Indiana leaders to gauge their thoughts on a Senator Schumacher or Governor Schumacher. Wiley never constrained his thoughts to one political office and kept pestering Anthony to set up an exploratory committee to test the waters for a presidential run. Anthony always demurred, stating the time was not right. Especially with a Republican in the White House.

Every Tuesday, Anthony and the Republican leadership in Congress would have a private lunch with Vice President Sutton at his office in the Capitol. It was a way for the White House to stay abreast of important legislation and brainstorm on how best to implement the President's agenda. The Vice President told Anthony he supported him on term limits but the President didn't care one way or the other, thinking it was a matter best left for the legislature to argue about. If Anthony thought it was necessary, the President would offer his public support however. The Vice President was concerned about the President's budget proposals and feared conservatives would be none too happy with the increased domestic spending and global-warming initiatives on the upcoming agenda. Vice President Sutton said he'd keep talking with the President in hopes of reining in his spending plans lest he simply morph into a big-government Democrat.

Their bean burrito and quesadilla lunch over, the Republican leadership excused themselves to return to pressing business. Anthony and the Vice

President sat around the office to talk baseball. Vice President Sutton enjoyed a Bud Light, his second of the lunch hour. He teased Anthony on his second Diet Coke, knowing Anthony did not drink alcohol. For goodness sakes it didn't even have caffeine in it. Did he have no vices?

"How can you call yourself a fan of the great city of St. Louis when you won't even imbibe once in a while in a good old fashioned A-B product? That's like slapping one of the Clydesdales in the face."

Anthony couldn't help but laugh. Beer drinking was just something he never grew accustomed to. It made him thirsty, which would then require another Diet Coke to wash it down. But he was a strong supporter of St. Louis businesses. And he would never slap a Clydesdale in the face.

"Boy, is it getting hot in here or what?" the Vice President asked. He brought his left hand to his chest like he had indigestion. Must've been that fire-engine style jalapeno sauce. The bottle came with a bright red warning label. He loosened his tie and stretched out the collar of his shirt. He wiped his forehead with his sleeve.

Anthony still had his suit coat on and didn't feel particularly warm. The food was a bit on the spicy side today but the Diet Coke had helped put out the fire. He then noticed the Vice President was perspiring heavily.

"Are you alright?"

The Vice President loosened his tie even more. He then put his right hand on his chest. The tightening caused him to lean forward and grunt.

"Mr. Vice President, are you okay?" Anthony said as he ran around the table. He didn't wait for him to answer. "Hey! We need some help in here!"

With the Vice President in attendance, help was never far away. The door to the office flew open with a thud and in raced four Secret Service agents. The Vice President was down on one knee with his right hand still clutching his chest. Anthony and one agent caught him before he fell over.

"I think he might be having a heart attack," Anthony said.

Two agents gave urgent directions into their portable radios. Yelling could be heard through the hallways. The table with the Bud Light and the Diet Coke was upended and thrown out of the way. The agents laid the Vice President on the floor and opened his shirt. The House physician, Dr. Aaron Rush, hurried in carrying an automated external defibrillator with him.

"I've lost a pulse!" lead Agent Michael Craig yelled.

Dr. Rush prepared the defibrillator and went to work. The Vice President was not moving and his eyelids were closed. Anthony put his hand over his eyes when the first shock was administered. Nothing happened. Still no pulse. Dr. Rush tried again, the press of the button sending the Vice President's naked chest into a spasm.

"I'm getting a faint pulse," Dr. Rush said as he held the Vice President's wrist. "We need to get him to the hospital."

Two breathless paramedics arrived with a stretcher and a bag full of supplies. With the help of Agent Craig and Dr. Rush, they lifted the Vice President's limp body on the stretcher.

The Secret Service then went into overdrive.

"Clear the hallways!" Agent Craig yelled into the cuff of his shirt. "Fast track to GW. Close all intersections. Northeast entrance! One minute! Move!"

They wheeled the Vice President, an oxygen mask now covering his face, down the empty hallway. Agent Craig was pushing on the back of the trailing paramedic on the stretcher trying to pick up the pace. The ambulance had backed up to the northwest entrance. The small opening between the Capitol building and the open bay doors gave a lone cameraman a split-second glimpse of the Vice President as he was lifted inside. The limousine sat in front of the ambulance. Two police cars idled in front of them.

"I'm going with you," Anthony said to Agent Craig.

The Secret Service didn't protest. Anthony was the last person with the Vice President and could have information that the doctors might need. Agent Craig snapped his fingers at his team and waved his finger. Two agents threw Anthony into a follow-up car.

"Go!" Agent Craig yelled from the back of the crowded ambulance. "GW! Follow the limo! Go!"

One of the paramedics and Dr. Rush huddled over the Vice President taking turns performing chest compressions. The motorcade flew down Constitution Avenue, the intersections blocked off by D.C. police cruisers. The sirens from two police cars, the Vice President's limousine, the ambulance, two Chevy Suburbans, a backup limousine, and two police SUVs pulling up the rear created a deafening wail as the vehicles raced passed. Employees from the Department of Justice and the IRS could be seen looking out their windows at the commotion. They were used to seeing a motorcade hauling some VIP around town, but not at these speeds. School kids and families exiting the American History Museum wondered what was going on.

The motorcade made a hard right on Virginia Avenue, the squealing hot tires startling the tourists taking pictures of the State Department.

"Go faster!" Agent Craig yelled to the driver who was falling behind the car in front of them. "Get up to the limo!"

Anthony was holding on in one of the Suburbans. Every so often, the four agents in the vehicle would put a finger on their earpiece to try and hear the commands coming over the radio. Their looks of concern indicated their protectee was in danger.

Anthony took out his cell phone and said he was going to call the Vice President's wife.

The agent sitting next to him grabbed Anthony's hand to stop him. "Sir, that's not necessary. We already have her en route."

The motorcade screeched to a halt at the emergency room doors of George Washington Medical Center, just a few blocks from the White House. The Secret Service agents already on site, with their guns drawn, cordoned off the entrance and prohibited all foot traffic except authorized medical personnel. The Vice President was wheeled in with Dr. Rush squeezing the oxygen bag every few seconds.

Anthony followed closely behind before he was stopped at the entrance to the emergency room.

"Congressman," said one agent with his arm outstretched. "Would you please put your congressional ID on where we can see it?"

Anthony complied, and the agent let him enter. He saw Candace Sutton rush in, a team of agents surrounding her. She looked scared, and it was obvious she had been crying on the way to the hospital. Anthony stood by a wall, out of the way, and started praying.

It didn't take long for the world to find out.

A flurry of "News Alerts," "Special News Bulletins," and "Breaking News" headlines flashed across TV screens. Web pages supersized the font on their news banners. The initial reports did not offer much.

"We have a breaking news story here in Washington," one news anchor said as she tried to read off her computer screen and talk at the same time. "At approximately one-thirty this afternoon, Vice President Sutton was taken by ambulance from his office on Capitol Hill and rushed to George Washington Medical Center in Northwest Washington. It is not clear the status of the Vice President's condition at this time. We have reporters heading to the scene and will have updates as soon as we get them."

The satellite trucks started lining the sidewalks and reporters were straightening their ties and fixing their hair before they went live on air. A few citizens lurked in the background across the street wondering what all the commotion was about and hoping to get on TV.

Anthony took out his phone and dialed Elle's cell phone. He figured she was probably in her lunch hour at school. The agent who told him to put on his ID came over to him.

"Sir, I'd ask that you refrain from making any phone calls," he said. He was polite and professional as one could be, but the look on his face indicated Anthony had best comply or he'd lose his phone for the time being. The Secret Service hated leaks about its protectees especially health-related concerns.

Given his law enforcement background, Anthony did not protest.

"Sure, no problem."

The agent went back to guarding the door. Anthony went into the men's room. He saw the look of fear and unknown on the face of the Vice President's wife, and it made him want to call Elle to let her know where he was. She knew what it was like to rush to the hospital because of a loved one's emergency. She had done that very thing after he was shot in the bank. He adhered to the agent's request that he not make a call and sent her a text.

"L, Schu w/ VP and C at GW. LU." (LU was Anthony's standard send-off for love you).

Anthony went back to the hallway and paced the floor. The agent at the door shook his head when Anthony asked if there was any news.

The Vice President's chief of staff and press secretary arrived and sought out Anthony in the hallway. He gave them all the information he knew. He grabbed his vibrating phone and read the text message.

"Schumi, Pray for VP and C. XO LU, L."

He flipped the phone shut. He missed his wife and wanted to wrap his arms around her. He started the morning thinking term limits for members of Congress was the most important issue confronting America. Now he just wanted to hug his wife. Someday one of them would lose the other. He had spent way too much time away from his family. He didn't want to spend another day without his Elle.

"Congressman Schumacher," the agent at the door said.

"Yes."

"Ms. Sutton would like to see you."

The agent walked through the emergency room doors. Outside the operating room stood Agent Craig blocking the doors. He had a solitary tear running down his stone-faced cheek. He nodded his head and let Anthony enter.

Anthony walked in and the Vice President's wife fell into his arms.

"Let's go to Lee Garner who is outside George Washington Hospital. Lee, what can you tell us?"

Garner held up his finger to the camera and looked at his BlackBerry. The buzzing that could be heard from the crowd of reporters standing nearby sounded like an angry beehive.

"Julie, I can tell you the Vice President was rushed to the George Washington Medical Center this afternoon after collapsing on Capitol Hill with chest pains. He underwent emergency surgery and it has been reported his condition is critical," he continued before a quick glance at his BlackBerry. His delivery then quickened. "Yes, Julie, we're just getting word, the Associated Press is reporting that Vice President Sutton has died."

Those final five words could be heard echoing up and down the line of reporters.

Once Garner caught his breath after the biggest announcement he had ever made in his young news career, he gave as much background material as he could.

"Vice President Sutton was seventy-two years old. He enjoyed a long and distinguished career in politics and some say was the reason for President Fisher's election."

The truck cut from the live shot and replayed the footage of the ambulance in the emergency room bay surrounded by Secret Service agents. Garner's producer was providing quick tidbits in his earpiece. "He is the first vice president to die in office since James Sherman, President Taft's vice president, in 1912. I can tell you his wife, Candace, was by his side here at the hospital. He is also survived by three daughters and six grandchildren."

The reporter next to Garner received a text message from a nurse in the emergency room who was an old friend from high school.

"My sources tell me Vice President Sutton had just finished lunch with Republican leaders, including House Speaker Spencer, Senate Majority Leader Kenyon, and Congressman Anthony Schumacher from Indiana, a close friend of the Vice President, when he collapsed to the floor with an apparent heart attack. He lost consciousness and was unable to be revived. Representative Schumacher is currently in the hospital with Ms. Sutton. We'll try to get a word with him when he comes out."

Anthony would make no public statement to the press on that day. He left out an underground entrance with the Vice President's wife and the Secret Service. He managed to get off one text message to Elle.

"L, Need U in DC ASAP."

After a quick thought, he hurried off another.

"LU."

CHAPTER 15

The Republican leaders in the House and Senate were quick to sign off on a concurring resolution.

"Resolved by the House of Representatives (the Senate concurring), That in recognition of the long and distinguished service rendered to the Nation by Robert Edward Sutton, Vice President of the United States, the Rotunda of the Capitol is authorized to be used for the lying in state of the remains of the late Honorable Robert Sutton. The Architect of the Capitol, under the direction of the Speaker of the House of Representatives and the President *pro tempore* of the Senate, shall take all steps necessary for carrying out this event."

The state funeral for the Vice President was everything Old Man Johnson would have wanted. His casket rested on Lincoln's catafalque in the Capitol Rotunda for thirty-six hours. A quiet steady stream of friends, colleagues, ordinary citizens, and those just wanting to be a part of history filed by the casket day and night to pay their respects.

A ceremony for dignitaries was held on a cool Saturday evening. The Rotunda was packed with members of Congress, five of the nine Supreme Court justices, all but one Cabinet member, and the President of the United States and the First Lady.

Danielle had flown to D.C. as quick as she could get a flight. Anthony took her to the Vice-President's Mansion where she offered condolences and support to Candace Sutton, her only real friend in Washington. Sutton could not stop thanking them for being so supportive. They were such wonderful friends, she kept saying.

Sutton sat in the front row with President Fisher, her daughters, and the grandchildren. Anthony and Danielle sat behind her, along with the Speaker of the House and the President *pro tempore* of the Senate.

The Marine Band played a soft version of *Hail, Columbia*, the entrance march for the Vice President, much like *Hail to the Chief* heralds the arrival of the President. The House chaplain followed with a reading from the Twenty-Third Psalm. Ms. Sutton had requested that four individuals give eulogies – the President, the Speaker of the House, the Senate Majority Leader, and Anthony.

Anthony followed the Speaker and the Majority Leader. Sutton had asked him to keep the eulogy lighthearted as she was unsure whether she could make it through the entire ceremony without crying. He left his seat in the second row with a copy of his speech. He paused briefly in front of the flag-draped casket illuminated by the overhead lights.

He took a deep breath and prayed he could make it through to the end. A good portion of the American public was watching.

"Mrs. Sutton and the Sutton family," he started off with a nod to the Vice President's wife and supportive clan in the front row, "Mr. President, my fellow colleagues in Congress, the distinguished members of the Supreme Court, and guests. It is with great sadness that I am here today to mourn the loss of a great American patriot, a colleague of many in this room, and a friend of all here and many throughout this great country."

Anthony wove in stories of the Vice President's vast knowledge of politics and his great love for America. He mentioned their recent tour of the country during the last campaign and how people would describe the white-haired Vice President and the youthful congressman as the father-son political team.

"The Vice President took some offense to that," Anthony said smiling. "He wondered why they didn't think they were the brother-brother team."

The audience enjoyed a much needed laugh.

"I was fortunate enough to spend a great deal of time with the Vice President over the past few years, and never would a day go by during the baseball season that we didn't talk about our beloved Cardinals."

Anthony then lowered his voice and did his best impression of the Vice President.

"'Schumacher, what's the Cardinals score?' he would ask. 'What's the score?'" Anthony smiled again and pulled the BlackBerry out of his pocket. The game had ended a couple of hours ago. "Mr. Vice President," he said, pausing slightly to keep from crying. "The score is Cardinals ten, Cubs zero."

The House and Senate contingent from Missouri could not help themselves and broke out in applause. The rest of the audience, even the Cubs fans, soon followed. Ms. Sutton gave a nod of delight.

Anthony then turned serious. "I just wanted to say one final thing. A politician's life is not the most conducive to a healthy home and family. The travels, the campaigns, people tugging at your sleeve. Oftentimes, the family gets lost in the shuffle. A politician's life can be a runaway train barreling out of control. But behind every successful politician is the politician's spouse. I have witnessed firsthand the love affair between Bob and Candace and all I can say is I hope that my wife and I have the same genuine love at that stage of life as the Suttons."

Ms. Sutton gave him a long hug after he finished. It was just the eulogy she wanted for her husband – a man who loved God, his country, and his family.

At noon the next day, the military honor guard carried the Vice President's casket out of the Capitol for the final time. The hearse and the motorcade headed for Andrews Air Force Base where Air Force One sat ready, by order of the President, to carry the Vice President back to Missouri. Dubbed Special Air Mission 29000 because the President was not on board, Ms. Sutton, her family, Anthony and Danielle, and House and Senate members from Missouri joined in the Vice President's final trip home.

The plane ride was somber and quiet. The pilot dipped the jumbo jet's wings as he crossed the Mississippi River and banked left for a final fly around the Gateway Arch, Busch Stadium, and the Brewery. The funeral took place at St. John's Lutheran Church in west St. Louis. The Brewery sent a Clydesdale to stand sentry outside the church. It was an inspiring sight, and the tears flowed when the beautiful horse appeared to bow its head in respect when the casket passed by. The organist kept the mood light with a few stanzas of *Meet Me in St. Louis, Louis* and *Here Comes the King*. The burial took place on a bluff in west St. Louis with a nice view of the western sky. The mournful playing of Taps and the 19-gun salute echoing throughout the valley closed the final chapter in the life of Vice President Robert Sutton.

It was a long sad day for both Anthony and Danielle.

Ms. Sutton stayed in Missouri with her family while a good portion of the D.C. types headed back to Washington even though Congress would be in recess for another week. Anthony and Danielle decided to rent a car and drive back to Silver Creek. They needed some time alone so they took the long way home.

They stopped at a bed and breakfast in southern Illinois and slept til noon. The proprietors of the establishment actually knocked on the door wondering if everything was okay with their guests. Yes, they were told. They were just catching up on some much needed sleep.

Anthony and Danielle spent the rest of the day walking in the woods, talking and holding hands. They sometimes wondered how life had passed them by so quickly. The kids were grown up and heading out on their own. Ashley was set to graduate from law school in a couple of months. She was engaged to an aspiring doctor. Michael was contemplating a career in law enforcement, and Anna would soon be off to college. Danielle feared it would be just her at home, with only her mother next door.

Anthony had noticed his absence and those of the children were weighing on her mind. She seemed depressed, a little less bubbly than usual. He had spent almost twelve years shuttling back and forth to D.C., and he was beginning to miss being home. They talked about his political aspirations, but even a run for Governor would require a move to Indianapolis. A part of him just wanted to retire.

"Maybe Wiley and I can start up the law firm again and we'll just settle back in to our normal lives."

Danielle liked the sound of that idea. They could travel and get ready to spoil some grandkids. There was just one problem with that scenario.

America needed a new vice president.

Wiley had quietly been working the phones in the weeks after Vice President Sutton's death. He called Governor Armstrong at the Capitol in Indianapolis and discussed the thought of Anthony becoming the next Vice President of the United States. Governor Armstrong, a staunch conservative, was all for the idea. Think of the good it could do for Indiana, he mused. He promised to mention the idea to other Republican governors.

The Republican members of Indiana's congressional delegation were next up on Wiley's call list. Most were strongly supportive of the idea. The lone Republican senator thought Anthony needed more executive experience to qualify for the job. Wiley dismissed the senator's concerns in private, knowing the senator hoped to find his own name on the President's short list of VP candidates.

Wiley then went to his Rolodex of conservative organizations who were already demanding President Fisher replace the late Vice President Sutton with someone having matching conservative credentials. Wiley's idea received glowing reviews from Christian groups, tax-reform advocates, and small-government supporters. Wiley would also happen to point out the Democrats' fear of the conservative congressman from Indiana. For goodness sakes, Wiley would remind them, the Democrats tried to kill him! He *must be* valuable to us conservatives!

In the past, a vacancy in the Vice President's office would remain just that. When Truman became President after FDR's death, he did without a vice president until the next election. The possibility of having a gap in the presidential line of succession all changed with the ratification of the Twenty-Fifth Amendment. Section 1 involves the removal of the President, while the second section deals with a vice-presidential vacancy.

"Whenever there is a vacancy in the office of the Vice President, the President shall nominate a Vice President who shall take office upon confirmation by a majority vote of both Houses of Congress."

In October 1973, Representative Gerald R. Ford became the second Vice President for Richard Nixon after Spiro Agnew resigned in the wake of a corruption scandal. When Ford took over after President Nixon's resignation in August 1974, he nominated former New York Governor Nelson Rockefeller as Vice President. Since the Nixon and Ford Administrations, the Twenty-Fifth Amendment hadn't seen much action.   Anthony began to know something was up when he started getting calls from Governor Armstrong and his Republican colleagues. The thought of him being nominated for Vice President was not even on his radar screen. And it sure wasn't on Danielle's. She was making plans for him to move back to Silver Creek for good in the next year or two. Although he thought his chances were slim, he thought he'd better talk to her about it because the ground swell would soon turn into a tsunami.

The cable news roundtables had something to occupy their time in the past few weeks. The question of who would receive the nod from President Fisher was a matter of frenzied speculation. The White House tried to say mum on the matter, saying the President was considering a number of candidates, male and female.

Through various leaks and insider information, the pundits narrowed the field down to four candidates. Louisiana Governor Kay Lafayette was the only woman. She was the popular lieutenant governor who took over after the former governor resigned in a bribery scandal. She was up to her armpits battling corruption and some thought the vice presidency would give her a much needed rest from Pelican State chicanery. Rumors of an extra-marital affair, however, continued to dog her time in Baton Rouge.

Utah Senator Thomas Sanderson was, like the former Vice President, seventy-two years old. He was, unlike the former Vice President, a teetotaler and devout Mormon. The latter would be, for whatever reason, a matter of contention with the hard-line Christian conservatives. Sanderson had run for President twenty years ago, but he never received much support outside of the Mormon stronghold in Salt Lake City.

Washington Governor Ted Kirkland was a former businessman and friend of President Fisher. He made a bundle of money during his days with Microsoft and parlayed that into a run for governor, which he bankrolled himself. Although labeled a Republican, he governed more like a moderate Democrat. Government bureaucracy spiked under his watch, unemployment rose, and revenue fell. His mismanagement led to higher taxes and an angry electorate. That and his push for same-sex marriage would ensure no support from conservatives. Some even vowed to vote against the President during his reelection campaign. But, Kirkland was a friend of the President, and thus he made the short list.

They were all up against a former FBI agent and six-term congressman with a beautiful family and strong conservative credentials. What could be considered his dirty laundry had been publicly aired and laundered and ended up backfiring on his opponents. Whether the conservative push would be strong enough to put Anthony over the top remained to be seen.

"Well, what do you think?" Anthony asked over a bowl of cereal.

He had asked Danielle to think about it over night. Nothing in life seemed to take its time. They had just gone through this roller coaster a week or so ago. She ran the scenario through her head over and over again, tossing and turning the whole night. The house was paid for. Their retirement plan was in good shape. The kids were looking for jobs or heading off to college. She decided she could retire from teaching and move to Washington. They'd never have to spend another night apart since she could travel with him wherever he went. Finally, they'd be together again. She missed her man.

"Why do you want to do this again?"

Anthony's eyes widened. "Think about the opportunity we'll have. I would be in a position to advocate for smaller government, lower taxes, and a strong national defense. I could focus on education and make sure every child in America has an equal opportunity to pursue their dreams, to help them believe that they can make a better life for themselves and the families. We, you and I, could make a difference in this world."

"Does this mean you'll end up running for President?" Danielle envisioned men with dark sunglasses and earpieces trailing their family for the rest of their lives. "You've thought about it, haven't you?"

Anthony swirled the remaining corn flakes around in his bowl. The thought of becoming Vice President always triggered the back of a politician's brain into believing a presidential run could be in the cards. He was only fifty four. With two years left on President Fisher's first term and his assumed reelection, Anthony would only be sixty years of age when the President left office. Not too old, he thought. Eight years in the White House and then he'd be ready for retirement and memoir writing at the ripe old age of sixty eight. Of course he had thought about it.

"It's a possibility," he said as nonchalant as he could. "But first things first. I have to get nominated before anything else happens."

She looked down at her uneaten toast and then started crying. Her tears were not of dismay but of pride. Her husband, the man she loved with all her heart, was under consideration for the office of Vice President of the United States. She believed he could make a difference.

"I think we should do it."

He smiled and winked. He left his seat, picked her up, and set her back down on his lap where they shared a warm embrace and a good long kiss.

"Let's do it then."

CHAPTER 16

Anthony and Wiley returned to Washington to resume their congressional duties. Responding to constituent requests and complaints helped them keep busy as they waited for the President to make his decision. Anthony had lunch with Speaker Spencer, who told him he'd try to bend the President's ear at their next weekly meeting. Spencer liked Anthony's chances, although he said the Senate Majority Leader might try and back Senator Sanderson. Wiley would intentionally bump into reporters on Capitol Hill and casually happen to mention that Congressman Schumacher had been receiving a great deal of encouragement to seek the nomination. It might be a story you would want to look into, he intimated.

The media caught wind of Governor Lafayette's secret plane flight to D.C. and met her with a crush of hungry reporters and live cameras at Reagan National. She tried to claim she was in Washington on state business but nobody believed her. She would only answer questions about the vice presidency with a playful smile and a shake of her head. Men in dark suits whisked her away in an SUV which pulled to a stop twenty minutes later in the west parking lot of the White House. The White House correspondents on the North Lawn, relying on sources who wished to remain anonymous because they were not authorized to speak on the matter, breathlessly started the countdown to the big announcement.

"Governor, come on in," President Fisher said. "Welcome."

"Thank you, Mr. President." Governor Lafayette extended a hand, and the President held it with both of his. She wore a red skirt with her long dark hair resting at her shoulders. Although she was fifty five, she looked forty. With her brown eyes and soft smile, she could mesmerize anyone who met her. Given her looks and conservatism, her ascendance to the Vice Presidency would send shock waves rippling throughout the land not felt since the appearance of Governor Palin.

"How was your flight?"

"Good." They sat down in separate chairs near the fire place, which crackled in the flaming heat.

"Would you care for a cup of coffee?" he asked. The President snuck a peek at her shapely tanned legs. Her toned calves indicated she was an avid runner. They cried out to be massaged and caressed by warm, gentle hands. She noticed his ogling.

"No, thank you."

She was nervous. So was he. The thought of working side by side with the Governor intrigued him. She had not been on the radar screen of any of the President's brain trust. His handlers thought her scandals might be a distraction. Some thought her ravishing good looks would be a distraction to the First Horn Dog, as he was called behind his back. They'd have to keep him on a pretty short leash.

"I think you know why I called you here." He leaned in closer, his folded hands inches from her bare knees. "What would you think about being the next Vice President of the United States?"

No sooner had he asked the question did the First Lady barge in from the President's private office like an unwelcome Kansas tornado. She was hopping mad and spitting fire.

"Ronald, dammit!" she huffed. She made a beeline right for him. The President didn't know what to do. His eyes pleaded innocent. He wasn't fooling around with the Governor, honest. Although it wasn't out of the question since the First Lady had caught him in the act on multiple occasions while he was Governor of New York. "We're supposed to be at the Kennedy Center in ten minutes!"

"Susan," the President interrupted, "can't you see I'm with the Governor." He hated it when she was on the warpath. He was the President of the United States for goodness sakes. Couldn't he get a little respect here.

Governor Lafayette stood, as a matter of respect but partly out of fear. The First Lady glared at her with contempt, like she figured the Governor was just another one of her husband's cheap tramps willing to drop her pants in hopes of a promotion. At least it was a step up from his call girl sluts.

"Ten minutes!"

The First Lady wheeled around and high stepped it out of the Oval Office without even acknowledging the Governor and leaving a path of destruction that only the President had learned to weather.

The President's face was as red as Lafayette's outfit. "I apologize for the First Lady. I completely forgot about my night at the Kennedy Center." It wasn't a surprise why. Three hours of sitting next to his bitch of a wife and any guy would be forgiven for having it slip his mind.

He walked up close to her and rubbed her right arm. "Can you stay until I get back?"

She took a step back. She was trying to think of the pressing business that awaited her in Baton Rouge. "Mr. President, I should be getting back home."

He inched in another step. It had been awhile since he had been intimate with such an intelligent and beautiful woman. His voice softened. "But we haven't even discussed my plans for us." His hand had now moved around to her lower back. "Just stay the night, and we can talk about it over breakfast."

The knock at the door startled them both. The President's hand took cover in his pocket.

"Mr. President," his lead Secret Service agent said, popping his head in the Oval Office. We're going to need to leave soon."

Governor Lafayette had given the President the slip and was headed for the open door. Before leaving, she turned to the President, thanked him for the invitation, but said she had to get back home. She would be in touch. Don't bother calling was her tone.

The ride to the Kennedy Center in the presidential limousine was a knock-down-drag-out verbal war between the President and the First Lady. He was sick of her tirades. She was tired of his whores.

"You're the President of the United States! Grow up and stop thinking with your stupid penis!"

The Secret Service agents in the front seat pretended not to hear anything. They had grown accustomed to the First Couple's profanity-laced outbursts. The lead agent wondered if he might have to jump into the back seat and separate the two.

"We weren't doing anything," the President pleaded. "I was asking her if she would be my vice president."

"Oh no! Hell no! That tramp is not going to be the next vice president!"

"She's a viable candidate!"

The First Lady wondered what type of work she was a candidate for – aide to the philanderer-in-chief? She was not surprised that her husband would want to fool around with Lafayette as Vice President. It would be more difficult since the President and Vice President can't travel on the same airplane or rarely share the same space outside the White House. But he would relish the thrill of the hunt and would probably just invite her up to the residence for a midafternoon quickie.

"The American people don't want another sex addict in the White House!"

"I should've divorced your ugly ass years ago!" the President snapped. "Then I could have found a real woman!"

The First Lady responded with a hard slap with the back of her hand to the President's cheek. She was winding up for another blow when the lead agent in the front seat turned around and started to make his way into the back to break it up.

"John," the President said, stopping him. "John. It's okay. It's okay."

The red-faced President and the fuming First Lady returned to their neutral corners and seethed in silence. Both were fed up with the other. Both wanted a divorce. But they would most likely be stuck with each other for at least the rest of the President's first term. Maybe even the second one, too.

"She is *not* going to be the next vice president," the First Lady fumed under her breath but loud enough for all to hear.

Governor Lafayette got the hell out of Washington as fast as she could. The bayou corruption scandal was more appealing than the soap opera being played out in the White House, and she wanted no part of it. The Fishers were a marital time bomb ready to explode.

The odds makers now put their money on Governor Kirkland and Congressman Schumacher. Senator Sanderson was a long shot, although he would not acknowledge the odds because of his aversion to gambling. Truth be told, the President thought Sanderson was too stiff and feared he might try to proselytize to him or pester him to repent of his sinful ways. The Christian right was demanding the President pick the conservative Schumacher, threatening there would be hell to pay if the President disobeyed (although maybe not in such demonic terms, of course).

Kirkland showed up at Reagan National full of smiles and handshakes. He told everybody in Olympia that he would soon be moving east. The White House photographer snapped a few shots of the President and Governor Kirkland chatting next to the fireplace. Kirkland told his old friend how he wanted the job so he could use Air Force Two to fly across the country without having to worry about getting his bags at the airport. He had thought about living at the Vice-President's Mansion but worried it might be a bit on the small side. He might just buy a small estate in Virginia and commute by helicopter.

Following the meeting, the President adjourned to the Cabinet Room to huddle with his chief of staff and political advisors. It was a done deal as far as he was concerned. Let's get the nomination process started, he said without another thought.

Peter Kennedy, the President's long time chief of staff, was such a yes man that he didn't know what to say. The President usually got what he wanted and everybody just went along with it. People who didn't were usually tossed aside. Kennedy's knees were shaking.

"Mr. President, I think we might have a problem." He bit his lower lip. He didn't want to do this. He then motioned to his deputy. "Go ahead and send them in."

The door opened and in walked the well-dressed and supremely confident long arm of the law – the Federal Bureau of Investigation.

"Aw shit," the President mumbled. "Not the FBI."

The President rolled his neck around and around like the tension was getting to him. Maybe it was just sore from his battle royal with the First Lady. Standing at the table before him in their fine tailored suits and matching ties were none other than FBI Director J.D. Bolton and Deputy Director Tyrone Stubblefield.

"Morning," Director Bolton said with a bright smile – a smile that indicated he had something up his sleeve that few people knew about and would most likely put the First Horn Dog in yet another foul mood.

"What the hell did I do now?"

Bolton opened his briefcase and removed a file. "Oh, it's not you, Mr. President. Our background check on your potential vice-presidential nominee has uncovered something that might be of interest to you."

Bolton opened the file and slid three undercover photos across the table. In crystal clear color, the photos showed Ted Kirkland smoking a freshly rolled marijuana cigarette on his private yacht. Another showed Kirkland admiring his smoke ring wafting in the air. Two bikini-clad young women were also shown enjoying a couple of hits much to the Governor's delight.

The President shook his head. "What the hell is this?"

"That's Governor Kirkland."

"So he smoked a joint with some girls a couple of years ago." That's what those West Coast types do nowadays was the President's rationale. He was probably using it for medicinal purposes anyway. "Don't you Boy Scouts have better things to do like catch terrorists or bank robbers?"

"Mr. President," Bolton said sternly. "We have a duty to scrutinize these candidates so the good people of America know who is running their government. And it wasn't a couple of years ago. It was last week."

"So what," the President responded. "Nobody's going to find out about it until after he's confirmed. He'll just apologize for his slight indiscretion and then we'll move on. The voters will have forgotten all about by the next election."

Bolton leaned over the table and pointed at one of the buxom bikini babes. "By the way, she's seventeen."

Deputy Director Stubblefield was next up. He opened his briefcase and pulled out a plastic specimen cup. "Mr. President, the FBI background check requires a urinalysis drug test. Do you want me to walk down to the Oval Office and ask Governor Kirkland to provide a sample now or should we wait for the cannabis to clear his system?"

The President glared at both of them. Nothing but a couple of damn choir boys. He then started rubbing his temples like he had a massive migraine. Life was a lot easier with Vice President Sutton around. Offer him a Bud Light and ask a few stories about St. Louis and he was happy as a clam. And there were definitely no worries about the FBI showing up with incriminating photos of him lighting up a doobie with underage hotties.

Kennedy spoke first. "Mr. President, what should we do?"

The President sighed and looked out the window. He couldn't stop shaking his head. "I'll go tell him." He put his hands in his pockets and issued his first executive order of the day. "Take your damn photos and piss cup and get the hell out of here."

Bolton and Stubblefield both responded with a sharp "Yes, Mr. President," and with a crisp about-face were out the door with a spring in their steps trying not to gloat.

"Mr. President?" What now, Kennedy was wondering. The President was 0 for 2 on vice-presidential nominees. The press would soon start with stories of his indecisiveness or poor judgment in picking qualified candidates. The liberals would mock him. The comedians would laugh at him.

"Go get Schumacher," he sighed. "And keep it quiet."

Wiley barged into Anthony's office bursting at the seams. The White House is on the phone! The White House is on the phone! He would have made Paul Revere proud. They want you over there as soon as possible. They're sending a van to pick you up. They want you to meet it in the underground parking garage. The White House wants you to be vice president! Wiley could barely contain himself.

Anthony took a deep breath, put on his suit coat, and straightened his tie. "I'll be back in a little bit."

The black van with tinted windows met him in the parking garage. It had no passengers so Anthony hopped in the front seat.

"Sir," the driver said. "If you could please sit in the back. Nobody is to see you enter the White House."

"Oh, sure," Anthony responded. The drive down Pennsylvania Avenue was slowed by noon-hour traffic congestion. It gave Anthony a chance to think about what might soon happen. The government professionals and tourists standing ten feet from the van at the intersection had no idea that the man who might one day be vice president was sitting inside wiping the sweat off his forehead. Nothing was said as they made their way to the Treasury Department just east of the White House. The van pulled to a stop in the underground parking garage and Anthony exited. He was met by three Secret Service agents and Chief of Staff Kennedy.

"Congressman, good to see you," Kennedy said.

"Pete, nice to see you."

Anthony smiled and raised his eyebrows. "What's up?"

They talked along the way. They walked into the basement of the Treasury Building then through the tunnel under the west side and entered the sub-basement of the White House. They headed straight to the Oval Office where the President was waiting.

"Mr. President."

"Congressman, come on in and have a seat." Kennedy and the Secret

Service left them alone.

The President sat at his desk – the Resolute Desk, the real one not like the Old Man's copy – and Anthony took the seat on the President's right.

"Schumacher, you're smart enough to know that you weren't my first choice for vice president."

Anthony was politically savvy enough to know he wasn't his second choice either.

"But right now you're the best person for the job. I want you to be my new vice president."

Anthony had dreamt of what he might say. He thought he might have to make an impassioned plea for the job. But here the President just came out and said it was his for the taking.

"Mr. President, I would be honored to be your vice president."

"Good," the President said. Finally, something had gone right in this whole mess. "We'll announce it as soon as you can get your family here."

"Yes, sir."

The President crossed it off his list. He acted like he had pressing business to attend to. Anthony stood and they shook hands.

"Thank you, Mr. President."

That was it.

Anthony hustled through the sub-basement and the tunnel to the garage underneath the Treasury Department. When Wiley saw Anthony's big smile upon his return to the office he took to dancing on the furniture. Anthony called Danielle and told her to quietly round up the kids and head to D.C. He didn't need to tell her why. Wiley would pick them up at the airport.

The announcement the following day in the East Room of the White House was a proud moment for the Schumacher family. A national TV audience watched as Congressman Schumacher from Indiana walked with his family and the President of the United States down the red carpeted hall and stood behind the podium decked with the presidential seal. Standing behind the President was a confident looking Anthony accompanied by his beautiful wife, two daughters, and one son. Although many had come to know of Danielle, this was the first time the Schumacher family as a whole was introduced to the nation.

"Congressman Schumacher's love for his country cannot be questioned. He has served the nation well as a member of the FBI and his home state of Indiana in the United States House of Representatives. He will bring a lot of energy and experience to his office, and the American people will be proud to call him their Vice President. It is my honor to introduce to you, my choice for the next Vice President of the United States, Anthony Schumacher."

Anthony shook the President's hand and removed a folded piece of paper from his suit coat. He cleared his throat. Now was not the time to sound overwhelmed or nervous. He thanked the President for this great honor and he promised to tirelessly work to better this great country. He thanked Danielle, who was wiping away tears. And he introduced his three children, all of whom he was very proud. He closed by remembering the great service rendered by his immediate predecessor and noted he had a wonderful chat early that morning with Candace Sutton, who had privately confided to him that she could think of no better man to be the next Vice President.

"I ask the American people for their prayers of support and I look forward to the confirmation process before the House and Senate."

The IRS combed through his taxes for the past twenty years. The FBI background check was just as extensive. Agents combed through Anthony's life since high school. His Spanish teacher still remembered his days in her class room and gave him glowing reviews. The FBI even interviewed Floyd Revson, who was still counting donuts and dollars as the manager of the Donut Palace in Silver Creek. Former colleagues at the FBI saw nothing that would raise red flags. A few disgruntled citizens from Silver Creek contacted the FBI themselves to complain about Anthony's heavy-handed tactics against their guilty relatives when he was state's attorney. Their complaints went nowhere.

The confirmation hearings began in the Senate Rules Committee. Anthony had spent the past few days in closed-door meetings with Wiley and the President's advisors to prepare himself for the intense questioning from senators. His political philosophy would be front and center. The Democrats would pester him on his ability to reach across the aisle and his inflexibility on abortion and same-sex marriage. When asked about his term-limits amendment, he smiled and said it was a matter best left to the legislature – which he was hoping to soon leave. The Republicans would offer their assistance with any needed rehabilitation and all in all indicate their approval for the next President of the Senate. The final vote was 76 to 24.

One down, one to go.

Anthony's road to the vice presidency would run into Democratic opposition in his beloved House of Representatives. The Democrats still held him responsible for Speaker O'Shea's ouster and their resulting loss of power. Most went before the press and said they fully intended to give the Congressman a fair hearing, but the liberal operatives were working round the clock to find any dirt that could be used against Anthony now or in the future. If he was going to run for President someday, now was the time to sow the seeds of doubt.

The Republican leadership in the House Judiciary Committee got Anthony off to a good start by asking softball questions and mostly letting Anthony describe his political beliefs and hope for America's future.

Then the Democrats fired away.

They started off questioning him about his days in the FBI and claimed he violated the civil rights of unnamed citizens on multiple occasions. Anthony could only respond that he would need to know the specific facts upon which they were making their baseless accusations. It didn't matter what the facts were to the Democrats, it was the damning nature of the charge that would play on the six o'clock news.

The Democrats scrutinized his legal career and asked for his stance on the death penalty. He responded it was a very serious matter, and a penalty that should only be used on the worst of the worst criminals. What about the death penalty for juveniles? He would support it in extreme cases but noted the Supreme Court has ruled otherwise and he would be obligated to follow the law. What about eavesdropping on terrorists? Torturing terrorists? Locking up terrorists without trial? Anthony responded he would adhere to President Fisher's stance on terrorist detainees and do everything necessary to protect the American people within the limits of the Constitution.

Liberal commentators scoffed at his responses, calling him a "right-wing dufus" and an "intellectual lightweight." Some claimed Anthony had been handpicked by Limbaugh. They, of course, would only be happy with a liberal East Coast type, someone with an Ivy League pedigree and not some second-hand education from a podunk school like Wabash State University. Multiple media outlets could be heard lamenting that the President's choice was just another Quayle from Indiana.

The Democrats' interrogation of Anthony had gone on for two whole days. At the end of each round, he would return to his town house and fall into bed suffering from exhaustion. Danielle worried this political anal exam would be bad for his health. He was too tired to eat, and even too worn out to take his early morning run.

Day three.

"Good morning, Mr. Schumacher," Congressman Robinson said.

"Congresswoman, good morning."

Anthony and Congresswoman Robinson, she of the blighted slums of Detroit, had well-documented run-ins on the House floor over the past twelve years. Now she was in the position of judging his qualifications for the vice presidency and she had no desire to take it easy on him.

It was payback time, and she could be as nasty as she wanted to be.

"Mr. Schumacher, have you ever had an African-American on your staff?"

"No, I have not."

"You cut off funding for expanded welfare payments and health care for the poor, isn't that true?"

"What time frame are you talking about?"

She didn't remember specifically. It was just ingrained in her mind that he voted against her welfare/health-care bill at some point. As did every other Republican in the House.

"A couple of years ago?"

"Congresswoman, I don't remember the specific bill you're talking about. But I can assure you I must have thought your bill was not the right way to fight poverty in the inner cities."

She was getting flustered. She really wanted to trip him up so he'd look like the racist she told everybody he was.

"Mr. Schumacher, why don't you just come out of the racial closet and just be honest with the American people that you hate black people."

The Chairman banged his gavel in disgust, asking the congresswoman to adhere to the rules of decorum. He wasn't going to put up with it much longer.

"No, it's okay, Mr. Chairman," Anthony said. "Congresswoman, I wish you and I could sit down for dinner sometime to discuss our different philosophies. It might come as a surprise to you, but I owe my life to an African-American."

Robinson didn't know what he was talking about. How dare he use a black person to make his point.

Anthony spoke softly, from his heart. "If it weren't for my good friend Ty, I would not have married the most wonderful woman in the world. I would not have had the opportunity to raise three wonderful children. And I wouldn't have been able to have served in this great House and had the privilege to sit before you today."

No one in the committee room made a sound.

"That friend I'm talking about just happens to be Tyrone Stubblefield, the Deputy Director of the FBI. He saved my life one Friday afternoon when I lay dying on the floor of a bank. I owe my life to him."

A few of the spectators in the gallery could be seen wiping tears from their eyes.

"Ty and I shared a lot of time together. He grew up poor on the mean streets of Los Angeles. But his mom demanded he go to school and get his education and make something of himself. He has made it to the highest levels of federal law enforcement. I want all the young Ty Stubblefield's out there to have the opportunity to reach for the stars and achieve their dreams. We can make that happen with government programs that encourage strong families and education. Lower taxes will enable poor parents to spend more time with their children instead of working a second job. A supportive parent at home will lead to better disciplined students, which in turn, will lead to less gang membership, less drug use, and less crime."

Anthony looked down at his microphone and then at Congresswoman Robinson.

"I want every child in America to have the opportunities that I had and Ty had. If you and I can work together to improve our nation's schools and encourage strong family relationships, America's future will be the better for it."

The Congresswoman started to speak but was told her time had expired. Anthony had talked long enough to weather the assaults from the Gentlewoman from Michigan once again. And he hoped for good.

After a break for lunch where the Democrats huddled for the final time, the liberal leaders moved away from Anthony and focused on his friends.

"Congressman, I'm concerned about the people you surround yourself with," said House minority leader, Ken Williams. "Your chief of staff William Cogdon has a history of alcohol abuse and womanizing. Will he be a member of your staff if you are confirmed as Vice President?"

Anthony stared into his microphone. He hadn't thought about Wiley's past dragging him down in these hearings. Wiley had turned his life around and Anthony had no concerns.

"Congressman, I have seen my friend, Mr. Cogdon, undergo a positive transformation in his life within the last few years. He underwent rehab, counseling, and now is in a committed relationship. I have no worries about him continuing as my chief of staff."

Williams scoffed at the response. "You're telling my you're going to let a supposedly reformed drunk and skirt chaser into a position that requires top-secret security clearance. Are you out of your mind?"

Three days. Three long days. Anthony had sat still while the Democrats twisted the truth and bent the rules in looking at every aspect of his life. What American would want to have to undergo such scrutiny? Anthony had had enough.

"Congressman, you and your fellow Democrats have dragged my name through the mud for the past three days. Now you're moving on to my friends. Maybe tomorrow you'll start in on my wife. It's true Mr. Cogdon once had a drinking problem and engaged in sexual relations with women to whom he was not married. But I know damn well that there are a handful of people that have served under this Capitol that have driven off that bridge once or twice in their lifetime. Yet, they change. They learn from their mistakes. I love my country. Mr. Cogdon loves his country," he said with his voice raising. The right fist slammed the table. "And we're ready to go to work for the American people."

The Republican spokesman gave a glowing argument in Anthony's favor. The Democrats tried to be civil and rested their argument that Anthony had no executive experience and was not ready to be a heart beat away from the presidency. The argument would sway few, and with the Republicans in the majority, Anthony's nomination was in the bag.

The final vote was 380 to 55.

Raymond J. Shannon switched off the TV in his office across the street from the U.S. Capitol. He had spent the good part of the afternoon with his feet on his desk wondering if he would be pressed into service. He rightly anticipated his phone would ring in the next five seconds.

"Mr. Chief Justice," his secretary said through the phone, "it's the Speaker of the House on line one."

Chief Justice Shannon had spent twenty-five years on the Supreme Court with the last ten in the middle chair. He had sworn in two presidents but Anthony would be his first vice president. He grabbed his robe and took the rear seat in a limousine driven by U.S. Marshals. The drive to the Capitol only took two minutes.

Anthony sat in a holding room with Danielle, her mother, and the three children. Anthony's eyes would every so often dart down to a preprinted card that stated the oath of office. He didn't want to screw it up. He and Wiley even practiced a couple times. They were all nervous, and in about fifteen minutes, each one of their lives was going to radically change.

They moved to the House floor which was packed with every member of the House and Senate. The galleries were overflowing. It felt like a State of the Union speech. The appearance of the Chief Justice caused a stir in the audience. It would be one of the few times the public would both see and hear the Chief Justice in the House chamber. Anthony and the family gathered in front of the Speaker's rostrum and greeted the Chief Justice.

"Congressman, are you ready to take the oath?"

"I am."

The Vice President collects a salary of $227,300 per year, the same as the Chief Justice and the Speaker of the House. It would be a nice bump for Anthony from his lowly congressman's salary of $174,000.

"Would you please raise your right hand and repeat after me. I, Anthony Joseph Schumacher, do solemnly swear."

Article II of the Constitution provides for the oath of office for the President but not the Vice President. Article VI states senators, representatives, judicial officers, and executive officials shall take an oath to support the Constitution.

"That I will support and defend the Constitution of the United States against all enemies foreign and domestic."

Title five of the United States Code section 3331 sets forth the text of the oath applicable to all federal employees, including the Vice President, members of Congress, and Supreme Court justices.

"That I will bear true faith and allegiance to the same."

The Chief Justice could give the Presidential oath in his sleep, but he carried a card and looked down after each sentence. He didn't want to screw it up on national television lest he be the newest YouTube sensation.

"That I take this obligation freely, without any mental reservation or purpose of evasion."

Anthony stood ramrod straight, his right hand at shoulder height, his left resting on the Bible held by a beaming Danielle. The Bible was opened to verse thirteen of Philippians chapter four, Anthony's favorite verse.

"And that I will well and faithfully discharge the duties of the office on which I am about to enter."

The weight on Anthony's shoulders would increase tenfold in the next few seconds.

"So help me God."

"Mr. Vice President," the Chief Justice said with hand extended, "congratulations."

"Thank you, Mr. Chief Justice."

The whole House burst into applause, although the Dems struggled to put their hands together with much energy. One of their own was now moving on. Anthony kissed Danielle and hugged his children and mother-in-law. He said a few words to his now former colleagues and pledged to work with them to better America.

After Anthony and family left the House chamber, they were confronted by seven men and one woman of the U.S. Secret Service. All of them were armed and ready to take a bullet for their new protectee. They would become like extended family now. They took the Schumachers via motorcade to the White House for dinner with the President. Tomorrow, Vice President Schumacher would start his new life serving his country in the Executive Branch.

CHAPTER 17

Anthony and Danielle spent their first night at Number One Observatory Circle in the Vice President's official residence on the ground of the U.S. Naval Observatory in Northwest D.C. They both awoke at around 7 a.m. and spent ten minutes wondering if it was really true. After all they had been through with the trial, the Speaker's expulsion, and Vice President Sutton's death, they really hadn't had time to decompress. They also hadn't had a lot of meaningful alone time in their own bed. A time when they could hold each other tight and remind themselves of why they were madly in love with each other. Their days of chasing each other around the bedroom might have slowed but they could still break a sweat between the sheets.

Between rounds of kissing and rubbing their hands over each other's body, the heat underneath the covers began to rise. The night shirts started coming off and the once forgotten joy of sweaty skin rubbing up against skin made them groan with delight. She wanted him, and he wanted her. She whispered to him, and he licked her earlobe. She threw the pillow to the night stand and dug her nails into his back. She then told the Vice President of the United States to make love to her.

His boxers were half off when the door to the bedroom flew open with a thud. Three armed men rushed in ready to fight to the death.

Danielle screamed.

Anthony looked over his shoulder. "Hey, what's going on!?" he yelled.

The half-naked couple then received an embarrassed morning greeting from the red-faced agents of the United States Secret Service.

"You guys need something?" asked Anthony, half of him on the bed and the other half straddling his naked wife. Both of them were holding the covers up over their chests.

Michael Craig, Anthony's lead agent, apologized profusely. He looked over at the night stand and then to the pillow on the floor. "Mr. Vice President, that Statue of Liberty figurine on your night stand is an emergency call device. It acts like a panic button. If it's knocked over, we come in. I'm sorry, I should have mentioned it to you last night."

Anthony smiled and told him there was no one to blame. They'd be more careful next time. He told Agent Craig he'd be out shortly. Once the agents left, Anthony and Danielle pulled the covers over their head and giggled like a couple of teenagers who had just been caught in the back seat of his father's car. Anthony gave her a long kiss and told her they would resume their play time later.

Anthony showered, shaved, and walked out the bedroom door to find Agent Craig standing guard outside. Michael Craig stood six-feet tall and had a slender frame. His hair was short, military style, and his jaw chiseled. He was a decorated former Indianapolis police officer before joining the Secret Service. Prior to his stint on the protective detail, he received numerous commendations in the Dallas field office. Anthony asked him to stay on after leading Vice President Sutton's security detail.

"Morning, Mr. Vice President."

Anthony gave him a half-embarrassed smile. "Morning." He threw an arm around Agent Craig. "How about you and I keep that one to ourselves?"

"Mr. Vice President, everything is kept between ourselves."

He winked. Anthony did the same. Time to go to work.

The trip from the U.S. Naval Observatory to the White House took less than five minutes. Of course, it's easy when you don't have to stop for red lights. The Vice President's speeding limousine was preceded down Massachusetts Avenue by two D.C. police cars and followed by two Suburbans, one with a communication command and the other with a counter assault team, and two more police cruisers. It made quite a racket. Anthony waved at a few tourists taking pictures. For the first time, he would be driven through the White House gates (no need for secrecy now) as Vice President of the United States.

"Shadow is in the Crown," said Agent Craig into the cuff of his suit coat.

The Secret Service assigns its protectees code names for quick identification. Each member of the family is assigned a code name beginning with the same letter. Anthony was Shadow and Danielle was Sunshine. A few protectees in the past have disliked their code names and requested a change, but Anthony and Danielle were content. The Schumacher children, who were either in the work force or attending college also had agents following them wherever they went. Ashley was Starlight, Michael was Shortstop, and Anna was Strawberry. The code word for the White House is Crown.

Anthony's first meeting as Vice President was in his West Wing office with the Secret Service. Agent Craig and his team instructed Anthony on the ins and outs of his protective detail. If he wanted to go somewhere, Agent Craig just asked that Anthony or a staff member give them sufficient heads up. The days of going to Burger King to read the paper and enjoy a Diet Coke would have to be curtailed. The Secret Service was well aware of Anthony's routine as a congressman. It would be best if he did his running on the grounds of the residence since it was a secure facility. Anthony was given a locator device that he was asked to have on him at all times. The Joint Operations Center would know his whereabouts twenty-four-seven. Danielle would have one as well. The agents showed him the panic buttons and had him come up with a secret word that would alert the Secret Service to a situation that the Vice President found potentially harmful. He chose "Harroun," after Ray Harroun, the first winner of the Indianapolis 500, and the name of one of Anthony's dear departed dogs from his childhood. Anthony took it all in and promised to make the lives of the men and women assigned to protect his life with their own as easy as possible.

Wiley walked in carrying a cup of coffee and a muffin that he had purchased from the White House mess. He couldn't stop smiling. He had showed up at the Northwest Gate at 5 a.m. saying he couldn't sleep and was itching to get to work. He proudly told Anthony he was the first staff member to arrive at the White House. Wiley showed Anthony around and introduced him to the staff, many of whom were holdovers from Vice President Sutton's team. The place reeked of power. It felt like a giant vortex where the center of the universe poured all of its energy into its swirling core. Anthony thought Wiley might need a sedative.

They walked over to the Eisenhower Executive Office Building to check out the Vice President's ceremonial office. There Anthony could have more formal meetings and sip coffee with big wigs and VIPs while TV cameras and still photographers recorded the moment for history. He tried out the Vice President's Desk, which had been used by every vice president since LBJ. In the top drawer, each vice president had signed his name and Anthony continued the tradition with his John Hancock. The White House photographer came over to take Anthony's official vice-presidential photo. The fun stuff over, now it was time to go to work.

9 a.m.

The National Security Council briefing began on time. The enormity of his new position would hit Anthony shortly thereafter. Upon entering the Situation Room, he was confronted with the Chairman of the Joint Chiefs of Staff, the National Security Advisor, the Secretary of Defense, the Director of Central Intelligence, the Director of Homeland Security, and the President's chief of staff. All of them offered their congratulations, but the hardened look on their faces returned quickly. For Anthony, it was his first full day as Vice President. For everybody else, it was Thursday.

And mad men around the world wanted to kill them and every one else in America.

They all stood when the President entered the room. He presided over a meeting that included a secure teleconference with the U.S. commander in

Afghanistan and the head of the U.S. Central Command. General Walter "Wally" Roe started the briefing with a recitation of the names of three service members who had been killed since the last meeting two days ago. Anthony made a note that one of them was a sergeant first class from Indiana. He'd follow up with a letter of condolence after the President did. The militants were putting up a hell of a fight, the general said. He needed more men. The head of the U.S. Central Command, General Donald D. Dukes, whose stars on his shoulders glimmered in the light of the room at the Florida Air Force base from where he was broadcasting, concurred in General Roe's proposal. They needed more men (and women) to fight for their country. More important, they needed more to win the fight.

The President took it all in and told him he'd get back to them by the end of the day through the Joint Chiefs. Once the teleconference was over, CIA Director Jillian Franklin, and Homeland Security Director Larry Starkey opened their briefing books. They would not paint a comforting picture. They were tracking two al-Qaeda groups within the United States and their contacts within foreign countries. Franklin indicated her agency had heard increased chatter among the Internet and authorized intercepts that an attack was imminent. East Coast transit hubs appeared to be the intended target, but they weren't sure how an attack would be carried out. It could be surface-to-air missile, a suicide bomber with explosives in his backpack, or a truck bomb. The worst-case scenario would be the release of a biological agent in a populated area. Hundreds of thousands of citizens could be at risk. Director Starkey believed raising the threat level was necessary. Law enforcement agencies would be put on high alert and random checks of passengers at subways, railways, and airports would be implemented.

The President nodded his head. He gave the go-ahead and authorized the Department of Homeland Security and FBI to ramp up the threat level. Tell the citizens to be alert and contact the police if they see anything suspicious, he wrote on his note pad.

"Anything else?" he asked, like it was just another ho-hum Thursday.

"No, sir," they all responded in unison.

"Mr. Vice President, would you like to add anything?"

"No, sir. Thank you."

The meeting adjourned and they all went their separate ways. Anthony took his briefing books and his notes and returned to his office. His head was spinning. Terrorists, suicide bombers, imminent attacks. He had always heard about it on the news and been privy to some of the information as a congressman. But now it seemed so much more frightening. The decisions that had been made in that Situation Room could have an effect on every American citizen as well as every soldier, sailor, airman, and Marine. And if for some reason the President couldn't make the decision, Anthony would have to make the call.

The Office of the Vice President might seem ceremonial to some – the more mundane parts being sent to some foreign leader's funeral or nominated to head a committee on education or space exploration. Others might even consider it a bit morbid – waiting around twiddling one's thumbs for the President to kick the bucket. Whatever the case, the Vice President had better be up to speed because lives might depend on the decision he makes.

Anthony could already feel his hair starting to turn gray.

11:30 a.m.

The President convened his legal advisers for an early lunch. He was confronted with a situation that every President hopes to encounter at least once in their term in office and, if they are lucky, more than once.

There would soon be a vacancy at the highest court in the land.

Over soup and salads, the President chaired the meeting that included the Vice President, Attorney General Claire Donovan, his chief of staff Peter Kennedy, and Patrick Clinton, his political advisor and campaign manager. The President exuded excitement, knowing his Supreme Court pick could carry out his legacy for the next thirty years. The Supreme Court was currently split with four hard-core conservatives and three reliable liberal justices. Two lone mavericks sat with their fingers in the air to determine which way they wanted to rule. One such maverick, Associate Justice Tobias M. McReynolds, had been lambasted by both sides long enough and wanted to retire to Florida.

The President was the first to throw out names of potential nominees. He wanted Mario Alonso, an old friend from New York who had spent the past year on the federal appellate bench. Judge Alonso had grown up poor and worked his way through law school working at a newspaper stand. He worked in the legal department at the global securities firm started by the President and showed great ambition and intellect. He followed Fisher to become counselor to the Governor and then New York Attorney General. When a seat opened up on the Second Circuit Court of Appeals, President Fisher nominated his old friend and promised him he'd be in line for a future Supreme Court seat.

Clinton was running the campaign commercials in his head, one replaying the President proudly announcing the first Hispanic male Supreme Court Justice. Clinton didn't care about Alonso's ideological leanings or how they would play out in the marble halls of the Supreme Court. Thirty percent of Hispanics had voted for the President in the last election. With that segment of the population growing, a five-percent gain would be huge.

Attorney General Donovan was on board with the President. Kennedy was too. The Vice President would be the lone dissenter in this room.

Anthony raised concerns about Judge Alonso's scant track record on the court of appeals. He had ruled in favor of a gun-control ordinance in New York

City, authored an opinion allowing for the liberal use of affirmative action in New York schools, and dissented in a case upholding a ban on partial-birth abortion. The Vice President noted Republicans would have problems with the nomination and it would hurt the President with his conservative base.

"Well, Mr. Vice President," the President sneered. "Who do you think I should nominate?" The President wasn't in a good mood. He had another fight with the First Lady last night and was always worried about the terror threat. He wanted Alonso and expected everyone else to jump on board.

"Mr. President, I think you should look at Judge Kimberly Tanner of the Seventh Circuit Court of Appeals. She's a native of Indiana, appointed as a federal district judge by the first President Bush, and then elevated to the Seventh Circuit by the second. She's pro-life, a strong supporter of the Second Amendment, and a believer in judicial restraint."

The President shook his head. "I've heard of her. I think she might be a little too right wing."

Anthony had never heard of anyone being "too right wing." Clinton thought there were enough women on the Court anyway. Donovan cleared her throat to remind him a female was in the room. She thought Judge Tanner was a fine choice and well-qualified, but she'd go along with whoever the President picked.

The President said he'd consider Anthony's choice. He wanted a few more names, people of color, if possible. They'd meet next week and make the decision.

Next order of business.

2:30 p.m.

The President invited the Vice President and the Secretary of Transportation, along with congressional leaders, to the Rose Garden for a signing ceremony for the highway bill. The reporters were told the President would take a few questions after the photo op. The President gave a short statement noting the need for a rebuilding of America's infrastructure and commended Congress for passing a bipartisan bill that would not only fix the nation's crumbling roads and bridges but would also put thousands of Americans to work. The President offered several ceremonial pens to the Speaker of the House and Senate Majority Leader after signing his name to the bill for all the world to see.

"Mr. President," Lee Garner yelled out, "how's your search for a new Supreme Court Justice?"

The President raised his hand and said he was working hard on finding the best candidate. "There are a lot of qualified Americans to choose from. We have plenty of time before the Court's term starts in October."

Other reporters asked the President about the war on terror. Would the

President ask for more funds to help the states combat terrorism? Did the President worry about a chemical attack? Did the President favor taking the fight to the terrorists' hideouts in foreign countries? What about sanctions in the United Nations against countries harboring terrorists?

The President answered all the questions in cool fashion, all the while making his way back into the White House. Kennedy ended the questioning and thanked the reporters.

The reporters were still hungry for some news.

"Mr. Vice President, how is your first day on the job going?"

Anthony smiled as if he was happy someone actually wanted to talk to him. He walked over to the assembled press corps and held court for twenty minutes. He noted the job was filled with great responsibility that could have a lasting impact on American society. So, he was not only humbled by the authority but looking forward to making a difference.

"I can't wait to start cutting some taxes," he said with a little too much exuberance. "Then we can start returning the government back to the people and keep it out of the hands of the bureaucrats."

The President and his chief of staff had returned to his private study off the Oval Office. Both of them were shaking their head at their new Vice President spouting off his conservatism to the cable networks.

They both thought they were going to have to keep a close eye on him.

6 p.m.

"Sunshine is in the Crown."

Danielle arrived in her best red evening gown and just happened to remember the Vice President's tuxedo. In an hour, they'd head to the White House Dining Room for a state dinner with the President and First Lady and their guests, the King and Queen of Sweden.

"So how was the Second Lady's day?" Anthony asked his wife.

"I spent half the morning with Brooke."

"Who's Brooke?"

"Oh, I mean Agent Harris. She's my lead agent." Agent Harris and her team of seven would shadow Danielle wherever she went. So far, she liked them. She spent the afternoon checking out the rest of the residence. She found the laundry room and pronounced it adequate. The Secret Service even showed her the underground bunker.

"I'm not sure if that's comforting or not?" Anthony responded.

Anthony changed clothes and both of them looked at themselves all decked out in the mirror. Here they were about to be introduced in the White House as the Vice President of the United States and Mrs. Schumacher. They giggled like school children. Arm in arm, they walked out of their holding room followed by Agent Craig and Agent Harris.

The dinner consisted of herb roasted pheasant and glazed vegetables, pecan rice, and broccoli florets. For dessert, the guests enjoyed cold praline souffle with caramel sauce. The King and Queen made excellent dinner companions and spent most of their evening talking with Anthony and Danielle. They had spent the previous evening in the Lincoln Bedroom and found the President and First Lady cold and uninteresting. It was uncomfortably obvious that the latter were having marital difficulties. The lovely and lively couple from Indiana, however, proved to be much more appealing.

When Anthony asked His Majesty whether he knew of a fellow named Kenny Brack, the King's eyes lit up.

"He is a national hero in my country," the King gushed.

Mr. Brack was also the 1999 winner of the Indianapolis 500, a race which Anthony had attended. He had met the Swede on a number of occasions and found him to be a wonderful champion. Although Anthony might have made it sound like he was long lost buddies with Mr. Brack, it was an easy icebreaker. Anthony learned the King had become a fan of auto racing and hoped to come to America's big race "at the Indy." When Anthony told him he could arrange for it, the King had a new best friend. When Anthony joined Danielle for their first dance of the evening, he learned the Queen had invited them to Stockholm. The Schumachers had a wonderful time.

At the end of the evening, the President and First Lady finally took offense to the Swedes' decision to diss their hosts and left for their separate bedrooms without even saying good night. Their resentment didn't stop with the royals. Both fumed that the new King and Queen of Indiana had best learn their manners when guests of the Fishers' house.

10 p.m.

Anthony and Danielle fell into bed. They were too tired to resume their morning make-out session. With a kiss on each cheek and one on her lips, he whispered he loved her and wished her a good night. The lights were off for at most a minute when the phone rang. It was Wiley.

"Mr. Vice President, I just called to tell you the CIA will be sending someone over tomorrow at 6 a.m. to drop off your daily briefing materials."

"Fine."

"How was your first day?" Wiley was itching to talk. He just had his final Red Bull of the day and wanted to tell his boss all the gossip and rumors that he had learned about half of Washington. He probably could have gone all night.

"Wiley."

"Yes, Mr. Vice President."

"Get some sleep. We have to do it all over again tomorrow."

CHAPTER 18

The first six months of Anthony's tenure as vice president were filled with national security meetings and strategy sessions with Republican congressional leaders on the upcoming budget. Anthony also sat with Speaker Spencer during the President's State of the Union address, giving him some national TV exposure in what Wiley liked to call "free campaign advertising." He also presided as President of the Senate on one occasion and, pursuant to Article I, section 3, he cast the deciding vote to break the tie on a bill allowing concealed carry of firearms on the grounds of national parks.

Anthony also had a blast as Vice President outside of Washington. He and Michael toured the Secret Service training center in Maryland to watch his bodyguards in action. Anthony even offered to work a live-action rope line to give the agents-in-training some first-hand practice. If a Secret Service agent would happen to write a tell-all book about the protectees, the Schumachers would receive glowing reviews. Shadow and Sunshine were always respectful of their agents and oftentimes invited them over for dinner. They also made sure to stay in Washington for Christmas to allow the agents a chance to enjoy the holiday with their families. They rarely went out on the town and mostly stayed in at night to watch TV or catch up on their reading. They were easy to protect and polite as could be. The Secret Service loved them.

In late May, Anthony returned to Silver Creek to give the commencement address at Silver Creek High School and visit the old hangouts – the Donut Palace, the Dairy Barn, and his beloved home overlooking the Wabash. Anthony may have abused the power of the office on one occasion to finagle the opportunity to drive the pace car at the Indianapolis 500. No Vice President of the United States had ever enjoyed the honor of leading the 33-car field to the green flag and Anthony pestered the Speedway management long and hard enough until they relented. Once he got the nod, the Secret Service actually balked claiming they could not protect him driving the latest version of the Corvette at high speed around a two and a half mile oval with 300,000 people looking on. On this one occasion, he overruled his agents and hauled ass down the main straightaway with the biggest grin on his face that anyone had ever seen.

Back in Washington, Anthony's mood wasn't as chipper. He was beginning to feel like he was losing the conservative battle with the so-called Republican President. Fisher was pushing for a tax hike on the rich to advance his global-warming agenda despite Anthony's argument to the contrary. The President also wanted to take over the banking industry arguing he could run it better than anyone. Even worse, freshly sworn Supreme Court Justice Mario Alonso was authoring his first High Court opinions and tipping the scales of justice to the Left.

"Just another damn Souter," lamented the angry conservative pundits.

Anthony's weekly private meetings with the President weren't all that pleasant either. He was constantly reminding the President that he was damaging his conservative base with his tax and spend mantra and the next presidential election was only a little more than two years away. The President scoffed at Anthony's concerns and told him he knew what he was doing. He also started calling Anthony "Big Boy," and it wasn't made in good-natured humor. It was more in the tone of "Hey boy, you're in the big leagues now so let us adults handle things and you just fall in line." Anthony would let the dig roll off, not worrying about silly name-calling. But he began to realize he would get little respect in the Fisher Administration.

The Fourth of July weekend around Washington is always a joyous occasion of fireworks, patriotism, and a flowing abundance of the Stars and Stripes. What could be more American than celebrating Independence Day in the nation's capital with family, friends, and fellow citizens? Happy families pushing strollers and elderly vacationers holding maps as they enjoyed the monuments to freedom and great American heroes and trying to find a place to cool off in the stifling heat. Old Glory, hot dogs, apple pie. God Bless America!

But there was another segment of the capital that found the Fourth of July to be a major headache. One million visitors huddled in a relatively small space. They all looked peaceful. But what about that guy sweating in the jacket and taking pictures of the Capitol? What about that moving van crawling slowly past the Department of Justice? Was that man really filming the subway trains entering the station? Two thousand law enforcement personnel from fifteen different agencies scanned the crowds with wary eyes. Surveillance cameras, biological sensors, random bag searches. O Say Can You See! the end of the line for that security checkpoint?

While the mood may have been festive outside, the movers and shakers inside 1600 Pennsylvania Avenue walked around with worried looks on their faces. The National Security briefings in the Situation Room were taking twice as long as they had in the past. The chatter had increased, and one plot to blow up a federal courthouse in Los Angeles had recently been thwarted. With their briefing books and classified memos, the Directors of the FBI, CIA, Secret

Service, and Homeland Security joined the President and Vice President to assess the current terror threat facing the nation.

"All right, whatta we got?" the President asked as he convened the meeting.

FBI Director Bolton took charge and pressed his remote control to bring up the hate-filled face of a Middle Eastern man on the flat-screen TV on the opposite wall.

"This is Mustafa Oman," Bolton said without looking at his notes. Oman just looked dangerous – beady black eyes that did not hide his hatred for the West. "He is a Saudi Arabian born business man who came to America on a work visa which has now expired. He has in the past expressed his hatred for America and sought to recruit jihadists to wage war against the United States. His group has had some meetings in Upstate New York. We've been tracking him for several months."

"But you lost him, didn't you." The snicker from CIA Director Franklin was not hidden very well.

Jillian Franklin was the first woman to head the Central Intelligence Agency. She had been President-elect Fisher's liaison after his election and prior to the inauguration and the two worked well together. Her long flowing dark hair showed no signs of gray. She also had a perky bust line that the President couldn't keep his eyes off of. She had been secretly voted the hottest CIA agent by her male colleagues, most of whom hoped to get stationed in some foreign land with her and then bed the sexy spy. When the President needed a new CIA chief, he bypassed more experienced men and women and chose someone he could have a good rapport with – someone who he'd have no problem meeting with on a daily basis.

Director Bolton and Director Franklin, however, did not get along. Both were career officers in their respective agencies, and both thought the other's agency was inferior to their own. Bolton railed in private at the CIA's feckless leadership and inability to gather hard and fast intel in countries like Afghanistan and Pakistan. What the hell kind of worthless spy agency is it anyway? he often fumed.

Director Franklin could not stand the high and mighty Bolton. She accused the FBI of stealing the intelligence gained by other agencies and claiming it as its own. She also thought Bolton was an arrogant publicity hog who only wanted to scare the American public thereby allowing him to demand more federal funds from Congress to combat the global war on terror and quench his thirst for more power.

"We don't know where he's at right now."

"So you had him and now you don't. Ergo, you lost him."

"Why don't you and your so-called spies go screw yourselves, Jillian," he shot back.

"Alright, alright," the President said, trying to calm the two combatants. Although he did like it when Franklin got snippy like that, thinking it made her look hot. "Should we post the guy's picture on television or what?"

Bolton shook his head. "Mr. President, Oman might have gone back to Afghanistan. We're not so much worried about him committing an act of terror as we are of him giving the order. We really need to find his friends."

"So what do you want?"

"We want you to sign off on a sneak and peek search warrant so we can secretly enter their hideout and search for clues."

"Don't you need evidence to justify that?" Franklin chided. "What ever happened to the protections of the Fourth Amendment?"

Under provisions of the USA Patriot Act, a judge can issue a surreptitious entry search warrant if federal agents show reasonable cause that notifying the occupant of the warrant's execution may have an adverse result – such as the destruction of evidence or if it would jeopardize an investigation. The warrant generally prohibits the seizure of the property – agents are just there to sneak and peek – and notice of the warrant's execution must be given within a reasonable time period unless good cause is shown.

President Fisher had campaigned against the use of such covert-entry warrants, claiming his predecessors had abused the power and violated the rights of ordinary citizens. Plus, he didn't want to upset his buddies at the ACLU, who were constantly calling for the repeal of the provision and threatening lawsuits.

"Mr. President, if I might," Vice President Schumacher interjected. "I agree with Director Bolton on this."

Director Franklin failed to suppress a muffled laugh. "What a shock."

Both Anthony and Director Bolton looked over at her at the condescending and disrespectful remark. The President pretended not to hear it.

"I've been reading these intelligence briefs and it just seems to me the chatter has been increasing day by day," Anthony said. "I think we need to take the chance. Better that we overreact than not act at all and have to clean up the mess afterwards."

The President leaned back in his chair and rolled his neck. He was more worried about the ACLU than the terrorists.

"How do you think an attack would be carried out?"

"Best guess," Director Bolton said, looking him straight in the eye, "small plane loaded with explosives or a truck bomb."

"But it's just your best guess?" Director Franklin mocked.

Director Bolton's voice amped up a few notches. "That's why we need to get into the apartments and houses of Oman's followers."

Anthony shook his head. "I agree, Mr. President."

"Easy now, Big Boy," the President said softly, putting Anthony in his place. The President didn't want to cause a panic if word got out that the FBI was sneaking around people's houses again, especially in his home state of New York. The Islamic community had contributed large donations in his campaigns for Governor and President and he did not want to cause an unnecessary riff.

He wanted stronger evidence. He then turned to Director Bolton. "Then you can go get your regular search warrants from a judge just like regular cops do."

Bolton bristled at the notion that his agents were simply federal "cops." And they sure as hell weren't "regular." He knew the President had little respect for the men and woman at the Bureau.

"Let's wait until we have a little more solid intelligence." This would give the President ample political cover. He then tried to kiss the FBI Director's ass. "I know your people are the best and will get what we need."

Anthony and Danielle welcomed the three kids to the Vice-President's Residence for the Fourth of July celebration. Ashley and her husband, Dr. Matthew Adams, brought with them the joyous news that they were expecting their first child in late February. Michael was preparing for the Indiana Bar Exam and then hoped to apply to the FBI or Secret Service. Anna brought two of her sorority friends with her and they planned to check out the night life in Georgetown. For an early evening dinner, Anthony fired up the grill and threw on burgers and hot dogs. Between keeping an eye on the meat, he joined in a spirited game of volleyball out on the lawn.

Before his second serve, he noticed Agent Craig and two other agents heading toward him. They were not looking to join in on the fun.

"Mr. Vice President," Agent Craig interrupted with a finger on his earpiece, "we need to get you to the White House."

"What's up?"

"We just need to get you there right now."

The agents didn't ask Anthony to follow them. Each had a hand on his waistband and another under his arm and practically carried him to the driveway. Danielle's two female agents did the same with her but took her inside the residence. The rest of the Schumachers were asked to quickly get inside. The burgers and dogs were left burning on the grill.

The agents hustled Anthony into his limousine and the motorcade put on its own brand of a fireworks show for the tourists watching it blow by them on Massachusetts Avenue. Anthony picked up the phone in the rear seat and was greeted quickly by Homeland Security Director Starkey, who reported two small planes had been reported stolen in Upstate New York near where Oman was last seen. Nobody knew where the planes were or who was flying them.

The nearing darkness of dusk accentuated the red and blue lights flashing on the roof, dash, and grill on every vehicle in the motorcade. Tourists around the White House clamored to see who was being driven in. Cameras flashes lit up the northwest gate. The Vice President did not give his normal wave.

"I'll be right in."

Agent Craig stayed in his usual seat to the driver's right and looked in his side mirror. He put his finger to his earpiece again. He then turned around to look out the back window.

"What's going on, Mike?" Anthony asked.

"Mr. Vice President, we're just waiting for the perimeter to be secured."

Anthony turned around in his seat. The tourists were being herded farther to the east. Anthony noticed the north grounds were crawling with Secret Service studs. Agents from the Emergency Response Team with automatic weapons stood at the ready begging for some asses to kick. A pair of Belgian Malinois prowled the grounds with their handlers hoping to gnaw off some terrorist's leg if one decided to make the unfortunate leap over the White House fence. The counter assault team that accompanied the Vice President exited their vehicle and had their automatic weapons locked and loaded. Two Secret Service counter snipers were manning the roof.

"Mike, I'm not running into the White House. And you're not carrying me in either." The last thing Anthony wanted was to have a camera shot of the Vice President running for cover into the White House.

"Yes, sir."

Once Agent Craig received the word that the perimeter was secure, he opened Anthony's door and a continuous feed TV camera on top of the U.S. Chamber of Commerce building just north of Lafayette Square offered a glimpse of them walking confidently toward the White House entrance.

Anthony headed into the Situation Room in his shorts and T-shirt to find Director Starkey and Director Bolton, both in suit and ties. They never had any down time.

How about those fireworks? Don't you just love patriotic music? There would be no such talk of the joyous Fourth festivities tonight.

"Mr. Vice President," Director Starkey started before Anthony sat down. Director Bolton was on the phone. The National Security Advisor, Jared Sherman, was on another phone and looking worried. "We believe we have found the two planes over eastern Pennsylvania. But they are not responding to air traffic controllers."

Director Bolton hung up his phone. "Mr. Vice President, I just received word that a large amount of ammonium nitrate has been reported stolen from an agricultural depot south of Buffalo and a university bio-chemical lab is missing two vials of anthrax."

"Stolen planes, stolen bomb making material, stolen chemical agents," the Vice President chimed in. "Coincidence?"

"I'm not willing to bet on it."

Anthony took it all in. Two planes were heading in his direction and possibility carrying explosives and biological weapons. And less than two blocks away sat tens of thousands of tourists up and down the National Mall looking at the fireworks exploding overhead. Decisions were going to have to be made.

And quick.

Anthony looked at the two Directors and the NSA and raised his eyebrows wondering if he was the only one who recognized that someone was missing from the room.

"Where's the President?"

Directors Bolton and Starkey looked at each other. NSA Sherman didn't make eye contact with Anthony.

"Where's the President?" Anthony asked once again. Since he was the highest ranking official in the room, he expected an answer.

"We don't know," Bolton admitted.

"What do you mean you don't know where the President is?"

Anthony looked at Agent Craig, who once again had a finger on his earpiece listening to someone tell him something.

"Mike, where is he?"

Agent Craig said nothing, one finger on his ear and the other asking Anthony to give him a moment.

"Mike, you make me carry this locator device wherever I go," Anthony said, as he pulled the oversized Lincoln penny out of the pocket in his jean shorts. "The President has one so the Joint Operations Center can know where he is at all times. Where is he?"

Agent Craig took his finger off his ear after hearing the last transmission. "We think he's on a boat in the Atlantic Ocean just off the Virginia shore."

"Well, get him in here or get him on the phone."

"Mr. Vice President, we have no agents on board."

Anthony cursed under his breath. "Where's the First Lady?"

"New York."

Anthony shook his head again. "Is he screwing around!?"

Agent Craig didn't respond before Anthony slammed the table with his fist. He didn't need to be told. He ordered Agent Craig to tell the President's security detail to get his sorry ass off the boat and to a phone.

"Do it. Now!"

Agent Craig left the room and yelled into his cuff. Anthony then turned to NSA Sherman and told him to get the Secretary of Defense on the phone. The Chairman of the Joint Chiefs was on his way in. Director Starkey was told to stay on the line with air traffic controllers and the North American Aerospace Defense Command. Anthony told him to ground all aircraft not in the air. Director Bolton asked if they should order the evacuation of the National Mall. Anthony asked where the people would go – to the surrounding streets, the subway, the Capitol steps? He didn't want to send the people into a panic.

"Mr. Vice President, NORAD is tracking the planes thirty minutes north of D.C.," Director Starkey blurted out.

Colonel Dusty Webster of the White House Military Office hustled in to the Situation Room and immediately set out to contact, Russell P. Javits, the Secretary of Defense. After two orders and in less than thirty seconds, he had the main man on the line. Anthony grabbed the phone and hurriedly ran the situation through with Secretary Javits, who was in London at a global defense conference. It was 3 a.m. in England, and the Secretary was slightly groggy. They were both patched in to the Pentagon where the Vice President and Defense Secretary gave the orders to scramble fighter jets from Andrews for possible intercept. The phone line then went dead. Anthony told Colonel Webster to get him back on line.

When the doors to the Situation Room opened, the lights in the room seemed to dim once General Huey L. Cummins, the Chairman of the Joint Chiefs of Staff, strutted in. His giant green dress uniform draped over his six-foot-eight-inch frame could act as a two-man tent in emergency situations. The Mississippian had more stars and medals on his shoulders and chest than any veteran alive. And with his slow Southern drawl and good manners, he could verbally disarm even the most anti-war of Democrats. He knew every inch of every branch of the armed forces, along with every weapons system, aircraft, warship, and troop carrier. He lived for these moments.

Anthony stood to extend a hand. Everyone else stood too. Although the civilians were not required to give the Chairman such deference, most people hopped to their feet when the decorated General Cummins marched in.

"Good evening, Gentlemen," he said calmly, like he was arriving to enjoy a round of poker with his buddies. He didn't take a seat. He just stood next to Anthony ready to do battle.

Anthony filled Chairman Cummins in on the situation. He nodded, and Anthony could tell the wheels were spinning in the four-star general's mind.

Agent Craig returned with no news. Anthony told him to make sure his family was safe. Craig told him they were already in the bunker. He then asked the Marine guarding the door to go to his office and get the suit, tie, and shoes out of his closet and bring them to him. A part of him thought business attire would help him focus more than a worn out Cardinals T-shirt.

Director Starkey, a phone in both ears, spoke up. "Mr. Vice President, we have two Navy F-18 Hornets tracking the two planes. The pilots have not acknowledged."

The Vice President looked over to the man cleaning his glasses. "General, what type of armament do we have available?"

Without a thought, General Cummins rattled off that the F-18s each had a M61 Vulcan 20-millimeter Gatling gun and four air-to-air AIM-9 Sidewinder missiles. If push came to shove, he recommended a single Sidewinder from each aircraft.

The Hornets approached close enough where the pilots of the Cessna 210 Centurions would be able to see them even if they refused to listen to them. Both F-18 pilots lit their cockpits and repeatedly pointed their index finger down – as in, if you don't respond or change course immediately you will be going down. Quickly and involuntarily.

"Put the map back up there," Anthony said. The screen showed four blips indicating the stolen planes and two Hornets were just west of Baltimore and heading straight south. The F-18 pilots reported each plane carried at least two individuals in their cockpits. They still did not acknowledge and their movements became erratic when the F-18s surged ahead and disrupted their airflow. The airmen had flown thousands of combat air patrols and intercepted dozens of rookie pilots who had flown their little Cessnas into restricted airspace. Once told to move out of the area, the novice pilots usually wet their pants and searched for the quickest place they could touch down and apologize for their idiotic mistake. That wasn't happening here.

"Whoever's in charge down there," one airmen calmly stated, "what are our rules of engagement?"

They would need to know quickly. Anthony finished putting on his tie and suit coat and started pacing the floor. Colonel Webster still could not get a connection with Secretary Javits in London. Agent Craig had heard nothing about the whereabouts of the President. The blips on the screen were twenty miles from D.C.

General Cummins looked at the screen. "Mr. Vice President, the ol' Sidewinders will do the trick."

"Mr. Vice President," Director Starkey said quietly. "It's your call."

In the absence of the President, the Vice President and the Secretary of Defense are authorized to make the decision to use military force to protect the country. If Anthony made a mistake, he would be ridiculed for overreacting. No President had ever given the authorization for military action that resulted in the actual shoot down of aircraft over American soil. If he was right, a handful of terrorists would soon meet their demise and thousands of American citizens would be saved. If he was wrong, a couple of idiot joyriders would be dead and the media and liberals would mock the clueless and trigger-happy cowpoke from Indiana.

"Mr. Vice President?"

Anthony looked at Director Bolton and Director Starkey standing next to each other at the end of the table. Colonel Webster was ready to give the order over the phone.

"Take 'em down."

Webster told the pilots they were clear to engage the targets. The hair on the back of Anthony's neck was standing straight up. He had just authorized the United States military to attack civilian aircraft in U.S. airspace on the Fourth of July. He should've been having dessert right now, maybe enjoying the fireworks.

It was all over less than thirty seconds later.

Citizens enjoying the summer evening quickly called 9-1-1 to report seeing two streaks of light in the sky followed by two explosions and then two more loud thuds shortly thereafter. The remains of the stolen planes were found in a smoldering heap ten miles north of Washington in a remote wooded area. Most of the tourists on the Mall who had just finished watching the grand fireworks finale had no idea what happened. Anthony ordered the Pentagon to remain on high alert and the FBI and Homeland Security Department would coordinate various agencies to monitor the transit system so everyone would get home safely. Investigators were on their way to the crash site. NORAD indicated there were no other known threats at that time.

Anthony sat down in a heap as did Directors Bolton and Starkey, both of whom loosened their ties. They were all exhausted. General Cummins excused himself so he could start work on a statement praising his fine military. From a secure phone, Anthony called Danielle, who asked if he had been watching the news about that plane crash north of D.C. Yes, he told her, he was aware of it. She said the Secret Service let them out of the bunker and asked what they should do. He told her to try and get some sleep and not to wait up for him.

He was in charge at the White House.

CHAPTER 19

The President arrived under the cover of darkness with a night landing of Marine One on the South Lawn. No television cameras caught him and the CIA Director scurrying into the South Portico of the White House. Director Franklin tried desperately to straighten out the wrinkles in her pants suit while she walked briskly with the President to the Situation Room. There, they found the Vice President, Director Starkey, and NSA Sherman stewing in near silence.

"Nice of you two to finally join us," Vice President Schumacher said with as much sarcasm as he could muster. He was tired and pissed.

The President didn't like Anthony's tone but let it slide considering the truth of the matter was he had been off banging the CIA Director when terrorists attempted another attack on American soil. They had worked on their stories on the flight back to Washington. The President would claim he was in constant contact with the White House and was making the tough decisions Americans elected him to make. He would also bite his tongue and praise the Vice President's handling of the situation. Per his direct orders over the phone, of course. The President said he would hold a news conference at nine and he hoped they would stand behind him to celebrate the great work of our military and law enforcement personnel in protecting America.

Anthony said he'd think about it and would get back to him. He then walked out of the room and headed back to the residence to get some sleep.

The morning airways breathed a sigh of relief that disaster had been averted. Besides the crash scene, the one still photo flashing across TV screens, Internet sites, and front pages around the world was one, courtesy of the White House photographer who always seemed to be on duty, of Vice President Schumacher in the Situation Room, clad in suit and tie, in command and pointing his index finger at some unseen individual and making some unknown decision in the heat of the moment. The President looked at it with jealousy. Wiley loved it so much he bought ten copies of the *Post* and the *Times* for the Schumacher scrapbook and with the thought he might be able to use the pictures some day in a presidential campaign. All the stories on the Vice President were positive and commentators praised his poise in implementing the President's orders. There were no whispers about why the President was out of Washington and his sudden affinity for high-level meetings on his private yacht.

Not yet anyway.

The investigators cordoned off a large section of forest land where the planes plunged into the ground in a ball of fire. The FBI was in charge and had twenty agents combing every inch of ground for any remaining pieces of the two planes. Five members of the National Transportation Safety Board were ready to provide assistance. Once the search began, two men in dark glasses from the CIA showed up and said they were there to supervise. The FBI agents on the ground called Director Bolton, who told them to keep an eye on the CIA and away from the crash site.

The FBI trucked the debris to an old airport hangar and shipped off collected residue to its forensics lab at Quantico. The initial reports indicated each plane contained seven hundred pounds of ammonium nitrate and fuel oil. A small amount of C-4 was also found. No anthrax was detected, and university officials announced shortly after the incident that the two missing vials were found in a locked closet after renovations of a chemistry lab had been completed. Still, the materials on board the aircraft could have killed thousands of citizens.

The four charred bodies were identified after fingerprint and dental analysis. Three of the men were Saudi nationals in the U.S. on expired visas. Ahmed Hazemi had worked part time as a computer specialist in Buffalo and attended a mosque known for its radical anti-American teachings. His brother, Khalid Hazemi, attended the same mosque and spent his time hiding out in the shadows of the U.S.-Canadian border. Abdel al-Fayemi had been a student at a Buffalo university where he studied to be a chemist. His roommate said he kept to himself and was often gone during the evenings. The fourth terrorist was an American-born Muslim from New York City named Moamar Salaam. He had served time in federal prison, where he underwent a radical conversion to blame America for all the world's ills. All four of the terrorists were known followers of Oman and had pledged to fight America to the death.

For days after the incident, the President convened his National Security Council on a daily basis and made sure the White House photographer was there to capture the moment for the press. He barked out orders and demanded results. When underlings reminded him that he had instructed them in the exact opposite fashion just a week earlier, he yelled at them and told them the safety and security of the American people were his main concern. Well-choreographed leaks showcased the President behind the scenes as in control and taking the fight to the terrorists. America need not worry with President

Fisher at the helm, the anonymous White House aides reassured.

The President then sent the Vice President and the appropriate security leaders to the networks to calm America's fears and reassure them that they were safe, and all in all make him look good. Anthony had no problem with the first part, the latter not so much.

On a cloudless late July afternoon, Vice President Schumacher walked the grounds of the U.S. Naval Observatory with Allison Bartow, one of the big three network news anchors sent to get the Vice President's views on and recollections of the attempted attack on America. Anthony did not mince words when it came to the threat al-Qaeda posed to the country and the need for Americans to be vigilant in their daily travels. Point out suspicious people and packages to law enforcement. Report incidences of stolen materials that could be used in making bombs such as fertilizer and dynamite. Sounds of gunshots in the woods might not just be hunters but terrorists practicing their attack. Help us protect America, Anthony implored.

Bartow stopped the two on their walk and looked up at the blue sky. She noted the planes had crashed not more than twenty miles from there. They may have only needed ten more minutes to reach the thousands of citizens watching the fireworks.

"Mr. Vice President, were you ever scared that night?"

"I really wasn't."

"Not even about your own family?"

"No. My family is protected by the finest bodyguards in the world. I knew I could focus on the situation with the full knowledge my family would be safe."

"What about the people on the Mall?"

"It was not a matter of being scared. You have to realize I was in the room with highly competent individuals who have practiced similar scenarios within their various spheres of influence. Joint Chiefs Chairman Cummins offered a cool and experienced head in the situation. Director Bolton and NSA Sherman gave me the facts I needed to make an informed decision."

Bartow wanted to dig deeper, to get a feel for what it was like in the Situation Room. Most Americans would never set foot near the place and definitely would not be faced with the decision of whether to shoot down aircraft loaded with weapons of mass destruction. What was the mood like? Did the men argue about possible actions to take? What would you have done differently?

"What did the President say to you before you ordered the military to shoot down the planes?"

Anthony did not hesitate. "I did not talk to the President before the F-18s engaged their targets."

Bartow looked confused, like she hadn't heard correctly or maybe she thought the Vice President misspoke.

"You didn't talk to him on his yacht?"

Anthony was not going to lie to make the President look good. And he would not be a part of any type of coverup. He would not offer anything more than necessary. The situation had been handled, and he hoped it would never happen again.

"I did not talk to him on his yacht. We were in contact with the Defense Secretary in London before the phone line was cut off. As time was of the essence, I had to make the decision in consultation with the Joint Chiefs, the FBI Director, the White House Military Office, and NSA Sherman."

Bartow looked at her notes. She thought the news reports indicated the President had given the order over the phone. Maybe she was mistaken. With the interview about to come to an end, she let the matter drop.

The President, however, would not forget it. When he watched the interview on his office TV, he threw a paperweight against the wall in disgust. He viewed it as an act of insubordination, and one that could seriously endanger his credibility if reporters started to dig deeper to uncover why the President and Vice President were not in contact when military action was ordered. He paced the room, always wondering what the latest news would do to his favorability ratings or chances for reelection.

Director Franklin, who was with the President watching the interview, tried to soothe his feelings.

"Everything he said was true," she pointed out.

"Why does that not make me feel better?"

"All you have to say is that you were talking with your national security advisor that evening." The latter part had an air of truth to it, something lawyers and politicians searched high and low to grasp on to if it would help their side of the story. The President did in fact talk to NSA Sherman on that evening – it just happened to be after the incident was over and the President was flying back to the White House on Marine One. But no need to worry, Sherman was too much of a team player to say the President was incommunicado when it really counted.

"What if that damn Boy Scout pops off again and says I was nowhere to be found?"

Director Franklin pulled him down to the couch and rubbed his thigh. "If necessary, we'll just paint him as a loose cannon, a power-hungry rogue who will say anything to get ahead. You were in control. Everything worked out. That's what you'll tell the American people. They'll believe you."

She always knew how to push his buttons and calm his nerves. The President rubbed her inner thigh to make himself feel better.

"You know, you'd make a damn fine First Lady someday."

The heat and humidity of August in D.C. caused most city dwellers to head for cooler climes during the summer recess. The President decided against a vacation this year, telling the American people he wanted to be on duty twenty-four hours a day at the White House. No need to worry, his staff would tell the press repeatedly. Even though the First Philanderer almost blew it on the Fourth of July.

Anthony and Danielle and their security entourage were ready for a break and headed back to Silver Creek. The Secret Service parked an RV at the end of the lane to the Schumacher house and watched half the town drive by, stop, point to the trees, and snap a picture. The gawkers would someday be able to tell their relatives that the Vice President lived somewhere behind that forest of leaves. The corn fields provided little buffer so the Secret Service had to install sensors all along the eastern edge of the property. One nutcase did try to find his way through the corn saying he had a present for Ashley. She wasn't there. He wasn't all there either. Agents arrested him and carted him off to a mental hospital.

While still hot and humid in western Indiana, the release of tension felt like a welcomed cold snap. The Schumachers spent their days beside her mother's pool holding hands and relaxing. Anthony would have a secure conference every morning at eight, wherein he would learn the latest terror alerts from the CIA. In the afternoons, he and Danielle would head to the Donut Palace or the Dairy Barn to enjoy an iced cookie or ice cream cone. Under the watchful eyes of Agent Craig and his team, Anthony would sit for over an hour signing autographs and posing for pictures with his hometown admirers. The evenings would be spent taking a walk by the Wabash listening to the chirping crickets and the corn popping in the fields. Then they would retire for the evening with a nice movie.

Sundays started off with church at St. John's Lutheran Church, the Schumachers' home congregation. There they begged off Pastor Stewart's request that the VIPs sit in the front row and instead headed for the fourth one, the row they always sat in. The Secret Service took up the rows in front and back. Afterwards, the Schumachers would head to the local hospital and visit the children's ward. The kids never seemed to be very impressed with that guy who just happened to have the title of Vice President of the United States, but the boys' eyes lit up when Anthony introduced his Secret Service agents (who overplayed the part well for the youngsters with their sunglasses, hidden radios, and serious manner on full display). The girls liked to talk with Danielle and several told her that their brother or sister had been a former student of hers.

Although Anthony tried to swear off the news and talk radio to clear his head of the everyday political bombardment, it was hard not to get pulled back into the fray.

Wiley wasn't much help.

He'd arrive at the house at six thirty every morning and fire up the coffee. He always brought with him every briefing book he'd ever read, highlighted and flagged with important notes for improvements here, changes there. He wanted to start dismantling some of the federal bureaucracy ASAP. Do we really need the Department of Education he would often ask? Shouldn't the states take care of education at the local level? What does the Commerce Department do that the Treasury Department can't? The Commerce Department has a budget of five billion dollars a year, wouldn't it be better for American commerce to give a few billion back to the American taxpayer?

But today, Wiley wasn't thinking about bloated budgets or big-government waste. He wanted to talk about winning the White House. That picture of Anthony in charge in the Situation Room appeared constantly in his head. He had a potential candidate who could lead in times of trouble. He had run the numbers. With a couple of breaks, Anthony could eek out a majority of delegates to wrestle away the nomination from the President. This is doable, Wiley thought over and over again.

Anthony had filled Wiley in on what transpired during the terror crisis and swore him to secrecy regarding the President's sexual peccadilloes. No leaks, Anthony demanded, not wanting to play politics with matters of national security. But Wiley always had it in the back of his mind that the President was in it for himself and unfit to be Commander-in-Chief.

"Mr. Vice President, I want to send out some feelers on the possibility of a presidential run, test the waters a bit."

Anthony put down the sports pages on the kitchen table. The box scores could wait. Wiley had poured himself a third cup of coffee. Anthony got up to get a Diet Coke out of the fridge.

"Wiley, I've only been Vice President for ten months."

"He doesn't deserve to be President."

"I don't think I deserve to be President either."

Wiley wasn't taking no for an answer. He was a reformed skirt chaser and knew the President's highly classified sexual excursions would not stop because the First Lady or Anthony lectured him about putting the American people first before his sexual desires. It could be a dangerous gamble in terms of national security.

"The election is just a year away. I'm not sure we'd have the time to set up a winning campaign."

"No, I think it can be done. I've been working on the governors in key battle ground states. They're upset with the high tax and climate change mantra the President's been spewing. They think it's going to be a job killer. We'll set up camp in Iowa and New Hampshire and talk to every voter that will listen. They'll love you."

Anthony paced around the kitchen, pausing out the window to look at the sun brightening the leaves on the oak trees. "Have you ever thought how difficult it would be for a sitting Vice President to take on a sitting President? I don't think it would work."

"You can do it because you're the best." Wiley was always good with the butt-kissing.

Anthony sat down again at the table. Wiley had that mischievous twinkle in his eye. He wanted to fight.

"I'll think about it."

The start of autumn brought in much needed relief to the swampy heat of the nation's capital, but the cool breezes didn't lower the tension inside the White House. The President decided he needed to put the Vice President to work so he sent him to Afghanistan to visit the troops and get him as far away as he could from Washington. Anthony took the assignment in stride and enjoyed his time with the troops. During his visits to various bases, he asked the soldiers on the ground to give him their unvarnished opinion on the war and what they needed to win it. They expressed their concerns about the lengths of their tours and the need for additional troops to hold the gains they had already made. Anthony praised them for their service and told them he would take their concerns to the President.

Anthony's meeting with the commanders was more frank and more dire. They complained the President had been dragging his feet on their request for more troops and it was putting a worrisome strain on the current mission.

"He told me last week he spoke to you in late August and you said everything was in good shape," Anthony said.

General Roe's back stiffened and his jaw clenched. He didn't like talking behind the President's back. But the truth had to be told. "Sir, I have not talked to the President since late June."

"Are we beyond the point of no return?"

General Roe looked directly at Anthony. "We're on the brink, Sir."

"Shadow is in the Crown."

Anthony returned from Afghanistan with a checklist of troop needs and requests from commanders on the ground. This should have been taken care of months ago. He wasn't in a good mood. The jet lag didn't help.

At 9 a.m., he arrived in the Situation Room armed with his briefing books for the daily national security briefing and an update on the terror threat within America. NSA Sherman, Director Starkey, Director Bolton, and a White House military aide were twiddling their thumbs waiting on the President. The Secretary of State was working on the *Times* crossword puzzle. Defense Secretary Javits was also present, and he wanted to personally congratulate the

Vice President on his superb conduct on the Fourth of July. Anthony thanked him and started going over his concerns after his trip to Afghanistan. At 9:20, Anthony could be heard tapping his fingers on the desk. His right foot was keeping pace underneath.

"Excuse me for a second."

Anthony stuck his head out into the hall and motioned for Agent Craig.

"Where's the President?"

Agent Craig spoke into his cuff. Ten seconds later came the response. "He's in his office off the Oval."

Anthony didn't waste any time heading in that direction.

"Shadow is on the move." Agent Craig had to step it up a notch to keep up the pace with him.

Anthony blew into the office of the President's secretary and headed straight for the Oval Office.

"Mr. Vice President," the trusty old secretary said, "the President is in a meeting with the CIA Director." She intimated he could not go into the Oval Office but she was in no position to stop him.

"It's okay," Anthony responded as politely as he could, "they're supposed to be in a meeting with us in the Situation Room anyway. I'm just going to stick my head in there and remind him."

The Oval Office was empty and quiet. The morning sunshine brightened the gold carpeting and white walls. Across the way, Anthony could see the door to the President's private study was slightly ajar so he waltzed right in.

Once inside, he found the President of the United States sitting on the couch with his trousers down at his ankles and the Director of the CIA mounted on top with her skirt hiked up over her waist going at it like sex-deprived prisoners in a conjugal visit. The citizenry would no doubt be amused to learn the CIA Director oftentimes wore no panties – a fact obviously overlooked during her Senate confirmation hearings but one that saved time when a quickie was in order and also amounted to one less piece of evidence to be picked up if a speedy getaway was needed.

The CIA Director's back was to the door, and the President had his eyes closed. Both apparently found what they were doing very agreeable, and it didn't have anything to do with national security.

"Oh yes, Jillian, yes," he whispered.

"Oh, Mr. President." As a first-rate spy, she had learned to stealthily suppress her moaning so it could not be detected outside the room.

Anthony let out a silent breath. If the American people only knew. He might as well get it over with.

"Is this where the national security briefing is being held?"

Director Franklin shrieked in horror. The President, in his fright, threw her off him and onto the couch. They both frantically attempted to cover up.

"Get the hell out of here, Schumacher!" the red-faced President yelled as he stood and hiked up his drawers. "Get the fuck out of here!"

Anthony spun around and walked back through the Oval Office. The look on his face indicated people had best get out of his way. The President's secretary was about to take cover under her desk.

The President was furious that he had been caught. That damn Schumacher, he kept thinking. Director Franklin was shaking in fear. They had been so careful. The private yacht in the middle of the Atlantic. Late night meetings when the First Lady was out of town. But they thought they were invincible. That they would never get caught. Especially in the President's own private study. Did he forget to lock the door?

The President called in his lead Secret Service agent and cursed him out for letting the Vice President in the Oval Office.

"Get the hell out of here, you worthless piece of shit!" he yelled at him as he slammed the door in the agent's face.

"What are we going to do?" Director Franklin whispered, straightening her skirt and repositioning her bra.

The President seethed, his heart racing and his chest heaving.

"That son of a bitch is off my ticket," he whispered back. "He will not be my Vice President after next year."

CHAPTER 20

The command post protectee log kept by the Secret Service indicated Vice President Schumacher departed from the Anacostia Naval Station at 1:31 p.m. It was the Sunday following Thanksgiving, and the President wanted to convene a meeting of his National Security Council at Camp David. With the Christmas and Hanukkah holidays approaching, the President wanted to be seen in charge so all Americans could go their merry way celebrating the season and jolting the sagging economy back to life with lots of shopping.

Camp David, the President's rustic retreat, sits tucked away high in the Catoctin Mountains and was once called Shangri-La by Franklin Roosevelt before President Eisenhower renamed it after his grandson. Its surroundings give the President a chance to walk outdoors and breathe fresh air without having to worry about tourists and gawkers lining the fences at the executive prison known as the White House. The constant wail of police sirens in D.C. was replaced by hooting owls and tranquil songbirds. Among its amenities include a pool, a movie theater, and a bowling alley. Plus, it is equipped with a helipad for quick aerial getaways for the President and his visitors.

Anthony and FBI Director Bolton shared a ride on Marine Two and discussed national security as the D.C. suburbs passed peacefully beneath them. Secretary Javits, Secretary Starkey, NSA Sherman, and Joints Chiefs Chairman Cummins were all on their way.

Needless to say, the CIA Director was already on site prepared to give the President hands-on briefings (or maybe it was hands-on debriefings). They had spent the past two nights together sipping wine and making love by the fire. They talked in whispers and smiled at the thought of their future together. They discussed different scenarios – secret ones that would allow them to quickly become the world's greatest power couple, a more modern and loved version of Bill and Hillary. During the day they would refine their plans and consider every angle. Just a few hurdles needed to be cleared before they could seal the deal.

One of those hurdles was the First Lady. She had showed up for the meaningless family gathering on Thursday and the White House photographer snapped the obligatory shots of the family with their fake smiles enjoying a perfectly prepared bird, hot stuffing, and pumpkin pie. Americans would no doubt be overjoyed at seeing the First Couple together for the holiday. Once the dinner was over, however, the First Lady hightailed it back to Washington to get away from her husband, while Director Franklin swooped in to take her place. A divorce was a possibility, but the President worried about his family fortune and his conservative supporters. He and Franklin would figure out how to make it work.

Anthony and the President had avoided each other the past couple of weeks except when national security matters required a high-level get-together. During Cabinet meetings in the White House, the Vice President always sits to the President's left, but gimlet-eyed reporters noticed the gap between the two seemed to be wider than usual. They rarely talked to each other and their Thursday lunches were no longer on the menu. Neither one of them missed the company of the other. The President thought Anthony was a Bible-thumping Boy Scout, and Anthony thought the President was a horny egomaniac with liberal proclivities. The Vice President went to Camp David just to do his job and then get back home.

The National Security Council met in the conference room of Laurel Lodge, a quaint wood-paneled room with a table large enough to entertain a whole host of government leaders in discussing the issues of the day. To the President's delight, CIA Director Franklin came dressed like a college coed – tennis shoes, tight blue jeans, and a Syracuse University sweatshirt, her alma mater. The latter was an early Christmas gift to her from the President. Her long dark hair was pulled tightly in a pony tail. Given the rustic nature of the place and with no chance of paparazzi catching a glimpse of his appearance, the President went with the disheveled frat boy look with matching gray sweat pants and sweatshirt. When the White House photographer showed up with camera in hand, the President quickly pulled on his navy blue windbreaker with the presidential seal for a more dignified look.

Once all the Council members were seated, the President turned the show over to Director Franklin. She was the only female in the room.

"Thank you, Mr. President. Gentlemen, what I am about to show you is highly classified. I would please ask you to not even write any of this information down."

She lowered the lights and clicked on the TV screen an image of a bearded Middle Eastern looking man, the typical picture shown on TV when reporters want to put a face on terrorism – either one who had done the dastardly deed or one who was inciting others to do it for him or in the name of Allah.

"This is Abdi Abdullah. He is probably our most important operative we have working for the Central Intelligence Agency. He's an American-born Muslim who majored in Islamic studies at New York University. He speaks fluent Arabic, Farsi, Urdu, and is conversant in Hindi as well as several minor local dialects of the Middle East. He has infiltrated an al-Qaeda network in eastern Afghanistan and western Pakistan and has been providing us with an enormous amount of intel over the last six months. To put it in sports terms, this man is our MVP."

She clicked off the image and on went the lights. She would now get down to the nuts and bolts of what she knew.

"Mr. Abdullah has been a part of a group of ten high-level Taliban and al-Qaeda leaders within Afghanistan who have connections to sleeper cells here in the United States. Under the direction of Mustafa Oman, we believe these cells were responsible for coordinating the attacks on the Fourth of July. Through various operatives and intelligence sources, we have picked up chatter concerning a possible terrorist attack around the Christmas holidays. Intercepted telephone conversations have mentioned operatives in the U.S. will soon be buying "presents " that can be unwrapped on Christmas Eve. Mr. Abdullah overheard one known terrorist seeking to buy a "candlestick " for his mother. We believe "candlestick " is a code word for shoulder-fire missile. There has also been mention of looking for "Santa's sleigh," and we believe that could be a generic term for passenger aircraft."

She folded her hands, exposing her red-painted fingernails, and waited for questions.

Director Bolton was still waiting for her assessment. It was a nice story, but he wanted more definitive intel. "So, what's your best guess?" he smirked.

"A possible terrorist attack on U.S. airlines using surface-to-air missiles during the Christmas holidays," she snapped. Did she really need to spell it out for him? Maybe she should have talked slower.

"I have heard none of this so-called chatter," Bolton shot back.

"The information has just arrived from the front lines. I wouldn't expect the FBI to know anything about it."

"What type of missiles?"

"Old U.S.-style shoulder-fire missiles used by Afghan freedom fighters against the Soviets."

"I have heard nothing about any smuggling of these types of weapons in the U.S. Trust me, if they were being moved by terrorists into this country, my people would have heard something."

"Well, maybe your boys let some slip through."

"Doubtful." Bolton rolled his eyes. He hated it when she called his agents "boys."

The President stepped in to keep the meeting civil. "Okay, what do we do about it?"

Anthony jumped in. "Why don't we raise the terror threat level and increase armed patrols at transportation hubs – airports, train stations, and border crossings."

Director Bolton had the Vice President's back. "I agree. I think we should also step up our covert surveillance, wire tap the phones of known Oman supporters here in the U.S. to get some concrete intelligence on any possible plots."

"Wo, wo, hold on there cowboys," the President said, his hands raised "There's that little thing called the Constitution I have to worry about. Did you two forget you have to follow it too?"

The tensions was beginning to rise.

"Mr. President," Anthony shot back, "I know damn well I swore to uphold the Constitution. I also know we're facing a terrorist enemy who is seeking to kill thousands of our fellow citizens. And if Director Franklin is correct, we need to act now."

"Mr. Vice President," the President said, his voice raising. "I don't need a lecture from you. We are going to follow the letter of the law."

"Mr. President, the law allows us to get the sneak and peak search warrants! It allows us to listen in on telephone conversations that originate from outside of the country!"

"Don't you raise your voice at me, Schumacher!"

Luckily, the President and Vice President were not sitting beside each other but across the table. The other Council members were becoming uncomfortable at the shouting. Anthony stood and pounded his fist on the table. Did the President forget his little screw up over the Fourth? "You're willing to take a chance on the lives of American citizens because you don't want to offend your campaign contributors."

"Listen here, Schumacher! I'm in charge here! We're gonna do things my way!"

Bolton couldn't resist getting in on the fight. "Even if it handcuffs us in doing our job. We'll be blind and deaf trying to catch these terrorists."

The President had enough. Schumacher would still be a no-name Congressman if it wasn't for him, he fumed inwardly. With spit flying from his mouth, he managed to give his last order of the meeting. "Both of you get the hell out of here! I never want to see you pieces of shit here again!"

Anthony sat with his mouth open in amazement looking across the table. Is this the way it was going to be?

"You heard me, get the hell out of here!"

The Vice President and FBI Director packed their briefcases and stormed out the door. The rest of the Council sunk silently in their seats not knowing whether the meeting was over or not. No one was going to take the risk of speaking up. Even General Cummins wanted out of the room but felt he couldn't walk out in front of his Commander-in-Chief.

Anthony and Director Bolton mumbled to themselves as they headed out of the lodge to the Marine Two helipad. Anthony was glad to get out of there and breathe in some fresh air. He kicked at a rock and spat on the ground. The two Marines flying the helicopter and four Secret Service agents said nothing as the two pissed off men stomped on board.

"Let's go," Anthony snapped.

Once the door was closed and the rotors sprang to life, Agent Craig indicated their departure time was 3:50 p.m. They had been there less than two hours, but the relationship between the President and the Vice President had deteriorated to such a low level that continuing on together would be nearly impossible. Anthony was fed up with him.

Director Bolton couldn't keep from talking. He needed to vent. "That prick is going to get people killed one of these days."

Anthony slammed his fist into his palm. "I don't know why he doesn't get it. His damn girlfriend's in there telling us that an attack appears to be imminent and he won't do anything. It's almost like she was making the whole thing up."

"Well, what are we going to do about it?"

Anthony didn't offer a quick response. He looked out the windows at the trees passing beneath him. He took a deep breath and let his head fall back against the headrest. He knew exactly what he had to do. It was time. He picked up the secure phone and made the call.

"Wiley, it's Schu. Yeah, I'm on my way back home. I just wanted to let you know I'm going to run for President of the United States."

A slight pause for a question on the other end.

"Yes, next year."

Director Bolton couldn't help but smile.

"Make it happen, Wiley."

Anthony hung up the phone and took a deep cleansing breath. He had a lot to do between now and next November. The campaign would have to start immediately. Maybe he should wait until after New Year's to make sure and not get drowned out by the holiday season. Yes, better to do it after the good cheer had subsided because he was going to lambast the President at every opportunity. The primaries would be tough fights in early February. It might come down to a late summer convention battle. He had no personal wealth. But he did have his office. And Air Force Two. Plus, he had Wiley, the political genius.

"You're in for one hell of a fight," Director Bolton said.

Anthony just shook his head. He was ready. The loud whistle caused both men to look at each other. Then the bells and alarms of Marine Two startled every one on board. Anthony noticed a streak of smoke fly past the rotors and through the clear blue sky.

"What the hell was that?"

"We're being targeted! We're being targeted!" the Marine pilot yelled.

"Evasive maneuvers! Countermeasures!" yelled his copilot.

Anthony cinched his belt tighter and Director Bolton grabbed the armrests with both hands as the helicopter suddenly went into a dive and then climbed before banking hard to the left and then the right. Anthony looked out his window wondering where the smoke trails were coming from.

Agent Craig turned around in his seat. "Attack on Marine . . . !" he managed to shout into his cuff before the missile blasted a whole in the tail rotor throwing shrapnel through the interior and causing the helicopter to vibrate so violently that the windows started cracking. The debris sheered off one of the main rotors.

"We're hit! We're hit!" yelled the pilot.

Anthony and the Director didn't need to be told. The deafening moan of a damaged motor desperately trying to keep the multi-million dollar machine flying kept getting slower and slower. They could see the blue sky out the rear end of the helicopter. They were now in a dizzying spin out of control.

"We're going down!"

Marine Two was filling with smoke. Anthony could feel his stomach churning with every drop in altitude. He said nothing. He heard people shouting but could not understand what they were saying. He kept seeing Danielle in his eyes. He had been near death before and she would have to go through her own turmoil again. He didn't get a chance to say goodbye to his kids.

"Brace for impact!"

The turbulent shaking jolted the occupants in their seats. If felt like the whole aircraft was going to break apart. The pilots lost control and the helicopter turned on its side before slamming into a lake high in a remote area of the mountain. Director Bolton, three Secret Service agents, and one pilot were killed instantly. They had been on the right side of the helicopter and took the brunt of the hit into the water. The force of the impact blew out the right side windows and the helicopter slowly sank to the bottom with the interior filling with the cold murky water.

Agent Craig and the Vice President sat stunned, their seat belts holding them in. The cold water snapped them out of their daze. The Vice President choked on the water he swallowed.

Agent Craig had been through something similar before. His training at the Secret Service included a crash water landing in a mock helicopter. He had practiced this very scenario two weeks ago, although in the Secret Service dunk tank the water was clear and the end result was assured. The darkness of the deep would soon envelope them.

Agent Craig unbuckled his belts and reached behind his seat for a canister of oxygen, which he attached to his face. A piece of glass had cut his cheek and blood ran down the side. The fully submerged helicopter came to a rest on the lake's bottom and he could partially stand up with his feet on the right side. He grabbed another canister.

"Mr. Vice President, we've got to get this on you!"

Anthony let Agent Craig put the mask on him as he tried to unbuckle his seat belt. He thought he might have broken a rib. His head and neck hurt from the whiplash.

Once Anthony got out of his seat, Agent Craig grabbed him by the lapel. "We've got to get out of here!" he yelled behind the mask.

The water was up to their necks.

"We've got to check on the others!"

Agent Craig nodded in agreement. He went to check on his agents, all of whom were gone. As were the pilots. Anthony checked on his friend. Emergency lighting showed the Director still strapped in his seat. There was nothing they could do. They needed to get out fast.

Agent Craig and Anthony tried to open the emergency hatch without success. Agent Craig grabbed the handrails and tried kicking out the window but to no avail. The pressure of the water on top of the left side of the helicopter was making it impossible to open the door. Agent Craig then grabbed Anthony, pointed to the hole in the rear of the helicopter, and told him he was going to try to squeeze through. He maneuvered his body through the mass of frayed wire and bent steel. He turned around, shined a flashlight back inside, and motioned for Anthony to follow him. Anthony made himself as skinny as possible and worked his way until a jagged edge caught on his belt. He couldn't move and he couldn't see. Agent Craig was on the other end pulling both of Anthony's hands. The oxygen canister was starting to run low, and Anthony was beginning to panic. Agent Craig tugged with all his might but the Vice President was still wedged in. He grunted in his mask. Anthony reached down to his waist to try and bend the piece of steel preventing his escape. He finally unbuckled his belt and whipped it off. With Agent Craig still pulling, Anthony shot out like a torpedo. Agent Craig grabbed him under his arm and they both swam hard to the surface.

"Oh!" Anthony screamed as he emerged from the watery depths. He was out of breath and scared to death. His arms were thrashing in the water. He threw off his oxygen canister and gasped for air. He feared he might be hyperventilating. He coughed out a bit more water.

Agent Craig still had an arm on the Vice President as they realized they were in the middle of the lake. "It's all right. It's all right. We just need to get to the shore," he said breathing hard. "Can you swim?"

"Yeah."

The water weighed down their suits. Anthony had little energy left and dog paddled a few seconds as Agent Craig tried dragging him through the water.

"Mr. Vice President, we need to swim to the shore."

Anthony got the hint, snapped out his dazed state, and was able to make movements with his arms to at least make it without much assistance from Agent Craig. They made it to a muddy shoreline and dragged their ragged bodies to the bank. They fell over onto their backs in exhaustion. Anthony put his hand on his sore ribs and coughed out more water. Both of them smelled like fuel oil.

It didn't take long for Agent Craig to spring into action – the Secret Service was always on guard.

"Mr. Vice President, I need to get you out of here."

"What?" Was he crazy? Why don't they just wait for the search and rescue teams?

"Sir, the people who shot at us cannot be far away. If they wanted to kill you, they're going to want to make sure you're dead. We need to get concealed."

He waded back into the water and fished out a piece of the fuselage and the red-painted end of one of the rotors. He brought them back on shore and buried them under a log. He then spread some dead leaves over them. A small oil slick from the leaking helicopter could be seen in the water, but there was little debris. It would give them a little head start from whoever was looking for them.

"Can you walk?"

Anthony wasn't going to argue with him or plead with him to just wait and hope for the best. They were now being hunted and needed to get moving.

He took a deep breath and nodded his head. "Yeah, let's go."

They bolted into the woods, both of them in their business suits and soaking wet. With the heavy canopy of trees, it would be dark in a couple of hours. After ten minutes of walking, they hid amongst the pines and whispered to each other trying to determine where they were and which direction they should be going. They figured they were ten to fifteen miles south of Camp David. Maybe close to Frederick, Maryland. Agent Craig knew Interstate 70 ran through Frederick to Baltimore. Interstate 270 ran southeast out of Frederick to Washington. The closer they hiked to Frederick, the greater chance they'd find a farm house where they could call for help. Agent Craig said they could not trust anyone they did not know. It was too dangerous to let their guard down. He checked his gun. It appeared functional despite the dip in the lake.

After half an hour of rest, they continued to walk, the terrain varying up and down, through ravines and over downed trees. The Thanksgiving weekend had brought in a cold front and a light drizzle began to fall. They heard no voices but helicopters and other aircraft could be heard beginning their search patterns to their north. They kept walking, stopping, and then listening. A couple of times they took cover near some fallen trees and underbrush, their dark suits and pants providing some camouflage.

With each cautious step, shadows would appear then vanish. They were constantly looking over their shoulders. From a short distance away, leaves could be heard rustling underfoot, sticks cracking in the silence. Flashlights searched the ground on top of the hill they had just descended.

After picking up the pace, they finally made it to a two-lane road running north and south. Anthony's watch read almost six. Emergency vehicles and government cars had no doubt whizzed by here in the last hour to bring search teams. Agent Craig and the Vice President began walking just inside the tree line, not wanting to be seen if some terrorist thought about stopping to ask if they needed his help.

A Chevy engine could be heard pushing its limit up the hill from the north. The speeding black sedan had flashing blue and red lights in the grill and more on the dash. Anthony and Agent Craig were behind two trees when the vehicle screeched to a halt thirty feet from them. Out stepped two men with closely cropped haircuts and off-the-rack suits – definitely government agents of some kind. Or at least that's what they wanted people to think. How did the two men see Anthony and Agent Craig behind the trees?

"Mr. Vice President, is that you?" one yelled, peering into the darkened forest.

Anthony and Agent Craig looked at each other in the growing darkness. Could they trust them? What if they took part in the attack and were looking to silence the survivors?

"Identify yourselves!" Agent Craig yelled out as he pulled out his gun. He chambered one round.

"Agents Kasten and Bartow, FBI," one yelled back. "Are you okay?"

Anthony took a chance and responded in the affirmative. The two obviously knew the Vice President was hiding behind the tree. He looked at Agent Craig, who held his gun up to his face. Anthony nodded, and the two appeared from the relative safety and security of the darkness. They looked terrible – cold, dirty, traumatized. Two hours ago their helicopter had been shot down and six of their comrades had died. They needed a hot shower, a wife's tender hand, and a strong bit of alcohol.

Anthony approached and shook both agents' hands. They didn't look familiar but who knows what field office they were coming from. Agent Craig stood off to the side, looking north and south. He was always on the lookout. That was his job. He watched their hands. It was difficult to see their eyes in the darkness.

"The Director sent us to make sure you're safe and get you back to Washington," said Bartow.

Both Anthony and Agent Craig zeroed in on the man. The Director? When did he send them? The Director's dead body was currently lying in a watery grave a couple miles to the north. Something didn't feel right. Anthony asked about his wife.

"Mrs. Schumacher has been taken care of," said Kasten, his eyes darting around for others in the trees. How many others survivors might be out there?

"What about my kids?"

"All three of them are at secured locations with their Secret Service details," Bartow said, putting a hand on Anthony's elbow to persuade him to get into the car.

"What about Harroun, my dog?"

Bartow stumbled slightly. "Harr . . Harr . . Harroun is just fine," he blurted out. "I saw him and Mrs. Schumacher together in the bunker."

Agent Craig did not hesitate. Harroun had been dead for forty-plus years. The two so-called agents never even saw him raise his gun and put a bullet in each of their brains. They dragged the dead bodies away from the road and dumped them on the right side of the car. Agent Craig frisked them for a flashlight and then reached in to turn off the car's flashing lights. Both could hear another car coming up the road.

"Move! Move!" Agent Craig said, as he pushed Anthony into the forest on the other side of the road. The car, another standard-issue government model, roared by without stopping. They plodded their way through the trees, slipping and falling as they went. Agent Craig stopped them to rest. He wiped the sweat off his forehead. They whispered to each other and wondered how the two men had found them in the near darkness.

The locator device.

Anthony reached into his pocket and pulled out the Lincoln penny, no doubt tracking their every movement. The signal the device emitted could not transmit through the dense forest the two walked through after they crawled out of the lake. Once the canopy of trees began to thin, the device would have allowed anyone tracking them to make a quick discovery. The Secret Service's Joint Operations Center was aware of the signal but considered it a false positive. Anthony and Agent Craig were presumed dead.

They continued on until they reached a rail line and crouched under a trestle. When the passing Burlington Northern train rumbled by, Agent Craig threw the penny into the car loaded with coal. Whoever was monitoring the locator device would soon think the Vice President was on his way to Baltimore at thirty-five miles per hour.

They continued on, until they reached a small river. They waded across and found a four-foot round concrete drainage culvert that funneled a small stream into the river. There was only an inch of water trickling through the bottom. Agent Craig and Anthony threw a dead log into the culvert and crawled in. There, they sat with their feet on one wall, their backs leaning against the other, and their butts out of the water beneath them. Unless a flash flood came roaring through, they would be dry. They leaned back and tried to catch their breath that they had lost three hours ago. They were safe.

For now.

CHAPTER 21

"We have breaking news to report to you," the breathless commentator said. The startling news was rolling in just in time for East Coast workers to get home and plop down in front of the TV. Dinner would be late tonight as citizens sat glued to the myriad of media outlets waiting for answers. The commentator could not believe what she was reading off her computer and hearing in her earpiece. The graphic at the bottom of the screen read "Vice President's Helicopter Down." The guy running the camera had to motion to her to keep going.

"The Associated Press is reporting Vice President Schumacher's helicopter, known by its call sign as Marine Two, has gone down south of Camp David. The Vice President had been attending a meeting of the President's National Security Council and was on his way back to Washington. It is believed J.D. Bolton, the Director of the FBI, was also on board." The screen showed taped footage of the beautiful Marine helicopter flying proudly in the sky over Washington along with still shots of the Vice President and Director Bolton. "At approximately 4 p.m., air traffic controllers lost radar contact with Marine Two. A massive search and rescue operation is now underway."

The frenzied White House correspondents repeated the same information on the North Lawn. The lights illuminating the Executive Mansion behind them took on an eerie feel in the growing fog and gloomy darkness. Some reporters noted the country had been on edge since the Fourth of July attacks and surmised the disappearance of the Vice President's helicopter was not simply a mechanical issue or weather related. They were awaiting word from the President. Other reporters were heading to Camp David or somewhere in between hoping to be the first on the scene of whatever had happened to Marine Two.

Danielle was nearly inconsolable. Once word came from Secret Service headquarters that Marine Two was down, her security detail whisked her into the bunker of the residence. They had no idea whether this was a coordinated attack to decapitate the executive branch of government or an isolated incident. Continuity of government measures were implemented. The President was under heavy guard at Camp David – helicopter gun ships hovering overhead. Combat air patrols were circling Washington and every other major city on the eastern seaboard. The Speaker of the House was on his way to a secured undisclosed location. Cabinet members were taken to safe houses.

But Danielle sat crying by herself in the bunker. "Schumi, please, Schumi," she prayed aloud. "Please be okay." Between prayers she would ask her lead agent if they heard anything. Her mom finally got through and both could be heard painfully wailing on each end. The Secret Service told her the kids were on their way to D.C.

"Please, God, let my Schumi be okay," she whimpered.

Wiley was almost as bad, although without the crying. He took the last call from the Vice President in his office in the White House. He kept trying to call Anthony's cell phone, pacing back and forth on the floor. He invoked the Lord's name in prayer for the first time in years. He also locked his door, not knowing who to trust. He feared the President's staff would try to throw him out. He didn't feel going back to his apartment would be safe. The whole city was on lockdown. He was content to just wait for the news in his office.

The President addressed the nation from inside his office in Birch Lodge. He wore his best suit and a somber face. The CIA Director was standing off camera. All of the President's advisors had stayed in D.C. for the holiday weekend so it was up to him and Director Franklin to write up the statement.

"My fellow Americans, tonight we have learned of an unspeakable tragedy. Terrorists have waged war on the highest levels of our government. It is my sad duty to report that Vice President Schumacher's Marine helicopter has been shot down by terrorists."

Shivers ran down the President's spine. Director Franklin was mouthing the words as the President read them off the TelePrompTer.

"The hearts and prayers of every American go out to the Vice President's family, his wife Danielle, and their three children. He was a faithful servant and a great American patriot."

The President offered condolences to the other passengers and crew of Marine Two. He then reassured the nation that he was doing everything in his power to keep them safe. Checkpoints were going up in a hundred-mile radius. Airports on the East Coast were being shut down. The National Guard was being called out to patrol train stations and bus depots to help catch the terrorists who committed this "cowardly act of terror." The President stated he had been in contact with the FBI and the Defense Secretary and vowed to use every tool in the government's arsenal to hunt down the perpetrators. Stay vigilant, he reminded the country.

"Our fight for freedom will go on and we will prevail. God bless America," he said signing off.

Anthony and Agent Craig huddled next to each other in the culvert. The cool wind whistled through the pipe. They were dry but shivering. There would be no sleep. Agent Craig was worried they would be found by someone with bad intentions. If necessary, he told the Vice President they'd jump in the river and float to who knows where. They agreed to head out at first light and search for a farm house. There they'd try to call the Secret Service or the FBI – people they could trust.

"Who do you think those two guys worked for?" Anthony asked.

"Definitely nòt one of ours. Not FBI either."

"Could they have been part of a Middle Eastern terrorist plot? Agents of a sleeper cell?"

"Doubtful."

"Director Franklin had mentioned terrorists were plotting to use surface-to-air missiles to shoot down a passenger jet over the Christmas holidays."

"I wasn't aware of those concerns," Agent Craig said looking in the darkness over at Anthony.

"That's exactly what Director Bolton said."

"Sir, if the Secret Service knew of a threat using surface-to-air missiles we never would have lifted off in Marine Two without three other decoys in the air. If the CIA had specific and credible intelligence, they did not share it with us."

"She mentioned some operative named Abdullah, but I got the impression from Director Bolton that he found the information speculative at best."

"Maybe the terrorists just got lucky and pushed up the date."

Neither one knew the answer. Anthony thought of the ousted Speaker O'Shea. She was serving forty years in federal prison, but she still had friends in low places. Friends that made up criminal syndicates that, for the right price, could make someone disappear without a trace like Jimmy Hoffa. Authorities are still digging up backyards and industrial sites in search of his body. Plus, the Speaker would love to pay back the man who helped put her in the penitentiary for most likely the rest of her life.

Anthony kept the possibility to himself. He and Agent Craig said little and huddled together for warmth.

The pictures the next morning proved everyone's worst fears. Marine Two had indeed been shot down. News helicopters hovered over the lake and its surrounding forests. Rescue teams in orange hats made it look like opening day of deer season. The FBI sent two-hundred agents up to the lake to investigate the terrorist attack. Five-hundred military personnel joined in the search of the forest looking for any debris. Navy divers submerged to the bottom and twenty minutes later conferred with the command post – a pontoon boat dropped in by helicopter. Six bodies were discovered still strapped in their seats. The command post requested more divers to look for the other two bodies. They also asked for another larger pontoon barge. Given the surrounding terrain, a Sikorsky skycrane helicopter was called in. The divers would secure Marine Two as best they could, and the helicopter would then hoist it from the depths and place it on the pontoon barge.

The news helicopter caught the first images of Marine Two as it was pulled from the water. The sight brought tears to the eyes of service men around the world and a large chunk of the American population. Attached to cables, the distinctive metallic green paint of Marine Two emerged from the dark water. The American flag above the main door was dented but defiantly held form on the crippled machine. The rotors were gone. Water poured out the gaping hole at the rear end. The skycrane gently maneuvered the remains onto the barge and a salvage crew placed a large green tarpaulin over the top. The crew hooked the helicopter's cables onto the pontoon and it was lifted off the lake and over the trees to the nearest clearing a mile away. There, the remains of Marine Two were placed on a flatbed truck for its final trip to Washington. Ten police cars on each end of the truck and two Marine AH-1 Cobra gun ships escorted the freight back to D.C. The procession had all the makings of a funeral train and drivers on Interstate 270 stopped their cars and took cell phone video of the shrouded remains of Marine Two. Overpasses were packed with locals, many rushing with their American flags to pay their final respects. Men removed their hats. Many wept.

The Vice President and Agent Craig had crawled out of their culvert and had been walking for an hour now. They would stop every so often and listen. Helicopters whirring overhead, vehicular traffic rumbling not too far away. The interstate must only be a mile or so to the south. They made it to the edge of the forest and found a lonely white farm house two hundred yards away. The fields had been cultivated some time ago, and the rain made them a muddy mess. A gravel road ran two hundred yards on the other side. Anthony and Agent Craig needed a phone. They looked each other over in the emerging daylight. The two had mud caked on the shoes and trousers. Anthony's suit coat had a good long rip in it. They looked like they had been wrestling with the pigs in the barn over yonder. Anthony used his handkerchief to wipe the mud and bits of leaves off his face and passed it over to Agent Craig. For some reason, both felt like they were behind enemy lines and grew apprehensive about proceeding. Approaching the natives always had its own hazards. If whoever shot down Marine Two had the wherewithal to occupy this particular farmhouse, then Anthony and Agent Craig would just have to hand it to them and give up.

"What's our story?" Anthony asked. Should he just come out and say he's the Vice President of the United States? Do you mind if I use your phone? They didn't want to raise any suspicions lest the enemy discover their position again.

"Vehicle trouble," Agent Craig suggested. No lie.

Anthony and Agent Craig scurried across the mud field and spotted movement in the window of the big red barn. The owner of the establishment appeared at the front of the sliding barn door and waved at the two strangers walking his way. For a second, the old buzzard wondered if the two were of this earth.

"How ya'll doing?" the eighty-two-year-old man said. He was decked out from head to toe in classic farmer regalia – a sun-scorched straw hat, red flannel shirt, torn overalls, and manure-crusted boots. The nice field of whiskers on his chin indicated he hadn't shaved in a couple of days. His back pocket contained a half empty pouch of Red Man, the other half was in his mouth and dribbling off his lower lip.

"Ya'll lost?" He wiped the tobacco from his mouth with the sleeve of his shirt and gave a good spit. He offered a welcoming hand and then another spit.

"We've had some vehicle trouble," Anthony said. "Name's Anthony."

"Virgil Gunderson," he said loudly, like he had a little trouble hearing.

"This is my partner Mike."

"Partner!?" Farmer Virgil shot back. Two nicely dressed men. Obviously not from around here. Instantly the old man's mind put the pieces of the puzzle together and surmised the two must be gay. Maybe they were out there fooling around in the mud. Damn city queers.

Anthony read the old man's mind perfectly and thought he'd better clarify. "Yeah, we work together in D.C. Do you mind if I use your phone to call my wife?" He held up his ring finger to show he had at least entered into some form of committed relationship.

Agent Craig chimed in too. "My wife's probably pretty worried too." He also showed off his wedding ring.

This seemed to appease ol' Virgil, who decided he needn't run to the house to fetch his Bible. Or his gun.

"The vehicle broke down a few miles to the northwest and darn it if we didn't take a few headers into the mud on the way down here."

Farmer Virgil let out a laugh. "You city folk ain't made for this country living. Come on inside and we'll get that phone for ya. Mother should have breakfast on any minute now if you're hungry."

After emptying his mouth of his morning tobacco, Virgil opened the back door to the farm house and allowed his guests to enter. Anthony and Agent Craig felt the warm blast of a furnace on their cold wet faces. The smell of bacon made them want to cry.

"Mother, we've got company."

Mother was actually Virgil's wife. But after having eleven kids, she had been called Mother enough times that it was used by everyone. Her given name was Mabel, and she welcomed the dirty duo into the kitchen wearing her blue duster and slippers like they were long lost sons.

Anthony and Agent Craig thanked them for their kindness but before either one could ask to use the phone, Mabel had them seated at the table with a plate full of bacon, eggs, hash browns, and toast. Virgil said the morning prayer, gave thanks for the bountiful harvest in the field and on the table, and asked God to guide the wayward strangers to their final destination. Mabel then implored them to eat, eat, eat. She said they hardly ever got visitors anymore. The kids were all grown up and moved away. She started rattling off the names of each one and gave a short biographical sketch. She was proud of them all. And she added they all made it to church on Sundays too. She asked Anthony and Agent Craig if they were church-going gentlemen. Yes, they responded, Lutherans. This pleased Mabel greatly. Not wanting to be rude, Anthony and Agent Craig did take a few bites of the finest down home country cooking they had ever tasted.

Agent Craig noticed two shotguns on top of the kitchen cabinets. That fire place poker in the living room could be used as a weapon. He heard the presence of no one else in the place. Anthony noticed the rotary dial phone on the wall. After more bites of hash browns, Mabel gave Anthony a quizzical look, her old wrinkled eye lids almost pressed completely together.

"I know you, don't I?" she smiled pointing at him. "You've been on TV."

Anthony blushed his cheeks as much as he could. You got me. The old bird had found him out. He couldn't hide it any more.

"You were on that *Dancing with the Stars,* weren't ya?"

Agent Craig choked on his toast. He grabbed a cup of coffee to keep from laughing.

"Mother, please!"

Anthony shook his head, almost upset that he was disappointing the old woman. No, he was not a dancer. He pulled out his wallet. Identifying himself to the Gundersons no longer seemed a concern. The black leather was still wet from last night. He opened it up and found a business card (the government actually made business cards for him). The card stock had softened and the ink of his name had begun to run ever so slightly. But the vice-presidential seal stood strong. He handed it across the table.

"I'm Anthony Schumacher, Vice President of the United States." He turned to Virgil, who had a piece of bacon protruding out of his mouth. He had suddenly lost the ability to chew his food. "Virgil, I really need to use your phone."

Virgil looked like he was ready to hand over the keys to the homestead. He thought the Vice President was dead. They had watched it on TV last night. He nodded his head at the phone on the wall, and Anthony hopped to it. Virgil and Mabel sat silent, like they wondered what the two government types were going to do to them. Uncle Sam was figuratively sitting at their kitchen table. Agent Craig pulled out his business card and identified himself as a member of the Secret Service. It was his job to keep the Vice President safe. No need to be alarmed.

Anthony called the FBI. "Ty Stubblefield, please. This is Anthony Schumacher."

Ty's secretary was in no mood for practical jokes this morning. A pall had been cast over the Hoover FBI Building at the loss of their beloved leader. She told the caller he might be breaking federal law if he was impersonating a federal officer or trying to obstruct the investigation or pissing off a federal secretary.

"Mary, doggone it," Anthony whispered into the phone so as not to offend old Virgil and Mabel, "I was on Marine Two last night with Director Bolton. He was in the rear seat right across from me."

Was that good enough evidence that he was the real Anthony Schumacher?

"Hold, Sir."

"Hello, this is Ty?"

"Ty, it's Anthony." He relayed the story as fast as he could to him – he and Agent Craig survived, their hike through the woods, their encounter with the two men, and their current location. Anthony wanted Ty to come get him. He could not trust anyone else. Before hanging up, he asked Ty to call Danielle on his way.

"Tell my Elle I'm fine and I love her."

Anthony and Agent Craig thanked Virgil and Mabel for their hospitality but they would have to leave soon. She hustled upstairs to find a copy of *Life Magazine* with Anthony's picture on the cover. She had every issue organized neatly in boxes right next to her collection of *TV Guides*. She was hoping for an autograph so she could show her friends down at the beauty parlor. She returned, and Anthony obliged with his John Hancock and gave her a big hug.

Always on duty, Agent Craig wasn't taking any chances. If someone overheard Anthony's phone conversation with the FBI, their last chance at getting the Vice President would be within the next twenty minutes. They explained the situation to Virgil, stating that until the coast was clear somebody might be looking to harm them. The terrorists could be out there trying to finish Anthony off. Ol' Virgil loved the idea of a little firefight and reached for his trusty shotgun. No terrorist was going to do harm to America on the Gunderson farm. Agent Craig was looking out the front picture window with sidearm ready for duty.

Always playing the gracious host, Mabel offered another cup of coffee to Anthony when the ground started rumbling and the house began to shake. It felt like an earthquake. Black sedans roared up to the farm house and two Army Apache attack helicopters appearing over the horizon hovered in the air looking to render hell-fire on anything that moved. Spot lights blinded the occupants and the windows started vibrating. Mabel's collection of antique salt-and-pepper shakers rattled perilously close to the edge of the shelf.

"Virgil! Virgil!" she yelled in fright, dropping the coffee pot on the floor. Fearing the rapture was upon them, she dove under the kitchen table and prayed for the Lord to save them.

Well-armed men poured out of military transports and ringed the property. A black helicopter landed on the front lawn and out stepped the massive six-foot-six frame of Tyrone Stubblefield. The rush of noise was having a hell of an effect on Virgil's hearing aid and on his cognitive abilities. He hadn't felt this alive since he took it to "those damn Krauts in the WWII."

"Is that giant black feller there one of them terr'rists!?" Virgil yelled as he cocked his shotgun and prepared to fight all comers to protect the Vice President.

"Virgil! No! Put the gun down! He's with me!" Anthony yelled. He ran over to the old man and pulled Virgil's pointed barrel down to the ground. It was okay. Ty's an old friend with the FBI. He can be trusted. The entire farm house was surrounded by federal law enforcement. Anthony would be safe now.

Ty made sure the Vice President and Agent Craig were okay and made preparations for their return to Washington. Before they left, Anthony checked on Mabel, who was receiving oxygen from the ambulance crew that had been dispatched to the scene just in case a bloodbath had ensued. All the commotion had given her heart a "pretty good start." He told her he'd have her and Virgil down to the Vice-President's Residence some day in the near future. She patted his hand with both of hers and smiled.

"God bless you, Mr. Vice President."

CHAPTER 22

"The Vice President is alive!"

Wiley bolted from his office and ran through the halls of the West Wing yelling at the top of his lungs. "He's alive! Vice President Schumacher is alive!"

The secretaries and deputies looked at him with wide-eyed amazement. The TVs on the wall were on twenty-four hours a day, and the only thing discussed on the morning news shows was what would happen when the recovery divers inevitably found the Vice President's body.

Wiley had spent the night in his office, his tie was gone and the top two buttons of his white dress shirt weren't being used. The dark circles around his eyes made it look like he had gone a few rounds. And lost. He didn't stop with those milling quietly about their work spaces and ran out of the White House onto the North Lawn and started yelling at the tourists in mourning lining the fence. Usually, the nutcases jump the fence and run toward the White House. Now it was just the opposite. The Secret Service marksmen on the White House roof had him in the crosshairs just in case. People thought the man with arms raised over his head and sprinting at full speed had gone mad. What was he saying?

"The Vice President is alive! I just talked to him!" he bellowed as he huffed and puffed along the fence. He went back and forth spreading the good news. No need for people to check their iPhones or BlackBerrys. They were getting their news straight from the source. Wiley just kept repeating the Vice President was alive. He then bolted to the line of reporters doing their segments from the west-side walkway. Reporters gathered around and jammed their microphones into the face of the Vice President's balding chief of staff who was now dripping in sweat. Between laughing and sobbing, he told the world that he had just got off the phone with the Vice President of the United States who said he and Agent Craig had survived the crash. They're on their way back to the capital!

News rooms in Washington and New York were exploding in action. "Breaking News" was a gross understatement. Obituaries for the Vice President were put on hold and every available reporter was sent to the White House and the Vice-President's Residence. Veteran newsmen were practically wetting their pants at the sensational news. Some went on air without makeup. Others looked like they had just been rousted out of bed. The terrorists had failed in their evil plot to kill the Vice President!

U.S.A.! U.S.A.! U.S.A.!

Four Marine helicopters lifted off from the Gundersons' farm and headed southeast. The two Apaches provided close air support. The news reporters breathlessly reported the Vice President was in the air and cameras zoomed in for a look. He wasn't in the air, however. Not wanting to take another helicopter ride just yet, he and Agent Craig were in an armored Suburban surrounded by every available agent the Secret Service had to offer. Three dozen government vehicles blew onto Interstate 270 intent on beating the helicopters to their destination.

The Vice President was heading back to Washington.

The motorcade found its way back to the Naval Observatory. The sidewalks were filled with citizens waving American flags and cheering the Vice President's return. They saw little given the tinted windows but they whooped, hollered, and generally made as much noise as possible to let their Vice President know how glad they were to have him back.

Once the motorcade came to a halt, there were no news cameras on the grounds. Anthony just wanted to have a private reunion with Danielle and the kids. The Secret Service had driven Wiley from the White House, although he said he could have sprinted there if he had to.

Anthony and Danielle met in the foyer. She was crying. She had been crying all night. She gave him an embrace that rivaled those given by lonely military wives whose husbands have been off to war for twelve months. She just wanted him to hold her, and he was glad to oblige. There were no official photos taken inside, the White House photographer unfortunately missing the event. But Wiley did capture Anthony and Danielle's loving embrace on his cell-phone camera. It would make a great campaign video, he thought. The kids all received big hugs. Even Wiley got in on the act.

Anthony had called ahead and asked that Agent Craig's family be driven to the Naval Observatory so they could have a rightful private reunion with their returning hero. Anthony would later push for Agent Craig to receive a congressional commendation for his valor in saving his life on more than one occasion during their ordeal.

Once the hugs were done and the harrowing stories told, Anthony begged for a hot shower and a change of clothes.

After a day of rest, Anthony and Wiley sat down in the residence living room to think of their next order of business. Anthony had not talked to the

President since he threw him out of the NSC meeting at Camp David. The President had made some comments that he was glad to see the Vice President was okay, but he kept the focus on hunting down the terrorists.

Wiley reminded Anthony of his last phone call before Marine Two was shot down. Remember? Anthony wanted him to start the Schumacher for President campaign. To Anthony, that conversation seemed like a million years ago. He barely remembered saying it, and the anger at the President had subsided slightly because of his near-death experience and the loss of life on Marine Two.

Wiley, however, had not slept for three days and his precious poll numbers were starting to trickle in. The Vice President's popularity had skyrocketed in the last twenty-four hours since his return. Ninety percent of the public viewed him favorably. Even fifty-one percent of liberal Democrats said Anthony would make a fine President. And they were saying this about a right-wing conservative!

"Now is the time," Wiley kept saying. "We can ride this wave of public support right down to 1600 Pennsylvania Avenue. Your message just has to be keeping America safe by taking the fight to terrorists and keeping spending low." Wiley was looking at his yellow legal pad full of notes. "The President will no doubt run a reelection campaign that focuses on fighting terror but we can get the Republicans to jump ship when they look at the big-government, tax-and-spend programs he's got lined up."

Anthony was giving it a good long thought. Wiley was making good points. Anthony's popularity and argument for a return to smaller government and balanced budgets might just pick off enough convention delegates to win the nomination. In the November general election, it would be no contest against the Democrats. If he could win the nomination, Anthony might be looking at one of the greatest landslides in American history. The Electoral College count would make Reagan's 512-vote margin over Mondale in '84 look razor-thin.

"I don't think I can do it," Anthony said, shaking his head. He could see the presidency within his grasp. But he was concerned about putting his ambitions before the good of the country. America needed to rally behind the President and take it to the terrorists. But if he were to go out and start campaigning against him, even if it were in an attempt to push harder against the terrorists, it might take the focus off of where it needed to be.

"Schu," Wiley implored, "we just can't miss out on such a great opportunity."

Anthony just shook his head. "It's not the right time."

Across town, another debate was going on. The President and Director Franklin were in the Oval Office. Both were in a bad mood for some reason.

The President had taken to yelling at his staff. His breath indicated he might have started drinking during the day. Maybe the pressure of the terrorists was getting to him. He and Franklin were pacing the floor of the Oval Office wondering whether now was the time for the President to file for divorce from the First Lady. He wanted his wife out of the way. That would make him feel better. He didn't want to wait until he was out of office in another five years if he was lucky enough to win reelection.

Director Franklin wanted the First Lady out too.

"Mr. President, now is the time," she said as they sat down near the fireplace. They wanted each other, and they were tired of fooling around in secret.

"I don't know."

"You have a seventy-five percent approval rating. You can just say the job has caused your marriage to fall apart. People will feel sorry for you. Here you are on call every day trying to keep America safe. It's no wonder why a marriage would suffer. Now is the best time. The country will be distracted by the attack and the holidays."

"Yeah, that sounds good."

The President ran the scenario through his head. He and the First Lady just couldn't go on like this. And it wasn't fair to the First Lady, he would say. She deserved a life too. One where they didn't have to put on the fake smiles before the cameras and the dinner guests. It sounded better the more he thought about it.

Anthony spent the next week attending the funerals of every person who didn't make it off of Marine Two. He thanked the grieving families and told them he would always remember their loved ones. Director Bolton's funeral was at the National Cathedral. The sanctuary was packed with government big wigs and law enforcement representatives from around the country. Director Franklin sent a deputy underling from the CIA. Bolton's two grown children and their families sat in the first row on the right. His ex-wives even showed up so they could be seen grieving on camera.

On the left of the sanctuary, the President sat on the end of the first pew next to his non-smiling wife. Both looked sad, but in reality they just didn't want to be there. And they especially didn't want to be sitting next to each other. Danielle, who got along well with the First Lady, sat next to her and Anthony. Agent Craig and his team sat behind Anthony ready to pounce in case the choir or the pastor tried something stupid. Acting FBI Director Stubblefield sat next to the Vice President.

Ty Stubblefield had been the second in command at the FBI for ten years, all under the reign of Director Bolton. They had similar styles, and Ty was ready to morph Bolton's legacy into his own. He had spent the last week looking for clues to pin the blame on someone. Once he found it, he hoped to unleash every available agent in the FBI to hunt down the perpetrators. He would not sleep until they were caught.

Prior to the start of the service, the small talk between Anthony and Ty centered on the investigation.

"The missiles were American made," Ty whispered in Anthony's ear.

Anthony gave him a quick glance. He had a flashback to the two streaks of smoke flying past Marine Two. He didn't see the other one, just felt its crushing blow. It was possible the terrorists bought the American-made missiles on the black market, probably left over from the Afghan war or stolen during the invasion of Iraq. The buyers could then ship the missiles on a cargo container bound for Canada or Mexico, where on arrival they would be smuggled into the U.S. through the porous border crossings that dot the northern and southern landscapes.

"Three of them were fired from an area north of the lake into which Marine Two landed."

Ty noted the FBI's investigation indicated the terrorists had most likely used all-terrain vehicles to access the highest point south of Camp David and waited for a Marine helicopter to appear overhead. They could have been there for days and gotten lucky that they hit the helicopter carrying the Vice President. Whoever it was, they left very little clues in the area.

"Have you found that CIA operative – Abdullah?"

"The CIA says they lost contact with him."

"What about those two suspected terrorists that Agent Craig capped on the side of the road?"

Ty looked Anthony directly in the eye. "Sir, we have found no bodies in the location that you and Agent Craig described. No abandoned cars either."

Their inner thoughts were interrupted when the organist began the opening hymn of *For All the Saints*. Neither Anthony nor Ty would hear much of the service, instead trying to put the pieces of the puzzle together.

Anthony's first press conference was a packed affair in the East Room of the White House. Correspondents from around the world wanted to hear the inside story of the Vice President's brush with death. The President opted out of the presser, saying Anthony should have the stage alone this time. He was busy anyway – the terrorists wouldn't take time off and neither would he. Danielle sat off to the left of the podium and watched her husband with eyes thankful he was able to stand before them.

The reporters wanted to know every detail – the missile's impact, the crash of Marine Two into the lake, swimming to safety, and then hiking for help with Agent Craig.

"Mr. Vice President, were you scared when you realized that Marine Two was going to make a crash landing?" an AP reporter asked.

"Absolutely. We were in a dizzying spiral that seemed to last forever. There was no panic from those on board, but definitely concern. The Marines were doing their job trying to land a crippled helicopter. I could tell my Secret Service agents were thinking about what they needed to do once we got on the ground. But it is true that one's life flashes before your eyes in those situations."

He reached inside his pants pocket and retrieved his handkerchief. He had told himself he wasn't going to need it.

"I saw the face of my beautiful wife," he said quietly, choking back tears and he turned to Danielle. She was crying again. The flashbulbs were popping like mad. Live cameras zeroed in on his moist eyes. "My kids were there too."

Anthony mentioned the terrible jolt they felt when Marine Two slammed into the water. The doctors said the only injuries he suffered were a cracked right rib, a sprained wrist, and superficial scrapes on his hands and face. He was still sore, however. He did not mention the two men that he and Agent Craig met on the side of the road. Only a handful of people even knew about that meeting. He did want to acknowledge the wonderful hospitality they received from the Gundersons in northern Frederick, Maryland. To him, they were great American patriots. Virgil and Mabel would soon become big stars.

"Mr. Vice President, what did the President say to you after both of you spoke for the first time after the attack?"

Anthony looked at the back wall of the East Room, the wonderful portrait of George Washington gazing over all who are lucky enough to enter. America would always come first to him.

"I'd rather keep those discussions private. I'll just say that personal matters were discussed."

After ninety-three minutes of questions and responses, Wiley had the privilege of saying the Vice President had pressing matters to attend to. Anthony thanked the reporters, told them it was good to see all of them again, and expressed his gratitude to all Americans who had reached out to him and his family during the last ten days.

"I am thankful to them. I am thankful to be an American. And may God bless this great country."

CHAPTER 23

The White House press release was sent out on Friday, December 23, the day before Christmas Eve. It simply said that the President and First Lady had decided to pursue divorce proceedings after twenty-five years of marriage. They asked that everyone please respect their privacy during these difficult times. The President's handlers hoped their dump of the marital bombshell at the start of the long holiday weekend would help take the sting out of any negative press coverage. Most reporters wouldn't get to the story until Monday, and by then the President hoped the American public would have something else on their minds.

The First Lady was apoplectic.

"That bastard," as she had taken to calling him, would rue the day that he threw her out during his presidency like a piece of rotten trash. She knew this day would come at some point, but she didn't think it would happen while he was still in the White House. "That bitch," as she referred to Director Franklin, would some day wish she had not messed with the life of Susan Randolph-Fisher.

Although the divorce papers had been filed in New York by the President's personal attorneys, he wanted things to move along quickly. Even his staff noticed the President was getting nastier by the day. Without any sense of decency or personal diplomacy, the President told the First Lady to pack her bags. He wanted her out of the White House by Monday morning, the day after Christmas. Since he and Director Franklin planned on spending the weekend at Camp David, he wanted the First Lady to get her things out of the lodge. He told her the Secret Service was waiting to take her up there. Be gone by three o'clock Saturday were his instructions. Santa would have to bring the First Lady's gifts somewhere else. She'd probably get the house in New York anyway, so the Secret Service would ferry her and her "damn things" up there once she was finished packing.

Danielle had a tearful goodbye with the First Lady, one of the few friends that she made while in Washington besides Candace Sutton. Not many women could understand what it's like to be married to a man who was constantly hounded by news reporters and photographers and followed closely by some of the heaviest armed guards in the world. The First Lady knew what Danielle was going through, and she promised to call once she got settled.

The First Lady's helicopter landed at Camp David at 8:30 a.m. on Saturday. It wasn't going to take her long to pack. She only had a few clothes and personal items. She entered the bedroom which she and the President had shared on a few occasions early on when the euphoria of being President and First Lady overwhelmed their sense of hatred for each other. The dresser drawers and closets were emptied and the contents stuffed angrily into suitcases. The First Lady did it all alone. She told her staff to enjoy the holiday weekends because it looked like they would be out of a job soon. She guessed she could continue showing up in her East Wing offices every day so long as she was still Mrs. Fisher, but the President would eventually force her out.

Once the bags were packed, she opened the glass doors of the TV cabinet. To the left of the TV sat shelves of DVDs for the First Couple's viewing pleasure. She liked the tear jerkers, the President enjoyed suspense. She took those she thought he wouldn't want. To the right of the TV sat shelves of books, almost all of them hers because the President said he had no time to read what with all the briefing books his staff made him sift through every night. She pulled out her mystery novels and books about First Ladies that caring citizens had sent to her. She would someday be a footnote in one of those history books, the first First Lady to be divorced while her husband was in office.

The last book on the shelf was the Holy Bible. No doubt untouched by the President. The First Lady had all but forgotten about it. She had purchased it online when she thought the President was cheating on her. But the purchase wasn't to soothe her wounded soul with readings of the Twenty-Third Psalm or to pray for the faithful husband found in the fifth chapter of Ephesians.

She wanted the video camera hidden inside.

Printing on the spine of the black Bible looked like every other copy of the New International Standard Version. But a careful check revealed a glossy film covering an inch-and-a-half portion near the bottom. Behind the film sat a one-inch lens. The camera worked like any digital game camera sold at outdoor supply stores or in hunting magazines. When the wild animal walks in front of the camouflaged camera attached to a tree, it takes a picture. The hunter or wildlife enthusiast returns later, opens up the box and, voila, a nice black and white of Bambi, color if you pay for the high-end model.

The First Lady didn't just want a camera, however, and one painted to match the trees and foliage would do little good in the bedroom. She wanted a video camera, one that would turn on when the wildlife entered the bedroom and engaged in the mating rituals rarely seen on the National Geographic channel. She went with the top-of-the-line version – built-in screen inside the Bible for quick replays of the boudoir action, zoom-in feature, infrared enabled, sound recording, USB cable, the works. The camera covers came in various styles – the Bible, dusty legal tomes, out-of-date dictionaries. Tolstoy's *War and Peace* was a top seller and one assured not to be picked off the shelf. After a minute of inactivity, the camera was programmed to return to sleep mode. It also came equipped with a slot for a thirty-two gigabyte memory card, sold separately, that in its current position in the TV cabinet would allow for one-thousand hours of recorded tossing and turning in bed or the occasional rounds of lovemaking. Along the right edge of the spine ran a microphone that could pick up a whisper within ten yards. Technically, recording voices without consent was illegal in Maryland, and on-line purchasers were required to promise they would not use it for eavesdropping or other surreptitious means. The First Lady, and every other purchaser, simply skipped over the legal disclaimer and hurriedly clicked "Yes, I promise." Good enough, the seller proclaimed. Proceed to checkout.

The First Lady had put the Bible cam out of her mind, since it was no longer a surprise that her husband had been engaging in multiple affairs while in the White House. She pulled out the Bible and opened it up. The memory card was still there, causing her to smile that wide mischievous smile. The smile cheated-on wives make when they know they have their cheating husband's balls in a vice-like grip. She would relish every minute of cranking that vice until the President screamed in agony.

It was only 11:30. She still had three and a half hours to kill before the President wanted her out. She thought she might as well put the card in the slot in the TV so she could start making mental notes to give to her divorce lawyer. This was going to be fun.

The First Lady fast-forwarded through a good portion of the early days. The video would show the President undressing after a long day and falling into bed. Sometimes he would watch a movie but the camera would usually shut off half way through because the President had fallen asleep. The mornings would usually show the President sipping a fresh cup of coffee as he read the *New York Times* and the *Wall Street Journal* in bed. He'd get up, take a shower, get dressed, and off would go the camera after he left the room.

The time-stamp for the longest recorded action was the Wednesday before Thanksgiving. The First Lady's breathing quickened when she saw Director Franklin enter the room behind the President. It didn't take long for the First Horn Dog to get down to business and he and his lover stripped off their clothes in record time. They pressed their naked bodies up against each other for a good fifteen minutes before the phone rang, requiring the President to dismount and answer it lest he miss yet another national emergency.

Once the call ended, Director Franklin lamented the fact that she had forgotten her nightgown. Although the President had the bright idea that she could just sleep in the nude, she protested. So the President, again with another of his bright ideas, told her to look in the dresser to see if the First Lady had an extra one. Director Franklin left the bed and walked toward the TV cabinet, where she stopped to fix her hair in the reflection of the glass. It provided a nice visual of the Director of the CIA and her buxom breasts as well as the President of the United States enjoying the view of her bare behind. She proceeded to rummage through the First Lady's drawer and complained that her wardrobe desperately needed an update into this century.

"Bitch," the First Lady whispered to the TV screen.

Director Franklin returned to the viewing area of the camera and modeled the First Lady's baby blue negligee. She also commented that it was way, way too big for her.

Another "bitch" in response.

Director Franklin fell into the President's arms and they fondled each other for another ten minutes. With the lights down low, they talked about the future. The divorce was a possibility. Then they could share the same bed in the White House without having to sneak around and pretend that high-level meetings were taking place from 10 p.m. to 6 a.m. every night.

"Once the divorce is finalized, then we'll get married and people will call you First Lady," the President said to her.

"I don't want to be First Lady," she moaned.

It was a boring title and such a let down from being CIA Director. She wanted power. She wanted a seat at the table. She wanted a hand in what went on in the world. She wanted more.

"I want to be Vice President."

What? The First Lady thought she must have heard wrong. She reached for the remote control and hit the rewind button. Then she turned up the volume.

"I don't want to be First Lady," the Director said, clear as a could be. "I want to be Vice President." Again, clear as a bell.

The talk between the sheets then turned to Vice President Schumacher. Oh, how they despised that goodie-two-shoes S.O.B. Nothing but a hick from the sticks who got lucky in life. Both of them feared what he might say about walking in on them having sex off the Oval Office. The First Lady rolled her eyes, although she wasn't surprised. The President and Franklin feared the Vice President's sense of patriotism could easily cause him to throw them under the bus if the opportunity presented itself.

"I can put you on the ticket for the next election. You could be the first female to be elected Vice President."

Director Franklin pouted like a four-year-old girl. "I want it now. I want it now."

She mentioned to him that Vice President Schumacher had excellent poll numbers and his performance on the Fourth of July only buoyed his credentials. He could take the President down in a primary fight. Then the

President would be one and done, and Director Franklin wouldn't even be allowed the opportunity to be called First Lady. She hinted the President might not enjoy their time alone in the bedroom if she didn't get her way.

"I can't just kick him off the ticket. That would be political suicide. The Christian conservatives would throw me to the lions and moderates in love with that country bumpkin would throw their support around him."

Director Franklin ran her fingers up and down the President's bare chest. The First Lady turned up the volume some more. She was on the edge of the bed wondering where the conversation was going next.

"I know of a way to get him off the ticket," she cooed.

"How?"

She looked deep into his eyes. "Oman."

The President's eyes locked on the TV cabinet. It looked like he was peering straight into the spine of the Bible. Was his conscience getting to him? The wheels were spinning fast in his head. Director Franklin had obviously thought this through.

Mustafa Oman was the world's most wanted man. The FBI had put a $50 million bounty on his head. Grainy images of Oman broadcasting his hatred of America were weekly occurrences on Arab television sets. He was ready to wage jihad on America and the President's laissez-faire attitude toward combat on foreign soil allowed Oman's followers to train at will.

"Oman is our way out," Director Franklin said, more caressing of the President's pectorals.

"How?"

"I can get a four-man team, black ops, no one will know. It won't even be on the books."

The President was shaking his head.

"We get the Vice President on Marine Two and take it down over a remote area. There would be two handling the missile firing and two ready to clean up any mess."

The First Lady dropped the remote control on the floor, scaring her. She ran to the door and locked it. It was 2:30 p.m. She was shaking, like it was damn clear she should not have been hearing what she just heard. She pulled a chair in front of the TV, rewound the video, and listened to the last minute again. She wouldn't have believed it if she didn't hear it with her own ears. She had hoped to use the recording of her husband's infidelity at the divorce hearing. Now she was watching the making of a conspiracy to murder the Vice President of the United States.

"What happens if we get caught?"

"We won't get caught," Franklin promised. "The team is a like shadow. Here today, gone tomorrow. We used them six months ago in Iran. No one outside of Langley knew what happened. I haven't even told you about it. Once the Vice President is taken down, we blame it all on Oman. We put his face on every TV screen. Then we bomb the hell out of his supposed hideouts in Afghanistan, promise not to stop until he surrenders or dies. The American people will line up in droves to kill Oman with their bare hands."

"And then what happens after we obliterate Afghanistan?"

"You'll be the hero that fought back against the terrorists." She smiled and kissed his lips. "Then you make me Vice President."

The President rubbed her upper arm. The camera lens could tell he was thinking about it. She pushed on.

"Once you're reelected with me as Vice President, then you file for divorce. I will then run for election to succeed you. After I'm elected, we get married. You'll still be in the White House and we will rule this world for sixteen straight years."

The First Lady sat stunned. She kept looking at the door, fearing the President or a hit squad sent by Director Franklin would barge in and take her out. She was now praying for her husband. Please say no, she begged. Maybe Oman's followers had gotten to the Vice President but missed. Surely, the President hadn't been in on it.

"Come on, think of the good we can do. We will end global warming, provide universal health care, and take care of every American's needs. We can do it with your one remaining term and my two that follow." She moved her hand underneath the covers. The President's body quivered. "Come on. We can do it."

He smiled and closed his eyes. Two of the most powerful forces in human nature – the unquenchable thirst for power and the unending desire for sex – were bombarding his mind and body. Forces that have felled many to their penitent knees, but in others could not be resisted. For a man who always got what he wanted, there was no fear in succumbing to the seductive call of the temptress.

"Let's do it," he said.

The First Lady buried her head in her hands. She couldn't believe it. When she looked up again, the video showed Director Franklin on top of the President. They were indeed doing it. The bed rattled and shook for ten minutes as two of the most powerful actors in all of government, nay all the world, let loose their inner demons and pounded away at each other's sweating flesh. Out of breath, they fell into each other's arms and drifted off to sleep. Then the camera turned off.

The knock at the door startled the First Lady out of her shoes.

"Who is it!?" she screamed.

"Ma'am, are you about ready?" came from her Secret Service agent.

She was still shaking. Her voice shook with fright. "I'll be out in five minutes, Steve."

"Ma'am, is everything all right?" Agent Steve asked through the door.

"Yes," she said quickly as she fumbled to get the memory card out of the TV. "I'm just finishing up."

She put the memory card back into the camera and closed the faux Bible. She would keep it close until she could figure out what to do with it. She grabbed her bags, walked out the front door for the final time, and boarded the helicopter with her security detail. Her mascara had started to run, and Agent Steve figured she was emotional over her departure. The clicking of seat belts, however, sent the First Lady into a sudden panic. She started hyperventilating. She feared she could be setting herself up for another attack from one of Franklin's teams. Those on board with her could be in jeopardy too. The rotors had barely turned when she spoke up.

"Wait!" she yelled through the cabin. "I want to drive back."

The whirring rotors slowed as Agent Steve turned around. "Ma'am, you can't expect us to drive all the way to upstate New York." He was practically begging her, please don't make us drive you all the way up there. It's Christmas Eve.

"No, I want to go back to Washington."

"Ma'am, we don't have the limo up here."

"I don't care if you have to take me down there on a motorcycle. I don't want to fly."

Agent Steve made the call into his shirt cuff. He wasn't that upset. The First Lady had generally been an easy protectee. She treated her agents with respect, and they in turn thought highly of her considering she put up with her husband's philandering. They exited the helicopter and piled all the First Lady's bags into two Suburbans and enjoyed a quiet drive back to Washington. She clutched her Bible close to her all the way.

Anthony had just finished wishing the hardworking agents of the FBI a merry Christmas at the Hoover FBI Building. They had been working night and day to not only catch the terrorists who committed the crimes against their Director but also prevent any future attacks. Anthony told him how proud he was of them and how proud the late Director Bolton was of them too. Anthony had the greatest admiration for their dedication, and America knew they were doing everything within their power to keep the country safe.

Ty walked Anthony to his office on the fifth floor overlooking Pennsylvania Avenue. There they unwound after a long day. Both sat down with a Diet Coke – Anthony asking for the caffeine free variety, Ty begging for extra because his day never seemed to end.

"I've mentioned to the President on several occasions to nominate you to head the FBI," Anthony said between sips. "That way you can get the 'Acting' out of your title." Anthony didn't know why the President was dragging his feet. It might have something to do with the fact that Ty was on the side of the Vice President and the late Director Bolton, two people the President had grown to dislike.

"I'm sure he'll get around to it," Ty responded. He didn't really care. His singular focus was on the investigation. "As I told you before, the missiles were American made. At the site of the shooting by Agent Craig, we recovered some blood off the leaves by the side of the road. The tests did not reveal anyone in our DNA database."

"I don't think I can give you much else. Two white guys, short hair cuts. It was dark and dreary out."

"You and Agent Craig said you thought the car was a government type?"

"Yeah."

"We checked the skid marks on the road. The tread patterns are consistent with government-issued sedans. The FBI, CIA, and Secret Service all use similar tires on their vehicles." Ty reached for a file with photos of the road and the skid marks. "There are another set of skid marks coming from the north. Like whoever was driving was heading south and came to an abrupt halt at the car left beside the road. We think these long marks right here are where the shoes of the two dead suspects were dragged across the road. No one we have talked to can remember seeing any suspicious vehicles heading south to Frederick."

Anthony shook his head. He worried the terrorists were still out there. He told Ty to make sure to get some sleep so he can stay sharp. The FBI will find out who did this, Anthony reassured him. Something will pop up.

The Schumacher family was slowly beginning to trickle back into Washington. Under heavy guard, Ashley, Michael, and Anna were set to celebrate Christmas at the Vice-President's Residence with their parents. Danielle's mother came up from Silver Creek so the whole family could be together. It was a joyous time, one that didn't seem possible a couple days after Thanksgiving.

They enjoyed a dinner of pot roast, mashed potatoes, green beans, and coconut cream pie. The picturesque Christmas tree had been trucked in from Indiana and was decked with angels and surrounded by presents. After dinner they sat around the fire and talked about past Christmases and their favorite memories. In the back of his mind, Anthony thanked God that he had been given this second chance.

At 8:30 p.m., when the Schumacher clan was preparing to turn in early, Agent Craig walked in the door and motioned for the Vice President.

"Sir, the First Lady is here to see you."

"The First Lady?"

"Yes."

"To see me?"

"Yes." Agent Craig threw a thumb over his shoulder. "She's out in her limo. She wanted to know if it's okay to come in."

"Sure, sure," Anthony said. He wasn't going to send her away on Christmas Eve. He motioned to Danielle. "The First Lady is here to see us."

The First Lady walked in white as a ghost. She looked haggard, like the President's sudden announcement of divorce proceedings had zapped the strength out of her. Maybe there was more on her mind.

"Mr. Vice President," she said almost in a whisper, her voice sounding hoarse. "I just wanted to stop by and drop off this gift." It had been wrapped in red paper with images of jolly ol' Santa Claus bounding from rooftop to rooftop with his trusty reindeer. A quick feel by Anthony indicated it might be a book.

Anthony and Danielle thanked her for her generosity and begged her to stay for a cup of coffee, maybe some pie. The First Lady declined, saying she was going to stay with her brother in Arlington this evening so her Secret Service detail would be near their families for Christmas. She hugged them both and told them she'd call on Monday.

"You be careful, Mr. Vice President," she whispered in his ear.

CHAPTER 24

Anthony began his Monday morning a couple of hours late. After having a big breakfast with the family, he said goodbye to the kids and Danielle's mother who were going their separate ways and back to their respective homes. Anthony sat down at his desk in the office of the residence and read over his mail and scanned the papers. Like every other worker in the country after a long holiday weekend, it was difficult to get back into the groove.

He looked up when he heard a knock at the door. "What's up, Mike?"

Agent Craig entered and stood before the Vice President's desk. "Sir, our technicians have picked up the presence of a recording device in the office."

"Which office?" He had four of them. One in the residence, one in the Old Executive Office Building, one in the West Wing, and one in the Capitol.

"This office."

The Secret Service conducts regular scans of protectee offices looking for bugs that someone might have planted in the walls or the phones after somehow penetrating the impenetrable barrier surrounding the Vice President, his residence, or the White House. Agents routinely find bugs in foreign hotel rooms where the Vice President is set to sleep. They usually just remove everything but the bed and bring their own fixtures. Once while in Moscow, the Secret Service instructed Anthony to enter into what looked like an aluminum foil, tent-like contraption set up in the room if he wanted to have a secured conversation. He was told it would disrupt any listening devices that even their technology could not find. Anthony didn't think much of Agent Craig's revelation.

"I'm the only one who's been in here," Anthony said looking around. "Do you want to X-ray my Diet Coke?"

To Anthony's surprise, Agent Craig actually picked up the can, swirled its contents, and set it back down. All clear. Drink to your heart's content, Mr. Vice President.

Anthony shuffled the mass of papers on his desk, throwing the *Journal* and the *USA Today* on the floor. Under his budget briefing book, the wrapped gift from the First Lady appeared.

"This was from the First Lady," he said, reaching for it. "I guess I should probably open it. She said she was going to call me or Danielle today."

Anthony took his letter opener and slid it under the tape. It had not been professionally wrapped. It was rather hastily done. He unwrapped the obvious book and threw the Santa Claus paper on the floor. His hand was covering the lens.

"Hmm, a Bible." It looked like a regular Bible on the outside. The outer pages looked and felt real. "What's your favorite Bible verse?" he asked Agent Craig.

"John 3:16."

"A good one. Let's see how this version gives it."

Anthony had to give the Bible a good tug to open it. When he removed his hand from the spine, the Biblical innards started buzzing. The contents startled him. "What in the world is this?"

Agent Craig practically lunged at the Vice President's desk, fearing it could be a bomb of some sort. "Sir, please don't touch it."

Since whatever was inside hadn't exploded in his face, Anthony disobeyed the request. They both hovered over the contraption. Anthony looked at the spine and the lens hiding behind it. He pulled out the memory card and the buzzing stopped. He gave a quick glance at Agent Craig.

"Why would the First Lady give me a fake Bible with a hidden video camera in it?"

Anthony handled the card in his fingers, contemplating whether he wanted to look and see what was on it. He had a pretty good idea. He unfortunately walked in on the President and the CIA Director and didn't need a tape to remind him of what he saw. He decided he had to know before he handed it over to the Secret Service so they could figure it out. The First Lady was obviously trying to tell him something. He hated to think the Secret Service would have to interrogate her. Maybe she was having a nervous breakdown.

The computer next to his desk was humming quietly and waiting for someone to press its buttons. Anthony put the memory card in the hard drive. He waved Agent Craig around the desk so he could get a good look.

The First Lady had stopped the tape just before the good parts. She wanted whoever watched it to see the President and Director Franklin going at it. That way the viewers' disgust would have a good couple of minutes to take hold. Anthony and Agent Craig watched uncomfortably hoping the boisterous lovemaking would soon end. Anthony turned the volume down lest Danielle walk by the office and think the two men inside were watching porn on the Vice President's computer.

When Director Franklin showed off her breasts to the TV cabinet and the camera inside, Agent Craig couldn't help but say, "Not bad."

Anthony did not disagree. Hey, they were red-blooded American males.

Anthony turned up the volume when Franklin jumped back into bed. He and Agent Craig sat wide eyed as the plot began to unfold. Oman. Covert hit squads. Marine Two. The CIA Director becoming Vice President. They strained to hear what was being said. When the President said, "Let's do it," did he mean the sex or the hit? They did not wait for the tape to end. Anthony stood up in front of the computer almost as if it were infected with a virus and should not be touched.

Anthony started out with the orders to Agent Craig. "I want your people to make sure the First Lady is secured." He feared someone might be looking to take her out. "Get Ty Stubblefield over here now. The Attorney General too."

Agent Craig didn't go for his cuff. He grabbed the Vice President's phone and called the Director of the Secret Service. He demanded the First Lady's detail be put on high-alert status. He also wanted ten more agents to secure the perimeter of the Vice-President's Residence. He would explain later. Call the FBI and get Stubblefield over here ASAP.

"Find the President and the CIA Director!"

The tinted windows of government vehicles started showing up in the driveway at the Vice-President's Residence. Anthony had been pacing the floor, wondering why his life couldn't just be boring like it used to be. Serious decisions, constitutional decisions, were going to have to be made soon. Acting FBI Director Stubblefield and Attorney General Donovan arrived with serious faces and quizzical looks. They were told to keep their travels quiet. Stubblefield noticed the Secret Service was out in full force, its agents prowling the grounds with automatic weapons drawn.

Anthony and Agent Craig welcomed the two visitors into his office. The Vice President struggled to find the right words for such a bombshell of an announcement.

"Ty, I think I know who shot down Marine Two."

Both Stubblefield and Donovan quickly sat down on the edge of the couch, wondering how the Vice President solved the crime of the century. Anthony ran through the story – the receipt of the First Lady's Bible, the video of the President and the CIA Director. The Attorney General sat shocked. She couldn't believe what the Vice President was saying. Agent Craig turned on the TV, plugged in the memory card, and played the video.

"I want to be Vice President."

"Let's do it."

Ty flew off the couch in a rage, his jaws clenched, his right fist pounding into the left palm. The CIA had killed the FBI Director! he fumed as he stomped around the office. The pieces were beginning to fit together. The CIA would have had access to the missiles. They could have been tipped off as to when Marine Two was taking off and its flight path back to Washington. The men who stopped on the side of the road could have tracked the Vice

President's whereabouts and tried to finish the job. Ty was ready to strangle someone.

The Attorney General started pacing the floor as well, although she was a bit wobbly in the knees. She cleared her throat and spoke clearly.

"Mr. Vice President, I think you need to invoke the Twenty-Fifth Amendment."

The Twenty-Fifth Amendment provides for the presidential line of succession. When the President cannot handle his constitutional duties, section four states as follows:

> *"Whenever the Vice President and a majority of either the principal officers of the executive departments or of such other body as Congress may by law provide, transmit to the President pro tempore of the Senate and the Speaker of the House of Representatives their written declaration that the President is unable to discharge the powers and duties of his office, the Vice President shall immediately assume the powers and duties of the office as Acting President."*

Surely it could be said the President was unable to discharge the powers and duties of his office given that he had conspired to kill the Vice President. The Attorney General said the Cabinet secretaries would sign off on the declaration considering the evidence on the tape. There was no precedent for the Vice President's assumption of power, but she was confident the situation called for action and indicated she would immediately contact Justice Department lawyers.

Anthony wasn't so keen on the idea. It had the makings of a palace coup. What if the President refused to go and holed himself up in the Oval Office? Would the FBI have to break down the doors and arrest him? This wasn't a situation where the President was simply having mental problems that prevented him from concentrating on his job. What if he implemented martial law and called out the military to do his bidding? The CIA would no doubt be on his side. It would be a constitutional crisis never before witnessed by the American public.

"Sir, if you follow the Constitution," the Attorney General said, "the military will follow you. Joint Chiefs Chairman Cummins will not stand with the President. I can guarantee you that."

The Vice President put his hands on top of his head wondering what his next move was. "Where's the President?" he asked.

"The White House," Agent Craig said.

"What about Director Franklin?"

"She's on the President's yacht off the Virginia coast. The President is supposed to meet up with her later today for an extended vacation."

Anthony sat at his desk and looked at the ceiling.

"Mr. Vice President, should I assemble the Cabinet?" Attorney General Donovan asked.

"Ty, what do you think I ought to do?"

Ty was still pacing. He held his tongue as to what he really wanted to do. "I think you, the Attorney General, and I ought to go have a talk with the President. And I think Agent Craig better come to."

Agent Craig wasn't sure what he meant by that. Maybe he would have to protect the President from the acting FBI Director.

"Alright. We'll go talk to the President. We'll confront him with what we know and bring the video with us. I will ask him to resign for the good of the country." Those in the meeting started looking for their coats. "Claire, if he refuses, then we'll get the Cabinet together."

As they prepared to leave the residence, Agent Craig indicated he was receiving a message in his ear. Something about the Director of the Secret Service wanting to be in the meeting with the President along with his lead agent so everybody was on the same page. Anthony concurred so they waited in the idling limousines. When Agent Craig received the word from his Director, they made the drive to the White House.

As they barreled down Massachusetts Avenue, Agent Craig received another message. He turned around in his front seat perch.

"Sir, the President is preparing to take off!"

"What?"

"Marine One is being readied for takeoff! The President is going to meet with Director Franklin on the yacht."

"Don't let him get on board, Mike! Tell your guys to keep him on the ground. It's urgent that we talk with him."

With sirens wailing and tires screeching, the Vice President's motorcade came to a halt on West Executive Avenue on the west side of the White House. The Vice President, Director Stubblefield, Attorney General Donovan, Agent Craig, and Secret Service Director Robert Newman hustled into the Oval Office and waited for the President.

He was not in a good mood. He could be heard yelling in the hallway that it better be damned important for him to get off Marine One. His lead agent, John Ewing, was trying to hurry him inside. No one told the President who would be waiting for him in the Oval Office.

His voice lowered when he entered the room. "What is this an intervention?" he asked, looking at everyone around him. His eyes zeroed in on the Vice President. "What the fuck do you want, Schumacher?"

He had cursed the Vice President at every opportunity. Once even in a Cabinet meeting. It was clear the President had been drinking. His eyes were glassy and his tongue heavy.

"Sir, we know about you and Director Franklin."

The President laughed out loud. "No shit, Sherlock." The President walked behind his desk. "Is that what this is about? Sex?"

He shook his head in amusement.

"Schumacher, I'm not the first President to have sex with someone while in the White House. And I'm pretty sure I won't be the last." He laughed again. "You're such a freaking Boy Scout."

The Vice President stepped forward. He stopped in the middle of the room on the shield of the presidential seal in the rug. The Secret Service was right behind him. They were armed along with Ty.

So was the President.

"Mr. President, we have reason to believe you and Director Franklin were directly involved in a conspiracy to shoot down Marine Two."

The President stopped laughing. No trace of a smile. "You're an idiot, Schumacher. Did Stubblefield put you up to this?" he snarled as he pointed at Ty. "You both have lost your minds."

Anthony cleared his throat. His heart was pounding. His lips were dry. "Sir, we have a tape of you and Director Franklin in bed at Camp David discussing the plot to shoot down Marine Two, kill me, and then make Director Franklin the Vice President."

"A tape? You are full of yourself, Schumacher. I'm not going to put up with your shit much longer. I'm this close to having the Secret Service remove you from the White House." The distance between his thumb and index finger indicated he was pretty close.

Anthony reached into his suit coat and pulled out the memory card. "Sir, this was in a camera hidden inside a Bible located in your bedroom at Camp David. It was placed there by your wife. It shows you and Director Franklin discussing Oman, the four-man hit squad, your divorce from the First Lady, and future marriage to the Director."

The President's eyes locked on the memory card. His slight buzz was gone, replaced by rage at his wife and that ungrateful jackass standing in front of him. Now he really wished the Vice President had been killed.

He jammed his hand into his suit coat.

"Sir, let me see your hands!" Agent Craig yelled, pulling out his gun.

"John! Tell him to put his gun away!" the President yelled at Agent Ewing. He continued to fumble around in his coat.

"Sir, take your hand out of your coat!" Agent Craig ordered again.

Agent Ewing didn't know what to do. Someone was actually pointing a gun at the President of the United States in the Oval Office, but the President appeared unstable. Processing that he had sworn to protect the President, he pulled out his own gun and pointed it at Agent Craig.

"Put the gun down, Mike," he said, his voice slightly quivering.

Ty unbuttoned his coat behind the two Secret Service agents. He might end up being the last man standing.

Feeling the need to calm things down, the Vice President reached out his left hand to Agent Craig and pulled the gun down. "Mr. President, it is time for you to resign."

The President's hand came out of his coat. It was shaking and holding a beeper. He looked at it and waited for the vibration. He sat down in a heap at his desk, cursing the Vice President and everyone in the room.

"You will not be President, Mr. Schumacher," the President slurred.

The world was crashing down around him. He kept looking at the beeper.

Director Newman said something into his cuff. Armed agents could be seen moving into position on the South Lawn. The President checked the beeper again.

"Sir, once this gets out. You will be left with no other choice," the Vice President said. "If you don't resign today, I will seek to invoke the Twenty-Fifth Amendment and take over as Acting President."

The public would be outraged at the revelation and call for the President's head. Some would argue the President's actions bordered on treasonous. He would most likely spend the rest of his years in a federal prison. He had trusted Director Franklin and wanted to live out his days with her, both of them sharing the power that fed them. He started to cry. He felt the end was near.

"Mr. President," Anthony said softly, "It's over."

The beeper started buzzing. Everyone in the room looked at it. Buzzing, buzzing, buzzing. The President opened up the top drawer of his desk and pulled out a bottle of tea. He could barely talk. His eyes were red and puffy. His hands shook.

Director Newman and his two Secret Service agents flinched and put a finger to their ears. Word was being spread quickly. All three of them looked at each other with wide disbelieving eyes. The Vice President could hear the voices in the silence of the room but not the substance of what was being said.

"What is it?" Anthony asked.

Direct Newman cleared his throat. The President struggled to open his bottle of tea. "Mr. President," he announced, "there has been an explosion on your yacht."

The President was well aware of it. The beeper told him everything he needed to know. Director Franklin gave it to him in case an emergency arose. In case someone found out. She also gave him the bottle of tea. That way they could go out together.

"Mr. Vice President, would you care for a cup of tea?" he asked, struggling to pour half the bottle in a coffee mug on his desk. "Then we can discuss how this is all going to play out."

Anthony took the mug, but he was in no mood to drink. "Mr. President, it's time to go."

The President took a good long sip and smacked his dry lips. It helped calm his nerves. He looked at Anthony, the man he made Vice President. He managed a smile before the foaming started at the corner of his mouth.

"Mr. President!" Agent Ewing yelled as he lunged over the desk. The President was convulsing, the foaming appeared to be choking him. "Get the President's physician in here!"

Agent Craig grabbed the Vice President's left wrist with one hand and the cup with the other.

The President's physician would be of little use. The six ounces of cyanide the President had ingested guaranteed a quick end. First the foaming, then the seizures. After twenty seconds, the heart would stop and never restart.

They called an ambulance anyway. At least the American public would know every effort had been made to save the President's life. Whether the people would ever know how he died or the reason behind it was a different story. The paramedics entered the Oval Office with the stretcher and found the cast of characters stoically standing off to the side. There was no show of concern on their faces. Only anger at the President. Ten minutes of resuscitative efforts failed to bring the President back.

After the ambulance left, Agent Craig walked the Vice President to his West Wing office. Neither said anything. Both were exhausted. Anthony grabbed a Diet Coke from the fridge and handed one over to Agent Craig. They both sat down in a heap. The TV was off, but the President's death was being announced and would soon reach every corner of the globe.

Ten minutes later, Attorney General Donovan showed up at the door and knocked. "Sir, I put in a call to the Chief Justice."

Anthony closed his eyes and shook his head. His swearing-in would take place in an hour.

In the Blue Room of the White House, Anthony and Danielle held hands as they waited to be announced into the State Dining Room for their first State Dinner as First Couple. The King and Queen of Sweden were back. The Schumacher's prayers for normalcy had been answered. Somewhat. As best as can be expected for the President of the United States and his wife. The government was running smoothly, the terrorists were on the run, and the American people were happy.

"I hope eight years in the White House will be enough for us," she said, hoping his terms would end quickly so they could go retire to Silver Creek and live out their golden years.

A tuxedo-clad Wiley leaned in from behind. "Nine years," he interjected. Anthony was finishing off President Fisher's first term and would have the opportunity to run for two more terms. Wiley had the exact number of days

Anthony could spend as President in his mind at all times.

Anthony turned around to find his trusted chief of staff with both thumbs pecking away at his BlackBerry. "Wiley, put that thing away. Try to enjoy yourself tonight."

With a muffled grunt, Wiley shook his head and turned away. He couldn't stop. He'd rather think politics than eat. Plus, he was determined to get Anthony elected. He promised himself his boss was not going to be another Gerald Ford, the only man to be Vice President and President without ever being elected to either office.

"Nine years?" Danielle sighed.

The Marine Band came to attention with Ruffles and Flourishes.

"It'll all be over before you know it," Anthony said with a wink. She didn't believe him. He gave her a quick kiss.

"Ladies and Gentlemen, the President of the United States accompanied by the First Lady."

THE END

Rob Shumaker is an attorney living in Illinois. *Thunder in the Capital* is his first novel. He is also the author of *Showdown in the Capital, Chaos in the Capital, D-Day in the Capital, Manhunt in the Capital, Fallout in the Capital, Phantom in the Capital,* and *Blackout in the Capital*.

To read more about the Capital Series novels, go to

www.USAnovels.com

... .‒

Made in the USA
Lexington, KY
02 November 2016